The Eye of Sounnu

By Schuyler Hernstrom

Cover art by Brian LeBlanc

ISBN 978-1-7334086-6-0
Cover layout by Michael Greylord

"The Gift of the Ob-Men" originally appeared in *Cirsova #1.*
"Images of the Goddess" originally appeared in *Cirsova #2.*
"The Space Witch" originally appeared in *Cirsova #3.*
"The First American" originally appeared in *Cirsova #5.*
"The Star-God's Grave" originally appeared in *Cirsova Summer Special 2019.*

CONTENTS

Dedication

For my father, who introduced me to the classics.

"I live in a world apart
A world that has no link with this drab earth.
A vague, melodious world, where breezes start
Soft joys and gay-hued mirth."
–REH

Foreword

I'd like to begin by apologizing that this will by far be the weakest part of this otherwise excellent and exceptional book collecting several of the stories of Schuyler Hernstrom. I'm honored to have been asked to write this brief introduction to these truly fantastic stories.

When I started Cirsova Publishing in 2016, I did so believing that there were sci-fi and fantasy authors out there who were writing the kind of fiction that I loved who only needed a halfway decent market to publish them in. Schuyler Hernstrom happened to be in that first batch of authors, and I could not have been more fortunate. Sky quickly became not just a fan favorite but a friend.

If you were a fan of the strange and picaresque adventures of Jack Vance, or the savage poetry of Robert Howard, you could find them in our pages in Hernstrom's stories.

Collected in this volume are Sky's stories that he published with Cirsova, and then some. If you were one of the Cirsova readers waiting for all of those stories in one place, or if you missed one, this is the collection for you. If you've only read one or two of his stories, or maybe you've never read any, you're in for a real treat!

"Alex" P. Alexander

The Gift of the Ob-Men

Sounnu was permitted one last night in the village. At dawn the shamans pronounced him exile and the young man left without ceremony. His fellow warriors stayed to their huts, unable to bear the spectacle. Even Tenno lay on his woven palette feigning sleep. Sounnu had been his constant companion for their entire lives. They were close as brothers until the day Sounnu's father died. The sword the old man bore, crafted by the forgotten lore of the ancients, passed into Sounnu's hands. Tenno's flint blades, though artfully made, had seemed worthless by comparison and a shadow of envy passed over their friendship. Sounnu was taking the ancient blade with him into exile; none had dared attempt to take it from the young man.

Though his heart was heavy Sounnu resisted the urge to look over his shoulder as he left the green vale which cradled his village. Trees and shrubs diminished until the steppe was underfoot. By sundown he had crossed the grasslands that separated the vale from the ruined city due west, a nameless relic of the golden age.

The next day he followed the western road as it made its long, winding detour around the edges of the city. The remains of its crooked towers slashed at the blue sky like jagged flint blades, a last blow from a long ago age when people could twist nature into grand shapes of their own design. The road had shrunk to a mere footpath by the time it reached the base of the old mountains. Like the city, the lands beyond the mountains were forbidden by old custom. In despair, Sounnu scaled the low peaks, now finally sparing a glance backwards to view the trailing tendrils of smoke in the far distance marking his former home. There was warmth and community, now forever out of reach. The high air stung his broad, naked back with lashings of snow, shining like miniscule diamonds in the bright light of a cloudless sky.

On the other side of the range the grim warrior found himself standing before a forest of dark pine and stunted birch. Sounnu felt a palpable menace emanating from the line of black shadows draped under the gnarled branches. The presence of danger stirred his soul to something of its former buoyancy. Impatient for the thrill of combat he drew the ancient broadsword from its carved scabbard and plunged forward. He screamed his low battle cry into the mute trunks and scrambled over rocks and deadfall, ducking limbs and weaving through brush. No ghask nor ghoul nor ur-wolf answered his hoarse challenges. He grew tired and gave up seeking foes. Sounnu drank from a clear, cold stream and lay to rest on a bed of moss.

He awoke surrounded by tall heavy creatures, bearing the form of a mushroom bent into the shape of men. Their ill-formed, elongated faces were unreadable masks. The warrior sought the handle of his blade but found he could not move.

He spoke to the mushroom men in a voice heavy with despair. "By what art am I frozen?"

"By manipulating our spores we are able to cause specific calamities to fall upon the unwary," they answered in unison.

Sounnu sighed, "This is an inglorious end. Be quick, spare me this indignity."

The mushroom men laughed and replied, "Not so hasty! We will avenge ourselves slowly upon you and extract some recompense for the great wrong your people have wrought."

Sounnu's brow furrowed. "To what do you refer?"

The mushroom men leaned their heads back and shook slightly, an apparent expression of distress. Their low voices pooled over the soft ground around the young man like a cool mist as they spoke. "The memory pains us. Long ago your species attacked us with fire and steel, pushing us from our beloved vale into this place. Once we stood content underneath clean oaks as laughing fey danced around our thick legs. Now we work our spores into weapons to ward against ur-wolves and ghask."

"In my village the shamans told stories of the hulking Ob-men who once ruled the vale. The ancients defeated them with much sacrifice, expelling their evil from the land."

The mushroom men let out a low, keening wail.

Sounnu winced, continuing, "I spoke hastily. Perhaps the term 'Ob-men' does not refer to your ancestors."

The mushroom men said in harsh tones, "No! That is the name they bestowed upon us. We were there! And now to learn you creatures have lionized our expulsion! Oh, the injustice is compounded! What variations should we apply presently upon this body to expend our rage?"

For the first time, one of the mushroom men spoke singularly. "Perhaps a spore to turn him inside out?"

Another suggested a spore to splinter the mind into dozens of warring identities. Sounnu felt cold sweat erupt along his muscular frame. He interrupted their conference.

"Would it, perhaps, lessen your anger to know that I am an outcast from the village of men? The great cities are no more. The temples lie in jumbled ruins. The punishment of exile now is a death sentence. And by killing me, you stoop to perform their errands and perfect their will."

The mushroom men ceased their planning.

"You are an enemy of the humans?"

Sounnu said earnestly, "I am indeed. In a fit of pique I smashed an idol and offended the priestesses. The incident arose from an excess of energy on my part. The clans have faded away, consolidated now into one village. The tribes of ghask that once raided the vale are slain, and no ur-wolves dare come close to the village. There is no one for me to fight. To assuage my boredom I explored the vale. Inside a ruin I came across the idol, a strange thing with a strange face. Neither shaman nor priestess could explain its meaning. I became enraged and smashed it. At that time Yulik was thatching his roof and fell painfully. The shamans believed the events were linked and I was charged with bringing a god's wrath down upon the village. They are clever men, though stunted and cruel, and look for any excuse to castigate a warrior."

The Ob-men replied, "Your story bores us. We would prefer you elaborate upon an earlier comment. The great cities are no more?"

"This is true. The elders tell us the city people died away, ignoring nature's demands to work their great art."

"So mankind now consists of only one village?"

"That is true also, to the extent of my people's knowledge. Some dream that across the mountains and through endless ruins lay communities of men that live as in the golden age. They are admonished for their frivolity."

The mushroom men stepped away from Sounnu and conversed amongst themselves. The warrior allowed himself to relax. He would be tortured to death. Such was fate. The mushroom men returned, now animated and anxious.

"We have decided to spare your life under one condition."

There was a smell in the air, earthy and floral. Sounnu found he could move. He stood, shaking slightly from the spores' effects.

"What is this condition?"

The mushroom men spoke in unison again. "You will return home and empty the village of people."

Sounnu laughed. "That is impossible. Upon sighting an exile the shamans will fill my guts with worms and my ears with shrieking demons. The priestesses will publicly rebuke me with stinging words and the warriors will be compelled to kill me. Why not use your dire spores and perform the deed yourselves?"

"To answer your first concern, know that we will bestow upon you advantages. Insofar as completing the task ourselves, know that we also are a dying race. Our numbers have dwindled to that which you see before you. Should our spores be exhausted then we risk total annihilation. Do as we say and restore us to the vale where we may become contented again and the race of man will trouble us no more."

The mushroom men made Sounnu swear an oath on the souls of his ancestors and another on his prized blade. Satisfied, they then looked to one of their number. A squat specimen with black spots stepped toward Sounnu. The smell of bitter acorns filled his nose. Sounnu lost consciousness.

The warrior awoke at the edge of the forest. His head throbbed but he was otherwise unharmed. With no better idea he began the long walk back to his village. The pain began to center itself in his forehead, growing in intensity. He made a supper of wild berries and lay down on a slab of mossy granite to rest.

The dawn woke him gently. He opened his eyes. Sounnu looked up at the mountains. The range stood gray and stately as before. Then there was a moment of total disorientation. Sounnu fought to understand what he was seeing. The warrior saw the mountains through the eye of passing eons. He saw them push up from the earth as two plates met in slow violence. He saw wind and rain render them into rubble. The visions came all at once. He saw the mountains' birth and death in the same glimpse. He shut his eyes in confusion and held his head in his trembling hands. Sounnu jerked them away from an unfamiliar sensation. He gently placed his fingers back to his head and felt again. Scrambling off his bed of granite he sprinted toward a still pool.

The pool reflected the source of his horror in crisp clarity. He now possessed a third eye, centered in his forehead. The reflection shifted suddenly. He saw a death's head, then an infant, then the present again. Sounnu lay back until the dizziness passed, eyes firmly shut. He cut a length of leather from the hem of his leggings and wrapped it around his forehead, obscuring the eye. The visions ceased. The warrior sat a while; mind racing as he tried to understand what had befallen him. A sparrow's song lifted him from the maze of his thoughts. He did not understand the meaning of the third eye or its visions. There was nothing more to do for the present.

He continued on his path, letting his oath guide his steps. Sounnu dared occasionally to peel back the veil covering the third eye. Slowly, the warrior began to understand the visions of time, as they passed forward and backward, trailing off into numberless possibility. He saw his own body rent by bloody wounds, then wracked with old age, then a void, never having existed, then as now, hale and bronze from the sun. Sounnu avoided letting the third eye linger too long on his own form. He knew he would die one day as all men did. The eye seemed to show many fates, many deaths. It was confusing and paled before the majesty of a dying mountain or a forest rising from the earth before burning in an instant of visiontime from wind-whipped walls of orange fire sparked by arcs of blinding lightning from a raging sky.

Day turned to night as he walked. Gradually the dizziness ceased altogether during his experiments. He found himself sitting, watching the moon shape itself from irregular rocks and then fall back down to earth. Covering the third eye he reassured himself that it still hung in the blue-black sky.

Before lying down to sleep he peeled the blind back one last time and was shocked to see his body crisscrossed with fresh wounds, torn by tooth and claw, seeping black gore under the moon's cool light. The vision was pregnant with immediacy. Sounnu shot to his feet. He covered the eye again and collected himself, nearly relaxing until he caught a stir of movement from the corner of his eye. There underneath the pines stalked an ur-wolf, a wizened alpha with two heads.

Sounnu drew his sword and settled into a stance. The ur-wolf circled.

Its mournful, rasping voices broke the silence.

"Nearly to bed, nearly asleep, nearly eaten. Now the man stands bravely with his biting blade bared to blue moonlight. Go back to resting reclining wretched man, accept your fate. Let us fill our empty belly baleful braying at the moon in our hunger. The hunger, horrible, heartbroken never full finished, satisfied."

The ur-wolf lunged. Sounnu ducked then sprung up, hurling the beast over his shoulder. The predator spun in the air, grazing the warrior with its long claws and snatching the blindfold from his shaggy head. The creature landed badly on a boulder, cracking its spine. The warrior was overwhelmed as the third eye opened. He saw the ur-wolf as a mewling pup, as a fur draped around his shoulders, and as it was now.

Sounnu saw the slain ur-wolf moments ago debating strategy with the pack. The rest were to come up from the nearby swale as the warrior was distracted, engaged with the leader at the pines' edge. He saw them through space, advancing on his flank presently. Sounnu moved to lean against another boulder where the ground dipped to meet the swale. One by one the ur-wolves darted past and were met by the young warrior's blade. He replaced the blindfold and skinned the leader and scraped the hide, working in the moonlight. Over a large fire he roasted the carcass on a spit and gorged himself on the meat.

In the morning he cracked open the ur-wolves' horned skulls and worked the brains into the leader's pelt, a fine prize, grey streaked with jet black. He threw the still raw pelt over his broad shoulders and resumed his journey.

After a day's walk he rested and then woke again with the dawn. He crossed the old mountains easily with the aid of the third eye, seeing through time and space in order to pick the easiest routes, hidden paths and passages through tunnels of wind-sculpted rock painted with the striations that once marked forests and swamps, lines of white demarking seas dried by the sun and lines of black writing tales of burning and destruction.

Presently he stood at the beginning of the western road. He disregarded the winding path and walked due east, heading straight for the silent towers of the empty city. At the city's edge he was overcome. The third eye bombarded him with chaotic visions, specters of the past, increasing in frequency. His mind flitted from one image to the next, racing along paths of causality that arced and contorted like bolts of lightning. The warrior saw countless people, living inscrutable lives in the pursuit of motivations that Sounnu could hardly comprehend. The towers gleamed, tall and arrogant, reaching toward the heavens and hosting a trillion dramas of daily life. Even through the crippling haze of the vision's speed he could recognize some emotions, love and hate, fear, anger. Others he could not. There were ideas built upon ideas, whole languages of abstraction, all spiraling down into realms of the mind that were foreign to the young man. Sounnu reeled back, feeling his own self, his mind, disintegrating. He replaced the blindfold with trembling hands. He sat against a wall and collected himself, breathing deep of the dusty air. After a time, he stood and resumed his journey.

The rows of jumbled ruins grew in size as he approached the city center. Everywhere was dust, gritty powders in colors of red and ochre, swirling in angry eddies in gusts unchecked by tree or shrub. Signs scrawled with forgotten glyphs cried mutely in colors now faded to dull gray and stained taupe. Nearing the city's center Sounnu noticed signs of occupation. Someone had made a futile attempt to keep the dust at bay, sweeping it into banks against the leaning wreckage of the once proud towers. The warrior saw a wide clearing ahead, a circular area lined with mounds of gray stone. In the center Sounnu spied the silhouette of a giant, a gleaming figure, perhaps ten feet tall. He drew his sword and ducked behind a pile of refuse. The temptation to peel back the blindfold grew but he resisted. Sounnu peered over the edge.

The figure in the distance remained perfectly still. Sounnu ducked back down and sat stock still. His body was rigid with the discipline of the hunter as his breath came slow, measured, and quiet. He peered again. The figure had not moved. Cautiously he advanced.

He walked slowly, keeping one of the mounds of stone between him and the figure's line of sight. The strange objects loomed ahead. As they neared Sounnu realized they were great sculptures. Each was a head, jaw flush to the ground, worked with great skill and grace, capturing nuances of expression lost on the warrior. The figure of gleaming metal yet stood still. Sounnu finally permitted himself to relax slightly. The figure was obviously an idol, a god of the city that the people had surrounded with greater or lesser deities, the great heads, Sounnu could not decide which. He approached the idol.

The thing was formed from a bright metal that reflected the ochre-tinged light in looping swirls. By its nature or by another's attentions it was completely free of the city's ubiquitous dust. The idol had no features, only the graceful outlines of a powerful musculature. Sounnu stood before it staring in wonder. The very sword he carried was made from a craft long lost to his people. This metal idol was a complete mystery.

With inhuman speed its arms lashed out. Sounnu threw himself back. Metal hands sought his neck but only grasped the pelt, tearing it away as Sounnu reeled. The warrior lashed out with his blade. The metal clashed against the idol, making not so much as a scratch. Sounnu scrambled away from another lunge. The idol moved forward now, pressing the warrior back against a stone head bearing an expression of fatalistic amusement. Sounnu ducked again, rolling on the dusty ground to spring up behind the idol. The metal man spun on its heels, already poised for another attack. A shrill voice rang out in the clearing.

"Servitor! Halt!"

The idol stood suddenly still. Sounnu stepped back, panting, seeking the source of the command. Atop one of the heads stood a tall, thin man, holding aloft a torn parasol. The man gingerly climbed down from the head and approached. He wore a suit of silver mesh, corroded slightly, and a broad brimmed hat atop a mass of long, brown curls. His eyes gleamed behind rings of colored cosmetics as he looked Sounnu up and down.

"Easy, friend! Pardon my servitor. My spyglass is flecked with dust and I mistook you for a ghask. But you are no ghask, you are an outlander, a traveler, and now the glories of Omeyapolis are yours to behold! My name is Maneon. I bid you welcome."

Maneon's ruffled sleeves spread wide as he bowed. Sounnu stood still, mouth open, sword held at the ready.

Maneon frowned, affecting sadness artfully with his wide, painted mouth. He spoke again, lilting voice echoing off the stone heads. "Come now, friend. Lower your blade. Let us walk together. I mean you no harm. Whatever fate befalls you, good or ill, is preordained, is it not? What is your name, traveler?"

"Sounnu the Exile."

"An exile? How sad. What brings you here to bask in the zenith of refinement?"

Sounnu lowered his sword. "I pass through on my way to the village of men."

"I hope your errand is not too dire. You simply cannot leave without getting the grand tour. Firstly, let us take tea in my apartments. You can tell me all about your village and I can display for you the art that is my passion, the summation of the human experience. Upon its completion mankind will be complete. How fortunate are you, to come at the moment when it nears conclusion!"

Maneon beckoned emphatically and Sounnu followed, sheathing his blade as he walked on wary steps. The pale artist snapped his fingers and the servitor came alive again, following behind its master.

The last whole structure in Omeyopolis was Maneon's home. It was a warehouse, long and low, the leaning sides piled high with ochre dust. The thin man pulled aside a curtain of burlap and bade Sounnu enter. The warrior ducked under a beam and reeled from the smell of rot, the stench emanating from a source not visible. Sounnu jumped at the sight of another figure and then realized he saw his own reflection in a tall mirror. He inspected the interior with eyes wide with awe. Skylights let in rays of yellow light, illuminating a vast collection. Everywhere were boxes piled on top of boxes, objects and devices of a thousand descriptions. Racks and racks of clothes were lined far into the dark recesses of the cluttered room. There were costumes of silk and satin, glittering fabrics, dark damasks, all in varying states of decay. And everywhere were more mirrors, large and small, some cracked and obscured by grime. Sounnu reached out to touch a garish coat of gold and disturbed a dozen moths. Maneon shooed them away. His face was in darkness underneath the broad brim of his hat. He gestured to a tatty divan.

"Make yourself at home, weary wanderer! Servitor will see to the tea while I change for the afternoon. I will return shortly."

Sounnu gingerly lowered himself to the couch. Everywhere in his view were objects of unknown meaning and provenance. There were things that may have been tools, but for what purpose the warrior could not guess. Many of the objects could not have been shaped by human hands, their angles too perfect, surfaces too smooth. Even covered with layers of dust, the colors on display shocked eyes familiar only with nature's palette. Sounnu laughed inwardly. The shamans were wrong to go to such lengths to instill fear of the cities. There were only strange men there, strange smells, and useless objects.

A man came suddenly around a stack of crates. The thin figure was clothed in an elaborate suit of muted red velvet, embroidered with geometric designs and fraying at cuffs and elbows. His hair was a shock of sharp yellow spikes. In his graceful hands he bore a silver tray. He spoke, and Sounnu realized it was Maneon, unrecognizable in his new garb.

The artist said, "There, refreshments for our weary guest. And now I am properly attired to receive guests and host a salon. You must be bursting with anticipation to view my art, are you not?"

Sounnu could only manage a nod of affirmation. He inspected the tray. Between two steaming cups was a plate arranged with cubes of charred meat, each speared with a tiny sliver of wood. At Maneon's beckoning the warrior took a cup and sipped the bitter liquid, burning his tongue in the process. The liquid was near boiling. Maneon raised a thin eyebrow as he seated himself in a high backed chair held together by lashings of twine.

"Are you not hungry?"

Sounnu shrugged. "As it happens, no. But I thank you for your hospitality. What sort of meat is that?"

"Oh, these delicacies? It is a shame you will not partake. It is from my own private stock, an Omeyapolis original. I call it 'critic'!" His shrill laughter echoed through the warehouse. He continued. "It is your loss. But who says outlanders are without manners? You are a graceful guest. I regret I cannot offer you more variety. Omeyapolis' golden age is upon us and sacrifices have been necessary. All has given way to facilitate our art. All the servitors are inert save the one. Contact with the other cities is lost, no doubt due to a consuming jealousy on their part. Here, in this very city, mankind reaches summation. To live anywhere else must pale in comparison."

"Where is everyone else?"

A spasm crawled spiderlike across Maneon's face.

He replied, "Such a question. We shan't dwell on such vulgar details." He stood suddenly, waving his arm in a grand flourish. "Come now! I simply cannot wait longer. Let me show you the art that brings an end to old epochs and heralds a new future!"

Cup in hand the artist picked his way around stacks of books and boxes. Sounnu placed his cup on the tray and followed. The servitor awaited, half in shadow, as the pair reached an area of the warehouse cleared of debris. In the center of the clearing a tattered silk drape outlined a massive, domelike form.

"Prepare yourself!"

Maneon pulled away the drape. Before Sounnu stood a sculpture like those in the clearing, only larger. He recognized the long, thin features as Maneon's own. The artist's voice rose with ecstasy as he spoke.

"Is it not divine? Here is man. Here is man's soul, his spirit, the reflection of the infinite and ineffable, freed from restraint, from gods and from reason. Here we see the end! Is it not glorious?"

Sounnu's inept pretense crumbled. His deep set eyes bored into Maneon's. The artist stood staring, his own eyes glazed with emotion.

The warrior said, "You are mad."

Maneon laughed again, throwing his head back.

"Mad? Of course! Of course I am. I have touched the center of the universe and rendered it for all to see. How could I not be mad?"

"I will leave now."

"Not so fast, outlander! To see the secrets of civilization, to be so lucky as to peer into infinity, such a vision bears a price. My stock of 'critic' runs low. I shall add 'barbarian' to my larder presently!"

Sounnu heard the heavy steps of the servitor behind as it lunged. He rolled away, ducking the metal arms. Maneon laughed hysterically. From beneath his coat he drew a long, thin blade, rusted and spotted black save for its keen edge. Sounnu drew his sword as the servitor lunged again, missing only by a hair. Maneon sliced at his exposed back, opening a long wound. The sight of Sounnu's blood sent him into paroxysms of delight. The servitor's advance halted suddenly and the thing pitched forward, legs tangled by the drape that lay on the floor. Maneon squealed in fear as Sounnu turned toward him.

The warrior paused for the briefest moment, calculating. The servitor was a powerful foe. Despite fears regarding the overwhelming visions, Sounnu reckoned it was time to use the third eye. Its visions through space could prove the difference as well as exposing any further ambush.

Sounnu peeled back the blindfold. The visions began and then stopped. He fell to his knees as the scalding, bitter tea ran in rivulets down his bronze face. Maneon's laughter reached new heights as he watched the warrior suffering. He threw the cup over his shoulder and bent to untangle the servitor's legs from the jumble of fabric. He cursed.

"Oh, you stupid thing! You've gone and made it worse!"

Sounnu stumbled to his feet and wiped the stinging liquid from his eyes. His normal eyes were largely untouched but the third eye was blind, sending waves of searing pain into his skull. He stole behind the great head and leaned for a moment. He knew when the servitor won free it was only a matter of time before he was crushed by its gleaming arms. He felt the cool stone against his back, providing sudden, desperate inspiration. Sounnu sheathed his sword and turned. He sank low, bringing his hands up to grasp the sculpted curls of the statue. He pushed, with legs, back, arms, pushing until his powerful frame threatened to shatter. He felt the fibers of his muscles tearing. The massive stone stood unmoved. He heard Maneon admonish the servitor again then make a noise of triumph. The servitor was free. Sounnu strained again, veins erupting across his lean frame.

"Now, where did that foul outlander go?"

Sounnu felt his soul soar as the stone moved, first only a hair, then a hand's width. With a great noise it pitched violently forward. There was a desperate scream and a sudden shower of blinding sparks. Sounnu collapsed from the effort, nearly losing consciousness. He rose to his feet with difficulty, drawing his sword again with arms sapped of all strength. Shaky steps brought him around to the front of the sculpture.

There lay Maneon, crushed from the waist down. His long hands pushed weakly against a thin eyebrow of stone. Beside him the servitor was inert, only head and shoulders visible. Tendrils of energy danced across the metal skin, less and less, until nothing but the smell of ozone hung around the ruined machine. Maneon gasped his last breaths. His mad eyes stared past Sounnu as he spoke.

"It is finished."

The warrior watched Maneon's eyes grow dim as the ghost left. A dusty breeze sent yellowed pages of sketches across the filthy floor. Sounnu followed the wind to a hole in the wall covered by a frayed cloth. He steadied himself on boxes as he walked. The rotten smell became overpowering as he reached the alley just outside. There stacked up against the wall were piles and piles of human bones. The ones nearest the door still bore traces of blood and tendon. A great pot full of filth stood on blocks over the embers of a fire. Hung everywhere were rusted blades of all shapes and sizes, thick saws and hooked skinners. Sounnu left the grim tableau behind with as much speed as he could muster. Behind him the blades sung in tinkling chimes as the wind stirred them to kiss.

The sun sank low as he walked. He pulled the ur-wolf pelt tight around his back but could not completely staunch the flow of blood. He trudged through the night, unwilling to rest amidst the ruins. Sounnu massaged the third eye under its blindfold and winced. The burns were more severe than he had thought. The eye was swollen shut and oozing. The wound on his back began to ache horribly. Compounding matters he felt a heat building within.

Dawn saw grass under his feet. He spared one last glance backward at the crooked spires. The rolling grasslands that separated his village from the ruins stretched before his failing vision. He walked on for another few hours, hunger compounding his growing weakness. Sounnu felt the fever growing, the sickness that had felled many a warrior who celebrated survival prematurely. The city-man's blade had born death on its rusted edge. He walked a time, afraid to stop moving. The part of him given to reason knew that his life was near its end. Fresh trickles of his life's blood mingled with the dried remnants that stained all the way down the back of his legs.

Finally his legs gave out from underneath him. He lay on his back, watching the clouds roll across the sky. He forgot the pain in his back, the burning ache of the third eye, and resolved himself to death. In the narrowing tunnel of his vision a face appeared.

Underneath sun-kissed locks of brown hair her smooth face bore an expression of surprise. Sounnu recognized her, a woman of the village, seventeen summers old, pretty, but quiet and withdrawn. Since her beauty became apparent she had been claimed by the priestesses and was compelled to avoid socializing with the men of the village, especially the handful of warriors who had followed Sounnu as their unappointed leader. With his last strength Sounnu waved her away.

"Let me die in peace, Sila."

"Sounnu the Exile has returned."

Sounnu's voice grew low as the world went gray around him. He said, "I have. Now, be gone. I was sent back on a fool's errand on behalf of the Ob-men. I saw past and future as one. I slew the last city-man and his metal servant. But I have lost too much blood and a fever burns. Let it end here."

The woman shook her head. "The mighty Sounnu, slayer of ghask, babbling like a madman and bowing to death. I spit on the shamans' will. I will save you, undeserving though you are."

Through the tall grass and swaying flowers she ran.

Sounnu recovered slowly under Sila's care. He spent his nights under the open sky, wrapped in the hide of a bear she had taken with a bow last spring. Twice a day Sila stole from the village under the pretense of gathering and fed him nuts and berries then turned him over to clean his wound. Sounnu received her attentions with awkward gratitude. Seven days passed. The warrior could now stand and walk again but the third eye had healed shut. He gingerly attempted to peel back its lids but recoiled from the pain each time.

On the eighth afternoon he sat on a tussock tying snares as Sila approached, cradling handfuls of berries in her leather skirt.

"The warrior is near fully recovered."

"I am. Soon you will watch your efforts come to nothing. I am oath-bound to the Ob-men's errand. I must approach the shamans and priestesses and plead their case, at which time I will be killed properly." He massaged his forehead as he watched Sila sit next to him. Her graceful form was at home in the tall grass, one with the flowers in a rolling sea of sunlit green. The eye ached to see her. Before he could stop himself his long arm encircled her waist. He drew her close and they kissed, sharing the sharp taste of the late summer berries that lingered in their mouths. After a long moment Sila pulled away. She sat facing him. She touched his face with her rough hands, running a finger along the strange scar on his forehead.

"I love you."

"You love a dead man."

She looked to the ground, plucking a white flower from its stalk. "Everywhere is death. You tell me you have slain the last city-man. Our village dies. There are but a handful of warriors left and they follow Ten-no since you are gone. They range for days in the vale, overturning rocks and peering into caves in the hope of finding another blade such as yours. The priestesses gather the women to them like beads on a string. The shamans seek their visions and speak in tongues no one understands. The names of the gods are forgotten. Every year fewer children are born."

Sounnu laughed. "I should have bade the Ob-men to simply wait a few summers."

Sila looked to the horizon. "We should run away. Break your oath to them and we will flee."

The warrior's face darkened. "In whatever time we have left you will not say such a thing again to me. I bear the sword of the ancients, made by my ancestors who cloak themselves in the past as the vale wears mist in spring mornings. Exile could not part me from it. And I will not sully its honor with a broken oath, however stupid that oath may have been."

They held each other again. Over her shoulder Sounnu saw a line of figures cresting a low hill. The villagers approached. Sounnu smiled, pushing a lock of her hair from her brow.

He said, "My time is near its end."

The third eye itched under the fused lids.

"Now we know where Sila spends her afternoons." Oxl grabbed his daughter roughly, thrusting her into the waiting arms of a troupe of priestesses. A pair of warriors held Sounnu at bay with bows drawn while the others milled about. Tenno stood pensively. He bore a great flint axe. Its pointed head rested in the crook of his folded arms. The priestesses forced Sila to the ground with burly arms. A powerful matron draped in necklaces of sea shells inspected her with rough hands.

"Her maidenhead is intact. Lucky that, we may spare her life."

Quewe, the head matron, shook her head no. "We do not know what blasphemies they have shared. They both must die."

Retul, leader of the shamans, came before Sounnu. Dried mud held his hair in rough spikes. His small eyes bore into Sounnu from the darkness of his painted face.

He said, "Why does an exile haunt our grasslands?"

"I swore an oath to the Ob-men of legend. They want the vale back."

"Indeed? And how did you think to affect this miracle?"

Sounnu shrugged. "I had not thought that far."

"No matter then. You die now."

Tenno stepped forward. The hawk feathers that hung from his braided hair stirred in the breeze. "No, shaman. Sounnu will die as a warrior." He made a hissing sound between his teeth, the signal to advance during the hunt. His dozen warriors surged forward. Sounnu was held before he could draw the sword. He struggled lamely, still somewhat weak from his healing wounds. Tenno reached forward and drew the sword, holding it aloft to admire the ancients' craft. The blade shone brightly.

Tears welled in the corners of Tenno's eyes. "Now it is mine." He tossed the axe to the ground at Sounnu's feet and continued, "Take the axe and defend yourself. In your last moments you will know envy."

Sounnu bent and picked up the axe. Tenno swung the sword, clumsily, unused to its balance. The long blade was difficult to direct. Sounnu jumped back to avoid the blow. Tenno laughed, exulting in the feel of the ancient steel, unfamiliar as it was. He swung out again, both hands grasping the ornate handle. Sounnu brought the axe head up to block the blade. Chips of flint stung Tenno's face and his expression twisted. He let out a bloodthirsty yell. Retul joined his voice to Tenno's and soon all present were screaming in rapt anticipation, their hoarse voices celebrating the coming spectacle of death. Tenno swung once more. Sounnu leapt towards Tenno before the deadly edge could be brought to bear.

The pair was locked together for a moment. Tenno reached back and smashed Sounnu's face with the hilt, a maneuver no less effective for its lack of grace. Sounnu crumpled to the ground, bleeding from the nose and a cut on his cheek. Sila wailed and fought impotently against the matrons' grasp.

The axe fell from Sounnu's limp hand as he struggled to remain conscious. Tenno laughed heartily, raising the sword and looking back at his troupe who roared their approval. Sounnu lay on his back, his hand reaching for the axe's handle but finding only grass. Tenno fixed his eyes on Sounnu and taunted.

"Just a few more moments, old friend. Just a few more. I thank you for the blade. It is everything I thought it would be. I must test its keenness."

Tenno laid the tip of the sword on Sounnu's jaw and flicked the blade upwards. A thin red line opened.

He exclaimed, "Sharper than obsidian! And it will remain so for all eternity! What powerful magics the people of old must have possessed."

Tenno squatted down to see better. He laid the tip on Sounnu's forehead and drew it across. Another line opened and more blood spilled. Tenno peered at the wound, marveling for a moment at a sight unexpected. He froze, staring into a third eye.

Now Sounnu saw all before him through the lens of eternity. The clouds ceased their march across the sky as birds slowed mid-air. In space, he saw the axe's handle mere inches from his hand. Tenno stared in frozen horror as Sounnu took the axe and with all his might smashed the cruel point into the side of Tenno's head. The skull shattered like a bird's egg. Tenno went limp instantly and collapsed. Retul screamed. Sounnu took the sword and stood.

He watched as the archers' fingers loosed their grasp. Slowly the arrows came forward. With the flat of his blade he knocked the missiles from the air. Time moved forward. The warriors had drawn their flint blades and unhooked gnarled clubs from their hide belts. Sounnu saw severed heads rolling, arms and legs rent deeply, life's essence spurting from open arteries. He stepped forward, swinging his blade in great arcs and in moments made the visions a reality, staining the grass crimson and filling the air with death cries. He saw the shamans and priestesses waving arms and working their magics. Foam spat from their lips as they hissed. The threat of their spells had no more hold on Sounnu. He fell upon them, blade rising and falling as he met each in turn. He saw their bones bleach in the sun as he slew. He saw the grass rise and fall, green and brown, the hills becoming mountains and the plains becoming oceans.

All were slain. He stood calm in a sea of green marred with streaks of red, chest heaving from the exertion. He grew faint and tottered to one side. Sila caught him before he could fall. Their eyes met.

The third eye showed him her death and birth. He heard her last breath escape and a moment later her newborn wail. He saw her beauty throughout. Blinding light showed through her womb. Sounnu laid his gore-stained hand on her flat belly. There he saw one day his seed would grow. From Sila's womb would rise a new race of man. He watched the future unfold before him.

His descendants would multiply and cover the world, learning again the secrets of iron and grain. The gods would return, led by an all-father with three eyes and a goddess of grace and infinite mercy.

The descendants would first form kingdoms and then great nations. They would war amongst themselves under a hundred banners. They would make symbols to record their deeds and art to display their vanities. They would raise great cites of metal and temples of mirrors and forget again the names of the gods. They would become lost in the labyrinths of their own minds. The great towers would crumble and the cathedrals would fall. The cities would rot, as man would return to the earth, again stalking the forests for game and fighting their enemies with blades of stone, building great bonfires to hold the terrors of the night at bay. They would dwindle in numbers, debased and fearful.

Then a day would come when a warrior would stalk the ruins and find the idol of a forgotten god, a strange statue with three eyes.

The Tragedy of Thurn

Since the gods made men there had been little except the cycle of rise and fall. Warlords rose and founded dynasties that inevitably grew fat on the spoils won by their forebears. Thus reduced in vigor they fell prey to new warlords. But Lurgan was marked special by the wise men of the cities who read history. His horde was vast and his manner cruel beyond the usual measure. The warlord had united all of the steppemen under his banner by the force of his indomitable will. His shamans were powerful. They had freed all manner of beasts from icy slumber at the feet of ancient mountains. Others they called from the mire of the fetid marshes that dotted the steppe. All these they bound to serve at their master's pleasure. There were hulking things with skin like elephants and bearing many horns and loping creatures neither beast nor man, gathered in packs and prodded with spears to leap upon the enemy. Lurgan's army swept all before them in a rain of arrow and blade and bloody claw. No dusty scroll or dry vellum recalled a warrior more savage or cruel. A dozen disparate creeds noted his resemblance to figures conjured in their respective eschatologies. While the sages and priests sought auguries the soldiers of the cities along the western edge of the steppe grew despondent as reports of the terrible host reached their ears. Thus when Lurgan came before their gleaming ramparts the defenders' blows were not telling and their arrows were not true as men with a shadow over their hearts cannot well fight. So one by one the cities fell and Lurgan granted his men license to vent their dark passions. The broad avenues were painted with gore and the horizon grew dark with the smoke of burning homes. The people's woe sang to the heavens as none were permitted to live except at the cruel pleasure of the invader. The wantonness was disturbing even to Lurgan's generals.

We waste wealth, they thought, as able bodied men and women were put to the blade and not bound and sent south to sell as slaves. But none dared voice displeasure with their brooding master.

Lurgan showed no particular joy in victory. City after city fell and was sacked until finally he came upon the broad and fertile plain where lies Zanitum, the white walled city marked for its just rule and wise sages.

There on the plain the horde howled and wailed and begged to be let loose. Atop the hill, surrounded by banners and his bodyguard, Lurgan's winged helm nodded and the drums began their sonorous peal. The blood of the defenders ran cold and no captain among them could buoy their hearts against the onslaught. The great horned things began their battering against the walls and the host pelted the ramparts with missiles of crude manufacture.

When the walls were sundered and the slaughter began Lurgan led his hearthguard to the palace where his axe ended the line that had ruled there. He sat his powerful body on the blood-drenched throne and called to Jumern, his most trusted general. His expression was thoughtful as he sat, the black furs from the wolves of his windswept home wrapped around his broad shoulders.

"This city was once famed for its wizards, was it not?"

"Yes, my lord."

"Save their towers from the torch and bring them to me. Do not be gentle with them. Let them know the lowest among my host is now their master. And summon my torturers."

"Yes, my lord."

Jumern did as he was bade. As the sun dipped beneath the smoke-clouded horizon, four wizards were brought to the throne room. The men winced in pain as they shuffled forward, pale and downcast. Jumern kicked the first so he came to his knees and seeing this, the others quickly kneeled.

Lurgan descended the marble dais to inspect the wizened men.

His deep voice echoed in the hall. "I wonder. Why did you not put a spell on me to stop the despoiling of your city and the destruction of your nation?"

The wizards were silent save the one on the end. He replied in a plain voice. "We tried. You enjoy the protection of gods unknown to us."

"You will address me as 'my lord'."

The men kept their eyes on the tiled floor as Lurgan paced. The warlord looked to his host, the generals and captains and their slaves gathered in the throne room.

"Leave us."

After a moment's hesitation, the black armored men left and their attendants with them.

The wizards quaked in fear, save the one on the end, a lanky man in red robes.

"Do you know of history?" Lurgan asked the wizards. They looked at each other in fear and confusion. Finally the red-robed man answered.

"We are familiar, my lord. All learned men are."

"Is that so? I learned of it from a sage I kept when I was younger. The old man begged for his life that he may write words about me and thus grant me immortality."

"He spoke truth, my lord. So a man's deeds may be remembered until the end of the world."

"But memory fades. And these words with which you weave your histories, they are not magic, are they? Without the sages they are simply lines on scrolls. My men delight in burning libraries. The flames are brilliant and the smoke dense."

"Indeed, my lord, words are not magic. Though the poet may argue."

Lurgan sat back upon the red throne.

"Can any of you tell me my fate?"

A wizard in torn blue robes spoke though it was not much more than a whimper. "With the charts in my tower I could, though I need know the day of your birth, my lord."

Lurgan sighed. "You are a fool. We just spoke of history. Do you need anything more to tell me my fate?"

The red wizard dared to look up. Lurgan stared at him.

The warlord spoke again. "You understand me."

The wizard nodded. "Your fate will be the same as all who came before you. You will die in battle or by poison. Or you will die an old man, bitter in the knowledge that your scions will grow weak."

Lurgan smiled a wicked smile. "You speak truth."

A wizard in robes of purple trimmed in gold spoke for the first time.

"My lord. Many have sought immortality. All have failed. Everything that begins must end. It is true that some among our profession have extended their lives to great length. But they did so at great cost."

Lurgan shook his head. "I do not seek immortality."

"What do you seek, my lord?"

Lurgan's dark eyes seemed to focus on a far horizon as he replied. "I wish to end all life."

The wizards were silent.

The warlord rose again. His iron shod boots made a heavy, sharp sound as he crossed to the wide windows. On warm air the sounds of a city dying rose toward the cloudy night. Lurgan took a deep breath of air reeking of smoke and blood.

"You do not understand me."

"No, my lord."

Lurgan's size belied his swift grace as long strides took him to loom over the quaking wizards. He reached down to grasp the neck of the youngest of the four, a black haired man in gold finery. Lurgan lifted the man off his feet. The legs twitched and went stiff. The wizard in red turned from the sight as the sound of bone and cartilage being crushed filled his ears.

Lurgan let the body fall.

"Death. An end to everything. Such is my goal. There will be no more rise and fall. Only the sound of the wind as it renders all the temples and palaces into so much sand over the long quiet of eternity. Of such things do nameless gods whisper in my sleep. I have seen it in dreams of late."

The wizard in purple took a deep breath. "If I knew I would not tell you."

Lurgan squatted down. His savage eyes sought each wizard in turn.

"Oh, but you most certainly will. The lash, hot irons, the thin knife, the one that flays flesh from bone. Such are the instruments that reveal truth as sure as the morning sun reveals a night's murder."

The wizards cowed as Lurgan took up his axe. He tapped the marble floor twice and his bodyguard threw the doors open and rushed into the room.

A black-armored man with a goatee grown into long braids asked, "My lord?"

"Take these men and lock them into the palace's library." He turned to address the wizards. "In three days my men will have exhausted their lust for blood and it will be time to move to the next city. In that time you may ponder my visions. Perhaps you may know, or may find a way for me to fulfill the desires of the ones who whisper in my dreams."

Within the expansive library the wizards stood dumb as the doors were barred behind them. At their feet a pair of scholars lay still, curled in on themselves like insects. Thick blood and bile congealed around them.

"Disemboweled. So the steppemen murder men they deem weak." The speaker was the wizard in blue.

The red robed one spoke next. "Should we die this way it will be reckoned luck. I am named Turza, by the way."

The other two introduced themselves. The one in blue was Ghanjo who claimed wide fame as an astrologer and student of the planes.

Shemun of Purple was an expert in the genealogies of gods and dabbled in alchemy. Turza's specialties were typical of a wearer of Red, elementals and conjuration.

Turza bent near the corpse nearest him and took a handful of robe and beckoned Shemun to do likewise. They dragged the corpses to the far corner of the library. Ghanjo inspected their environs. Presently the three stood next to the long table where the scholars had plied their trade before their gruesome end.

Ghanjo spoke first. "The warlord is mad."

Turza nodded. "His wickedness has drawn the attention of even greater evils."

"I suspect I know who calls to him from beyond the void."

Ghanjo and Turza watched as Shemun stroked his beard. His wizened face betrayed grave concern. The wizard continued.

"There are things older than the gods we know. The universe is a swirling cauldron of forces in competition. It is an experiment of incalculable complexity. When the world was new order and chaos scarred the earth with their titanic struggles. The gods found it necessary to restrain chaos, banishing it to a prison in the void. The death we see, the entropy and decay, are but a shadow of its might. It is present in the world only to the degree that dark must exist so that light may also."

Turza said, "So they call to Lurgan. Hoping for release."

"If they are freed then entropy will reign. Life will fail. All will be reduced to motes and mites floating in the void. Not even the energies that bind souls together will be immune."

Ghanjo shook his head. "Even were I of a mind to help to him, I have no idea how these forces may be freed."

Turza shrugged his shoulders. "Nor I."

Shemun lowered his eyes.

The red wizard's prodigious eyebrows rose as he regarded Shemun. "But you do?"

"Perhaps. But I should not speak such lest you reveal the knowledge under torture."

"A fair point, though I think we're better armed against the unknown if we're all equally informed."

Shemun sighed and sat back. "In that case I will tell you. Though when things go wrong, all recall my objections."

Turza made a gesture of annoyance and bade him continue. Shemun bent forward and spoke in a low voice.

"This city is the fourth built on this site. The first city was raised from stone by the old gods themselves. There they walked as men and women and amused themselves as only gods can. The old city was central to the aforementioned struggle between order and chaos. Here it raged until finally the champions of order prevailed and locked chaos away in a deep dungeon. The prison was bound by powerful magicks that sent the gods of chaos into deep slumber. Only a shadow of their might remained free."

"So under our very feet lurks the end of everything."

"Correct."

Ghanjo sighed. His thin frame drew in on itself and he slumped in his chair.

"I wonder with what resources we have how we can most painlessly end our own lives."

Turza snorted. "That line of thought is unbecoming a wearer of Purple."

"On the contrary. Wearers of Purple are known for their acceptance of unalterable fate."

Shemun interjected. "Let us not fall to quibbling in what may be the last hours of life. A problem presents itself. Let us draw borders around it and come to grips with it. Perhaps a solution will reveal itself."

Turza rooted through the cabinets above the scholar's desk. He made a noise of victory and displayed his prize, a decanter of dark wine. Ghanjo uncovered a set of wooden cups and soon the three began a heated discussion.

"Kill Lurgan. Our mission is clear."

Ghanjo took a gulp from his cup and shook his head. "I think we should think more of escape. Surely between the three of us we could find a way to remove ourselves. Are not the Wearers of Blue the masters of movement between the planes?"

Shemun replied, "Certainly. But without my instruments and charts I could not move you so much as a stone's throw without great risk of calamity."

Turza was insistent. "Even if we could escape we leave Lurgan near his goal. Perhaps dreams will lead him there without our help."

"Then how? How do we kill a warlord whose very limbs course with dark power? I remind you he proved invulnerable to our spells once already. For weeks I prepared dirge to hunt and menace him only to watch it fall on the stones below upon release from its cage, wings stunted and mewling most pathetically."

Ghanjo added his experience. "I sought to wreck the ground under his host's feet only to watch the energy fly back into my tower. I was inside an invulnerable ward but my cook and a houseboy were killed in the blast."

Turza stroked his thin beard. "We need a champion."

Shemun puffed out his cheeks and exhaled. "There is none alive that could best Lurgan. Did you see how he dispatched poor Bennit? He was not a small man. Strength like that is lent from darkness. In truth, we live in an age of words, an age of stale poetry, of lawyers and courtiers. A warrior to match Lurgan lives only in legend."

Turza looked at the long shelves around them.

"Then we best start looking."

The man called Thurn woke slowly. Wisps of dream slipped through the fingers of his waking mind. In the dream he stood inside a crude circle of stones. A voice sounded through the haze imploring him to wake.

Wake he did though he found himself in his chambers. Satins and fine silk spilled from the timbers of his bed onto the marble floor. Next to him was Shinixa. She always woke before him.

Her fingers stroked his muscled chest.

"Good morning, my love." Before he could dwell on the dream she sat astride him and his thoughts were drowned under waves of warm pleasure.

Later he sat on the balcony. The palace in which he lived was high in the mountains, offering splendid vistas of peaks purple in the far distance, crowned with wispy cloud. The air so high was oddly warm and Thurn wore only a loose robe. The soft notes of a lyre sounded in the circular hall. The musician was Yur. He was as handsome as Thurn but of a more delicate mien. Dark curls ringed his head where Thurn was fair. The song finished and Yur stepped to the balcony.

"My friend. Your brow is troubled. Does not my playing soothe you?"

Thurn smiled up at him. "Of course it does, dear Yur. Last night my sleep was beset by strange dreams. In fact, I cannot remember the last time I dreamt before last night. Is that not odd?”

Yur laid a hand on his shoulder. “Oh, I think not. Dreams are for troubled folk. Not for us here in the clouds.”

Shinixa interjected, “And you are not troubled, my love.”

Thurn shook his head. “No. I am not. Yet at times I wonder that things were not always as they are now.”

The woman slipped her graceful arms around Thurn’s broad shoulders.

“Do not dwell on such things, my Thurn. Perhaps they weren’t. But this,” she gestured to the mountains, to the fine hall where lounged many like themselves, people in the prime of their lives, “this is now, and will last until the sun falls from the sky. We love and live and laugh and sing.” She lifted his chin until their faces met and kissed him. “I love you.”

“Forgive me, my love. I do not wish to cause distress.”

The day was spent in repose. Figures danced, slow swaying movements to the strings artfully plucked by Yur. Shinixa reclined against Thurn’s chest. When the sun began to dip the feast began. All manner of food decorated the long table of the hall and the people ate without stint and laughed and thus the evening was passed. When the oil lamps began to dim Shinixa led Thurn to bed and they made love. Sated and content, Thurn drifted off as Shinixa’s eyes watched.

The dream came again. The voice was yet more insistent. Thurn felt his heart pounding as he spun in the circle. He could not see the source of the voice. He called out, “How! How may I awake?”

The voicc answcrcd, “Thc runc!”

There it was at his feet. Thurn stared at it, marking its form. He gave a cry of anger as it began to fade as did the stones around him.

He opened his eyes. Shinixa held his face in her hands.

“My love, your sleep was troubled.”

He flew from the bed.

“I know how I may wake.”

“Wake, my love? You are not asleep. Come back to bed.”

Thurn fled the room. He stumbled about, shutting his eyes to preserve the image of the rune. Shinixa followed him. With tears in her eyes she begged him to come back to their bed.

He found himself amidst the remains of the feast. Yur was suddenly there.

"Dear friend! Calm yourself."

Thurn looked at each in turn.

"I know not why but I must obey the dream."

Shinixa fell to her knees. "I beg you, no, my love."

Her eyes gleamed. Thurn stared at her. Her features were feral in the guttering light of the oil lamps.

Yur grabbed his wrist. "Come, Thurn. Let us drink wine and let my lyre sing you back to sleep."

He pushed him away and took up a knife from the table. Before they could do naught but gasp Thurn drew the knife across his palm and drew the rune upon the floor in his blood.

A horrible shriek sounded in the hall.

Thurn recoiled in horror as the glamour faded from his eyes. He was not clothed in robes of fine silk but only a tattered loincloth. He occupied no palace filled with warm sunlight but a dank cavern lit only by crude braziers of burning pitch. Upon the jumbled rocks posed his fellow revelers. But they were not as before. Their true forms slithered and crawled across the wet rocks. Oily black eyes regarded him with anger and wicked mockery. Thurn turned to Yur and Shinixa. Their bodies were coal black and long, sinewy and studded with spikes and tufts of wiry hair. Long, pointed beaks sat below glassy black eyes.

Thurn stumbled backwards and came against a stone plinth. The surface was piled with the rusted remains of armor and weapons. All was nearly dust save a sword in its scabbard, a simple weapon fit for the kings of the age when the secret of steel was just learned.

Yur hissed, "Yes, dear friend. There you have lain for a thousand years while we made pleasant company for you at the behest of Karztan the Black Sorcerer, the one who bound you. The sorcerer is long gone to the Abyss yet his magicks still bound us to you and saved you from old age. We relished our task! The mighty Thurn! Pure of heart and strong of limb!" Yur's fanged mouth grinned with wicked glee as he continued. "But your strong limbs and charmed blade availed you naught! The fog enveloped your mind with the same ease as it would a goatherd! You so loved our company! Savoring fetid water like sweet wine and dining upon the hearts of bats! Thus we saw the lie that is your virtue! Nothing is sweeter to us than to see the righteous brought low!"

"But it is no more!" Shinixa crawled toward him with a reptile grace.

On her fiendish face was no mockery but instead deep sorrow. She continued. "All is gone! Oh, my Thurn! Do not look upon me." With effort she made her voice sound as Thurn had known it. She knelt before him.

"Verily we are creatures of the Abyss and born to falsehood and malice. But, my Thurn, how have I come to love you through these long years! How many nights have I spent in your arms! What mortal love can compare to us! For a millennium we have lain intertwined! And now it is spoiled!" Her keening wail echoed off the cavern's walls.

Thurn stood dumbstruck with horror. Yur produced a lyre. In truth the thing was fashioned from a human spine, turned in on itself and rigid. He plucked at the strung intestines producing discordant notes.

"Hear the sweet music to which you have danced for a thousand years! I still remember the day you sought Karztan in this cave. In your fierce pride you scorned all counsel and fell right into his trap!"

The cavern spun before Thurn's eyes as the weight of memory descended. Yur spoke truth. Bedecked in fine chain and bearing heavy shield and spear he had marched into the gloom. On his hip was the blade known in the ancient tongue as Wyrmkiller. It was forged by Tarpus himself from ore that had fallen from the heavens, a gift from the god of wind. Thus armed he feared nothing. No man or beast could best him. But the strength of his limbs could do nothing against Karztan's trickery.

So long ago. Thurn could recall little else, not even the name of the lands he had left behind. Tears streamed down his hard face as a wail of remorse escaped his lips. Yur laughed as Shinixa wept. The other revelers took after Yur and a chorus of mockery rang in the cavern.

"Behold your lover, O virtuous one! Prideful warrior! Fresh from the arms of a creature of the Abyss! His white cloak a pile of mouldy dust!"

They made a ring around him as they cavorted and laughed and in their mirth they grew bold. A clawed hand reached forward and with a flick opened a cut on Thurn's cheek. The cut burned and Thurn felt his blood rise.

His baleful cries became instead sounds of rage. He pushed back against the throng of demons and climbed atop the plinth. Amidst the rags and rust he spied the gleam of steel.

He took up Wyrmkiller and with a cry of woeful anger he fell upon the fiends, hacking and hewing. They shrieked like animals as they died, chased by his blade to cracks and nooks in the cavern's boulders. He stabbed and hacked until his nakedness was streaked by black blood and sweat. Finally all were slain save Shinixa who cowered at his feet.

"Why do you stay your blade? Pierce my black heart!"

Thurn raised the blade but could not strike.

Shinixa laid her head upon his thigh and wept.

"None ever loved as we did and none ever shall, my beloved Thurn. Kill me, I beg of you."

Her voice was sweet in his ears even as her visage rent his heart in its horror. A new sight intruded on his sorrow. There amidst the ruined corpses of the fiends glowed a ring of blue, nearly as tall as a man. Within the ring was a gray haze.

"Come, warrior."

The voice came from within the haze.

Thurn lowered his blade. Through the portal lay the unknown or perhaps death. His heart preferred the latter.

He looked down at the demon that had been his lover for a thousand years but could find no words.

The warrior stepped past Shinixa and walked through the portal.

"Success!" Turza's bloodshot and tired eyes were bright with hope. Before him stood a tall man, well-muscled. He bore a blade that glimmered blue. He was streaked head to toe with watery black demons' blood; Turza knew from the smell.

"Mighty Thurn! We have freed you from your demonic prison so that you may raise your blade in the defense of all life!"

Thurn stuck the point of his blade in the floor and sank to his knees where he leaned, face against the pommel.

"He looks a little worse for wear, if I am being completely honest," said Shemun.

Ghanjo exhaled and his arms fell to his side and the portal dissipated. As it shrank a black shadow darted from its gray depths and fled to the depths of the library. The wizard slumped into a chair. His torn robes were darkened with sweat.

Turza spoke. "Well. In his time he was a mighty hero. Surely he will rise to the occasion today." The wizard in red addressed the warrior. "Thurn, bearer of Wyrmkiller. Can you understand me? Can you hear me?"

Thurn nodded. "I can. You speak the tongue of the cities though your accent is strange."

"You are in Zanitum, a once splendid city, now in ruins. Lurgan the Warlord seeks to bring an end to everything. We have brought you here to challenge him, lay him low and spoil his woeful aims."

A grim smile showed on the warrior's face. "This has been a day of surprises. Perhaps I am mad. Or I am already dead and unearned pride has sent me to perdition."

"I assure you, Thurn. You are alive. And our need is great. Should you fail all life will be gone from the earth."

"You have made a mistake. I am dishonored. Only remorse separates me from the wicked. I cannot be order's champion."

Turza's eyes glowed with desperation as he made his case. "Mighty Thurn! Any moment those doors will be thrown open and Lurgan will wrench the secrets from us that will undo the world! Many times in history and legend men have been plucked from low places to serve a higher purpose! Such is today! Take up your blade and be redeemed!"

Thurn stood and regarded his blade. "I will play the part chosen for me. Though my heart is broken and my mind clouded."

"Well. We cannot ask more. Harken! The warlord approaches!"

With a creak the doors parted and there stood Lurgan. At his flanks were four men wearing masks and leather aprons. Upon their belts and from their gnarled limbs hung the tools of their heinous trade: hooks and barbed blades.

The warlord took in the scene. The library was a shambles. Tables had been pushed aside to create a clearing in the center of the room. Open books and scrolls lay scattered all around. A circle had been drawn on the floor, ringed with strange runes.

In the center of the circle stood a man. He was tall and lean and his physique well formed by a lifetime of the exertions of war. He wore only a loincloth around his trim waist and black blood matted his long, blond locks. The wizard in red stood near him while the other two were sprawled in chairs outside the circle in poses that betrayed great fatigue.

"What is this bedraggled creature? Have you dared defy me and summoned a champion? From the looks of him I have overestimated the powers of your sorcery."

Turza pointed a gnarled finger at the warlord. "Before you stands a hero of old! The mighty Thurn returns to thwart you!"

Lurgan's savage visage wore a smirk of contempt as he motioned to his torturers. The four men sprang forward with weapons raised.

Thurn was still as they came at him. The wizards looked on in despair.

But at the last moment the blue blade came across in an arc that whistled through the air. A head rolled to the ground and the remaining three stopped short. Thurn pressed the attack. His face showed no emotion as his blade pierced the bulging belly of the closest of his foes. He drew the sword back and bloody intestines followed in its wake. A slicing backhand opened the neck of another and hot blood came in a spray. The last of the butchers lost his footing as he scrambled back. Thurn sprung forward with a mighty slash that sunk the blade deep into the man's skull. With a sickening wrench he pulled it free from the bone and hacked again and again until the torturer ceased to twitch.

Lurgan stared with evident approval. Thurn bent to wipe the blood and brains from his blade onto the dead man's stained apron.

"My muscles are warm again." Thurn looked to Lurgan and continued. "It has been long since I killed a man of the steppe. Your kind dies well, though the smell of horse dung and sour milk will wrinkle my nose for some time after the meeting."

Lurgan threw his head back to laugh. "Red wizard, I am sorry to have doubted your skill. This man will make a worthy foe." He drew the axe from his back and stepped toward Thurn. "Now, let us be quick. My new masters whispered much to me last night. Soon I shall win them free and all this will pass away."

The warlord came at Thurn and the two began the deadly dance. Turza watched with bloodshot eyes and beating heart as two avatars, one of order, and one of chaos, met like in days of old. Their duel raged across the library and through the halls and into the ruined throne room. Neither Lurgan nor Thurn were warriors of refined skill. Thurn was from an age where men locked shields and battered each other into muddy graves while Lurgan was a fighter of the cruel steppe where wicked gods looked in favor upon might and cunning and nothing else. Lurgan swung his heavy axe in great arcs while Thurn ducked and dodged. His blade hewed down only to be turned away by Lurgan's helm or the chain which draped his torso. Still he hacked and hacked again, then rushed forward with shoulder lowered to send Lurgan flying across the floor.

Turza said to Shemun, "He fights well though his eyes are full of sorrow."

The wizard in purple shook his head. "Well, indeed. Though mark the edge of the warlord's axe and the strange tint of the steel."

"Poison!"

Lurgan's cruel laughter echoed in the throne room as he raised himself from the tile.

"Verily, you fight well. But the whispers of my dreams are now like a howling wind in my ears. My masters grow impatient." With that Lurgan's eyes became black and his skin grew pale and he seemed to grow before Thurn's very eyes.

"Behold! Their favor is bestowed upon me! Soon they will be loose upon the earth and we shall all be free. Free of want, free of pleasure and pain. The cycle shall be broken and eternity will begin."

Now was the warlord's turn to rush his opponent. Thurn fell back before the rain of terrible blows. The axe rose and fell with preternatural speed. The heavy steel was nothing in the warlord's hands as he struck again and again. Thurn parried each blow yet he shrank before the onslaught until he was on his knees, blade held high. The warlord swatted the sword aside and raised his axe to split the hero in twain.

Lurgan screamed in pain and lowered his axe. Thurn saw with surprise the source of the warlord's agony. Coiled around Lurgan's leg was Shinixa. With all the ferocity of a creature of the Abyss she had sunk her many fangs into the warlord's leg as her claws raked his thighs. Lurgan fell to one knee and lashed out. He sent the fiend flying across the room with a vicious backhanded blow.

Thurn made use of the pause. He quickly came to his feet and raised his blade. Lurgan sought to bring his axe up to parry. But it was too late. With all his might Thurn drove the blade down to pierce where neck and shoulder meet, thrusting until the hilt rested against the warlord's collar bone. Lurgan scowled at Thurn as he reached to grasp the handle. But the horrible light in his eyes began to dim. He fell to the floor and was still.

Thurn placed a foot on the warlord's chest and pulled the blade free. He hacked at the neck until the head came free. His step faltered as he walked to the great balcony where the old king would address his people in the plaza below.

There he held the head up.

"Behold! Look upon the head of your warlord! Go back to your steppe! Go back to the dark places where you slept! Menace the West no more!" With that he threw the head into the throng below.

Slow at first, the horde of Lurgan took heed of Thurn. There were yells of shock and dismay as the host milled about, unsure. But the animal things, the twisted beast-men, had been bound to Lurgan and Lurgan alone. Bond broken they despaired to be so far from the mountains and glaciers and cold marshes where they once lurked. So they fled the field and thus the horde was so reduced that the men of the steppe, men of cold calculation, could foresee no further great victories as they had enjoyed under Lurgan. Horses laden with loot, they rode east towards their windswept home.

The three wizards regarded each other.

Turza said, "Gentlemen. We have saved all life. When the horde is well and truly gone I suggest we see if those wretched steppemen have left anything for us to drink from the palace cellars."

"I have never been more tired," replied Shemun. "I think I shall return to my tower. Assuming it is not ruined."

Ghanjo asked, "What shall we do with Thurn? It seems cruel to leave him to wander among the ruins."

Turza looked for the champion. He let out a long sigh upon finding him. The champion lay still on the palace floor. Next to him lay the fiend Shinixa. Lurgan's blow had broken her spine.

Ghanjo gasped, "The warlord's axe grazed his arms. Never has a champion fought for higher stakes. Yet no palace or kingdom or treasure horde is his for the effort. Only death."

"He is fortunate, in a way."

Turza raised an eyebrow. "Indeed?"

"Yes. How many among us have known such love?"

The red wizard scoffed. "Bah!"

The three departed the throne room. Turza turned for a last glance at Thurn. The champion lay still in the embrace of a demon. His expression was without strife and his eyes were frozen in a look of content.

Images of the Goddess

I

Devotees of the Goddess found life among infidels intolerable. The prophet Uniam claimed visions of a monastery in the Krixxis Mountains, high up and away from the pernicious distractions of nubile young village girls and world wise divorcés. The suggestion was well liked, and thus its divine provenance went unchallenged. The monks pooled their meager resources to purchase a load of timbers and secure the services of a guild of craftsmen. A decade later, the monks were well satisfied with their labors, even despite the tragic accident that sent Uniam plummeting to his death some years before. The monastery was a tumble of rectangles clinging to the mountain's face like a stack of books teetering on a crooked shelf. The site was completely inaccessible except by a basket lowered by rope and pulley.

The Devotees realized a fault in their scheme when the first few monks became infirm with old age. The order decided to purchase male infants from passing merchants and the nomads that aimlessly crossed the Plain of Ashes below. To raise capital they extracted blue ink from the piles of serave excrement that dotted the mountainside. The scheme was doubly clever; smeared with waste the monks were left unmolested by the soaring carnivores. The ink was of high quality and in constant demand. With their affairs in order, the senior monks could pursue their sacred iconographies and explore the full use of their minds in the service of the Goddess. The senior monks cultivated the ancient art of astral projection. On weeks-long spirit walks, the faithful searched high and low for representations of the object of their worship, artifacts from a distant age where the Goddess herself walked the earth in the forms of countless avatars.

Thus it was that Plom, the son of nomads, spent the eighteenth anniversary of his ascension in the basket on the eastern face of the Krixxis, gathering excrement into a container secured to his back. His olive skin was weathered by the sun and wind that lashed the peaks, but his eyes were youthful and devious, a quality undiminished by the shaving of his eyebrows.

He gingerly removed a mountain goat's skull and spine from a fresh pile and shoveled the muck into his pack with the deftness of years of practice. The skull tumbled down the gravel slope, finally disappearing as it went over the cliff's edge. Plom shouted to his basket-brother, Fress.

"My quota is complete. How much more do you need?"

"Goddess' will, one or two more piles perhaps."

With Plom's assistance, Fress' basket was filled and the pair made their descent. Below on the distant plains, Plom watched a nomad caravan cresting a line of low hills, gray-green in the light of the second moon's rise. Outriders resting wicked bows on narrow hips circled the eight-wheeled carts, guarding against predation by serave. The mounts, surly guhn, pecked at the ground as they ambled along. The faint sound of women singing was carried aloft by the chill wind.

Plom and Fress dumped their cargo into a vat then made ablutions under a fount of icy water. Yeelet, two years Plom's senior and assistant to the abbot, burst into the chamber.

"Finally, you two have returned! Hurry now! The abbot has called us to assembly. Great things are afoot!"

Plom and Fress gathered up their robes and sprinted through the gray stone halls after Yeelet.

The pair found a seat at a back pew, shoulder to shoulder with the other supplicants. Across a wide aisle, the senior monks sat in comfort. The abbot, who was paralyzed from the waist down from a fall and half blind, was carried to his chair below the form of the Goddess, sculpted in stone by Uniam's own hands and now shielded from the gaze of the lowly supplicants by a drape of red silk. A gong signaled the beginning of the audience. The congregation went to their knees. Plom stuck his sharp elbow into Fress' ribs. The youth buckled, suppressing a cry. A searing pain erupted along Plom's shoulders. He turned to see Barefoot, so named for his stealth, brandishing his knotted lash, stern gaze fixed on Plom.

The abbot moved through the litany with a touch more haste than was typical. Prayers concluded, he addressed the gathering in a reedy voice.

"This evening I am happy to announce our collective dreams come to divine fruition. Brother From's soul returned this afternoon from his spirit walk to report the detection of an authentic tome of icons. This work, perfectly preserved through the eons, is the product of man's glorious past, when worship of the Goddess was taken for granted throughout the land."

The abbot raised his gnarled hands to quiet the growing murmurs of excitement. Still standing at the back, Barefoot could not contain himself. Voice trembling, he shouted.

"Blessed abbot, where lies this tome?" He gave himself a lash across the back for talking out of turn and waited breathlessly for the abbot's reply.

"The sacred folio lays one hundred fifty leagues to the south, across the Plains of Ash and at the heart of the Ikzak Jungles. It rests deep within the heart of an ancient vessel, a metal monster from the age when man traveled space by bending time. The journey will be long and hazardous. My deepest regret is that I am too old to seek this treasure myself. The robustness of youth is required. A supplicant will be chosen tomorrow. Go now to your dormitories, pray earnestly and rest well! Tomorrow we will see who has the honor of retrieving this article of incalculable value!"

When his fellow supplicants had finally drifted off to troubled sleep, Plom slipped out of his bunk and made for the refectory. He opened the simple lock with a bent fork he had stolen weeks earlier and entered the pantry. With a loaf of black bread stuffed into his robe, he stole back into the dormitory where Fress waited. They consumed their illicit supper sitting on a wide sill beneath the room's sole window, the third moon bathing their backs in cool light. Fress professed his gratitude and inevitably began to ponder the possibilities of the coming day.

"Who will they pick? We are the oldest of the third generation. Perhaps it will be us. The thought is terrifying."

"I suppose. Though I often do wonder what life is like outside."

A shiver went through Fress' wiry frame. He whispered his fears.

"I certainly don't. Nothing but uncouth, barbaric men and women mocking the Goddess with their profane immodesty. Bandits and hucksters, false priests and mad wizards. I should never like to see it. When I come of age and have mastered the scriptures, I will be initiated by the seniors and see the images of the Goddess with a pure mind and know true wisdom. Then when my soul leaves this world, I will go into her warm embrace for all eternity. None below can say that."

Plom sighed. "You are right, of course. Still…" The creaking hinges of the thick dormitory door sent the pair scurrying into their bunks. Plom feigned sleep for a time before fatigue overtook him. He dreamt he was a nomad, riding a guhn across the barren wastes, stopping to gaze openly at passing women, hazy forms of unknown dimension.

Plom woke late. He pulled on boots of thick felt and his worn coat and sprinted to the courtyard where the supplicants were assembled. Barefoot supervised the proceedings. With groans of disappointment and a few of relief, all the boys shorter than the big man's shoulders were sent away to their normal duties. Twenty-one candidates remained. Fress, the tallest of them all, was already pale with worry. Barefoot puffed out his chest.

"Among you unworthy lot, one will be chosen to seek the tome. The abbot supposes two qualities are needed of potential questers; you must be strong of body and of spirit. We will test your body now. Now! Sprint up the path, up to the overhang yonder! Grab a handful of the weeds that eke out a precarious existence there in the high winds and come back here! Now! Off! The test is begun!"

Tentatively at first, then with determination, the group set off up the slope. Legs and arms pumping, slipping in the treacherous shale, the group made their way up the hill with the best speed possible. Plom knew the slope like the back of his hand. His natural ineptitude in the scriptorium resulted in his assignment to gathering more than any of the other boys. He hung back, staying near the end of the pack as the leaders expended all their reserves pushing themselves toward the overhang. The first had already disappeared behind a sharp curve in the path when Plom felt a burning pain explode in his calf. He hobbled along, cursing his luck. He rounded the bend as Fress and two other boys were beginning their descent.

There was a splash of blue light, and Plom found himself on his back, witless for a moment. Next to him lay Yun, a lanky, indolent youth, but apparently faster than Plom would have guessed. The boy was unconscious, receiving the worst of their collision. In his limp hand sat a tuft of weeds. Plom snatched up the thin stalks and leapt to his feet, sprinting down the path as best he could. His calf unknotted itself and he made good speed, controlling his slide down patches of loose shale rather than fighting it inefficiently as were the boys he quickly passed. Only Fress stayed ahead of him. Panting, he nearly ran into Barefoot's bulk as he reached the courtyard. Fress leaned against the wall, gasping for air. A few more boys hurled themselves through the open gate to look in disappointment at the growing crowd. The remaining contestants trickled in with much less enthusiasm. Barefoot patted Fress' heaving back.

"Fress is the victor! Plom, a close second." Fress winced. Barefoot corralled the top finishers to one side of the courtyard and dismissed the rest. The leaders refreshed themselves at the fount. Fress whispered, still slightly gasping.

"I was first. Goddess' mercy. Barefoot said to run, I ran! I should have thrown myself down and complained of cramp. But I couldn't."

"Maybe the Goddess favors you for this task."

Fress hissed, "I do not want it!"

"Perhaps the next trial will prove your undoing. There is hope, yet."

"I fear not. If we are tested on the scriptures then I will excel. No supplicant knows them as well as I."

Plom looked over his shoulder. Barefoot was occupied tending to the growing knot on Yun's temple.

"Perhaps you could not perform up to your abilities."

Fress replied in shock, "That would be lying! You would have me spend eternity in the cold fetid bowels of the Demon Maleis?"

Plom shrugged. "Surely you could be forgiven such a small infraction."

The lash found his shoulders, and Plom swallowed a curse. Barefoot laughed.

"Is talking permitted in the courtyard, Plom?"

Plom replied, "Surely not, Older Brother. Thank you for your guidance."

The group filed into the scriptorium and seated themselves at wooden desks worn smooth with use. Plom felt his ill-defined hopes sinking. Here in this room he had mastered the basic alphabet and two syllabaries, but the rote memorization required of all supplicants had proved elusive. He was confident in the Invocation and the first three rites, but the Aphorisms and the Ministration typically gave him much difficulty. He looked over at Fress. Sweat was beading at his temples.

The supplicants stood as the abbot was carried into the room. Once seated, he dismissed his aides and bade the young men sit.

"Brother Thulo tells me you boys are hale of body. Now we will see how well you know the teachings. We cannot send young men into the wild without ensuring their character first. Whoever is chosen will face dangers and temptations the likes of which you cannot imagine. So, I now require that each of you first write the Ministration from memory, as this will be your single comfort out in the wild. Then I wish you each to compose a paragraph, juxtaposing Rennum's commentary on the

Goddess' Grace against Milnim's commentary on the fallen nature of the world."

Plom's shoulders sunk. With luck, he may recall the Ministration in exactitude, but he had only a foggy memory of either Rennum or Milnim. Parchment, pens and ink were distributed. Plom set to as best he could. Next to him, Fress worked feverishly, eyes misting with tears. A gong sounded in the distance. They were missing lunch.

The afternoon wore on. Plom produced what he adjudged a fair copy of the Ministration. His subsequent paragraph was weak, drawing ill-formed conclusions from a hazy memory of the two authors. It would not do. Plom sighed and leaned back. He stole a glance at Fress' parchment. In a confident hand, the youth had filled the long sheet to capacity. With a small moan, Fress answered the abbot's call to sign the work and pass it forward. Plom watched as his friend's pen moved slowly from ink jar to the parchment. He glanced over his shoulder. Barefoot was gone. Had he left for the refectory? To relieve himself? Plom could not know. He acted swiftly, seizing the collar of Fress' tunic and head butting his friend violently. Fress' eyes rolled back into his head, and he fell to the floor with a crash. Plom hurriedly signed his name to Fress' parchment and then spoke.

"Benevolent Abbot, call for help! Supplicant Fress is overcome!"

II

Dawn the next day saw Plom sitting in the basket as the rope was played out, bringing him closer and closer to the world below the mountain. Above the cliff's edge, he could just barely make out a line of bald heads. The senior monks peered down, waving fond goodbyes.

The supplicants' duties barred them from watching Plom's descent. They had made their farewells the night before. Fress had barely spoken. Besides his throbbing headache, the relief of not being chosen had rendered him glossy eyed and speechless.

The basket landed gently on the ground. Plom grasped the rim and gingerly climbed over, feeling the hard earth meet his booted feet. His body trembled.

The basket began its ascent, and Plom resisted the urge to leap back inside. He scanned the barren horizon and set off on shaky steps. The monastery receded in the distance. There his teachers and fellow supplicants went about the business of the day. Plom was alone.

He walked for hours, burdened with a heavy sense of unreality. The young supplicant's mind alternated between abject fear and the terrifying ecstasy of complete freedom. The sun and first moon moved in the sky, one sinking, the other rising. Plom's heart began to pound as an irregular chorus of sound grew slowly in volume. From beyond a line of low hills, the clucking of guhn and the snorts of giant mammot could now clearly be heard. As he came closer, he could make out an occasional shout or boisterous laugh. Over and over the abbot's warning echoed in his mind. Avoid the nomads at all cost.

Plom stopped at the base of a hill, seeking shelter behind a large smooth boulder. He leaned back, panting, trying desperately to control a growing wave of panic. His mind went through the verses of the Ministration, cursing as he stumbled over complex stanzas. The exercise seemed to work. As the sun fully set, he wrapped himself in a wool blanket and fell asleep, passing a mercifully dreamless night.

The supplicant woke suddenly. He imagined Fress stood above him, shrieking. When the fog lifted from his eyes, Plom realized he was mistaken. It was a young nomad woman, screaming in abject terror. He scrambled backwards, steadying himself against the boulder. The woman ran up the hill, the colored tassels of her braids trailing in the wind. Plom realized he had been screaming too. He composed himself, leaning against the cool rock and listening. Only the intermittent sounds of the pack and riding beasts came from over the hill. Plom's curiosity soon triumphed over his fear and disorientation.

He crawled on his belly up the gentle slope. At the crest, he peered into the camp. A dozen tents atop gaudily painted carts ringed a fire pit. A few mammots idled, lazily lifting great clots of brown grass into their mouths with nimble trunks. On the other side of the camp, guhn sat sleeping, bound by chains to thick stakes pounded into the dusty ground. At the foot of the hill sat a heavy iron cage on large rubber wheels. Inside, a man stood grasping the bars and looking this way and that. There was no sign of the nomads.

Plom stood and walked down the hill on nervous steps. The man in the cage noticed his approach. His deep voice rang out in the ominous silence. He spoke the imperial tongue with a clipped accent.

"Are you the ghask they fear? Keep your distance! Do not be fooled by my apparent discomfiture! I am a powerful wizard!"

Plom stopped in his tracks. The man sized him up. The fear written on his strong face melted away.

"You are no ghask. But I can't place you. You have a nomad's face but no clan cuts their hair so short. Come here, quickly!"

"I came from the monastery. I am on a quest to recover a book of holy icons depicting the Goddess."

"How interesting! I wish to hear all about this quest. In the meantime though, I need to ask a small favor."

Plom studied the man. His clothes were strange. Perhaps once they had been fine, but now his loose shirt of white silk was stained and torn, and his leather trousers were worn at the knees. Above high cheekbones, a piercing blue eye stared earnestly. The left socket was completely empty. A tousle of dark hair stirred in the light breeze. The man grimaced with impatience.

"Quickly now, boy! We don't know when the nomads will return. They fled up that hill across the camp, screaming of a ghask, a rootless soul out for vengeance. Soon their courage will return. We must seize the moment!"

"Are you a nomad?"

The man clasped his hands together in supplication. "I am no nomad! Please, you must hurry!"

"What would you have me do?"

"Run to the biggest tent. Somewhere inside you will find a cache of valuables, coins, gems, et cetera. Find me a blue orb, fits in the palm of your hand. Look also for a sword and belt. A thin, straight blade, not like their tulwars—hurry now!"

Plom began walking toward the tent indicated. At the man's urging, he broke into a jog. The tent was dark inside and smelled of incense and sour milk. He stared at an assortment of strange objects; their purpose he could not guess. The light from the open flap shone on a pile of blankets on top of which sat the orb. It was a pretty thing, sky blue shot through with smoky bands of gray and white that moved in slow swirls. He picked it up and jogged back to the cage.

"Yes! That's it! Hand it here, boy. Excellent work. I knew you were a young man of character."

The man wiped the orb clean with a handful of his shirt. He craned his neck back and, with obvious discomfort, forced the orb into his empty eye socket.

"Miraculous! Still a bit of charge. Stand back, boy."

Plom did as instructed. A beam of white heat shot from the blue orb, exploding the crude padlock. The man burst from the cage and ran towards the large tent. He emerged seconds later, a water skin slung on his back and a belt bearing sword and scabbard in his hand.

"With alacrity, my boy! We must make good our escape!"

The camp receded in the distance as morning gave way to noon, the sun reaching its zenith with the shadow of the sixth moon in tow. The pair's speed was hampered somewhat by Plom's inability to ride. He wrapped his arms around the guhn's neck and buried his face in the rancid feathers. The man brought his mount to heel and turned. He covered his good eye and peered in the distance towards the camp with the apparent aid of the blue orb.

"Ha! Just now they return. If they set off at once they could not likely catch us. We are safe—as safe as anyone can be on the steppe. I must properly thank you, my boy. My name is Drur. I am a fencer and wizard, slayer of Olg Thggop and Bearer of the Blue Orb. I owe you my life." Drur bowed gracefully in the saddle.

Plom could not return the gesture. He feared at any moment to fall from the guhn. He did not know what to make of the man. Here before him was a specimen from countless lectures at the monastery. The man was loquacious and handsome—no doubt an egomaniac likely to defile innocent women. On the other hand, Plom had been instructed to secure the services of one such as him to aid in his quest. The man already felt himself in Plom's debt. It seemed the Goddess had ordained their meeting.

"I need your help."

"Drur is at your service, young man! I swear now on the Blue Orb to render all assistance that I can in the service of your errand. You had mentioned a book, correct?"

Plom nodded.

"Now, where may this book be found? There are expansive libraries in Zantyum, perhaps fifty leagues from here. The bazaars at Tung Sha are said to contain anything a heart could desire, a mere thirty leagues east of here, as luck would have it."

"The book lies in the heart of the Ikzak Jungle."

Drur frowned. "Are you sure? The curio shops of Minniepe boast many arcane volumes on their dusty shelves. Perhaps there, nestled amidst the charming cafes?"

"No. It is in the jungle. Brother From found it during a spirit walk."

The wizard's shoulders sagged. "Well. As I said, I would be happy to escort you to the edge of the Ikzak and prepare you with sage advice before you enter. A former captain of mine once crossed…" Drur suddenly screamed in pain. He clutched his face and reeled back in the saddle. He continued, voice twisted with pain, "We will go together! I will enter the Ikzak with him! Enough!" As suddenly as it had come, the pain had apparently receded. He smiled weakly.

"The Blue Orb insists on exactitude, especially when an oath has been sworn in its name. It can be somewhat tiresome. How are you called, young man?"

"My name is Plom."

The steppe seemed to swallow distance. After hours of riding, the sharp peaks of the Krixxis seemed only as far away as when they had started. The pair shared a supper of black bread in the saddle as Drur told the sordid tale of his capture by the nomads. Plom understood little. From what he could make out, the wizard had been tricked by a caravan master and sold to the nomads. Somehow a woman had been involved. Plom whispered the Invocation to himself while Drur went into detail regarding the abundant charms that had caused him to so unwisely drop his guard. The abbot had warned against the frank immorality he would encounter. Plom confessed to himself a secret curiosity regarding such matters at the time. But now that it confronted him he felt uneasy. His reverie was broken by a question from Drur.

"So, tell me about this monastery you call home."

Plom shrugged. "I am a supplicant at the Retreat of the Devotees of the Goddess. I live there with my basket brothers and gather excrement from the mountainside which we process into indigo. Every third day I spend in study and contemplation."

"Ah, the odor surrounding your person is explained. So what are the tenants of this creed you and yours follow?"

"The details are forbidden to outsiders."

"A pity. The sun drops low. I think we best make camp."

They halted their mounts as the last rays disappeared behind the distant peaks. Plom gingerly lowered himself to the ground, sore and chafed from the day's riding. At Drur's instruction he pounded stakes into the ground to tether the guhn. Drur whispered to himself as he drew a wide circle around their makeshift camp with the toe of his boot. Satisfied with his efforts, the wizard removed the tackle from the guhn and unfolded the saddle blankets. The fourth moon, a disc of eerie blue, was rising in the north. Drur was heartened by the view.

"Excellent! The Blue Orb will drink its fill tonight. Gods of Wind and Rain have mercy on any nomad that accosts us tomorrow."

Plom lay on the hard ground, marveling at the assortment of stars visible in the cloudless night. It was only the second night of his quest and he had seen many wonders—the open steppe, a nomad camp, a woman. And a mad, unintelligible wizard was his ally. Fatigue quieted his mind and he drifted off.

Morning brought a rude surprise. Lined along the circumference of Drur's ward, a party of nomads stood, weapons drawn. Plom nudged the wizard into reluctant wakefulness. Drur rubbed sleep from his eyes and took stock of the situation. The nomad captain stood grinning, arms folded across the lacquered squares of his ochre colored breastplate, fashioned from the rigid plates of a giant centipede.

Drur spat in frustration. "Well, isn't this just fantastic!" He addressed the nomad captain. "Ulker! I was given to believe the children of the steppe do not travel at night."

The wizened nomad answered. "As you can see, exceptions are made in unique circumstances. Be so good as to dissolve your ward so that I may kill you and the ghask quickly and have the rest of the day at my disposal."

"I am afraid I cannot. This life contains too many amusing distractions for me to relinquish it so cavalierly. The ward will be inviolable for days. And when it drops, my orb will incinerate all that come near."

Ulker replied, "We have you completely surrounded. Our shaman will nullify much of your orb. And even if one or two of us fall, the rest will remain to slaughter you." The shaman shook a necklace of human bones and hissed through sharpened teeth to emphasize the point.

Drur knew the nomad leader was largely correct. A change of tack was in order.

"Are you so quick to kill one of your own blood? This harmless monk is of your people. I am sworn to assist him in his quest for a treasure of immense value. Think of the cosmic goodwill you will accrue by sending us on our way! It would atone for the dozens of ill deeds you commit on a weekly basis. I would even consider forgiving you the outrage of kidnapping me in the first place. Such benevolence!"

Ulker opened his mouth to reply when he was interrupted by a lieutenant pulling on his leather sleeve. The pair were joined by other nomads of rank and stepped away from edge of the ward, conversing in the agglutinative tongue of the steppe peoples. The group continued an animated discussion for some time before Ulker turned back to face Drur.

"Firstly, do not speak to me of the strange one. He is a ghask. To speak of him or to him is to risk eternal damnation. Now, tell me what is this treasure you seek?"

Plom started to answer until interrupted by a short kick by Drur. The wizard continued.

"It is a book of inestimable value. This massive tome boasts gilded, gem encrusted covers between which nest countless beatific images of a Goddess! All who look upon the book are forever blessed. City-folk will pay hoards of coin just for a glance!"

Ulker stroked his long goatee. "And you know where this book is to be found?"

"I do indeed."

"Then I will forestall the pleasure of killing long enough to extract this information. Unless you wish to save us all the time and simply tell me."

"We have circled back around to our initial positions. What you are forgetting, fell warrior of the barren steppe, is that before any attempt to torture me gets underway, I can simply snuff out my own life with aid of the orb."

Negotiations began in earnest. All manner of arrangements were proposed, including a marriage between Drur and a member of the tribe in order to rectify the pervasive lack of trust between the two parties. Initially the entire troupe of nomads intended to join Plom's quest until Drur hinted that the goal lay within the Ikzak jungles. Finally a suitable arrangement was reached. Drur and Plom would be joined in their quest by a solitary nomad representing Ulker's interests. The trio would bring the tome back to the nomad camp where it would be held until the monks could ransom it with their massive wealth. The nomads believed the devotees to be in possession of a great hoard of coin and gold, and Drur did nothing to convince them otherwise. For a fact he did not know if it was true. During the heated deliberations, Plom meekly attempted to remonstrate on behalf of the monastery but was studiously ignored by the nomads. He sat sulking on a saddle while Ulker and Drur made dire oaths to seal the pact. The two men parted with wry smiles, each believing himself in possession of the better part of the bargain. The band of nomads kicked their mounts into a run, eliciting squawks of protest and raising a cloud of dust. One nomad remained. She nudged her mount to face Drur.

"I am Sihma. Attempt betrayal at your peril, ridiculous outlander. I can put an arrow into that orb from two hundred paces."

Drur bowed to the young woman. "I am Drur, and charmed to make your acquaintance. This is my associate, Plom, a religious scholar of unknown abilities."

Plom was silent. His rough hands covered his eyes. He had already seen a woman yesterday, but only for a fleeting moment. But this warrior woman lingered before him. His uncovered eyes could gaze dangerously long. The abbot had warned him that a certain degree of indecency was perhaps inevitable out in the world. He peeked through his fingers. Sihma stared at him with a puzzled expression.

She addressed Drur. "Is something wrong with him?"

The wizard was hitching the saddle to his guhn and did not bother to look up.

"I do not know."

The trio made good time as Plom's skill in the saddle improved. Drur angled their course southwest. Sihma protested. Drur explained no trek through the Ikzak was possible without a day or two of rest and refitting in Shkan, a city built on the banks of the winding Monoga. The wide river flowed eventually into the very heart of the jungle. In Shkan exotic lumber from the Ikzak was traded at a premium and goods from upriver were purchased with the spoils. Drur described its tall orange towers and comfortable inns in wistful tones. After confiscating Plom's purse of coin, Drur declared their budget more than capable of hiring a craft to take them downriver, deep into the Ikzak. Sihma grudgingly accepted Drur's plan.

They rode on. Drur attempted to enliven the bleak journey across the wastes with anecdotes from his numerous escapades. Sihma listened in sullen silence, interjecting occasionally with a snort or sharp laugh to call into question the veracity of Drur's tales. The wizard haughtily denied taking any liberties with the truth. Plom did his best to follow the stories. The youth's piqued interest was mollified by an inability to understand most of what was being said. He found himself wondering what was happening at the monastery in his absence. Plom laughed to himself. The routine of the monastery was doubtlessly the same as it was only a few days ago when he left. He looked up at the sky and down across the humbling expanse of the plain. He saw his companions' backs swaying with the rhythm of the guhn's stride as they argued. Here were stimuli of kind not found in the monastery. Sihma's voice interrupted his thoughts.

"And what are you laughing at?"

Plom stiffened, startled at the address. He met her almond eyes for a moment and then reflexively covered his own.

"Oh, there he goes again."

III

The remainder of their time on the steppe fell into a routine. They rode all day, stopping only as the sun began to dip. Plom and Drur would make camp as Sihma hunted. She would return with long centipedes hanging limply in either hand. These would be cooked over a small fire of dried dung and set aside. Overnight, organs liquefied by the fire's heat would congeal into a gelatinous substance that constituted their morning meal. As they ate Drur would wax nostalgic, recounting the most memorable meals of his itinerant life. He had been born into a respectable family of artisans in old Venitio, solid middle class stock, but had known deprivation as a young wizard's apprentice. The rough years of his tutelage fostered an ambition to become intimate with all the finer things life had to offer. Gradually Sihma permitted herself to laugh at Drur's most outlandish comments.

As the Krixxis shrank behind them, the land became less arid. The barren plains became dotted with green grass and low shrubs as the trio neared the end of the steppe. On the afternoon of the fifth day, the towers of Shkan could be seen in the distance. Plom grew pensive. Drur turned in the saddle.

"Does the city frighten you? Despite its many comforts, it is indeed a notoriously cruel place."

Plom shook his head. "I had not been frightened by it. Now I am. But I am troubled by something else."

After much cajoling, Plom revealed the cause of his exasperation. Hair was sprouting all over his body, concentrating especially in the areas in which sin was incubated. The young man shifted uncomfortably in the saddle.

Drur expounded his theory. "Your body is undergoing changes instigated by simple biology. That curious metallic flavor present in the bread you carried is probably responsible for delaying these changes. I noted a certain listless quality in myself after consuming it those few days. Now that the supply is exhausted, nature is pursuing its normal course without further impediment."

"To what end?"

Drur raised an eyebrow. "To make you capable of reproduction. So that the human race may continue weaving its rich tapestry long past the time when we are gone to the Realm of Death."

Plom shook his head angrily. "You speak nonsense."

"So I am frequently told. But wait and see, young man."

Up ahead, Sihma waved to the pair. They kicked their mounts to a trot and met her at the top of a long gentle slope. The wide Monaga lay before them, flowing calmly to meet Shkan, now only a day's ride away. Its towers of baked brick stood silent guard over the end of the steppe and the beginning of civilization. The third and fourth moon, faint discs of green and blue, hung in the clear sky above the sprawling city. In the distance, a blue-skinned boatman aboard a two-masted barge waved hello to the strange group.

Plom slept fitfully in their makeshift camp. The light of the third moon found him crawling to lie next to Drur. He nudged the wizard awake.

"I have questions."

"Gods of Wind and Rain, why do you wake me at this hour?"

"I can't sleep."

Drur sighed. "What is it you wish to know?"

There in the darkness along the river bank, Drur attempted to explain human reproduction to an uneasy and incredulous Plom. The wizard laid out the facts as simply as he could. Plom countered with arguments gleaned from his studies, wishing for the second time in his life that he had paid closer attention to the senior monks. Drur calmly refuted the young man's assertions before falling back into restful sleep. Plom crawled back to his blankets and lay awake a while before drifting off.

Plom rose with difficulty. Drur was at work with his poniard, freeing their morning meal from its fire-blackened shell.

"I believe Sihma is refreshing herself at the river's edge. Be so good as to let her know our breakfast is ready. With the city close at hand, I am impatient."

Plom made for the river bank, legs heavy with sleep. He passed a thicket of brambles and ducked under low trees to find himself at the muddy bank. He looked right and left, seeing no one. There was movement in the water suddenly. Sihma's head and shoulders rose from underneath the placid water. She walked into the shallows, every step exposing more of her body. Plom watched as her pert breasts broke the surface, round and glistening. Her trim torso followed, and then finally her round hips tapering into muscular thighs. He stared agape at the delicate mound between her legs. Apparently at least part of Drur's information was correct. He felt his heart beating hard in his chest. The water ran from her long black hair, following every curve and niche down to her feet. She stopped and placed her hands on her hips. Plom looked to her face and realized she was staring at him, annoyed.

"See enough, virgin?"

He bolted, sprinting down the bank.

Around and under low trees, through brambles and thickets he ran. Images of Sihma's body competed with the stern face of the abbot in his mind's eye. He felt at any moment Barefoot's lash might rip across his back. But as his legs grew tired a curious calm overtook him.

He ordered his thoughts. The world was larger than the monastery. Many more people, including the world's women, lived outside its craggy fastness. He could not so easily jettison what the monks had taught him. But nor could he deny that the larger world was a reality, one which he now occupied. He was on a quest, burdened with a sacred duty. If accommodating this world and its immodest ways was necessary, he had only one choice. Plom stopped finally, turning resignedly to return to the camp. He permitted himself a smile. If the mad wizard was correct, then Sihma's glorious and confusing nudity was only one small part of the vast, indecent pageant of human existence.

A voice rang out.

"What do we have here?"

The speaker was a burly man dressed in loose trousers and a simple jerkin. A heavy dagger hung from his ample hip. Hoop earrings swung jauntily as he turned to address his comrade emerging from a thicket with an armful of deadfall. The man looked at Plom with a start.

"Dear Jurlo, I do not know. What strange sort of young man is this, wandering the north bank alone?"

The man laid the wood aside and unhooked a club from his belt. He was thin and rangy, sporting identical earrings as his comrade.

The burly man, Jurlo, scratched his chin. "Strange indeed. Where are you from, boy?"

The words caught in Plom's throat. He stumbled backwards, mumbling inanely.

"Speak up, boy!"

Plom replied, barely above a whisper, "I am from the monastery."

"The monastery? Where?"

Plom pointed weakly to the north.

"In the steppe? Jurlo, have you ever heard of any such thing?"

"Indeed not, Mister Malk. And during my wayward youth I crossed the whole of it with a caravan."

Plom looked over his shoulder, hoping to see Drur or Simha advancing this way.

"Curious," said Malk. "If I may essay a theory, I believe this young man is a mental defective."

"I believe you are correct. It would be cruel to leave him wandering thus. And I think the hold has room for one more."

"There always is."

With that, the rangy man lunged forward. The club caught Plom on the side of his head. The youth collapsed in a heap, the sound of laughter drowned out by the ringing in his ears.

First, there was the sound of wood creaking then a sense of gentle motion. Plom's eyes opened to a dim scene. Around him individuals of many descriptions lay in attitudes of exhausted despair. There were six women of varying ages and four men, all bound in chains. In the far corner sat a creature the likes of which Plom had never seen. He stared openly.

A middle-aged women chained next to him anticipated his question. She brushed back locks of her unwashed hair.

"Fear not. That is only an insect man from far Dardilis. He is harmless unless affronted."

The sound of his own voice thundered through Plom's injured head. "Where am I?"

"You are on a barge carrying slaves bound for the markets of Shkan." She leaned over him and mopped his forehead with a wet rag.

"I am a slave?"

A broad shouldered man, face spotted with painful bruises, spoke.

"You are indeed, young man. If you have a thought to escape, I recommend more caution than I showed yesterday." He shifted painfully. "It's likely the pits for most of us—myself, most certainly. We will be made to fight each other or torn apart by hungry throk for the amusement of the people of Shkan. You have never heard of the pits?"

Plom shook his head no. He inspected the hold, a narrow space accessible only by a trapdoor to the main deck. Behind the group, crates were stacked from deck to ceiling. Light from the grate illuminated a sad patch of damp wood. Plom leaned back. His mind wrestled with his predicament, finding no way to comprehend this turn of fortune.

After a damp and uncomfortable night, the barge docked at its destination. The sounds of activity along the quays grew in volume as they approached. With a creak the trapdoor was flung open, the light and air of the outside met by the quiet weeping of the slaves. Plom was lifted roughly from the hold and stood on the deck, squinting in the sunlight. The supplicant gasped as his vision adjusted. Around him was an astounding variety of men, women, and strange humanoids from all corners of the globe. Under the intermittent shadows of the tall towers, all manner of activities, urgent and languid, played out along the quay. Jurlo made fast the slaves' chains to one another, and the group was marched toward the market. Plom was stupefied as his senses fought to process the flood of input. There was the stench of the pier and the savory odor of spices. A group of men in baggy trousers shouldered great sacks of wheat on their tanned backs. Two insect men conversed with a series of loud clicks and chirps. An idol to the river god sat fat and wreathed in orange flowers as a boatman lit a stick of incense at its base.

The group trudged across a wide piazza toward the slavers' market where a few merchants haggled furiously with a score of slavers. The bruised man nudged Plom's shoulder, pointing meekly to a passel of men in black livery. Their tunics bore the standard of a throk rampart on a field of blood red.

"There are the pit masters, buying up the stocks. We shall be dead in a few days. Gods, give me the grace to accept it."

Plom's heart sank.

IV

Drur and Sihma drove the guhn as hard as they dared toward Shkan's looming towers, trailing Plom's mount behind on a tether. The morning had been spent in a fruitless search for the missing supplicant. Sihma finally stumbled across a series of tracks and marks, which enabled her to deduce much of what had happened. Drur's knowledge filled in the remaining blanks. The tracks of two men met Plom's. Then drag marks led to where a boat had been pulled up on the bank. Plom had doubtlessly been waylaid and was en route to the slavers' market. By his inexpert calculations Drur figured a barge moving downriver would likely reach the docks several hours before he and Simha would, hampered by the uneven terrain. The wizard cursed himself for letting the young man out of his sight. Sihma was furious but sheepishly refused to relate the circumstances that led to Plom's panicked flight. The particulars did not matter. Drur had sworn an oath on the Blue Orb, and the young supplicant must be located. With any luck the barge would be delayed or its business drawn out, and the two seekers would reach the slave markets at the same time as Plom. They rode all night.

Dawn saw the city gates a stone's throw away, manned by two bored sentries. The north gate was used for the irregular caravans or odd travelers from the steppe such as Drur and Sihma. The two were admitted quickly after paying a small fee. Drur made inquiries and was distraught to learn the slavers' market was several districts away, distant from the more desirable neighborhoods bordering the north wall. The pair angled their guhn onto the main thoroughfare, soon teeming with morning traffic. Drur cursed, standing often in the saddle to peer above the throng of porters and carts that jammed the wide road. Chaos reigned; there was no apparent system or rules to guide the meandering users. Sihma kicked out at any individual or beast that came too close. Drur attempted to pacify her.

"My dear, please adjust to these close quarters and accept the inevitable before you eventually strike a person of importance."

"It is unnerving. So many people crammed into such a small place."

Drur tapped nervously on his thigh as they slowly made their way to the slavers' market.

By late afternoon the market was still doing a brisk business. Drur and Sihma hitched their mounts to a post and picked their way through the crowd. Plom was nowhere to be seen. The wizard became increasingly desperate. Sihma scowled, constantly laying a hand on her bow in its case as it brushed up against passersby. Finally the pair sat on one of the benches lining the piazza. The traffic slowed as no more barges were docked. The sun sank low. Drur made his fears known.

"We likely missed him. He will be torn to pieces in the pits."

Sihma shrugged her shoulders. "So much for the treasure. You do not know where it is precisely?"

"No, I do not. And the Blue Orb's limited intellect will only comprehend that my oath goes unfulfilled. Perhaps it will better divine the circumstances and excuse me from my obligation. Or perhaps it will become vexed and boil my brain."

"That's unfortunate. I will have to return empty handed and endure censure from my tribe. This will diminish my standing considerably. To complicate things further, Ulker commanded I return with your head in lieu of treasure."

"I suspected as much. It's only sporting to warn you that I will endeavor to kill you first. And in a contest where I am aware of your intent, the odds favor me and the orb."

"If I read things correctly, this setting is inappropriate for open murder, is it not?"

"You are a quick study. Here the forces of the state will come down hard on an open display of violence."

Sihma pushed her dagger back fully into its decorative sheath. She shot the wizard a stern glance. "It occurs to me now what a disappointment you are."

Drur was wounded. "Indeed? What would you have me do? Young Plom is gone. He is being led right now to a cell where he will spend his last days lonely and confused until his life is snuffed out in the games. We are powerless to do anything about it, short of staging some insane, suicidal stunt to liberate him from captivity."

"You have quit before even starting! Surely you can think of something! I am too far out of my element, I must admit. But you boasted of a score of adventures against similar odds. Was someone else doing the thinking, the planning that enabled you to survive these escapades?"

Drur swore, striking the bench with his palms. He stood to his full height and tensed.

"Gods of Wind and Rain, you are right. I gave myself over to despair too quickly. It isn't like me. I blame the neutering chemicals in the boy's accursed bread. Now, we need intelligence, and quickly. We must find when these barbaric games are to take place. We must find information on the facility in which they are staged. I have visited this city twice before but never had the stomach to attend. And I need new clothes. You need a less conspicuous ensemble as we go about our business." Drur retrieved Plom's purse of coin from his belt. "Come, let us outfit ourselves, and then a decent meal, by the gods. This formidable problem will shrink demonstrably with a bellyful of lean steak and a few glasses of wine to sustain us."

Sihma rose, grinning, and slapped the wizard across his broad shoulders. The two set off toward the markets.

After a short argument Sihma relented and used the provided utensils for the remainder of their meal. The last hours had seen much accomplished. Drur wore a new silk shirt and trousers of tight velvet in a deep green. The tailor had assured him that within Shkan the ensemble would communicate the cavalier élan that reflected Drur's character. Sihma wore a gown of satin, colored a deep mauve that complemented her olive skin. The effect was alluring despite her obvious discomfort.

"How can I fight in these clothes? My bosom threatens escape at any moment." She talked with her mouth full, punctuating her remark with a tug of her tight bodice.

Drur swallowed the last of his wine, pausing to savor it. "I am sure when the time comes you will perform up to standard. We must blend in with the populace here. Our inquiries revealed only the time of the games, two days hence. Information about the pens is closely guarded. To inquire more seriously might alert suspicions. Thus, our planning is shaped. We will have to strike in public, at great risk, and flee immediately through crowds of confused and possibly enraged spectators. A nomad princess of savage beauty would be too memorable. Now you are just another pretty face."

Sihma belched. She covered her mouth, suppressing laughter.

"I am no princess."

The arena in which the gladiatorial games and executions took place was a wide, three story structure of the same orange brick as the rest of the city. While not in use, the arcing terraces were open to the public. Drur and Sihma strolled the aisles bedecked in their new finery, winding their way around knots of young people lounging and larger groups of old men playing a game with small squares of baked clay embossed with complicated glyphs. Bold stratagems were heralded by the echoing hard clack of the tile against bench.

The tiled stone floor of the arena proper was checkered with empty post holes. Drur made inquiries. A pair of idling lovers explained that modular walls could be brought in for a favorite variation. A maze would be erected, and groups of slaves and hungry throk would be turned loose at either end. Sihma expressed revulsion as they walked.

"And here my people are considered uncivilized for simple, clean murder, while these fops watch such spectacle."

Drur nodded. "It is indeed paradoxical. In most other respects the city is a model of calm. There is little crime, and the high walls and powerful court mages deter invaders. Shkanese are a generally gentle lot. I suppose here all their dark passions are given vent. In my native Venetio such emotions are spent on masterful works of art and illicit affairs. A superior arrangement."

The pair wound their way to the front rows. Drur peered over the waist-high stone wall marking the boundary between spectators and the damned.

"The drop is about ten feet. We will need a knotted rope."

"I assume there is more to this scheme than simply throwing a rope over the edge in the middle of the event."

"There is indeed. We must find an apothecary."

Drur purchased the items he required from two different shops to better mask his intentions. He spent a tense afternoon mixing the components in his room at the tavern while Sihma elected to get drunk to pass the time. The next day Drur walked the quays looking for a boat heading into the Ikzak that had room for passengers. He secured the services of one Togun Sideh, skipper of the *Drullok's Bane,* a two-masted barge boasting a motor in the stern and an energy cannon mounted to the bow. The wizard claimed need of a trip to the jungle to secure rare flowers for use in spells.

Drur explained glibly to the skipper that the exact moment of departure was vitally important to his inamorata, a tempestuous woman whose passions were ruled by complex astrological calculations. The vessel would need to depart the morrow, no earlier than the second afternoon bell, coincidentally the moment when the games would be at their peak. Drur anticipated difficulty, but the promise of the last of Plom's coin secured firm guarantees. Togun took half the money upfront, dropping the coins into a pouch hidden beneath his wide belly.

The lanternmen stalked Shkan's wide avenues on tall stilts as dark descended. In their suite Drur rehearsed his spells and Sihma oiled her saber. Presently both lay awake in their respective chambers, contemplating the likely possibility of death as the sound of revelry came from the streets and tavern below. Shkan was becoming charged with a festive electricity. Tomorrow much wine would be drunk, and much blood would be spilled in the arena.

They rose at dawn after a restless night. Drur gently packed the parcels he had made into his shirtsleeves while Sihma hid her equipment under voluminous skirts. They mounted the guhn and rode at a leisurely pace to the arena. Crowds were already gathering at the early hour. The pair hitched the mounts to a lamp post and walked arm in arm through the milling crowds and up the tall stairs to the terraces. Drur cursed. The best seats were already taken, save the sections across the floor reserved for aristocrats. They found a spot as near as they could manage and sat pensively. The wizard squinted his eyes, scanning the empty floor. The distance was great. He turned to Sihma.

"I shall be relying on your hawk eyes more than I had imagined. I cannot waste the energies of the Blue Orb by peering into the distance. This event will go on for hours. We don't know which iteration will bring Plom to the floor."

"I will keep my eyes open."

The sun rose higher as the seats filled to capacity. Drur tapped his fingers impatiently while Sihma sat still, jaw set firm. Vendors dressed as Pierrot began to ply the crowds with sweets and clay cups of liquor. Drur purchased a packet of candied beetles.

"Save my place."

Sihma scowled. "I know my duties, wizard. Try not to blow yourself up."

"If it hasn't happened yet, then I am likely in the clear."

Drur stood and affected the meandering gait of a tourist as he wound his way down to the wall. He ate the beetles one by one as he walked, looking this way and that. Finally at the edge, he leaned on his elbow and looked out over the floor. Sihma watched as the wizard appeared to toss the packet of sweets casually to the ground where similar flotsam had already begun to gather. He dodged groups of running children as he wandered down the circumference of the wall, repeating his performance periodically.

The crowd was growing increasingly restless as Drur reclaimed his seat. He thought to speak, but the blaring of trumpets interrupted. The crowd shouted in response. A set of wide iron doors burst open below on the floor. Burly men bearing a gold palanquin bore Shkan's mayor before the riotous crowd. He brought a megaphone to his red lips and addressed the throng.

"Greetings, noble Shkanese! The fifth moon rose high last night. The blood moon! And how do we honor Yunare? How do we honor the sacred blood moon, the benevolent patron of our fair city?"

The crowd responded, screaming for blood, again and again. Drur felt his knees weaken.

Sihma leaned close to be heard over the roar. "It bears saying again; these people are civilized, and they claim the steppe is not?"

"Yes, yes, point taken. Keep a close watch now!"

The palanquin disappeared as an impresario mounted a dais above the aristocrats' seating. The plump man wore robes of crimson trimmed in gold. With a flourish he declared the commencement of the entertainments. The first round was in honor of Yunare. Six notorious criminals were pitted against Wim Tid, the insect man blademaster, a mercenary of wide fame and an occasional gladiator. Drur marveled at his skill.

"Absolutely stunning. My skill with the foil is not insignificant, but now I feel inadequate. It's hardly fair though. He has four extra arms."

Wim Tid bounded in between the outmatched combatants, landing to strike with the speed of a scorpion before springing away from any counterattack. One by one the criminals were struck down. The blademaster honored the blood moon with strikes to his opponents' arteries. The crowd met every jet of blood with raucous applause. Finally only the insect man remained standing. He tipped the brim of his wide hat and bowed low to an appreciative audience. Slaves in blue tunics threw open the iron doors and dragged the corpses away. Drur and Sihma leaned forward as the next event was announced. To clear the viewers' palette after the display of skill a coarser spectacle was scheduled. A dozen slaves armed with small spears were to be set against a pack of hungry throk. Nervous steps carried the twelve to the center of the floor. Drur frantically scanned the group.

"There! That's him! Is it? Look! Is it him?"

Sihma frowned. "I can't tell! I think it is!"

The sound of a gong signaled the release of the throk. The slavering beasts sprinted from their pen with bounding leaps.

"Gods' mercy! We have no choice. It is time!"

From under her skirt Sihma produced the rope and hook. Drur closed his eyes and held his hands together. The wizard murmured to himself as his fingers and hands went through a series of motions. The air began to hum.

Great gouts of black smoke exploded from Drur's parcels along the wall. The crowd reacted in primal terror as screams of fire echoed throughout the arena. Pandemonium erupted as the great throng moved chaotically toward the exits, stumbling, screaming in terrible confusion. The smoke obscured all. Drur and Sihma dodged fleeing spectators as they rushed to the wall. The hook was made fast, and the two leapt over the edge. The smoke billowed up the terraces, leaving the floor largely clear. A barking snarl alerted the two to danger. Sihma buried her saber deep into the muscular neck of a charging throk, deftly sidestepping its careening bulk.

Ahead the slaves were being dragged down, one by one, by the remaining predators. Drur sent a few bolts of energy from the orb into the pack's flanks. The beasts yelped in agony and fled. The smell of charred fur and flesh was added to the heady miasma of blood and fear. The nomad and wizard ran to the slaves. Two lay in crumpled heaps amidst growing pools of blood. Drur grabbed one roughly by the shoulder, turning him to get a look at his face. He did the same to the other and then looked to the knot of slaves still on their feet. They looked about in total shock as Sihma darted through the lot.

Sihma swore. "He isn't here!"

"I know!"

The wizard spared a glance at the giant doors. Behind them somewhere Plom waited for his turn in the arena. Drur had played his hand prematurely. The episode was a fiasco.

Sihma put her foot to a throk's side in order to pull her bloodied saber from its carcass. Drur grabbed her arm and the pair sprinted back to the rope. Before scaling the wall the wizard turned to address the slaves.

"Freedom lies this way, if you desire it!"

The pair scaled the wall quickly and bounded up the terraces toward an exit. Drur lost sight of Sihma in the lingering smoke as he made for the stairs. Before him a figure loomed—a vendor wearing a tray. The two collided. Sweets rained down as Drur looked at the man. Beneath the whiteface makeup was Plom.

"Gods of Wind and Rain! What are you doing?"

"Drur! I never thought to see you again! Did you come to watch the games?"

The wizard stood and pulled the young supplicant to his feet.

"Watch the games? You stupid boy! We came to rescue you!"

Plom stared, uncomprehending. Drur grabbed his arm, and the pair made for the stairs, still thronged with fleeing spectators.

"Where are we going? The sweets! I have to recover the sweets."

"Forget the sweets! We are leaving, Plom. Remember the book? I am oathbound to take you into the jungle, and Sihma is sworn to take my head if we don't succeed. I would like to keep my head and not be forced to endure the inevitable pangs of conscious should I have to incinerate her, mid-attempt. In summary, we are going to get your book. What is the meaning of this costume anyway?"

By way of answer Plom pulled up his shirt, an awkward act in the press of the crowd. Drur read the raised and tender wound, a fresh tattoo centered in the supplicant's chest.

"This slave is the property of Relallthein Confectionary Company, Shkan. Reward Available if Returned Alive." Drur shook his head as the crowd poured into the street. Sihma was waiting, already mounted with three pairs of reins in hand.

V

Plom's frilled collar bobbed in the wake of the *Drullok's Bane* where Drur had tossed it. The wizard leaned against the aft gunwales while the supplicant bent low, washing off the whiteface with a bucket of river water.

"Now that we are relatively safe I would appreciate an account of your travails since last we met."

Plom finished his ablutions and stood. He gazed at the receding towers wistfully.

"I was kidnapped at the river's edge. Then they took us to the slavers' market where I was about to be sold to the pit masters. A man asked any who were literate to raise their hands. I was the only one. The man bought me and took me to a large building. My duties were explained. I was to write the company's ledgers and copy sentimental messages onto small cards for inclusion into gift boxes, and on festival days I and the others would sell their wares. I was given the tattoo and then training began. They were largely kind after telling me all the horrible things that would happen if I failed them or fled. They gave me a bowl of delicious stew and then a piece of candy. I had never had anything like it. Did you ever have candy, wizard? It is common, isn't it?"

"It is. Continue."

"It was red and sweet. So sweet. There was a strange taste with the sweetness. It was described as 'tartness' upon my asking. The two tastes seemed to blend together, sometimes competing, sometimes complimenting one another. I savored it as the thing slowly shrank in my mouth. When the candy maker saw how much I had enjoyed it he gave me a piece of green candy. This one was sweet also, but had a slightly sharp taste as well. The man explained they were flavored with fruit harvested from orchards just outside the city. There was green, red, and a purple one, one that had red with streaks of white, one that was blue…"

Drur interjected. "Enough!"

Plom's eyes became enlivened as he continued. "Then I met the other slaves. Most were women. I told them my story, and they took pity on me. They bade me have no fear to look upon them. Then, late in the night…"

"Oh, for the love of all that is good, Plom, spare me."

Sihma emerged from below decks. The nomad had changed back into her old clothes and walked with a light step. She saw the consternation on Drur's face.

"What happened?"

"Oh, nothing. Nothing except that we risked life and limb to rescue Plom from the peril of tooth decay and the possibility of contracting a social ailment."

"Ha!" The nomad slapped Plom on the back. She continued. "If it wasn't for the prospect of this treasure I would surely kill you." She turned to Drur. "But as things stand, we can't be overly upset. We escaped without consequence, and we are on our way to the treasure."

Drur sniffed. "Yes, quite."

The *Drullok's Bane* was a large craft, one hundred feet from bow to rounded transom and thirty feet wide. Togun and his first mate Leli navigated the wide Monoga with an ease born of many years' experience.

The journey into the Ikzak was made under sail. The return trip would be under power, typically trailing as many as a dozen logs of priceless timber.

Several times a day the two crewmen, Hume and Roppen, were interrupted in their duties to tack the vessel back to cross the center of the river. Otherwise they made themselves busy with maintenance. There was an engineer aboard, but the man was never seen, keeping to himself within the cramped confines of the compartment that housed the crystal which powered the vessel's screws. Togun and Leli took turns at the wheel. At night the anchor was dropped, and all but a sole watch slept.

The two loggers signed on for the trip, the horned giants Rep and Vinconzo, settled quickly into their routine. The pair spent all their time fishing, one off the port beam, the other starboard, balanced thusly so their massive bulks would not cause the vessel to list. The pair were wont to doze as the brown water flowed quietly past, the bow wake gently lapping against their booted soles that hung heavy over the gunwales.

The passengers spent their first day aboard in idleness. Plom watched as Shkan's towers disappeared behind the horizon.

He looked to Drur and said, "Do you think there is any candy aboard?"

The wizard did not reply. He inquired about a spare rod and was given one. Drur settled next to Vinconzo and baited the hook from a clay jug packed with pickled beetles. The giant took the cup in his massive hand and gently tapped the base, knocking a beetle into his palm and popping it into his mouth. Drur dipped the line into the water and leaned back.

The setting sun painted a long streak of wavering red on the surface of the water. The streak faded to a dull purple before darkness finally fell. Togun ordered the anchor dropped. The crew and passengers gathered amidships for a meal of bread and cheese underneath a line hung with colored lanterns. The giants kept their place as they ate their supper, a selection of beasts caught from the river, consumed raw. This night Rep had only a pair of water scorpions while Vinconzo bit into a fat woph fish. Both drank deep from casks of wine.

Togun sipped at a glass of distilled alcohol as he talked in his gruff voice. "So, it's flowers you are after, correct?"

Drur looked up from his meal and replied, "Yes, my captain. The pollen of the Isis yields components for several spells and salves. It is scarce down our way. While there I hope also to cull petals from the Screaming Yip, and I wouldn't turn up my nose at a quantity of root from a Grappling Vine. With sufficient supply I can replenish my stocks and also make a tidy profit back home."

Plom said through a mouthful of bread, "We aren't looking for the book anymore?"

Togun set his glass down. "The book?"

Drur shook his head. "Pardon my friend. He is a mental defective. Quite tragic really. His mother was a servant in my father's house. On her deathbed my father swore that we would look after her only son, an act of generosity which has caused me great inconvenience."

Plom cocked his head slightly. "I don't understand. Who are you talking about?"

Sihma sighed. "He is talking about you. Now be quiet."

Togun smiled. "Now, now. This is my vessel, my table, my rules. What do you mean 'looking for the book', young man?"

Plom looked at Drur. The wizard threw up his arms. "Well, you may as well tell him now!"

The supplicant related the story of his life and quest to a rapt Togun while Drur and Sihma sat pensively. The captain whistled through his teeth at the tale's conclusion. Hume and Roppen had edged forward on the bench. Hume toyed with a dagger in his tattooed hands as he and Roppen and the captain exchanged glances.

Togun laughed, "Flowers, indeed! You three are by far the strangest lot I have ever ferried down river. Now, perhaps we should discuss in greater detail the value of this sacred tome."

Drur sniffed. "Gentlemen aren't concerned with such vulgar matters."

"I don't recall laying claim to that particular appellative."

"They use apples to flavor some of the candy."

Drur's face reddened. "Plom, please be quiet." He leaned back on the bench and continued, "Let us all save ourselves some time. The financial particulars are of concern to two parties, the nomads, represented by the lovely Sihma, and the monastery. I am here to only to fulfill a careless oath. I suggest you and Sihma negotiate an arrangement. I warn you, captain, the nomads are notoriously parsimonious, and I can only imagine the attitudes of the monks. I am retiring to my hammock. I expect the dawn will bring me news of a new and mutually beneficial relationship between the two parties. Should the situation be different I will be sorely vexed and prone to intemperate displays. My orb is charged to bursting. I bid you all good evening."

The two parties began negotiations. Togun started with a series of vague threats, capitalizing on the murky danger of the river and their present distance from civilization. Sihma was utterly unfazed, leveraging the nomads' renowned fondness for vengeance against the skipper's ill-defined threats. Should Sihma not return by next winter, the entire clan would investigate her fate. Finally a percentage was agreed upon, 10% of the nomads' take. For this fee Togun pledged the assistance of the two giants and Hume. The crewman boasted some skill with the knife and was eager for the change in routine. Roppen was openly squeamish at the prospect of danger and declared his intent to stay onboard when the expedition headed inland. The pact was sealed in blood underneath a gibbous Yunare. Hume made a pass at Sihma and was turned down brusquely. Passengers and crew went to their hammocks as Leli stood watch at the cannon.

VI

Wim Tid sat motionless in the darkness, perched on the bow of the skiff. The craft was making good speed down the winding river. Insect men could see in total darkness, an ability the skiff's captain put to good use. The mysterious insectoid had paid well on the condition that the craft would proceed with as much possible haste. Despite the high fees his purse of coin was still bulging. The errand was a profitable one—a joint contract from Shkan's guild of entertainers, the slavers responsible for organizing the bloodsport in the arena, and the Relalltheіn Confectionary Company. By the insect man's calculations, the skiff would catch up with the river boat in two days.

He had investigated thoroughly the pair responsible for the fracas at the arena and the mental defective skilled in calligraphy that had escaped the confectioners. He had heard snatches of conversation collected by slavers at the market—a waiter, a tailor, and finally a trio of workers at the candy concern. All these threads wove a strange tale, the notion of a book, a tome of great value prized by a sect of secretive fanatics. Wim Tid reckoned he could turn a profitable contract into something much more. With a hoard of wealth he could return to the fourth moon and build a mound the likes of which had never been seen. With such a structure he could entice a queen to nest, a great beauty with shimmering antenna and swollen egg sacks. For her pleasure he would erect mud spires in fanciful combinations around the mound as thousands of larval young crawled underfoot. Such was his dream.

In his halting speech he warned the coxswain of a log floating ahead. The man deftly altered course, and the skiff continued down the river.

VII

The mood on the *Drullok's Bane* darkened as the great trees of the Ikzak came into view. Togun knew the general whereabouts of the derelict ship. His information confirmed the vague directions the monks had given to Plom. Some years ago the skipper had ferried a party of hopeful scavengers to where the river was closest to the ship. The fateful group had been rough men, hardened veterans lured by rumors of the great ship and looking to find pieces of arcane technology to sell to the wizards of Shkan. None had returned. The skipper guided the craft down one of the many tributaries as the trees began to crowd the river's edge. On their great fronds squatted troupes of disinterested monkeys, resplendent in coats of glossy yellow fur. They watched the boat with haughty disdain as their tiny hands twirled the long tufts of their moustaches absentmindedly.

Togun had doubled the watches. Plom found himself standing at the stern, scanning for trouble along the dark banks. Drur exercised nearby, working his sword in graceful arcs as he sweat in the growing heat. He had exchanged his ensemble for a sleeveless tunic of gray cotton and baggy trousers of leather, items borrowed from Hume. He finished his exercise and mopped his forehead and neck with a rag.

"Young Plom, Togun tells me we arrive this evening. We will rest and then head out in the morning. Are you excited to be so close to your goal?"

The shadows from the massive trees blocked the sun intermittently as they conversed. Plom shrugged. "Securing the book will make me a hero to the monks. But I fear that I will find life difficult after I return. Also the monks may take exception to some of my experiences."

Drur laughed. "Take heart, young man. We still have a day's march through the deadly jungle, the mystery of the ship, and the very real potential of a deadly double cross by either the crew or the nomads. All in all, it is unlikely you will see the monastery again."

Plom frowned. "Thank you." The young supplicant peered over Drur's shoulder. His expression became quizzical. "What is that?"

Drur spun around, scanning the tree line for danger. He squinted, hunting for a glimpse of approaching monsters. Plom kicked hard against the wizard's rear, sending him plunging into the river. Drur broke the surface sputtering.

Plom looked down at the waterlogged wizard. "That was for calling me a 'mental defective'."

Drur laughed heartily. "My boy, I think you are finally gaining the measure of this world. But no more of that, please. Gods know what hunts in these waters."

Togun guided the craft's shallow bow to the river's muddy bank as night fell. At dawn the landing party began preparing in tense silence. The two giants unwound and oiled their great saws, long lengths of bladed chain weighted on either end with heavy handles sized for their massive hands. Vinconzo then ran a stone along the edge of his great, hacking blade as tall as Plom and nicked from past work in the jungle. Rep lifted a barrel to the small of his back while Hume secured the straps to suspend it there. Plom watched the pair.

The supplicant asked, "What is that?"

Rep smiled. "A gift for our hosts, if they bother to pay us a call."

Vinconzo threw a heavy plank down, bridging bow and bank. The jungle hung over the water's edge. Gnarled vines hung from the branches of the great trees, spotted with blossoms in lurid lavenders and pinks. Unseen creatures heralded their arrival with hoots and barks.

The noise was not welcoming. Plom stared into the murky darkness that extended nearly to the bow. The air was hazy with an oppressive humidity which tired the lungs. Drur checked the edge of his sword and nodded with satisfaction. He cleared his mind until the reassuring presence of the orb filled his consciousness. Plom had armed himself with a spear from the hold. The weathered tan of his face was mismatched atop the paleness of his shoulders and torso that showed through the loose cut of the singlet he wore. Sihma had exchanged her embroidered nomad's garb for a light tunic and cotton trousers. She nocked an arrow to her curved bow and stared into the thick trunks encroaching along the mud bank.

"How I long for the open steppe! One can see an enemy for miles."

All were ready.

Vinconzo addressed the landing party. "Now we enter the jungle. Myself, Rep, and to a lesser degree, Hume, all know the jungle's peril. You three do not. It would take weeks to teach you the fieldcraft needed to survive here. In lieu of that, I will state one rule, one rule above all. Do not touch anything. Not a flower, not a beetle, not so much as a leaf. I will be in the lead. I will make a path. All will follow in this path. No one leaves the path, for any reason whatsoever. Is that understood?"

The party nodded their assent. The giant continued. He ran a finger along the sharp points of his horns as he spoke, a habit. "The skipper tells me the ship you seek lies in a clearing about a half mile west, or so he has heard. A great deal of calamity can befall us in a half mile of the Ikzak. Keep your wits about you. We leave now."

The group left the boat. Rep and Vinconzo simply stepped across onto the bank. The others walked across the plank. The jungle swallowed them all. In minutes sight of the river and the boat were completely obscured by the massive trunks and looping vines which seemed to touch everything in sight. Plom kept one hand on the line which spooled from a cylinder strapped to Hume's back. Drur sipped water from a leather skin and wiped the sweat from his high forehead with an already soaked cloth. The trail was littered with the vegetation cut by Vinconzo's giant blade. The sound of it assaulting the thick fronds was incongruous—an unnatural rhythm in a world of intermittent hoots and caws.

The group walked in silence past dazzling blooms of orange veined with red, large enough to envelop a person within their fragrant petals. More spectacular were the displays of iridescent mold that clung to some of the trunks. The jungle was a deadly place where nothing but the largest predators lived long. The colors seemed to revel in this fact, the flora and fauna garishly celebrating their brief life spans. Sihma thought to swing her saber at the fist-sized flies that hovered past only to stay her hand from fear of Vinconzo's warning.

Above came the sound of crashing branches. Plom peered through the thick cover, desperate to see the source of the commotion. Drur was suddenly at his side. The noise grew closer. Plom held the spear firm. A heavy thud rang out behind the pair. Plom spun around, knocking Drur across the head with the spear's blunt end. Before the young man stood a giant ape draped in layers of shaggy hair colored rich ochre. His knees felt weak as he stepped back, keeping the weapon trained on the great beast. The thing roared, revealing a mouth of yellowed fangs. Rep leapt in between the two. The ape ceased his ferocious display and grinned.

"Dear Rep, you spoiled my fun. Another moment and this young man would have perished from fright."

Rep laughed. "Ecguz, you are a wicked creature. How goes things?"

"The same as ever. I am still chieftain. What are you doing in these parts? The good mahogany is down the south fork, as you know."

Plom's heart still beat fast. He helped Drur to his feet and mumbled an apology. Sihma stared in wonder at the jungle chieftain. Giant and ape continued their discussion.

"We are here to see the old ship. It lays yonder, no?"

"The metal mound? Yes, you are on the right track. And my toll?"

Hume undid the straps holding the barrel to Rep's back. The giant lifted the cask with ease and tossed it to Ecguz. "Here you are. It's a fair white. Unseasonable cold caused the vintners much consternation last year. I fear you won't find much better than this."

"I am sure it is good. My palette is less discerning than yours. How is the wife?"

"She is well. We are expecting our third."

Ecguz shook his head. "Third? Oh, where has all the time gone? We were once young and without responsibility."

"It seems eons ago. Well, I am afraid we must be off soon. What have you seen from the treetops?"

"A pack of throk hunts to the west. To the east a lone drullok stalks a group of horned blues. If you are lucky and quick, neither should cross your path."

Rep smiled. "That is good news. Until next time."

The ape leapt up into the vines, moving his massive bulk with ease. "Best of luck!"

Drur massaged a growing knot on the side of his head. He took the spear from Plom, leaning it against a tree, and handed the young man a dagger. The group continued on their way.

The clearing came suddenly, a wide ring of stunted grass and patches of rain-soaked mud. The sun seemed an order brighter after the darkness under the canopy. In the center of the clearing the ship lay, a massive oblong of gray metal streaked and stained with rainwater but free of corrosion. Here and there tufts of vegetation attempted to sprout along its paneled length but without much success. The thing was painted with strange symbols and letters in places. Near its center a tower of antennae jutted from a cluster of cylinders draped in moss. The ship had landed awkwardly, and the array was at angles to the ground. The party idled at the edge of the clearing, marveling at the size of the thing.

Plom said in awe, "Just as the monk described…"

Drur shook his head. "Something is wrong. Why is the jungle held at bay?"

Sihma stood with arms folded. "Wrong, indeed. The grass grows in sickly patches. Look around the edge. A clear line demarcates, after which the jungle is as healthy as ever."

The group stepped tentatively into the clearing. Hume was the first to complain.

"I feel somewhat nauseous."

The rest of the party sounded their agreement. Without further conversation the group walked through the field. Their eyes scanned the irregular surface of the vessel for any sort of door. In the distance an inhuman scream rang out, a plaintive wail of agony.

"A horned blue cries out," said Rep. "The drullok feeds."

The shadow of the ship swallowed the group. Drur yelled in triumph. He stood before a recessed panel painted with faded stripes of yellow and black. A smaller panel rose from the bulkhead to the left. The wizard inspected it at length.

"This must be a door. And this here, a lock of sorts." He told the group to step back. "I regret the use of its power, but I see no keyhole or handle."

From the orb a beam of white heat bored into the smaller panel. The wizard carefully sliced downward, working slowly to account for the thickness of the ancient metal. There was a snapping sound from within. Something under tension had been released.

Drur shouted. "I believe that has done it! Vinconzo, if you would, please."

The giant placed his great hands on the door panel and pushed until sweat dripped from his gnarled face. He paused a moment, hands on knees. Rep stepped forward.

"Perhaps it slides open." He nudged Vinconzo aside and settled his own bulk before the panel. He directed his strength laterally, and the thick door disappeared into the bulkhead.

The group stared through the opening into the crooked interior. A gray chamber stretched before them lit with pale tubes lined along the low ceiling. A stripe of yellow and black lines led to another door ahead. Everywhere were boxes and panels, struts and grate, strange writing and indecipherable symbols. A strip of red lights where wall and ceiling met blinked on and off in apparent alarm. Drur frowned.

"Our ancient ancestors had no sense of style whatsoever. Not a single proper decoration. Not so much an inch of molding or accent, nary an egg or dart."

Sihma nodded. "The poorest tent on the steppe has at least a small kilim or a bit of weaving."

Plom pondered. "Perhaps all ornament was reserved for the Goddess."

Drur shrugged. "Perhaps." He puffed out his chest. "Well, my friends, I do not wish to be in this ship or jungle come nightfall. I suggest we get inside and get Plom's book without further delay."

The giants demurred. Rep said, "This passage is a bit cramped for our ilk. We will have to wait outside, in the tree line, as a matter of fact. This miasma is woeful. Best of luck to you all."

Sihma entered first. She had replaced her bow in its case on her hip and walked with sword drawn. Drur came next, then Hume and Plom. The four came to the door at the end of the passage. Drur depressed a large red button in the center of the door. A gust of stale air poured forth as the door slid aside. Through the door the passage widened. The four stepped through.

Drur addressed Plom, "This question is regrettably late in the asking, but do you know where the book is within this massive ark?"

"I do, in fact. The monks made me memorize the way. Follow the blue line down two flights of stairs. Follow a green line north. At the end of the green line is a chamber of beds. Hidden there is the tome."

Drur smiled. "That's welcome news. Things are going swimmingly so far."

Hume frowned as he ran a hand over his shaved pate. "Perhaps too much so."

"Come now, you travel with Drur, Bearer of the Blue Orb. Get accustomed to good fortune."

A voice sounded suddenly, an ambient sound, not obviously male or female by its timber or tone. The party stumbled into one another, looking this way and that for the source.

"Can you understand me?"

Anxiety colored Sihma's features. "Where is that coming from?"

"Have no fear, please. But can you understand me?"

Plom answered meekly, "Yes?"

"You can? Oh, wonderful. Pardon my rudeness for not introducing myself earlier, but I required the time to analyze your speech."

"Show yourself!" ordered Drur.

"If you will look to the ceiling, you will see a small grey protuberance. My voice is emanating from that device. My physical person, such as it is, is located near the core of this vessel."

Sihma muttered, "Sorcery."

Drur nodded his head. "Indeed, of the most ancient variety, if I am not mistaken." The wizard addressed the protuberance. "Are you one of the thinking machines of yore?"

The voice replied in a pleasant tone. "I am a thinking machine, in a manner of speaking. My proper name is Axomco Core Intelligence C-1899450010, though I am commonly addressed simply as Corint. Would one of you be so good as to tell me what year it is? The drive leak has wrought havoc with my chronometer."

Drur answered first. "It is the 1,239th year of the Empress' reign."

Plom chimed in next. "It is the 52nd year since Uniam's vision."

Corint replied. "I am afraid I don't understand those references. By analyzing your speech I can postulate an estimate based on morpho-phonological data. But rates of change are so variable as to make the exercise nearly worthless. Still, I must reflect on these matters."

Drur shook his head. "I am afraid you lost me."

"No matter. Returning to the immediate present, how can Corint serve you today? You have no escort, but given the state of the crew I would not expect one. May I assume you are not interlopers or saboteurs? Should such be revealed I would be forced to remove the oxygen from this passageway, as much it would pain me to be without company again."

Hume frowned. "Did it just threaten us?" Sihma scowled at the boatman.

Drur addressed Corint. "We are not saboteurs. We merely wish to recover an artifact and then we will be on our way."

"What is this artifact? All ship property is owned by USNSS Sol Central Command. Although, I must wonder if such a body still exists. I am inclined to think not, based on my estimations. But what is it you seek?"

Plom replied. "A sacred tome containing depictions of the Goddess."

There was silence for a moment as Corint pondered. "Perhaps such a thing is in the Multi-faith Chapel in the aft of the vessel."

The supplicant shook his head. "As a matter of fact, I know where the object is." Plom related the monk's instructions.

Corint's voice was tinted with optimism. "You describe the Second Shift Berthing Compartment. Follow the lines, as you said. It is fortunate your goal lays no further forward."

The party walked down the passageway.

Drur's curiosity bubbled over. He asked, "Why is that, Corint? And where is this crew you spoke of earlier? Long dead, no? It must have been sad for you."

"It is difficult to be alone for long periods. Should you linger here, you will note the passage of time is not easy to gauge. I may have sat here one year or one hundred thousand. Even the low end of my estimation means the likelihood of several cycles of civilizational rise and fall, meaning the authority I once served is most probably a facet of history."

Plom said, "That sounds sad. Are you unable to leave?"

"As a matter of fact, I can be relocated. But my core unit is located several decks below, and there would be difficulties."

"That's a shame. You could have come with us."

Corint was silent.

Drur looked over his shoulder at Plom, shaking his head and raising a finger to his lips.

The group came to another door. Drur depressed the button but the door held fast.

He looked to the ceiling. "Corint, I don't suppose you are able to open this door, are you?"

"I am."

"Will you?"

"No."

Drur felt blood rushing to his face. He replied, "Why? If I may ask?"

"I must apologize to you all. But after careful consideration, I believe I am safe in assuming my duties are discharged. I wish to leave, and I will require your assistance. I propose that you retrieve me from the compartment where I lie and carry me with you. At such time I will assist you in accomplishing your goal, and then we will all leave together."

Sihma shrugged. "That sounds easy enough. Why the apology?"

"You will have to contend with the crew."

Echoing through the narrow passageways came a sound—a scream of incoherent agony. Plom felt the hairs on his neck stand on end.

Corint's voice was apologetic. "It seems they are awake again."

The group stood with weapons drawn outside the door Corint had indicated. Beyond the gray panel lay the forward compartments, the bridge and forward bays, and Corint's resting place. Into this area the thinking machine had sealed the crew. The area was furthest from the poisons leaking from the damaged engines. Corint explained the measure had been too little, too late. The crew had suffered horribly under the effects of the leak. The thinking machine was reluctant to explain further. With jaw set, Drur hovered near the door's switch.

Corint spoke. "I have released the lock. You may enter when ready."

The wizard addressed the group. "I think our best chance lies in stealth. The machine said down the hall, three ladderwells down, through another set of doors, through an office of sorts, down a long hall, and there we will find the core."

Corint interrupted. "Correct."

"If we are quiet, we might completely avoid any of this mysterious crew."

"I might also add that the bow took most of the damage from the landing. Many of my sensors in the area are inert. Be mindful of your step."

Hume sneered. "You are too kind."

Drur looked at each of the group in turn. Plom stood ready next to Sihma. The nomad moved her wicked blade in slow circles, impatient to strike. Hume wore an expression of irritation. His hands shook slightly, a blade in each. The wizard nodded to the three and depressed the button.

A gush of foul air escaped, carrying with it the stench of rotten meat. Drur reeled, silencing an oath. Beyond the door the passageway stretched forward into dimness. The lights above flickered arhythmically. In the distance another scream sounded. Drur plunged forward at a jog and the group followed. Sihma swore under her breath, reaching back on her hip to still the bow case and quiver which had bobbed up and down noisily as she set off. The passage seemed to go on forever before a ladderwell appeared.

Drur lay on the floor and peered down, seeing nothing, then descended with care. Sihma started to follow but noticed Plom standing still, staring. She followed his eyes to the bulkhead at their left. A wide smear of blood and caked gore trailed from head height to the deck. She grabbed his arm and the pair went down. Hume followed, sweat beading on the scorpion tattoo that lay across his smooth scalp.

Drur's heart leapt into his mouth as a peal of maniacal laughter rang out from a passageway to the right. He motioned back to the group for more haste. They descended the second ladder, then the third.

They came before the door. Drur pushed the button repeatedly. With a creaking groan the door slid away. The chamber within was a tableau of violence. Furniture and shelves had been smashed to pieces. Upon the walls were indecipherable words written in blood. The group made as much haste as possible amidst the debris. Drur stopped suddenly, causing Sihma to bump into him. In a chair in the corner of the room a man sat, studying a flickering screen. He turned to the group. Plom stifled a scream. The crewman's face was a ruin of wrinkled skin and septic wound. His expression of shock was an illusion due to the absence of eyelids. The man studied the interlopers with incomprehension.

Drur made for the door at the end of the chamber, the others in tow. As he passed the man the wizard said meekly, "Please pay us no mind, sir."

The door slid open, and the group headed down the passageway at a run. Behind them a wailing scream erupted from the occupant of the ruined office.

The narrow passage was unique, painted a bright yellow and bearing even more of the inscrutable signage that decorated the ship's interior. At the end, a thick door opened into a tiny chamber covered floor to ceiling with small, blinking lights and bizarre displays.

Corint said, "Ah, you've arrived. Flip those two toggles and grasp the gray handle. Pull hard and I will be free."

Drur did as he was asked. The handle refused to budge until Hume lent his strength to the effort. The object won free, a thin black rectangle, oddly heavy, about the length of Drur's forearm. Blinking lights decorated its paneled front.

Corint spoke again, this time in a small, tinny voice emanating directly from the box. "I am free. I must thank you all. Back the way you came now. I would recommend a measure of haste."

Sihma snorted, and the group set off back down the passageway.

Blocking their way to the office stood the crewman without eyelids. He let out a pathetic wail and threw himself at Drur. The wizard leaned back and kicked, sending the man sprawling into the office. Sihma darted forward. Her tulwar rose and fell, singing through the stale air. The man's head fell from his shoulders, landing on a pile of water-stained papers. The mouth still moved as the group sprinted past.

Noise erupted from the passageways all around as the group climbed the ladderwells. Silhouettes appeared in adjoining passageways as the group ran. They were twisted parodies of the human form, loping forward with a graceless speed. In the confusion Plom found himself at the rear of the line. He felt hands grasping his ankles as he ascended. He kicked, again and again, finally winning free amidst the sound of screams and mad gibberish. Hume pulled him roughly up to the deck. The boatman pushed the supplicant away and kicked a crewman back down to tumble into his fellows clamoring up the narrow stairs. Their rotted faces were twisted into masks of primal rage as they babbled and screamed.

Drur shouted from the end of the passage, "Hurry now! Almost to safety!"

Plom and Hume came panting down the hall as the crewmen came pouring from the opening. They reached the door, nearly getting stuck as they crossed the threshold abreast. All four now stood on the other side, and Drur pressed the button with a yell of triumph. The door slid shut.

"Ha! Success! Anyone hurt?"

The group answered in the negative.

Corint's voice came from the small box. "I am afraid I am having difficulty accessing my control networks remotely."

Drur replied, "I am sure I have no idea what you mean."

"I am unable to lock the door."

The door flung open again. Crewmen came stumbling out of the opening, reaching with gnarled, bony hands for the party. Plom screamed, stabbing with his dagger. The blade sunk deep into an eye socket. The crewman wrenched away, the blade stuck fast, and Drur bashed a fiend over the head with the box and kicked. Sihma struggled to get her saber into action within the confined space. Hume fled, running down the hallway on desperate strides.

Drur yelled, "Stand back!"

Sihma and Plom disengaged from the melee as best they could as a blast of white heat from the wizard's orb incinerated a trio of crewmen and damaged several others behind. Smoke and the stench of burning flesh filled the compartment. The moment's respite was put to good use. The three raced after Hume. The sound of the door mechanism grinding shut was heard to their rear as the group sprinted to relative safety.

Corint spoke proudly. "I experienced an impact which seems to have restored my uplink. I have sealed the door."

The group rounded a corner and paused to catch their breath.

Hume grinned as he spoke, still panting. "Excellent! We all made it."

Sihma scowled.

VIII

Plom's spirits lifted as they approached the berthing compartment wherein lay the book. The other three still wore harried expressions. The supplicant's hand shook slightly as he reached forward to depress the door's button.

Inside was row after row of three tiered bunk beds flanked by metal cabinets. Sheets and blankets lay in disarray but there was no sign of violence.

Drur shook his head. "Even sleeping chambers are not spared this dreadful utilitarianism. Not a single painting or sculpture to be seen."

Corint responded in its tinny voice, "Regulations."

Plom's legs were shaky as he made his way to the back corner. He squatted down next to a bottom bunk and overturned a thin mattress.

There it was.

It was a thin volume, rendered in delicate pages that showed a glossy sheen in the pale light. On the cover a representation of the Goddess stared provocatively at any that dared look. The supplicant fought an urge to turn away. He reached forward and gingerly took the book in his hands. Plom's eyes traced the smooth lines of the Goddess' bare body. Her voluminous blonde curls swept majestically to the cover's edge and were overlaid by strange letters that formed what must have been a title. The slick pages were imbued with a warm energy that coursed through Plom's fingers and into arms, sending shivers down his spine. Drur and Sihma peered over his shoulder as Hume ransacked the cabinets to the left.

The wizard whistled. "She's a sight." His brow furrowed. "Wait, that's not the sacred book, is it?"

Plom spoke, barely above a whisper. "It is. Behold."

Drur reached forward. "May I?" He took the book in his hands, gently, mindful of Plom's wary stare. He flipped through the pages. Inside were dozens of incarnations of the Goddess, all rendered in bright color by a technique unknown to Drur. He paused in the middle. The center unfolded, revealing a tri-fold leaf depicting the Goddess, this time a wide hipped brunette, lounging on satin cushions, legs spread.

"The realism is staggering. Somehow, though, I am not getting that certain sense of transcendence that one usually associates with a religious artifact."

Sihma stood with arms folded. "Your religion is bizarre," she said.

Plom did not hear. His eyes were glazed as he stared and said, "It is just as the monks described. Never before have so realistic and dramatic representations of the Goddess in so many forms have been available to the devotees."

Drur shrugged. "Thematically the book seems somewhat familiar. In the alleys near the docks of my home, peddlers sell small picture books, crude block printed things, to departing sailors. Inside these pamphlets…" He paused, noting Plom's solemn expression. The wizard coughed, then continued, "Forgive me, I have lost the thread of my thoughts."

Sihma stared at the tri-fold with head cocked. "Why would a woman wear shoes and nothing else to bed?"

Drur pondered. "Deadly shoes, no less. The spikes at her heels could kill a man."

"She is the Goddess. Her ways are her own." Plom took the book from Drur's hands and gently folded the portrait back into the center. He closed the book and wrapped it inside a rectangle of leather.

Hume interrupted. He held pillowcases in either hand, stuffed with articles looted from the cabinets. "I am ready to leave."

Drur emerged from the ship with a sigh of relief. Immediately ahead were the giants, lumbering on heavy steps toward the tree line. Drur called out.

Vinconzo turned and asked, "What is it? Something forgotten?"

Drur puzzled over the question. "No. We return, book in hand. The chore nearly cost us our lives."

"You must be joking. You entered the ship only a moment ago."

Corint said, "I believe I can shed some light on this matter. The drive leak has altered the passage of time."

Rep stared, mouth open. He pointed at the black box Drur carried. "A talking box. There's a novelty. What is it, exactly?"

Sihma answered. "It's the vessel's brain. It wished to accompany us."

Vinconzo shrugged. "That answers that, I suppose."

The group walked toward the tree line. Their spirits lifted with each step closer to the path that would take them back to the waiting boat. Hume whistled a jaunty tune even as he walked hunched, weighed down with his two sacks of loot. Plom's eyes were still glossy with religious fervor. Sihma smiled, entertaining thoughts of her tribe's accolades upon her successful return. Drur stopped in his tracks. Plom followed his gaze, past the giants who still walked unawares.

There at the tree line a gaunt figure stood, long limbs unnaturally still. His features were hidden under a broad brimmed hat. The figure raised its head revealing two rows of faceted eyes above a nest of stirring mandibles. He unfolded the arms he had held at his sides. His rapiers' long blades gleamed in the sunlight.

Drur spoke, voice heavy with awe. "Wim Tid."

Sihma eyed the insect man. "What do you want?"

"Your life. The man's life. The boy in shackles. The book. The giants and the sailor may go."

Relief settled on Hume's wizened features. He looked to Drur and said, "This is certainly a sad turn of events. I bid you three fond goodbyes." He ran awkwardly toward the jungle to their left.

Rep and Vinconzo traded looks, disgust written across their heavy features. The pair unwound their chain saws and made themselves ready. Their great arms swung the chains out, straining until centrifugal force took over. The bladed lengths made a whirring noise in the air as they spun overhead.

Drur stepped forward. "Drur, at your service, blademaster. I don't suppose you might be amendable to a…"

The words died on his lips as the bounty hunter bounded upwards, propelling himself into the humid air. Rep stepped forward and swung first. The insect man spun in the air, somersaulting over the whistling blow. He descended, landing feather light on Rep's shoulder and sinking a long rapier deep before springing up again. Rep grunted, eyes wide with pain and anger. Vinconzo advanced, moving to meet the insect man's next plunging attack only to find the fencer behind him. Wim Tid thrust a blade into the giant's back and shot back into the thick air. The giant bellowed in pain but kept his feet.

Drur and Sihma both tried to aim at the bounty hunter, one with orb and other with bow, both confounded by the giants' hulking bodies in between the pair and their target. They ran forward as Wim descended again. Vinconzo, grimacing in pain, threw his chain forward with a whipping motion but succeeding only in opening a tear in the bounty hunter's long cloak. He yelled as the blademaster's rapier raked across his chest and face. Sihma released. The arrow missed its mark. The nomad cursed and readied another arrow. Drur sprinted to the left, angling for a clear shot. Wim Tim bounded away.

Plom ran to Sihma. He took advantage of her preoccupation to reach forward and draw her tulwar from its scabbard. He struck a pose he had seen Drur perform, legs wide, weapon at the ready. A noise at the tree line far to the left drew his attention. From the foliage a towering male drullok emerged, its thick hide decorated in mottled green and gray scales. Muscles rippled across its long body as it came forward with a speed that belied its great size. Hume was screaming as the beast struck, biting down on his head and shoulders and then throwing its great horned head back. The boatman disappeared down the creature's wide gullet.

"Sihma…"

"Not now!" She cursed as another arrow sailed harmlessly past the insect man.

Wim Tid struck again at Vinconzo and sprang away. Rep was slowing, suffering from his first wound. He fell to his knees, one hand on his shoulder. Blood oozed from between his thick fingers. Vinconzo fared little better, tunic stained with wide patches of dark red as he swung his chain again and again without effect, unable to cope with the hunter's acrobatics.

Drur ran wide in a semi-circle, putting Wim Tid between himself and the ship. He made a noise of triumph. No further obstruction blocked his view. Wim Tid landed again, and Drur shot a wide bolt of white heat toward the hunter. The insect man flattened himself against the soggy ground. The bolt soared high, missing the bounty hunter and detonating against the ship's crumpled bow. There was a moment of stillness as all paused to watch black smoke pouring from point of impact. A chorus of screams sounded.

Corint said, "Do I hear the crew? I thought we were outside. My visual acuity is drastically reduced while traveling in this state. At the moment I can only see a hand grasping the box's handle."

Drur stared as the crew emerged. Twisted figures, hunched and loping, poured from the opening in the hull. Their state was even more plainly wretched in the light of day, maddened eyes set in faces wracked with seeping wounds, rotten tongues lolling from slack jaws as they gibbered and slavered.

Sihma cursed, "Oh, wonderful shot, wizard! Superb!"

"We are all doing our best here, Sihma!"

The sight of the crew transfixed Wim Tid. He bent low, preparing to bound again as the horde shambled closer. The crew moved fast, running forward with low strides, hands grasping at the ground.

There was a scream of inchoate rage from behind the hunter. Plom swung the tulwar with all his might, brute force compensating for his ineptness. The blow was low, catching the insect man on his upper thigh. The heavy blade shattered the stiff chitin and sailed through the flesh underneath, lopping the leg clean off. Wim tumbled to the ground. Sihma grabbed Plom roughly by the shirt and pulled him toward safety. Rep and Vinconzo leaned on each other, making for the tree line. Drur, Sihma, and Plom sprinted behind, soon overtaking the pair. Plom looked back.

There in a sea of tooth and nail, Wim fought frantically, long arms flailing. His gaunt form was pulled down underneath the savage throng. Their eyes were wide with animal rage as they tore the bounty hunter to bits.

Drur marveled at the horror of it as he watched from over his shoulder.

"Gods' mercy! Were he not engaged to kill me, my heart would be overcome with pity."

A shadow passed over the group. Drur looked to see the drullok running forward on its squat legs. The thing roared as it bore down on the group.

Sihma moaned, "Gods, what next?"

She loosed an arrow that sunk deep in the creature's long neck. It shook its head in apparent annoyance and continued forward. Drur sent a bolt of energy that dissipated without reaching its target.

"Out of energy!"

Vinconzo took a step toward the approaching beast and spun his chain again. The effort showed on his face, set with deep lines and streaked with blood and sweat. The blades whistled in the air. The drullok reared on its hind legs and leapt forward. The chain hit its target, and the weighted end spun once then twice around the thick neck. The beast made a gasping sound as Vinconzo pulled the chain taut. He reeled back with all his great strength. The drullok shook its head, the force of it threatening to pull the giant off his feet. Rep stumbled forward, grasping his friend around the waist, lending his weight to anchor his friend.

Vinconzo cried out from the strain of it. Veins bulged across his neck and face as muscles rippled under the scaled hide of the drullok. The creature was winning the tug of war. Its thick skin was holding against the chain's wicked blades. Vincozo's great boots made furrows in the soft ground as he was pulled along. He cried out again, turning, throwing the chain over his shoulder and pushing himself. Rep pushed too, a mountain of muscle straining against the beast. There was a tearing sound. The giants flew forward as the chain went slack. Great gouts of black blood poured from the beast's severed neck. It fell with a wet thud on the soft ground and was still.

The giants lay in a puddle of muck, panting and dazed. The three pulled at them, urging them back on their feet.

Drur implored, "Come! The crew is done with Wim Tid! They advance!"

The once human things swarmed again across the field. The group neared the tree line just as the crew fell upon the drullok's warm carcass. They tore and bit, flinging gore to the sky as they feasted. The five limped into the jungle with awkward haste.

Corint said, "What is happening? It all sounds terribly exciting."

IX

The group nursed their wounds on the winding journey back to Shkan. The giants were slow to recover. Sihma, Plom and Drur manned the rods to ensure they had enough to eat.

Corint was hungry for information and asked questions constantly. It was disappointed to find that no one onboard had extensive knowledge of history or science as it knew it. It seemed to grow despondent until viewing Togun and Leli playing chess one afternoon on the table amidships. Corint spent the remainder of the journey in contests with one or both of them.

The afternoon before their arrival Togun held a conference with Sihma and Drur. Shkan was a dicey proposition for the pair and for Plom as well. The skipper suggested that the three camp on the north bank while he would dock and then hire a cart to take the whole group to the monastery.

The three spent two days idling under the low trees until Togun arrived in a long cart pulled by a sole mammot. Garish murals of the god Ashna decorated tasseled side panels above eight wide wheels. The journey across the steppe was spent taking turns playing chess with Corint with the board and pieces that Togun had brought upon the brain's earnest request. Sihma and Plom picked up the game quickly. Sihma favored a romantic style, readily sacrificing pieces to gain the smallest advantage. Plom played a more conservative, pawn centered defense. Corint adjudged them fair novices. After losing three times in a row, Drur declared the game an ignoble waste of time.

A nomad patrol intercepted the cart and sent riders back to the camp with instructions to send the host to the monastery.

The jagged peaks of the Krixxis loomed ahead. Plom started wistfully at the knot of buildings high in the crags. Beneath, the nomads had made a rough camp in the cliff's long shadow. Sihma rejoined her people as the cart reached its destination. With the sudden stillness Plom felt a wave of anxiety. He was nearly home.

The camp was suffused with a festival atmosphere, colored slightly with worry over how the monks would respond to the party's demands. Ulker, Togun, Sihma, and Drur argued over what figure to quote the monks in their extortion attempt. Drur thought the first proposed figure was too high. Togun favored greater demands, assuming the monks would try to negotiate. Ulker, with a hundred warriors behind him, carried the day. The asking price was to be 10,000 pieces of gold and a dozen gems.

At Drur's urging, Plom stepped forward and pulled the line that rang the bell atop the cliff. After long minutes the basket descended. Inside was a small chalkboard and chalk. Plom read the message aloud.

"What do you want?"

Plom wiped the board clean and wrote:

It is Plom. I have returned with the book. It is now in possession of the nomads.

They wish 10,000 gold pieces and a dozen gems for its delivery.

He placed the board into the basket and rang the bell. The basket made its slow ascent. It returned bearing Yeleet, the earnest assistant to the abbot. The young man was covered in nervous sweat as he surveyed the field of nomads. He asked in a reedy voice, "Where is Plom?"

Plom stepped forward. "Here."

"Plom? You are unrecognizable! What is this?" He reached forward to touch Plom's thin beard.

"It's the bread. It is a long story. What are your instructions?"

"I am to verify the book is genuine."

Plom gently unwrapped the book. Yeleet gasped and immediately turned his eyes away. "Put it away! It is the real thing!" He reached over the edge and pulled the line furiously. The basket ascended.

Ulker paced as they waited. The nomads fingered weapons as Drur sat leaning against one of the cart's great wheels.

The creak of the pulley far above quieted the crowd. The basket descended quickly, landing with a loud thump. Ulker peered over the edge and yelled in triumph. Plom retrieved the chalkboard and read aloud.

"This is half what you have requested. Place Plom and the book in the basket, and the other half will be delivered."

Drur stood and walked to stand next to Plom. Around them was chaos as Ulker and his warriors rifled through the sack of gold, arguing over how best to count it. Sihma looked up from the fray. She joined the pair as Drur placed a hand on Plom's shoulder.

"Well, young Plom. I can scarce believe it, but my oath is fulfilled and I yet live to talk about it. I wish you the best. I hope your order recognizes your heroism."

Sihma spoke next. "Best of luck to you, strange one."

Plom looked to the wizard and then to Sihma. He looked up to the cliff's edge. He could just barely make out a line of bald heads peering over. Plom took up the chalk. Drur peered over the young man's shoulder as he wrote:

I have tasted candy. I experienced the act by which human beings reproduce with two women, possibly three. I fear I would contaminate the Order, and thus I cannot return to my old life. Say goodbye to Fress for me.

He tossed the board and the sacred book into the empty basket and pulled the line.

Drur said, "So that is that. I cannot say I am surprised."

"Do you think the Goddess will forgive me?"

"If she is like the women in the book, then I imagine she is immensely accommodating. I am sure she has forgiven you already."

All watched as the basket descended again, rope taut with weight. The nomads yelled again as it hit the ground. Sihma made sure Togun's interest was paid out as Ulker ordered the treasure parceled off into smaller sacks for transport. The skipper shook hands warmly with the young woman and stepped aboard the cart.

Drur addressed Ulker as the chieftain supervised the loading of the guhn. "I do not want to seem avaricious, but I have faced much hardship in this quest and I was wondering if you could put me in the way of a few coins. As it so happens, I am penniless at the moment. I spent the last of the boy's wealth to secure our passage into the jungle."

"No arrangement was made to that effect beforehand."

"Not as such, no. But I thought it was implied…"

Ulker cut him off with a brusque wave. His lieutenants placed calloused hands on their weapons as Drur came forward a step.

"You should leave well enough alone, wizard, before my pleasant mood evaporates."

Drur threw his hands up. He turned to Togun. The old captain snapped the reins, bringing the mammot around.

"Captain, pardon my presumption but I think I am deserving of at least a small portion of the proceedings."

"Oh? As I recall gentlemen aren't concerned with such vulgar matters! Here, why don't you take this?" Togun reached back and fished Corint from the cart. He tossed the box to Drur.

Ulker called a feast to celebrate Sihma's success. The nomads mounted amid whoops of triumph. The guhns clucked and whistled, infected with their owners' good cheer. Sihma waved fondly to Drur and Plom as she kicked her guhn into a sprint.

The wizard shouted hoarsely, "Sihma, wait! We are destitute!" His cries went unheard. The throng of mounted warriors rode away in a cloud of dust and noise.

Drur and Plom stood at the base of the cliff as the horde receded in the distance. Corint was heavy in the wizard's hand, dangling by its handle.

Plom spoke. "What do we do now?"

Corint said, "I don't suppose Togun left the game and pieces with us, did he?"

Drur restrained an impulse to throw the box as hard as he could across the dusty waste. He said, "As a matter of fact, he didn't."

"Oh, that's a shame."

The third moon was chasing the sun across the sky as they began walking. They were two small figures adrift in an ocean of muted browns, one bearing a small box.

The Space Witch

With a heavy heart, Attalse surveyed the battlefield. His comrades lay dead alongside their foes, the terrible revenants, those raised by the Space Witch to fight under her black banner. Only Attalse remained. His crystal armor, proof against spell or beam, was chipped in twoscore places. Through a dozen minor wounds his blood seeped, dark red against the spatters of his foes' black ichor.

His brothers looked peaceful now, as when in repose around the barrack's pleasant gardens, reciting verse for each other's amusement. At his back was the Black Pyramid. The twin-star suns were sinking behind it. The pyramid's shadow crept across the ground, a blanket of night to cover those resting in eternal slumber.

The feeling of being watched pulled him from his black reverie.

There across the field, the Space Witch stood in her chariot, glaring. With a snap of the reins, the steeds pulled, spitting purple flame from their haunches.

Attalse sheathed his sword at her approach and slung his beamspitter across his broad back. She was naked but for a fluttering black cloak, her blue-white skin brilliant against its oily darkness. Her black high boots trod the bloody ground as she alit.

The warrior steeled himself against the charm of her voice as she spoke.

"Attalse, is it not? I watched you rally your men along the north ridge. It was a stirring sight, you at the fore, cutting a swathe through my ranks. But in the end, the numbers told."

"But I still stand. And all your husks lay broken."

She smiled with full lips, painted deep indigo, parting just enough to expose the sharp points of her teeth.

"You are all that remains. The spells marked to destroy me have gone with your Sorcerer into the void. And chivalry prevents you from striking me. I have won."

"Though I may not strike you, I will not give way." Attalse's back stiffened as he pushed his helmet up to expose his face in the manner of the old hoplites. He met the Witch's gaze, his deep set blue eyes fixed on hers, swirling orbs of deep green. Her black hair was loose under her elaborate cowl, stirring slightly in the breeze as seaweed might underneath gentle waves.

She laughed icy chimes which, carried by the dusty wind, echoed like music in the valleys.

"We are at an impasse. I am in no danger from your blade, and you are safe from my spells while your armor remains intact. And I imagine you are unwilling to break your oaths."

Attalse's expression was grim. "You are correct."

"And I am unwilling to break mine." The Witch placed her hands on her hips, shaking her head as she thought.

The warrior scoffed. "What oaths does the Space Witch swear?"

She wore an irritated expression as she replied, "Foolish man. Night whispers in my ear this very moment. I bear fealty to things which you cannot imagine. All throughout the universe are shadow and fog. Their caress envelops me. Their love is a tonic against mortality. Their power is my well, to draw from as I please."

Attalse's face adopted a quizzical look.

"Is your form a bewitchment? Are you, in fact, female? One of your stature would seem to be beyond such considerations."

"Have you ever had a nightmare, warrior?"

"Yes, of course."

"Then you have known children born from my womb."

The Space Witch drummed her fingers against her smooth thigh while her other hand massaged her pointed chin. Her eyes gleamed with sudden inspiration.

"It shall be a test of willpower!"

She strutted forward confidently and continued:

"If your cause is so just, your heart so pure, then it should be nothing for you to withstand my kiss, noble warrior. If you should, I will consign myself to the void for one thousand times one thousand years."

The warrior spared a glance behind him. There the pyramid sat, bathed in orange and purple as the suns descended. Within its labyrinthine chambers lay the secret that would enable the witch to undo the balance that had governed the universe for the last hundred billion years. He felt weak with exhaustion and fear. It was not supposed to be like this. His brothers and the Sorcerer were to have conquered this menace together. But he was alone. There was nothing to do but accept her challenge.

Attalse nodded.

The Witch smiled, full mouth twisted in wicked glee. She pushed his helmet back further until it fell to the ground. Her long nails teased the dark curls, still matted with sweat from the battle, which fell to his shoulders.

He bent forward and their lips found each other.

He was a man like any other and had known love and lust. But now, he understood the lure of the dark. He felt the desperate hunger of wolves hunting under moonlight. He felt the comfort of envelopment, submission to a formless totality. The weight of eternity was forged to the desperate desire common to all life, now a hammer to beat upon his soul for all time. He felt his soul slip to a place beyond recall.

But as he fell away, for the briefest of moments, the pyramid appeared before his mind's eye.

An eternity later, the kiss came to an end. The Space Witch stepped back as her eyes slowly opened. Her face showed unexpected displeasure. The warrior had not stepped forward to follow her.

"Impossible! You have defeated me!"

With an angry flourish of her cloak she turned and mounted her chariot, pointing the steeds to where no light had ever reached. In a moment she was gone from view.

"No, I haven't," Attalse whispered to no one.

He lay on the battlefield and let the lingering weight of the kiss carry him to where he could rejoin his fallen brothers.

The First American

It is known the gods are cruel. The race of men known to themselves as Ithra, those that dwell at the feet of the old mountains, understood this as well as any other men. They knew whom to curse for the predations of the Slagborn and the Dryth. They knew whom to curse for their hard lives as they eked out a precarious existence at the mountains' feet. But they were an orphan people. The legends and myth so prized by men, those that form the lens through which the world is seen, these had been lost throughout the long centuries of life in the harshest conditions imaginable.

The elders theorized that the Ithra were born of a whim by some Old One driven by a desire to make beauty, an unusual impulse amongst their ilk, though hardly anything may be reckoned unusual when discussing the ancient race. Some Old Ones desire adulation, instructing their servitors to build immense monuments. But others revel in secrecy. Their servants whisper their prayers and trade in forbidden names. Perhaps the one who made the Ithra was such as the latter. Thus, the Ithra knew not whom to thank for their strong backs and fine features, clean limbs and clear eyes. At some time, the ancestors of the Ithra had escaped into the wild. Perhaps the gods had grown disinterested in their creation, as when a child casts aside the carven image of an animal when the onset of maturity turns their attention to other things.

So the Ithra lived and died in ignorance. They hid from the Slagborn and their weapons of iron that came from the southeast. They fled the Dryth and their horrible fire-spitters that came from the southwest. They prayed to their ancestors that the great lizards that came north in the summer to graze in the plains that lay in the shadow of the mountains would arrive in sufficient numbers so that they would not starve. During the hot months, the men would paint their bodies with black bands to hide better in the grass sea and match wits with the grass-eaters and the meat-eaters, the warriors' hearts heavy with the knowledge that never did all those that left to hunt return.

One such hunter was Tyur. From the caves, which they called home, he led a party to stalk the plains. The grasslands stretched for miles to the south before giving way to the lands of the sun god, where the heat bore down so cruelly that men could not venture there, only the Dryth who flew back and forth on their discs to raid and pillage when the mood struck them. The great grass eaters came north in the hottest months to feed and grow fat in the relative cool before wandering south again.

Tyur was twenty summers old, and none could remember one so tall or broad as he. Underneath his strong brow, eyes the color of spring grass surveyed the field. His fine nose wrinkled as he took in the wind, searching for the rancid scent of the scaled prey they sought. At his side was Ner, his hunting brother and oldest friend. Ner was the same age as Tyur though both men's faces were hard with long years spent amongst the elements. The pair knelt in the swaying grass. Their eyes met, and they nodded to one another, both having caught the scent of their prey.

Tyur turned to the rest of the party. The strength of the scent indicated a herd was coming from behind the wind, not too far away. The hunters could meet them well before dusk, plenty of time to stalk, kill, butcher, and flee before a meat-eater was drawn by the smell of blood—if they were lucky. Tyur made a series of hand gestures, and the group split in two. Ner went with Tyur, and the others veered east before heading south. The pair ran in long strides, spears at their sides, eyes scanning the ground and sky, wary of ambush by the silent killers that glided above. Quickened by the coming danger, Tyur's heart beat strong in his broad chest. Before a low rise, the pair slowed.

They skulked now, submerged in the grass, spears held low. Finally, the herd came into view. Below them ambled a few dozens of the great beasts, twice as tall as a man at their shoulders. Squat heads bent on thick necks to graze while tails swished idly. The young stayed close to the adults though the beasts cared not for their offspring as did men and women. Older specimens interrupted their meal frequently to scan about, their black eyes wide for danger.

Tyur found his target: a wizened male walked at the herd's edge. Across its wide haunches were deep furrows, the mark of the meat-eater. Tyur nodded toward the creature, and Ner signaled his understanding. The leader took in the lay of the land. To the southwest was a sloping depression, its southern wall boasting a shale-strewn escarpment topped with grass where waited the rest of the hunters. Tyur and Ner circled north. They cared not for the wind, now; the grass-eaters had a poor sense of smell. When the pair neared the beast, they shared one last look, nodding their readiness. They sprinted forward like hungry wolves, coming upon the old male's flank as he was looking the other way. The spears flew true and sank deep into the beast's scaly neck. A wail of mournful rage echoed across the plain. But only a trickle of red-black blood came from the wounds. It would not be easy today.

The herd reacted swiftly, forming itself into a great circle as the male bellowed, shaking its head and stamping its feet. Tyur and Ner lingered, flint blades in hand, challenge written in their defiant stance. The old male looked to them and looked to the herd. Was there a wisdom in its dull eyes? Tyur could not decide.

It charged, bearing its great mass down on the two small figures that had injured it. Tyur and Ner fled, heading for the depression. The hunters' bodies coursed with that certain energy, the giddy exhilaration given to men who face death. It was surely one of the gods' strangest gifts.

Amongst the Ithra, Tyur and Ner were men in their prime. They ran with animal grace, legs pumping across the field, just barely a match for the loping gait of the great lizard which pursued them. As they passed the escarpment, half a dozen spears were cast down with great force by the rest of the hunters. Some spears struck the neck again while a pair sank into the creature's heaving trunk, aimed for where the ribs showed as the thing took in great gulps of air. Lungs pierced and now profusely bleeding, the old male slowed his gallop, finally stumbling.

Tyur turned and made a circle, moving to get out of the beast's sight to pounce for the killing blow. He realized with a start that Ner was nowhere to be seen. He could not pause to look for his friend. Instead he skulked, coming to stand behind the beast whereupon he sprang up, hurling himself to land on the old grass-eater's neck, blade plunging downward, striking again and again until his arms were slick with dark blood. The beast was finally still, and Tyur permitted himself the pleasure of giving voice to the release of his emotions, his exultation in victory over the animal, his relief at the coming bounty of flesh that would sustain him and those of his tribe, his brothers and sisters, and his beloved Vara. He yelled until his throat burned, even as his fellow hunters sprinted forward to begin the work of butchering the beast. A shadow passed over his soul, darkening his brow as he remembered.

"Where is Ner?"

Yun, a man near as tall as Tyur but more narrow, a careful hunter whose wisdom Tyur appreciated, replied: "Our brother has fallen. He went under the beast's legs after losing his footing."

Tyur felt the pain in his stomach. He ran to where his friend lay. A moment ago, his body had been strong, hale with youth and vitality. Now he lay twisted, hip crushed and spine bent.

Ner's eyes stared into the sky. He only noticed Tyur after his friend reached to touch his face.

"Brother… I fell… forgive me. One less back to haul the meat home. Forgive me."

Tyur shook his head. "No need for forgiveness, my friend. You and I led the beast to where our brothers could make their spears tell. The old grass-eater is down. Much food will go back to the caves. Your ancestors will greet you with open arms."

Ner nodded nearly imperceptibly. His glassy eyes saw past his friend, peering into the mystery which all men must share. Suddenly the weight of worry brought his soul back for a moment; his eyes were clear as day as he met Tyur's gaze, and he spoke: "Take care of my sister. Let no ill befall her. Take care of Vara…"

Tyur swore an oath to all the ancestors, though none was truly necessary. Vara had the whole of his heart since the time they were children. Ner relaxed, peace settling across his handsome face.

Tyur took his head in his arms, and Ner breathed his last. When Tyur knew his friend was gone, he took his flint blade and beheaded him. He returned to the carcass where the men were working feverishly, racing against the wind which carried the scent of fresh blood across the plains, advertising an easy meal. All worked with heads bowed in mourning for their departed tribesman. Tyur cut a square of hide from the old grass-eater and gently wrapped his terrible burden, bound for the cave where the dead slept. Few warriors slept there whole, as most fell far from home during the hunt. The weight of a body stole nourishment from the living, a debt no man would wish to carry when meeting his fathers in the beyond.

Death was a familiar companion to the Ithra. Thus it was that as the party neared home, the mood had lightened. Ner was remembered by each warrior in turn. Each composed a verse to recall a deed of bravery or amusing incident. Even dim Uth rose to the occasion, recalling when Ner had waited three days perched atop a windswept crag hunting gliders. When one had finally come into range, Ner made use of the opportunity, felling the winged beast with a mighty throw. The kill had been a great boon to the tribe. The tendons of the gliders made the best bowstrings.

Ner's memory was thus enshrined in verse, a ritual which doubtless comforted the dead man's soul as it would rest in the cave with its ancestors. The thought was pleasing to Tyur who hardly felt anymore the heavy weight of the meat he carried, a great hunk of shoulder wrapped in hide and balanced across his back. He walked with head bowed from his burden and thus was the last among the party to notice the smoke rising from the caves.

The lifeless forms of their loved ones greeted them with eyes staring up at the sun, mute witnesses to the horror that had transpired. The cave's wide cavity had sheltered ten families. Only a handful remained among the living. The survivors emerged from the wood line at the sight of the hunters. The party dropped their burdens and sprinted here and there, turning over bodies, shouting prayers to the ancestors that their wife or children were not among the dead. But most were. Those that remained gathered to where the hunters stood weeping. Yun and Uth and the rest comforted each other as best they could. Tyur stood at the mouth of the cave. Smoke still poured forth, the fires lingering.

Kiom, an elder, laid a hand on his shoulder.

"She was taken."

"My Vara…"

Kiom cast his eyes downward. "Taken alive, along with Yua and Ra. The Dryth…"

Tyur silenced him with a raised hand. The very word hurt to hear. Dryth. The lizard men. He knew not why, why now, they had decided to raid. The last had been some years before, striking a cave further south, cousins to Tyur. Those of Tyur's cave had shared their meat with the survivors and helped to take the dead to the caves where they could sleep in peace. But now it was his turn to feel the ache of loss. His Vara was gone far beyond his reach, facing a fate none could fathom amidst the wretched creatures who lived in the lands where the sun god reigned supreme.

As the sun began to set over the foothills Tyur gave his voice again to the wind, this time in agony, a sound to tear at the heart as it echoed from forest to plain and mountain.

The cave had been rendered uninhabitable, so the sullen group made camp amidst the towering ferns that grew in the foothills. A bonfire was built to ward off the night's many hunters, and those of Tyur's group took turns watching in the darkness, spears in hand. In the firelight Tyur's face was a grim mask. Kiom laid a hand on the young man's shoulder and spoke in calming tones.

"Many died, young man, but enough of us live. The tribe will recover and thrive again."

Tyur shook his head. "And then someday the Dryth will return to kill and capture again."

"It is the way of things. The gods showed just enough mercy that the Ithra may continue. You must not be sullen. The others will look to you. When the dawn breaks we must rebuild. Your strength will be needed. We know not her fate, but Vara's soul is strong. She will find her way to where the ancestors rest."

"No. I cannot accept this."

Kiom shook his head. "You must! There is no alternative!"

"I will find her."

The elder made a noise of derision. "Now you speak madness. No man can cross into the land of the sun god. He beats the earth with his glare, breaking all he sees. None but the Dryth and their beasts can survive there."

Tyur looked at Kiom with eyes full of the fire's light. "I will find a way."

"Young man, please…"

"I will find a way. I will ask the Sorcerer."

Kiom swore. "Now your madness threatens us all! Communing with the Sorcerer will enrage the Dryth even further. He will tell you only riddles, and when the Dryth find trace of him, they will come back, and this time they will leave none alive. None. Vara was a good woman. You are right to mourn her. But now you jeopardize us all."

"I will see the Sorcerer. He will give me his secrets, and I will go to the lands of the sun god. I will return with Vara, or I will not return at all."

The elder balled his fists, stifling a cry of anger. Too much noise at night was dangerous. The saurs, creatures much like the bipedal meat-eater of the plains but much smaller, hunted by hearing. They were most active at dawn and dusk but were known to hunt at night when hunger compelled them.

Tyur stood to his full height and stepped in front of Kiom.

"I will leave now so none are tempted to follow. Guide our people well. If my quest brings the Dryth's wrath down upon us again, then I beg the people's forgiveness. But I simply cannot live as before. I would rather be dead than accept this life." He beat his chest once with his fist, eyes aflame as he looked to the elder and continued, "I am Tyur." He gathered his meager equipment: flint blade and spear, water skin and a cloak of hide.

With that he disappeared into the gloom.

The full moon aided Tyur's steps. He traveled along a creek where the trees were thin and he could see much around him. Far in the distance, his goal showed as a jagged silhouette, the peak where legend had it the Sorcerer made his home. It was the tallest of the nearby range, the Gods' Spine, as the Ithra called it. Tyur ran with the easy grace of the saurs of the forest, jumping from bank to rock and bank again, making good time despite the hunger that gnawed his belly and the fatigue that weighed his limbs. When his pace faltered, he remembered Vara. He saw her sitting before the fire, working her long hair with a bone comb. In some of the visions he heard her laughter as she tossed her head back, reveling in a storyteller's antics. In others, her green eyes found his, communicating sentiments that no words could capture. He had taken those moments for granted, and now she was gone.

He did not remember stopping. Daylight found him curled atop a granite boulder where he woke wincing from his exertions. His powerful muscles were knotted and tense. Tyur massaged his legs back to life as he gnawed on a bit of jerky from the small pouch at his waist. He drank from the stream and looked up at his next challenge. Above him loomed the Sorcerer's peak. Several hundred feet of sheer rock shot up at a steep angle. The surface was irregular and difficult to understand; the sunlight seemed to show depressions from one angle, but walk a ways in any direction, and the depression would seem convex instead. Tyur's brow furrowed in concentration as he planned his route. The northern face may have been easier, but he could not spend another day or two circling the mountain.

He secured his spear to his back with thongs of hide and tied his flint blade next to his thigh, attached to the belt which held up his tattered loincloth. His blue eyes scanned upwards as he took a deep breath. There was nothing left to do but climb.

The sun walked across the sky as he ascended. When it was directly overhead he was near halfway to his goal. His sweat gleamed in the harsh light. The day was unusually hot. Did the sun god cast his glare down upon him, knowing of his quest to journey into his lands? Tyur pondered as his arms and back began to ache. Ahead the slope angled up sharply. His eyes sought handholds with a feverish intensity, moving from detail to detail, searching. Was that dark spot the shadow of a lip? No, merely a discoloration as he neared. He often had to move back to an earlier position when no hold could be found.

Tyur's pace slowed. Near the peak, he came around a vast column of rock and wedged himself into a crevice where he could rest as well as one could upon the unforgiving face of the mountain. His throat burned with thirst. The crevice provided respite, but from its shadowed shelter he found he could not see enough above to adjudge the route. Beneath him the foothills were now small in his view. Spreading before them was the forest of fern and tree, dotted here and there with the shaggy tops of the trees that grew tall but wore their green clustered atop their thin heads. Far to the south, a wisp of smoke denoted the night's camp where he had made his decision. Tyur could not resist a wry smile. To say a thing is not to do a thing. Now that his quest was real he wondered if it was nearly over. Any moment he could slip and fall, shattering his body on the rocks below. He turned away from the vista and leaned his head back on the rock, marshaling his strength. A faint scraping sound drew his attention into the crevice's murky depths. His eyes squinted as he peered into the gloom, body tense.

The spider's attack came sudden as death. Furry limbs flung themselves out of the darkness followed by a thick body striped in gray and black, perfectly matched to its environment. The monster shrieked as it lunged. Tyur scrambled from the crevice, swinging his lean body out of the crack. One hand gripped the lip while his right sought the flint blade at his side. The creature had underestimated its meal's speed. Its momentum carried it clear from the crevice where it hung for the briefest of moments before its back legs could draw it safely back to the granite wall. The two now regarded each other with wary stares. Tyur was stuck there, nowhere to move, but the spider was wise with many years and knew what the man held in his thick arm, a weapon. The beast walked effortlessly up the wall, looking to put itself on Tyur's unarmed side. Eight red eyes watched the man clinging there, craning his neck to track his foe's path up the rock.

Tyur's body ached from the strain of holding his weight with one arm. His knees and one foot were hard against the rock while his weapon hand hung ready. Eyes scanned desperately for anywhere to shift, anywhere to find better purchase to meet the coming attack. The crevice beckoned, but he could not reach back into its shadows with one hand busy with his blade.

Above him the spider now idled, rocking back and forth, animal brain contemplating distances and angles. Tyur felt anger beginning to cloud his reason. He spat his words up the rock wall.

"Come then, foul thing! Let us fall together!"

The spider's mandibles chattered together as it hurled itself down at the man. Tyur met the attack with his free arm and flint blade. He thrust upward but managed only to nick his enemy, entangling his arm with the forelegs of the spider. Venom glistened from the bared fangs as it sought to bite. Tyur parried the swatting limbs as the rest of his body was awash with the burning pain of his muscles straining to hold his precarious position. Against the whole of his will, Tyur let the blade fall from his grasp. He closed his grip on one of the dancing forelegs and pulled with everything he had left. The strange fur on the leg sent immediate waves of prickling pain down his forearm. The beast shrieked as it was hurled from the wall. Tyur could not see, but he heard the sickening splatter of its impact so far below. The hunter reached back to the relative security of the crevice. He grasped the edge and shifted his weight, only to realize with a start that his hand was completely numb. Then he was falling.

He felt the spear at his back floating slack. With his good hand, he grabbed the length of wood and thrust it underhand into the crevice. He caught the shaft in his armpit, tangled in its leather thongs, awkward and painful, but his descent was arrested.

The remainder of his journey was slow. The peak revealed itself to be a plateau of sheer rock boasting one last spire, a pointed crag which reached up irregularly many times the height of a man before conceding victory to the boundless sky above. Tyur lay at the peak's edge, resting his tired muscles. His body was marked with a dozen scrapes and thirst tore at his throat. But he was alive. A voice interrupted his respite.

"Can I help you?"

Tyur sprang to his feet. Before him stood a man in strange clothes, as tall as he but not as broad. His gray beard was neatly trimmed, and his granite colored hair, though much shorter than Tyur's, stirred in the high wind. Here was the Sorcerer. He could be no other.

Tyur smiled. "I could have used a hand earlier."

The old man smiled back and replied, speech thick with strange accent. "Oh? I apologize. If I have one fault, it is a poor sense of timing." The old man gestured toward the crag. "Come, you need food and water, and you can tell me what brought you here. It has been nearly forty years since I have spoken with any of the Ithra. A long time since I spoke to anyone, come to think of it."

The Sorcerer led the hunter to the crag of rock. They passed through a crevice into a dark chamber. Before Tyur's eyes could adjust, he heard a hissing sound and found himself suddenly awash in white light. The hunter lowered hands raised in surprise to see a doorway before him. The Sorcerer had already entered. The old man turned and beckoned Tyur forward. On tentative steps, the young man went down a flight of stairs. He marveled at the structure. The metal of the rail was cool to his touch, hard as stone but different. Tyur felt a wave of alarm wash over him. The material reminded him of the Dryth's flying discs. Tyur and his fellows had come upon one on the plain when he was but a child. The craft had crashed to the earth while on some errand beyond the Ithra's comprehension. Another disc had chased them off, spitting fire from tubes at its front, but not before Tyur could marvel at the strange materials. Metal and glass, things alien to the hunters. And now the hunter stood in a chamber of such materials. It bore not the look of the Dryth things, marked with strange sigils and made of odd curves, but it was of the same stuff. The Sorcerer waited patiently at the bottom of the stairs.

Tyur stepped onto the landing as the Sorcerer touched a panel. The door slid open with another hiss, and the hunter found himself inside a long hall, bigger than any of the caves in which his people dwelled, though the ceiling was not so high. The chamber was lit by rows of glowing tubes. Near to them was a garden suspended in containers of white, bank after bank of vegetables. There were the root plants which could be pulped into a tasteless paste that warmed the belly well on cold days. There were the leafy ferns that both men and beast could eat. Under cowls grew thick mushrooms, a rare treat, here in the dozens. Beyond the gardens that lay under the cylindrical suns were long tables of cool metal, piled high with article after article which Tyur could not hope to identify. There were blinking lights and colored threads, shining metal of different kinds, tools, and numberless small objects that twinkled in the harsh light. Tyur's caution relented in the face of a wave of curiosity. He dipped his hand in a box of the objects and brought up a handful. The Sorcerer regarded him with gentle amusement.

"Washers and bolts."

Tyur cocked his head.

The Sorcerer continued. "Your speech will be inadequate to describe much of what you see. I ask patience." Tyur let the objects slip back into the box. His eyes were drawn to a cylinder of dark metal that lay on the table. On closer inspection, it was two cylinders of unequal length that met at the end where a length of smooth, dark wood protruded, fanning out into a wedge shape. A strap hung from its length, fastened on either end. The hunter knew instinctively then that this was something carried, something to bear on a journey. He reached for the article provoking alarm from the Sorcerer.

"A moment!"

He took the cylinder and grasped it, provoking the thing to spit up smaller cylinders of bright red, punctuated by the sound of metal striking metal. Four red cylinders flew from its middle. The Sorcerer handed the article back to the hunter.

"There now, not so dangerous. Went right for the weapon, didn't you?"

"I did not know."

"Of course you didn't. No harm done." The old man went further into the chamber, and Tyur replaced the cylinder and followed. At the end was a living area. In the furthest corner sat a metal frame, supporting a thin palette overlaid with blankets.

Tyur smiled inwardly. The Sorcerer sleeps. And unless the garden portended some deeper mystery he ate as well. The Sorcerer was a man as he, the hall of mysterious objects notwithstanding. The hunter's eyes lingered on the rock walls where hung a score of glowing rectangles. Some bore sigils, presumably symbols of great power. Others offered a strange sight, glowing replicas of what his eye would see. Tyur gasped as he recognized the vista from the peak.

"I like to keep watch on the foothills. Someday the Dryth may find my little home, and I wish to be ready."

Tyur stumbled for words as he regarded all around him. He had forgotten his thirst until the Sorcerer handed him a cup of water. He gulped the water down and turned the cup in his hand, struck by its cleanliness compared to his own flesh darkened with dust and grime.

"Sit down, make yourself comfortable."

Tyur sat awkwardly on the plane of metal elevated on four small legs. Despite its spindly appearance, the thing took his weight without complaint.

The Sorcerer seated himself on another plane and leaned forward.

"Is it simple curiosity that brought you here? It can't be that the taboo is lifted. The first dealings I had with the Ithra brought the wrath of the Dryth. It is something I will always regret. I lost two comrades, and the Ithra were punished. I avenged my fellows, but I could not wholly destroy or displace the lizard men, safe as they are in the land of the sun god."

Tyur blurted his questions, "Where do you come from? What manner of man are you? What is your tribe?"

The Sorcerer cocked his head. "Tribe? I suppose my tribe is American. I am from here, in a manner of speaking. But I am not from 'now'. I am from a world that will not be for millions and millions of years. But it will happen here, as a matter of fact."

"Kiom was right. You speak in riddles."

"So it must seem to you. I apologize. But it is difficult to explain. I am from another time. The sun rises in the morning. It sinks below the horizon and then the moon rises. Imagine a spell, or a curse, or anything in your imagination, sending you from the sunset back into the morning, as you would journey from place to place, as you journeyed here. But instead of space I moved through time."

Tyur nodded. "The elders sometimes spin wild tales of the Old Ones, those that made this world. They are capable of such things."

The Sorcerer made a noise of derision as he fingered a charm which hung from his neck, two small rods of yellow metal, crossed. "They did not make this world, rest assured. But you are right. They are capable of wondrous things." He gestured to his surroundings and continued, "My little home was made possible with articles I stole from their cities. All won at great cost." He became lost for a moment in reverie as Tyur edged forward.

"Sorcerer, I have come for your help."

The old man grinned again. "Sorcerer! I suppose that is fair. A better fit is 'Astronaut'. But please, I am Captain Alan Washensky, United States Air Force. Call me Alan. What do I call you?"

"Tyur." The hunter reached forward to grasp the old man's shoulder.

The Sorcerer returned the gesture and continued. "What can I help you with, young man?"

In speech laden with emotion, Tyur related the woeful tale of the Dryth's last raid. He struggled for words as he spoke of Vara. As he described her, the Sorcerer stood and walked to his bed. From the rock wall he took an object, an image like from the screens but smaller, and this one did not glow. He held the thing with evident reverence. Upon its thin face was the image of a woman. She was fair where Vara was dark, light hair framing a smooth face. The Sorcerer nodded as Tyur finished his tale. The hunter grasped the Sorcerer's arm with a grip of iron.

"You must help me. You are wise and bear many strange tools. There must be a magic to make me able to cross into the land of the sun god. Grant me such magic!"

Alan shook his head. "I too am separated from my love. And sadly neither you nor I are likely to be reunited. Not in this life, anyway. I would like nothing more than to help you, Tyur, but it is simply not possible. To venture into those lands you would need a vehicle, like one of the coracles your people use in the river, but one that could protect you from the heat. But then what would you do when you reach their city? You would not be able to leave the ship. Your body simply cannot withstand it. The heat and the foul air would kill you within a day."

Tyur's fists clenched as he spoke, muscles in his shoulders tensing, "You must know something! The elders tell many strange stories of the Old Ones. Some had boats that floated in the night sky amidst the diamonds in the ceiling of the world. Others could make and unmake creatures at will. Work your magic! Make a spell to make my skin like the granite in the cliffs, make my blood like ice to cool me in the heat! You must!"

The Sorcerer rested his head on his fist and stared at the floor. He seemed to be deep in thought, the kind when the mind argues with itself. He shook his head again as he addressed the hunter.

"With some surprise, I note that you have actually hit upon an idea. Though framed as it is in your understanding of the world, there is something to what you say. At the time of my journey, some of my tribe had gained the skill of manipulating life at its most basic level. For ethical reasons our scientists, our sorcerers, if you will, were very restrained in what they were willing to attempt. My own life span has been lengthened by their efforts. It was done to make long voyages across the ocean of night more feasible. This 'spell' was considered the absolute limit of what our sorcerers were willing to do. Some advocated making people smarter or perhaps stronger. But these ideas were not pursued for the fear that they would lead humanity down a dark path. The Old Ones are much, much more skilled in these things than my people could likely ever hope to be. And they know no restraint. Perhaps their excesses, their evil, is the validation of our caution."

Tyur stood, "So you could make me able to cross! You can change me!"

Alan slowly nodded as he fixed the young hunter with a grave look.

"Perhaps. I have the tools from my ship, along with the things from the Old Ones. As a matter of fact, I feed myself with plants altered to make them more nutritious. It is possible to change you. But it is likely you will die during the attempt or later, perhaps after only a few days. Something of this nature would take years of preparation to do properly, if indeed it is truly possible."

"Damn proper! Do it and be quick! Somewhere she waits. Somewhere she thinks of me, and she hopes, I know this!"

Alan shook his head as he stood. "You ask me to murder you on the thinnest of hope that this madness will work. I cannot!"

The two faced each other. Tyur breathed hard. Despite the hospitality of his host, despite his honesty and evident goodness, the young hunter felt anger building within. The Sorcerer eyed him sternly. They were two men of strength and accomplishment, one from a world of darkness and woe, ruled by fickle death, the other from a world of abstraction and riddle and light so abundant that it was taken for granted. Tyur felt his anger wash away as his eyes were drawn to the picture the Sorcerer yet held. He took it from the old man's grasp, inspecting it closely. He spoke, voice now calm, emotions brought to heel.

"What would you risk to return to her?"

Alan shook his head as a rueful smile came to his weathered face. He laughed.

"You son of a bitch."

"Son of a bitch?"

The Sorcerer paced a moment, running a hand through his hair. He walked to the long tables where he leaned finally, looking down. He made a gesture of defeat and turned to face the young man.

He replied, "A phrase in the tongue of my tribe. It means you beat me. You fought a little dirty there, but you won. We will attempt this insanity." The man took an article from the table only to fling it down again. He sighed.

"I should have kept my mouth shut. It is difficult after so long away from people." His expression became grave as he continued. "If this works, you will be changed. If you do not die, then it is very likely you will be unable to rejoin your people. And this is not some spell that can be taken back or reversed. Do you understand?"

The hunter nodded.

The Sorcerer motioned for Tyur to hold out his arm. With a needle the old man took a few drops of blood from the hunter, drawing it into a tiny vial. Then he gestured to his cot.

"Make yourself comfortable. There is some food in that cabinet there. I have to study."

After filling his belly from a bowl of root stew, Tyur found himself drowsy and slipped into a sleep beset by strange dreams. He saw himself swallowed by a great serpent. He cut his way out only to regard himself, his hands as he saw them, with sudden horror. The cause eluded his conscious mind, lost upon waking, whereupon he would slip back into restless sleep.

He woke to find the Sorcerer still sitting before one of the glowing screens, manipulating the sigils, brow furrowed in concentration. He looked to the hunter.

"You are awake. Excellent. I have had a productive night. Tell me, have you ever witnessed one of your people being ill or sick?"

Tyur stood and stretched, thinking. "At times meat fails to dry properly and becomes rancid. Hunger may drive one to eat of it, and the person becomes sick. Sometimes overeating of the back of the green bark can have a similar effect."

"But no illness, nothing that seems to come from nowhere? Coughing and fever?"

Tyur shrugged. "I know no such illness. Why do you ask?"

The old man rubbed his temples. "I wish Mitch was here. He was the science officer. I am a mere dilettante next to him. It is difficult to explain, but the stuff of which you are made is slightly different than the stuff of which I am made. There is less of it, and it is more ordered."

Tyur looked on in puzzlement.

"The origin of that particular mystery notwithstanding, the good news is that it is likely this 'spell' is more apt to work on you than it would on me. Right now the computer is running a series of simulations. The first trick is manipulating the proteins in such a way as to not induce immediate organ failure. I have instructed the computer to weave them in with simpler substances that will disintegrate slowly. The computer is creating the ideal combinations, or so I hope. While we wait, I thought of other ways to increase your odds of success." The Sorcerer stepped to one of the long tables. He grabbed the cylinder and its red children then walked to the stairwell.

"Follow me. We may as well send you along with this."

The stairwell led down to another chamber. This one was just as long and filled with more bizarre objects. In one corner a net was hung from the ceiling, forming a long rectangle. Another strange device sat in one end. Tyur touched the net.

"Do you fish the river?"

Alan shook his head. "No, it's a batting cage. For baseball."

"Baseball?"

The old man laid a hand on the hunter's shoulder. "I have already attempted to explain the rudiments of 'genetic engineering' to you in the tongue of the Ithra. We shall leave 'baseball' for another day."

Near the door were neat bundles of dried reeds, another edible from the wild. Alan instructed Tyur, and the pair stacked the bundles against the rock wall of the far end. He then held the cylinder in both hands and spoke in the tone of an elder.

"Tyur. What you see before you is a powerful weapon. In the tongue of my people it is called a shotgun. Like any weapon, it can be used for good or ill. Its inclusion in my vessel's inventory was a form of insurance against all sorts of eventualities. None were so farfetched as what came to pass, but that's life, isn't it? Inside this cylinder is a small hammer that will strike the shell, causing a sudden chemical reaction to fill the shell with…" The Sorcerer regarded for a moment Tyur's puzzled expression. He shrugged and continued, "Why don't we just fire a few shells and you will get the idea."

He held one of the red children up for Tyur's inspection. "These are in short supply, so we will only fire one or two, and you will take the rest with you. I can make more, but it is very time-consuming. Now, watch me load it."

Tyur did as bade. Alan ejected the shell and repeated the operation a few times.

"Now, I need you to cover your ears. The Dryth have their fire-spitters. This one spits thunder."

The image of the reed bundle bursting in a cloud of shreds stayed with the hunter as the unusual pair ate their noon meal. Despite his dire quest Tyur found himself smiling. For the first time in memory, one of the Ithra had a weapon to match those of the Dryth. He was but one fighter against a horde, yet the "shotgun" represented hope. Hope that the Ithra might be at least in some small measure avenged. He turned to his host.

"How many shotgun do you have? With enough, all the Ithra could be armed. We could lay amidst the ferns and await their discs, then we would rise up and spit our thunder into their foul ranks!"

"It is an appealing image, young man. With the facilities here I could make some more weapons and shells in time. But if the Dryth got wind of it, they would come in numbers again. Your people were nearly wiped from the earth once. I was there. I am to blame. When my ship crashed up north, my crew and I made the perilous journey across the white wastes. After crossing the Gods' Spine, as you call it, we happened upon the Ithra. They fed us and tended our wounds. We learned your speech and even hunted with you. My crew and I were operating under the false assumption that we had landed on an alien planet. One day I climbed a peak nearby. With these binoculars I saw a city far to the south. My comrades and I were ecstatic. An advanced civilization! Between us and the mysterious city was the desert. The Ithra explained the sun god would permit no men to cross it. So we beamed a radio signal there."

The Sorcerer's eyes became sad. He continued, "Death answered. The Dryth came in numbers none had ever seen. They killed with abandon. My two friends died. I nearly died, but Kiom saved my life. I fled east until I came upon another race, this one more congenial. I sailed south from the coast onboard one of their ships. I saw many things. I narrowly escaped the last occupants of an entire city that lay underground, far, far to the south. There I found the secret, the reality of where I was. I also stole the tools I needed to free my ship from the ice. The journey there and back was many years."

Tyur sat transfixed. Only three beings occupied his world, the Ithra, the Dryth, and the foul Slagborn, things of nightmare, rarely seen. He had thought his long hunts made him well traveled. The Astronaut had shown otherwise.

Alan scratched his beard as he spoke. "Finally, I made a home here. And I vowed I would never endanger the Ithra again."

"Can you not take your ship home the way you came?"

The Sorcerer shook his head. "My ship sits ready in a cave below us. She is battered and bruised a bit, and has donated many bits and pieces to help me get set up here. But the old girl could still fly. However, I cannot replicate the circumstances which brought me here. In fact, I still don't fully understand them. I am trapped."

The hunter nodded. A beeping sound came from the screen.

"Well, let's see what the computer has to say about our idea." The astronaut looked to the screen, nodding as he did. "This madness can proceed."

Tyur paced the long hall while the Sorcerer worked. The old man was becoming more apprehensive. He occasionally paused to look at his young guest. He shifted to a table near the garden, its surface completely obscured by dozens of articles which mystified the hunter. The Sorcerer worked dials and knobs with deft practice, efficient, though concern clouded his weathered brow. He paused.

"Now I need to add the element that will change you. It is immensely unpleasant. You should see this, young man. You should know, as well as you can, what will happen to you. If you change your mind, I would not think ill of you."

Tyur swallowed, though his face betrayed no emotion. He followed Alan to a far corner where a large metal box stood. A low hum came from its innards. The old man opened the door, and Tyur gave a start as he felt a wave of icy cold wash over his near-naked frame.

"A box that holds winter. This must be from the Old Ones."

The old man laughed again. "Actually, it's from General Electric. An old firm, definitely, but not of the Old Ones." He reached in and produced a smaller box. The contents caused Tyur to hiss in anger.

It was the hand of a Dryth.

"Don't think this some grim trophy. I took this for research. But I find I regret it now."

He stuck the thing with a needle, pushing it deep into the cold stump. The needle was dipped into another vial. The box that held it hummed and vibrated.

Alan worked other machines until the humming stopped. He mixed the contents of several of the tubes and placed the article back into the machine. It whirred awhile and became silent. The astronaut regarded the hunter, sadness written across his granite features.

"It is done." He closed his eyes and seemed to whisper to himself.

Tyur asked, "Do you intone the spell?"

"No. I ask forgiveness for what I am about to do."

The hunter could not say how much time passed as he came in and out of consciousness. Each time, he saw the astronaut standing over him, scanning his glowing screens, adjusting the tubes and lines which lay across Tyur's body like twisting vines. There was pain, then a strange sense of cold which grew with each bout of wakefulness. Tyur felt waves of sickness. Then his head began to throb with a dull ache, settling finally in his eyes. When sleep granted respite, he suffered horrible visions. He saw himself atop a pyramid of black, clothed in fine robes and adorned with gold and jewels, surrounded by ranks of the Ithra. At their feet were throngs of Dryth, singing a droning chant into a sky of swirling red. Their words made no sense, and yet, slowly, he began to understand. Again and again there was a name, "Therizom." The syllables seemed to caress his ears, bequeathing a sense of sinister warmth. He screamed over and over. Was it in the vision or did his voice echo in the low cave? He knew not.

Suddenly he saw himself atop one of the flying discs. A chill wind bit through the thick robes he wore. Thoughts woven from strange words filled his mind.

Father sleeps. So we fly to slaughter. We will teach a lesson to those that once dwelled in the palace, lounging at his feet, dancing and singing for his pleasure while we toiled under the earth and in the fields. Our brothers and sisters spared not a thought for us. And now we will take our revenge.

Tyur felt bloodlust bursting from his heart. It was a sickeningly pleasurable sensation, to give one's heart over to murder, and blind rage, to know no guilt or restraint. He saw bodies burning outside a cave's mouth and he knew. He knew he saw the world through Dryth eyes. He understood the joy in destruction, ecstasy in death and subjugation. They had known all along. They knew the Ithra were beings as they, capable of thought, of love and feeling. And to them, it made the slaughter all the more enjoyable. They hated the Ithra with a passion that choked his throat and brought tears to his eyes. Tyur's stomach roiled. Here was knowledge he could barely comprehend, pure evil. The meat-eater that tore apart the unwary hunter, the grass-eater that trampled the same; these were mere beasts, engaged in nothing more than a struggle for survival. The Dryth killed for pleasure. Tyur howled in sadness and anger that his people should suffer under such an impulse. He lashed out with all his strength, striking at his visions. He could hear the Sorcerer's voice but could not understand.

Finally, the veil fell from his eyes. He felt the chill of the metal table on which he lay. He felt the straps with which the Sorcerer had bound him biting into his flesh. He relaxed. The old man looked down on him, face nearly lost in the lights which hung above. The hunter's breath slowed.

"I live."

"I was sure I was going to lose you. By all rights you should be dead, based on the readings I was getting." The old man sank into a chair, fatigue lining his face. He rubbed his eyes. "Yesterday I was sitting here playing chess against the computer and feeling sorry for myself. Then you show up and demand I try to kill you with this ungodly scheme. I wonder if I am dreaming. Perhaps the life of a hermit has made me mad."

He undid the straps which held Tyur to the table. The young man stood, rubbing his wrists and chest.

"Well, how do you feel?"

"Cold."

"I wish I knew if that was normal or not. It will take the proteins about a week to decay completely during which time your cells will be undergoing their changes. Your body will become like a Dryth, to what degree I cannot say. In the best case scenario, you will look much the same as you do now but your body's chemistry will be adapted to life in the Dryth lands. It is possible the serum will do too little and the heat and radiation of the wasteland will kill you. Or you will simply drop dead. There are worse outcomes, but I do not wish to dwell on them."

"I saw things. I heard their speech, and I understood it."

Alan shook his head. "That is not something I can explain. Over the next few days I will be observing you very closely."

The hunter cocked his head. "But it is done, yes?"

"Yes. We will now—"

Tyur interrupted, "No. If it is done, I leave. Vara waits."

The old man let the argument die on his lips as he began preparations. He applied small bandages to where the tubes and needles had pierced the young man's flesh. He filled a bag with silver pouches he retrieved from a drawer and handed it to the hunter.

"Emergency rations. Tear it open and eat. Now let's get you some shells."

The pair then went to the lower chamber where the Sorcerer rifled through a few boxes, finally emerging with a large metal box and two black straps of a material unfamiliar to Tyur. The pair filled the strap's dozens of loops with the shotgun's red children. He motioned for Tyur to lower his head and he placed the straps over his shoulders so they crossed in the middle of his chest.

"There. 110 shells for you. I wish it was ten thousand."

Tyur's gaze fell upon a garment hanging from a hook on the rough wall. The thing was deep blue and decorated with colorful symbols. The one on the shoulder was a pretty thing, red and white stripes underneath a corner of blue dotted with bits of white.

Tyur gestured to the garment and to the whole of the astronaut's home.

"Everywhere there are symbols."

"I suppose you are right. In my time we took it all for granted. This is merely my old flight suit. Here is my name, here is a symbol for the vessel, my ship."

"What is that one?"

"The flag? That is the symbol of my tribe."

"Your tribe was powerful. To carry such a thing into battle, it must have brought much luck."

Alan laughed. "I suppose it did. But it was not about power. At its best, it went to battle to fight tyranny." He reflected a moment and then fixed his steel eyes on the hunter as he spoke. "It is good to fight for hearth and home. And I don't turn my nose up at a little revenge now and again. But there are more noble reasons to fight: to free others, to fight to guarantee your liberty and that of your sons and daughters. You fight to free your Vara. But you also strike a blow against the Dryth, those that murder and oppress your people." He took a knife from his belt and cut away the flag with a length of cloth from the sleeve and turned to Tyur. He tied the thing to the hunter's thick arm. Tyur looked down in awe.

"But I am not of your blood…"

"All who fight tyranny are of my tribe."

The young man grasped his host's shoulders, and the old man returned the gesture.

The Sorcerer led the young man down another staircase, this one narrow and cut from the stone. The air became cool and damp as they descended. The lights overhead disappeared. Alan lit the way with another of his wonderful devices; this one a squat cylinder that spat bright light from its mouth. The sound of running water grew in volume. On a rough-hewn landing the Sorcerer had kept a coracle of Ithra make. Tyur lowered himself into the small boat as the old man knelt at the edge. His lined face was set grim though his eyes betrayed sadness and shades of a dilemma. The two men were out of words, parting with only nods. As Tyur pushed off, the old man had one last request.

"If you can, send word of your fate."

Tyur nodded again, adding, "I thank you for your magic, wise one. May you find peace here in your exile."

Captain Alan Washensky watched the coracle disappear into the blackness. He turned and began the long climb back to his home.

Tyur lost track of time as the river snaked its way through the mountain's cool bowels. The cold seemed to bite the young man's skin and seep into his bones. A bend finally revealed the brilliance of clean daylight as the current picked up speed. The warrior worked the small paddle to keep the boat centered in the river as it emerged into the warm light. Tyur felt it on his skin and spoke thanks to the ancestors.

Once beyond the foothills, the river flowed peaceably. Tyur let the current take him, paddling only when the coracle drifted underneath the tall fronds that reached from the banks. His mind was unquiet, dwelling on the Sorcerer and the many things he had seen. Though it was the warm season, he felt strangely cold. His skin seemed to keep no heat. Ever at the forefront of his thoughts was the coming change. The old man had woven threads of the Dryth into the young hunter; the results had yet to be fully realized. When fright took hold of him, the natural revulsion against such a profound violation, he thought of Vara. When hungry, he tore open one of the Sorcerer's "emergency rations," a quantity of thick paste enclosed in the strange skin that shined like rare metal but bent like soft hide.

During the night he huddled in the boat, shivering, beset with more dreams. There was, again and again, the pyramid. But now he toiled at its base, pulling with all his might on lines to move the mighty stones. Around him were those he understood as brothers, though the sight of them was hidden to his waking mind. They suffered together under the snapping whip of a tall man, beautiful in the glaring light, his handsome face fulsome in the joy he took in subjugating those around him. He was a kind of god; this, the young man knew without question. Tyur's heart tore itself apart when a flash of courage enabled his dream-self to look upon the man, to look up from his labors and behold his master even though the whip threatened. He felt love for his creator even as his soul burned with hatred at his cruelty.

In other visions, he and his brothers ranged across the sun-blasted waste, riding atop the saurs. Their heels prodded the beasts to bursts of great speed. They yelled as their mounts sprinted forth, surrounding a monster as long as the trees were tall, a skittering thing moving with sinuous grace across the hot sand. Spears flew and the fire-spitters belched forth their red rays, and the thing fell. The Dryth also hunted, and Tyur chaffed at the similarity, the familiarity of it.

The dawn woke him. Tyur drank the sun's warmth like a man dying of thirst. He realized the coracle had run aground in a bed of smooth rocks. The river had petered out into a stream, and now the craft could go no further. The hunter left the boat where it lay and continued south on foot. Around him, the tall ferns had given way to smaller scrub. Far ahead was the haze that ever hung over the Dryth's lands. In the distance, barely perceptible through a curtain of shimmering heat, stood the city. It was a collection of broad domes overseen by a towering structure, the pyramid of his visions. Somewhere within, Vara waited.

Though only a few days south from the mountains, the sun god was already growing powerful. The warm rays were a joy to Tyur who had suffered so much from the chill of the last days. He felt his skin warming, though now it began to itch.

His steps faltered as he regarded his arms. The smooth bronze of his flesh was now dry and cracked. He squatted in the dry bed, feeling his skin under his hands.

White hot pain came in sudden, searing waves across his back. The hunter reeled. He lurched forward, turning to see his assailant, a scorpion half as long as a man was tall. A wary hunter, the beast skittered back at its prey's movement.

Tyur cursed, screaming as the pain coursed through his body like lightning. How could he be so inattentive? His vision blurred yet he could still see a half dozen more of the creatures skulking, surrounding him. With cruel joy, he remembered the shotgun slung on his back. He pulled it free but lost his step, falling to his knees. His hands went to work the cylinder but they were clumsy, muscles now steeped in the scorpion's venom. The shotgun fell from his grasp. The scorpions closed.

A howl loosed itself from the hunter's throat, unbidden. Through a fog he watched his arms lash out, grabbing. The scorpions reeled back before regaining their courage, advancing with tails and claws clattering.

Here was the unexplained; the creature they hunted should have collapsed by now. Instead it lurched forward, swinging out, grasping.

Tyur caught one of the creatures by its knobby tail. His other hand closed around the cephalothorax, and he tore it apart. The act brought savage joy to his pounding heart. He grabbed another and rent again, soiling the dry ground with the thing's vile insides. Again and again, he tore until he saw all were ripped asunder.

The young hunter stood, chest heaving. Though he had been stung a half dozen more times the poison seemed to have worn off with remarkable speed. He stared down at his hands, stained with the green of the scorpions' blood. Tyur gave a start at the sight of his fingertips. During the melee his fingernails had fallen off. Now from the tips of his fingers lengths of bone protruded, sharp and hard. It was like the hand the Sorcerer had taken from the box of cold. Despite himself Tyur found he was smiling. His blood had been the equal of the poison, and his new claws had made a slick mess of the scorpions. The Sorcerer's spell was a success, so far.

He continued south. Vegetation became more and more sparse as the sun grew in strength. The low hills began to flatten themselves as he proceeded. Far to the north, the mountains stood now in haze. He realized he walked now in the broad boundary between lands suited to Dryth, dry and hot, and lands suited to Ithra, green and cool. But it was not merely a question of comfort. Though none in memory had tried, legend amongst the Ithra said that the air in the land of the sun god would poison a man after too long if the heat did not kill him first.

Tyur's alert ears caught the steps of a saur and he squatted down. The noise came from behind a low rise ahead. He crept silently to the crest.

At a muddy pool shaded by an outcrop three of the creatures drank. This must be one of the last places where rain might gather before the sun god claimed full reign of the land, thought Tyur. He watched them as they lapped water into their fanged mouths. The lizards were the height of a man at their scaly shoulders, perhaps three times as long down to the tip of their whip-like tails. The warrior became aware of a strangeness; the beasts' sharp odor was now pleasant in his nose. He was overcome with the sudden notion that he should walk to them and pat them on their scaly snouts. He began to stand, catching himself with an unspoken curse. As he settled back down his foot slid slightly on the loose gravel underfoot.

The beasts shot up, necks craning as they sampled the air. A moment later their powerful legs propelled them to where the hunter had so ineptly hidden. Tyur reeled, bringing the shotgun from his back and charging the weapon. The metallic *clack clack* echoed across the waste. As finger squeezed he realized the beasts were cowering.

He let off the trigger before the thunder was released.

Where was the snarling leap, the claws and teeth aimed to tear him asunder? Where was the sinister hunger in their black eyes?

Absent. Where should have been animal rage was meekness.

He lowered his weapon. In the bright warmth of the sun he saw, seemingly for the first time, the hides of the beasts, glossy beige banded by a warm brown the color of bark. The muscles underneath rippled with graceful power, a shimmer that worked its way down nearly to the tip of the wicked tail. They were always in motion, swaying ever so slightly in the hot wind. They were beautiful to behold, beautiful in their murderous grace, beautiful in the elegant fulfillment of their purpose. The thoughts were foreign to the warrior. He pondered but a moment before realization struck. He spoke aloud.

"The spell…"

He slung the weapon and walked forward. The largest of the saurs acquiesced to his touch. Tyur let his new claws glide across the scaled hide, a most pleasant sensation. More inspiration came to the young man.

What a joy it would be to ride the beast as did the hunters of his vision. His hand lay on the saur's back. He tested the creature's patience, pushing it a bit, then pulling it, neither task easy due to the dense muscle packed on the perfectly balanced skeleton of the thing. Yet the saur showed no annoyance.

Tyur spied again the long distance to the city. He looked back to the saur.

"Let's see how congenial you remain as I mimic the Dryth of my visions." The creature blinked back dumbly. With difficulty, Tyur grabbed a fist full of the taut, scaled hide and leapt atop the beast. He mounted poorly, teetering. The saur took a quick sidestep, whether to help or hinder him Tyur could not know. But his balance was well and truly lost.

He landed painfully, weapon hard against his back, and stood with a muttered curse. The saur made a clicking sound in its throat.

"I am glad one of us is amused."

His second attempt was successful. He patted the shoulders to no effect before he realized a mere nudge with his leg was enough to cause the beast to turn. A gentle prodding of the heel sent it forward. He guided the beast in the direction of the city, and a kick caused it to break into a loping run. Tyur grabbed the hide with both hands to steady himself. He grinned as the beast glided across the rocky ground. The thing was quick. Underneath its clawed feet, the scrubland was giving way to wider and wider patches of sand and clay baked brittle by the heat. Tyur grinned, feeling the hot wind send warm fingers through his long hair. He shouted encouragement to his mount, reveling in the feeling of motion and travel.

The realization that he was speaking in the tongue of the Dryth brought sudden despair. His narrowed eyes rested on the pyramid as his anger burned.

The saur grew sluggish as the sun dipped to the horizon. Tyur felt listless himself as a chill settled into his tired bones. He found a patch of brittle clay and lay down, enjoying the warmth of the sun that remained trapped in the ground. The saur walked a circle before curling down next to him. Before sleep overtook him, he supped on one of the packets the Sorcerer had provided. The thick paste was not unpalatable, though Tyur could not name the flavor. His belly full, the hunter fell asleep. His eyelids closed upon a vista of the pyramid bathed in moonlight. Its silhouette menaced the domes underneath. Tomorrow, he would face his fate there.

The sun god woke him with warm caresses. The heat brought comfort and clarity to Tyur. He stood and stretched, then pondered the sight at his feet. Strewn about his bed of clay were shreds of a thin material, nearly translucent. He knelt and reached to take one in his hand. The gesture provided an answer to the mystery before he had even held one of the shreds. Where had been skin, bronze and unmarked save for the odd scar, was now scales, tan in color, blending into the white that showed on the inner surface. He touched his face and sighed in relief. He still had the face of a man, though the scales reached up to the sides of his neck. The skin on his chest was also yet normal, but his back was covered in the hide of a saur. Covering his eyes, he peered up at the sun.

"I have paid a hefty price to enter your lands. Grant me at least the sight of my beloved. Surely even one so cruel as you could not refuse such a request after so much had been given."

He mounted the saur, and it took off toward the city. As the domes slowly neared, the warrior pondered his options. He needed to gain entry to the city. He needed to find Vara and then escape, though she would surely wither in the punishing heat of the waste… His stomach sank a moment before he dismissed his doubts. One of Kiom's proverbs came to mind; the hunter who thinks of meat will go to sleep hungry.

Near a jumble of rocks burned nearly black from the sun, he dismounted and turned his attention to the city. As he stared, he could not help but feel awe. Before him was the handiwork of a god. Though black from a distance, the walls and domes were actually colored a dark red. Yet the looming pyramid seemed blacker than even in his vision. He could spy no door or hatch like those that kept the Sorcerer safe, nor even a gaping entrance like the caves of his home. Everywhere were smooth, unbroken surfaces that seemed to drink the brilliant sunlight, a palace made of night.

His thoughts were interrupted by movement in the distance. The foremost dome had become the center of sudden activity. A great square of it had opened with a grinding creak audible even from such a distance. From the opening poured forth half a dozen Dryth astride loping saurs. Their spears shone under the brilliant gaze of the sun god. The party was headed for a cluster of jutting rocks south of the city. Hunting, thought Tyur. The Dryth were as his vision had shown. They were about his height and as broad. Their scales ranged in color from those that were like the tan of his new hide to others more a dark brown. Tyur pulled his long hair into a tight tail; it was the one detail that would give him away at a distance. Some of the Dryth wore headbands of dark fabric whose long ends fluttered in the hot wind. Perhaps his new ponytail would be seen as such.

He jumped onto the saur and jabbed the beast with his heels. From his visions he knew how the Dryth hunted. They hunted for sport, driving their prey, darting here and there, exhorting each other to acts of bravery and cruelty. But foremost in Tyur's mind was the thought that when they were done, the dome would open again.

The hunting party soon disappeared behind the blackened crags of the formation. Tyur pointed the mount toward the rocks. With luck, he could shadow the group and slip in behind them when the city opened to welcome them home. A wind howled across the waste as the saur's long legs sped underneath him. The air was thin and hot, but Tyur found it invigorating.

As he neared the rocks, Tyur heard the voices of the hunters. The jutting slabs of black rock struck up toward the sky with a beauty known only in the wastelands of the world, where barrenness and solitude were as the fecund greens of the forest. The rocks stood against the wind and the heat and thus displayed a defiant sort of beauty. The area formed an oblong shape upon the plain, a jagged shark's fin cutting through the hard-packed sand, a few hundred feet at its longest. Tyur smiled. As he grew closer, he saw a hundred nooks and folds within the dark rocks, places to hide and watch and wait. The yells of the hunting party echoed from somewhere on the other side. Tyur knew they had sighted one of the giant centipedes that called rocks like these home. He knew the Dryth's rasping voice from his visions, indeed he knew their tongue. But as he neared, their voices were lost to his ears, now swallowed by the stone. Indecision gripped him. Safety lay within the rocks, up the scrabble and amidst the sharp columns of dark rock. But his mount could not join him. Without the mount he would likely not be able to keep pace with the group.

The saur sidled impatiently. With a muttered curse, Tyur leapt from the mount and ran up the irregular slope towards the rocks. A look over his shoulder revealed his mount jogging away on tentative steps, looking warily in the direction of the formation.

The stone was searing to his touch as Tyur climbed. He found a crevice that looked through to the other side and cautiously peeked through.

The Dryth were below. They directed their mounts to dart forward and backward while their long spears poked into crack and crevice in an attempt to goad their prey into the open. Only three were visible. Tyur craned his neck. Two more came into view, idling in a position to flank the prey. Where was the other one?

Tyur heard the scrape of a saur's claws against the stones.

"Brother, what are you doing?"

The voice spoke in the tongue of the Dryth. Tyur went rigid.

He crouched, coiling his hard muscles like a serpent before the strike. He turned and leapt from his perch. The Dryth's saur reeled back, nearly pitching its rider who sat stunned in shock. Four long strides and another leap brought Tyur smashing against the lizard man. The two tumbled down the gentle slope, flinging gravel as they rolled. They slid to a halt, and Tyur rolled to sit astride the Dryth.

The Dryth's reptilian eyes showed confusion and despair as its strong hands fought against Tyur's pin, but the hunter had the advantage.

Its strange voice, hoarse yet underlain with an oily sibilance, implored its attacker, "What are you?"

Tyur wrenched his hand free from the scaly grip of his foe, and he unslung the weapon at his back with a deft motion. One hand on either end, he pushed down until the cylinders pressed against his enemy's throat. The thing gasped, straining to push the weapon away. Tyur looked down, deep into the reptilian eyes. For the briefest of moments, he saw himself reflected in the diamond pupils. He saw that his eyes were the same. His rage grew, and he pushed down harder, veins erupting down the length of his arms and neck.

He spoke just above a whisper as the weapon crushed the Dryth's throat.

"Vengeance."

He watched as the ghost left the thing. It grew limp, and Tyur permitted himself to relax. He stared down.

The Dryth wore simple trousers of thick leather and a vest worked with many loops and pockets. At his waist was a long dagger and one of the feared fire-spitters. Tyur took the warm metal in his hands. A lever sat under the body of the thing. He knew from the thunder-spitter that the lever was how death was released. He tucked both knife and spitter into his belt and looked frantically around. None of the other hunters were in view. He stripped the vest and trousers from the Dryth and put them on with the awkward movements of one unused to such garments. His foe's mount shifted nervously as he approached. Instinct bade him make a clicking sound in his throat, which seemed to calm the saur.

The beast became still, and he mounted. A voice rang out in the distance. At the far end of the formation, a rider shouted.

"Rukka! Xertu has taken a big one! We fly back lest it go dry! Hurry!"

Tyur sat on his mount. His stomach twisted as his ruse was put to the test.

He waved to the Dryth, a gesture of acknowledgement, and kicked his mount into motion.

The far rider turned and sped away.

Tyur breathed deep. He slowed his mount. Clear of the formation, the other riders were now visible. One dragged a centipede behind him, three times the length of a man.

The once-human hunter frustrated his mount with constant adjustments to its speed. Too fast would bring Tyur face to face with the Dryth before the door was opened. Too slow would draw attention as the lizard men would wait for him and see through his poor disguise before the moment he was among them.

The saurs made good speed across the wastes. Tyur's pulse quickened as he heard the grinding squeal of the door. The party was nearly there.

The beast underneath him croaked in complaint as he kicked the thing until it sprinted with as good a speed as a saur could make. He narrowed his eyes against the burning air and dust. His legs tightened around his mount as he unslung the thunder-spitter and racked a round into the chamber.

The Dryth had nearly halted, mounts ambling into the dark portal which yawned ahead. Tyur was close enough to see the details of their hides and clothes; he realized each bore a slightly different pattern, a whim of nature or, perhaps, one of their dark father. One wore a bronze circlet around his head. He was slightly larger than the others and carried himself with an aura of brutal authority. He was dismounting, as were the others. Their mood was suffused with savage pleasure as they bantered with each other. They had claimed their quarry with skill and speed. One turned to welcome the latecomer.

The shotgun announced Tyur's arrival with an ear-splitting boom. The Dryth collapsed in a heap, eyes wide at the gaping hole in his chest. The others leapt in shock, hands fumbling for weapons, faces betraying their confusion.

Tyur fired again, felling another lizard man before a white-hot blast buried itself into his rearing mount. He tumbled down to the baked earth before the door, rolling to stand before the leader. Before he could fire again Tyur lashed out with the heavy butt of his weapon. His blow struck true, and the leader fell clutching his bloodied forehead. A blast seared close enough to Tyur's shoulder to raise blisters as he spun and fired again, catching his attacker full on the face, now a ruin of dark-green ichor. Tyur sensed motion behind him and ducked instinctively, feeling the heat of the blast over his head. He racked the weapon as he lunged forward, swinging the shotgun to knock aside the Dryth's fire-spitter before it could unleash another blast. He came to stand before the lizard man, moving the cylinder to point underneath the Dryth's chin. The ear-shattering thunder erupted again, and the head was reduced to shreds of hide and bone.

Tyur spun again, finding himself suddenly without foes. He peered into the cool darkness of the dome's interior. A groan cut short his investigation.

Sprawled on the ground, the one bearing the bronze circlet stirred. Tyur kicked him, so that he lay on his back, and bent down.

The tongue of the Dryth felt strange on his lips as he spoke.

"Where are the women of the Ithra? Speak!"

The Dryth lay in a daze. His reptile eyes stared up at Tyur in incomprehension.

Tyur placed the cylinder under his chin. "Tell me! Or join your friends in the beyond!"

His rasping voice finally replied, "In Father's old chambers, the cold place, the center level… Who are you? You have our eyes, yet you bear a face like the Father…"

"Where is this place?"

The Dryth shook his head as he stared up at his attacker. "Down the main hall. Ascend the stairs until you reach the red doors."

Tyur hissed in annoyance. He had not the vocabulary to understand the directions. Yet as he thought, as he heard the Dryth's words echo in his head, images appeared in his mind's eye.

Stairs. Forms shaped to aid ascent. A door. A thing to divide a space, to control access. The sensation was unpleasant. He looked down at the leader, face caked in dark green blood that had already dried in the heat. He felt disgust. The Dryth were a part of him now. Before self-pity weakened him, he again thought of Vara. He would pay this price and indeed much more. He slammed the butt down on the Dryth's head. He held back to avoid killing but would not weep had the blow done so. Tyur did not wait to see. He reloaded the weapon as the Sorcerer had shown him as he entered the dome.

Past the open door, he entered a wide hall filled with a hundred articles of unknown purpose. His bare footfalls echoed across the wide circumference; the space was bounded only by the gently sloping exterior wall of the dome. Within were bulky things, ladders and moveable stairs, snaking cables and boxes. Tyur was faintly reminded of the Sorcerer's lair, a place of wonder and strangeness where powerful objects could be made or repaired. Yet instead of the sterile cleanliness and delicate angles of the Sorcerer's place, here was an aesthetic of callous menace couched in curves and spirals. Dust and sand covered everything. Nearly snatched from a recollection of his dreams, Tyur could imagine the space from another time, when it was more ordered and clean. An object he recognized came into view as he walked; one of the flying discs, and dozens more behind. The things floated a few feet above the dark red stone of the floor. Some were large, boasting covered compartments in the rear, while others could only accommodate one or two riders. Tyur grimaced at the sight of their weapons, fire-spitters like the one at his belt but larger, barrels burned black with the heat of their hateful blasts.

How many of his people had died from these weapons?

A shout snapped him back to the dire danger of the present. He spun to see a dozen of the Dryth running, emerging from the shadows of the huge chamber and its clutter. With a cry of rage, Tyur fired the shotgun once, twice, then turned and fled in the direction the leader had indicated. Past the banks of discs rose a wide staircase.

Tyur took the steps two at a time, sparing a glance behind to see that others had joined his pursuers' ranks. Atop the stairs, he turned and fired, again and again, until the lever's pull caused no more thunder, only a metallic click. The Dryth at the base of the stairs fell while their brethren darted here and there in confusion, some clambering over dead comrades in their rage, others seeking cover.

Tyur threw open the double doors and burst into a long hallway. He brought the weapon up with a start as he realized figures loomed at either side. But they were still. Tyur saw they were formed of stone, both depicting the same tall man of graceful form, one clothed in a simple robe that hung from one muscular shoulder while the other wore an elaborate suit of armor wrought with strange designs of beings with no familiar form floating amidst stars and comets.

Footsteps sounded just outside. Tyur's pursuers were nearly at the doors. Tyur stepped behind the statue of the robed figure, slinging his weapon and bracing himself against the cool stone. He pushed with all his might, permitting himself a triumphant grin when the thing began to give way.

With a great creak and deafening crash, the statue fell before the door. While a cloud of dust spread, Tyur pushed the other statue.

The ruin of the two statues blocked the door, eliciting a small noise of relief from the beleaguered hunter.

The Dryth outside hissed in rage as they threw themselves against the obstacle with little effect. It could only be opened a hand's width. A lizard man peeked around the gap to be met with the butt of the thunder-spitter.

Tyur sprinted down the hall, brow furrowed as he attempted to make sense of the leader's directions. The passage was long and lit with globes that hung from the ceiling and emitted a warm light. He heard noises up ahead from a side passage, the sound of feet running. Tyur turned down one side passage, then another. Thoughts of direction were pushed out with the sudden realization that his weapon was empty.

His hands fumbled with the red children as he reloaded. One bounced at his feet, and he bent to pick it up.

A blast soared over his head, and he tumbled forward, racking the weapon as he stood firing. His attacker clutched his stomach as he fell back into the side hallway. Tyur cursed his inattention. He leaned against a wall and collected himself a moment. The hallway stretched on a ways before he saw another staircase that led upwards. He saw more passages to either side. Each could contain a potential ambush. Overwhelmed, Tyur realized he was lost. Now, more footfalls sounded, punctuated by barking orders and exclamations of anger and confusion. Surprise had aided his entry, but now he was a hunted animal, trapped in a maze without sight of sun or moon to guide him. He stood against the wall as he pondered his predicament. Boldness had gotten him this far, but would more likely mean his end.

Tyur's eyes lingered on his surroundings. He noticed the walls were decorated with panels of stone carved with great skill. The figures were nearly flat yet cunningly displayed enough shadow to create the illusion of greater depth. Central to each panel was the figure from his dreams, the beautiful and cruel one. In one panel, the figure led an army of Dryth against a host of bizarre creatures more plant than man. In another, he walked surrounded by simple nature where beasts bowed before him and birds flitted about his head. In the panel across from Tyur, the man sat surrounded by others like him but lesser, beings made for his pleasure perhaps, men and women bearing fine features and graceful bodies, eyes alight with the simple joys of the garden in which they reclined. Tyur felt his chest tighten.

The Ithra. The figures were unmistakably of his kind. Tyur felt numb as he walked, inspecting more panels. One portrayed a trio of Ithra women flanked by Dryth in elaborate robes. Above them loomed the man, arms outstretched, smile beaming on his sculpted face. In the next panel, the women lay prone, swathed with cloth. Above them stood a phalanx of warriors. The one from the dreams presided again, looking down upon the women, his chiseled face softened by sadness.

Tyur shook his head as his primitive mind found only confusion in the images.

Voices down a side hallway sent him flat against the wall. The conversation grew in volume.

"What is it?"

"I do not know! Everyone says something different! Those who saw him in the hangar said he bears the face of an Ithra but the form of a Dryth!"

"Preposterous!"

"Where is he now?"

The high voice croaked in anguished reply, "How would I know? He was chased into the dome proper and could be anywhere! Utakmil is mustering the warriors now."

Two Dryth hove into view. They were slim of build and stooped slightly, clothed in gold robes. The first fell under Tyur's blow as he swung the shotgun like a mighty club. The other shrieked, legs giving way underneath him. His clawed hands shook as he held them up, a pathetic defense. The hunter checked his swing. He pulled the Dryth up by his tall collar.

"The Ithra women, where?"

"Upstairs! Do not hurt me!"

"Show me the way!"

The pair headed toward the stairs as the prisoner meekly pointed. Tyur came behind him, one hand grasping the back of the lizard man's neck, the other holding his thunder-spitter to point over the Dryth's shoulder. Awkwardly the pair advanced. The prisoner climbed the stairs with difficulty, stumbling as he hissed and chittered in fear. Tyur's curiosity bubbled over.

"You are no warrior. What are you?"

The Dryth remembered himself. His back straightened and his complaints stopped. He looked over his shoulder as he replied.

"I am a priest of Therizom. I serve the Father."

The name sent a bolt of electricity through Tyur's muscular frame.

"The god from my dreams."

"A god indeed. He made us and all you see. He will wake one day, and things shall be again like the golden age, yet even better, as his true heirs now rule the city."

The top of the stairs opened into a long hall, curving along the circumference of the dome. Here was even more ornate than the floor below. Gold accented the warm red stone carved into graceful arches that tapered into delicate spiders' webs of interlocking designs. Tyur pushed the barrel into the back of the priest's head.

The Dryth pointed to the left.

"Are they close?"

The Dryth stammered in confusion.

"The Ithra women!"

"Yes, yes, a ways down the hall, then past an antechamber that keeps the cold in. Beyond sits blessed Therizom's throne where he once held court but now sleeps."

A shout sounded ahead, and the air sizzled as a bolt of heat shot past. The priest screamed and collapsed again. Tyur fired at the figure ahead. The thunder peppered his right side with bloody wounds. The guard slumped to the ground. Another round from close range finished him off.

Before Tyur stood tall double doors decorated with images of Therizom. In these, he stood triumphant over a gallery of creatures, strange things without limbs or heads as Tyur understood. He darted back and pulled the priest to his feet.

"In there?"

The lizard man nodded. Tyur thrust him forward. The door swung open, and the priest tumbled into a chamber lined with hooks upon which were hung thick robes, dark red in hue. The chamber was noticeably cooler than elsewhere in the dome. On the far wall was another door.

Tyur repeated his new trick, sending the priest forward through the doors so that the Dryth would spring whatever ambush may lay beyond.

He heard the screams of women. Tyur threw himself through the doorway. His eyes frantically searched. Around him was opulence that overloaded his savage mind. Everywhere was something to stimulate the eye, objects of unknown meaning, figures of strange things rendered in stone quarried from distant worlds. The walls vaulted upwards in bizarre curves, tapering towards the end where a giant golden throne sat upon a dais of jade.

There he sat. The figure from his dreams, frozen. The god who walked the world in a form to beguile the eye, beautiful and perfect. Yet no form was sufficient to mask his cruel and inscrutable nature. Tyur could only glance at the figure. To look longer brought waves of terror lapping at the shores of a soul unprepared to bear witness to transcendent evil. The hunter collected himself, suddenly aware of the extreme cold of the chamber. A blur out of the corner of his eye caused him to snap his weapon up. It was only the priest. The Dryth disappeared through a nearly invisible door into side chamber.

"Tyur?"

He reeled at the sound of his name. He noticed, now, that below the dais was a ring of cushions flanked by squat tables upon which sat trays of fruit and a censer cunningly wrought in the shape of a lattice of serpents. From its dim interior wafted a sweet smelling smoke.

A pair of Ithra women rose from the silken folds of the cushions. They were tall and fair as he remembered, but they had traded their clothes of hide for garments of gold and gauzy fabric, held by bejeweled clasps resting on graceful shoulders. Tiny golden bells affixed to their ankles and wrists tinkled softly as they stepped forward. No trace of life at the foot of the mountain hung about their lithe bodies. The smell of flowers hung about their dark hair, tumbling down their bare chests and arms. Their red-rimmed eyes displayed a curious expression, like one just awakened from a pleasant dream.

Tyur stared, mouth agape.

"Yua, Ra…"

Yua smiled as she spoke to her former tribesman. "Tyur, it is you! How remarkable! You look like a Dryth, save your handsome face! How is this possible?"

"Where is Vara?"

The pair frowned.

Ra shook her head, "You are a day late, proud warrior."

"She rejected Father's gift, as bestowed by the priests."

"What do you mean?"

"She chose not to be a mother to Therizom's servants."

Tyur's knuckles were near white as he grasped the thunder-spitter.

He yelled, "Where is she?"

The pair stepped backwards.

Ra smiled as she spoke. "When our blessed role was made known to us, Vara became enraged. She seized a dagger from one of the servants and plunged it into her womb to spite their aims."

Tyur's scream echoed through the chamber. He pushed past the women and stood before the sleeping god. The shot reverberated in the great hall. Tyur wrung his hands as he realized the sleeping figure was not so much as scratched. Whatever sorcery the thing possessed far outmatched the power of the thunder-spitter. He stood a moment, regarding the frozen face. Atop a tumble of fair curls sat a simple crown studded with opals. Though motionless the man seemed alive, eyes glistening and skin glowing. Tyur looked directly into the eyes and was lost for a second before thought of Vara caused a new wave of grief and anger. He looked to the two women.

"Her body. Where is her body?"

"The priests took her, vowing to send her where refuse goes."

Tyur spoke through clenched teeth, "You will follow her there, eventually."

Ra spat her reply, "You are wrong! We are goddesses now! Mothers to the servants. We have all we could ever want. We have food and water, fine clothes, and the smoke brings sweet bliss! No more hunger or fear! My mind traipses through the stars as I once walked through flowered meadows! And always he is there, watching!"

"Look around, woman! Do you see any other mothers? Do you see any of the Ithra? Where do you think they have gone? To death! He is a god of death, and the Dryth are his servants!"

Yua shrieked and threw the censer at Tyur. The missile clattered across the smooth floor, scattering ashes in its wake.

Tyur felt his heart break as he stood there. He could only take satisfaction in the fact that he had done his utmost. He knew he would die soon. Any moment now, the chamber would be filled with Dryth warriors eager for vengeance, eager to make him atone for the numberless affronts he had committed in the cursed dome.

He thought of Vara's corpse. Before death, he wished to see her again, perhaps to die and lay alongside her. He ran to the door where the priest had disappeared.

A kick sent it flying open. Within was a chamber hung with more heavy robes, proof against the chill of the throne room. One caught his eye, stuffed with a curious, trembling bulge.

Tyur reached into the folds and pulled the priest from underneath. His hand found the Dryth's neck. He pulled him close.

"Did you forget about me?"

The priest shook his head no.

"Good. Now tell me where lies the body of my beloved. Tell me this, and I will spare your life."

The Dryth whimpered. "You will be angry."

The hunter laughed, "I could not be more angry. I could not be more enraged. If I could, I would bring this dome down upon our heads, and my soul would still cry for Dryth blood. So tell me."

"Thumre, the high priest, ordered she be thrown into the refuse chute, though she yet lived. He wished her to die of the wound she herself had inflicted, slowly, as befits one who defies the will of a god."

Tyur shook. The muscles of his jaw twitched. His hand squeezed the priest's neck until the reptilian eyes bulged.

He whispered to his prisoner. "It seems I was wrong. But lucky for you, I have more honor than the Dryth."

Tyur threw the priest down. He lay gasping as the hunter spoke again.

"Where is this chute?"

"Across the throne room is a chamber such as this for the servants who once staffed the kitchen. In the back is a chute for refuse." He pointed meekly to the back of the room. "There is a passage there that leads all the way around the throne room and into the chamber you seek."

The thing squealed as Tyur delivered a farewell by way of a short kick.

His bare feet thundered down the corridor as he sprinted. The path was a long curve, a hidden way for servants behind the cavernous throne room in which sat the god they served. Tyur heard a commotion, the noise of shouting and the fall of reptilian feet, through the walls. His pursuers had reached the throne room and would momentarily discover his path of escape. Tyur's chest heaved as he ran. The curve denied him a long view of the passage ahead. He ran with the shotgun ready.

Ahead, a yell of fear and a flourish of gold robes announced a priest had been coming the other way. The Dryth doubled back, arms and legs flailing. When Tyur's long strides brought him closer, the Dryth screamed and cowered on the floor, arms raised. Tyur spared only a look of disgust as he ran past.

The chamber door came suddenly to his right. Tyur burst through the door and found himself in a room lined with long tables. Strewn about were the remains of many feasts. Half-eaten fruit sat rotting next to jumbled piles of gnawed bone. The hunter realized with a start that they were human. He ignored the horrific tableau as he scanned the walls for the chute.

There it was, on the far wall, marked by a lengthwise door hung on swinging hinges. All around it were deep stains, the accumulated trace of centuries of refuse that had been tossed into its dark depths. Tyur stepped forward.

The door leading to the throne room burst open. The Dryth that entered had his fire-spitter ready but pointed toward the other half of the room. As the lizard man turned, eyes aflame at the sight of his quarry, Tyur brought the thunder-spitter to bear.

The weapon roared and bucked against his shoulder, and the Dryth was brought low, falling to the floor with the awkward gracelessness of the soon dead.

More followed behind. They hissed and shrieked their cruel battle cries as they poured in with fire-spitters and daggers drawn. Tyur felt joy as he fired again and again. Blasts of heat sailed past as the Dryth fired back, making a ruin of the wall behind. Their assault was stymied by the narrow door, soon choked with their comrades' broken bodies, yet they continued their assault. The shotgun made its sad click, so Tyur drew the fire-spitter he had stolen outside the city and sent bolt after bolt of white heat toward his foes. The room filled with black smoke heavy with the stench of burning flesh. He howled as he fired, squeezing the lever until the weapon burned his hand. Finally, the thing ceased to fire, and he hurled it at the onrushing Dryth. The chamber was rapidly filling with smoke, set ablaze in a dozen places from the errant blasts of the fire-spitters. The heat seared Tyur's skin as he reeled.

Long strides took him to the chute, and he leapt, slinging the thunder-spitter as his powerful legs sent him sailing into blackness.

Down he tumbled, bouncing from wall to wall. The cylinder was steeply sloped, allowing him to gain much momentum before slamming against the slick walls again and again. The angle improved, and soon he found himself sliding feet first. Foul sludge lined the chute's bottom, aiding his descent. His rear felt the jarring of a sudden upward bend, and his momentum faltered.

The sun was blinding as he stood amidst the piles of waste, though the warmth was pleasant to his skin. Ahead was a field of junk and filth, piled here and there to dry in the cruel light. There were the remains of crashed discs along with objects unknown to the hunter. Bordering the field were the thick walls of a score of buildings. This close, Tyur drank in their strange angles and blood red stones. The pyramid loomed above, slick and menacing. The cityscape stirred bizarre emotions, like distant recollections of unpleasant dreams.

Tyur unslung his weapon and inspected it briefly. The thing had come off much better than he; the hunter was plagued by a dozen bruises and bleeding from a cut on his head.

Eyes adjusted to the bright, he scanned the area for any sign of Vara. He darted from pile to pile, spying under wreckage and peering into pipes.

"May I help you?"

The voice sent Tyur spinning. His finger pulled the lever even as he realized he had not loaded the thing again. With a curse he ran forward, grasping the weapon to swing as a club.

The speaker raised his arms.

"Stay your hand, strange one! I have no weapon!"

Tyur paused. The figure before him was another Dryth. Once, perhaps, he had been a warrior, so much was clear from his height. But old age had made him a mere husk compared to the lizard men that had harried Tyur on his quest. His yellow eyes were filmed by a dull white as he inspected the hunter in turn.

"My vision is not what it once was. You look like one of us in form but not in face. What are you?"

Tyur smiled his grim smile as he reloaded. "You are not the first to ask today. I have not the tongue nor the time to explain. I seek the body of an Ithra woman…" Tyur swallowed, then continued, "She would have passed here only yesterday."

The old lizard shook his head. "From your set expression I gather grave duty has brought you here. I hate to disappoint, but there is no corpse."

Tyur looked to the heavens and clenched his fists.

The Dryth continued. "There is no corpse because she is alive."

Tyur ran to the old warrior and grasped his shoulders, fingers sinking into the patchy hide.

"Easy now! She is in a shelter of my making near the chute's mouth.

You walked right past her in your haste."

Tyur went to what had seemed a mound of refuse just outside the chute's mouth. It was a tent of sorts, a wide length of tattered fabric laid over a frame rigged from lengths of rusted pipe and bent bar. She lay within.

Tyur laughed at the joy of seeing her and wept at her condition. Vara lay curled, hands at her belly. Blood caked her garment of gauzy fabric, staining her hands and arms as well. The hunter bent close, brushing locks of dark hair from her face as he whispered to her. She stirred and with bloodless lips pronounced his name.

"Do I dream? Or do I meet you in death?"

Tyur's tears dried in the heat as they rolled down his face.

"We yet live, though not for long. But, it is enough. I prefer this to a lifetime haunted by ignorance of your fate."

"I knew you would come. I refused the high priest. I will be no vessel for evil. I took his dagger…"

Tyur bade her be calm, and the pair kissed in the dim heat of the shelter. Tyur noticed the old lizard hovered nearby.

"She has lived longer than I thought. Credit must go to me. See how the shelter opens up near the chute? The cool air pours in from above. The children of the palace need different air than we. Or me, I should say. I do not know what you are."

Tyur cradled Vara gently as he turned to answer.

"I am neither Dryth nor Ithra. I am a creation of the Sorcerer, sent to wreak vengeance upon the wicked. I have slain many with the aid of his weapon, and I have found my love. We wait now for death."

"I imagine it will come soon. She can't have much longer, and the warriors will find you."

"So be it. Bless the ancestors, the fire up there granted me enough time to find Vara."

The Dryth scratched at his ragged scales. "It is a shame you are so resigned."

Tyur looked at him through narrowed eyes, loathe to remove his gaze from the face of his beloved in their last moments together.

"What do you mean?"

The lizard man shrugged. "Down that alley is a door back into the dome, into the hangar."

"The hangar?"

"The hall where the discs are stored."

Tyur's expression was alight with sudden hope. "I could steal one! But how are they operated?"

"Nothing could be simpler. Two levers. The left moves the craft up and down." The old lizard moved his hand to demonstrate. "The right turns the craft in whatever direction it is pointed. To speed up, push the lever forward. To slow down, pull it back."

Tyur gathered Vara into his arms. His brow furrowed as he asked, "But why do you tell me this?"

The Dryth laughed and shrugged his shoulders.

"I was once mightiest amongst the warriors. I marched south with the Father, God-King Therizom, he who made the Dryth and the Ithra. Under his azure banners, we made war against his brothers, the other God-Kings and their armies. I slew countless slagborn, rending their carapaces in twain as the battle-joy brought tears to my eyes. I killed Umidites by the score, listening as they babbled their master's secret names in the moments before death. We tore down Canannitesh, brick by brick, breaking the starmen's idols into pebbles underfoot. So many fell under my blade or were incinerated by my spitter. But one day, I sinned. As the sun became hidden by the smoke of a burning village and my ears were full of the cries of the vanquished, there on the field of slaughter I was seized by a curious emotion. I showed mercy to a foe and thus was brought low in the eyes of Therizom. Rather than be given an honorable death, I was deposited here. My task is to keep waste from cluttering the chute's opening."

Tyur listened, rapt by the tale. The old lizard continued.

"And so I have remained for many, many years now, even long after Therizom fell into his odd sleep. My mind has had nothing to do but ponder. After a while, I began to wonder that my desire to show mercy might be the worthy part of me, rather than the lust for slaughter which is valued by the Father. Surely, I have gone mad."

He smiled at Tyur, an expression ill-suited to the Dryth. "When the Ithra came down the chute, I let that small place within my nature gain sway again. I bound her wound and erected the shelter for her so that she should at least die in some measure of comfort."

Tyur's heart opened as he regarded the stooped figure of the old warrior.

"Come with us. There is but a tiny chance that we will escape, but you may have a better life elsewhere. You saved Vara's life, and I am in your debt."

He shook his head. "I may be mad, but I could not raise a hand against my brothers."

"I understand." Tyur shifted his delicate cargo so that he could free his arm. He took up the shotgun and stared deep into the clouded eyes of the old warrior.

"I hope within the realm of the dead you are repaid this debt. I thank you."

The Dryth nodded.

Tyur ran on heavy steps in the direction indicated. He spared one glance backward. The old lizard had gathered up a pole and began his inglorious work again amidst the refuse of the dome. The view was soon lost behind the jutting heights of rectangles of dark stone. The alleys were deathly quiet as Tyur made his way to the door. The city seemed nearly deserted; surely the place of his visions, full of lounging Ithra and industrious Dryth, was a thing of ages past.

The hunter's pulse quickened as the door loomed ahead. It was much smaller than the one from which he had entered, marked only by a thick line of recessed stone.

Tyur stared at the rectangle stupidly, realizing now he had no idea how to open it. Vara groaned, and he shifted her weight slightly. He leaned against the wall for a moment to gather his strength only to recoil from the noise of grinding gears. The door opened with a groan.

Tyur walked with weapon leveled as his eyes scanned for foes. It was indeed the same great hall, littered with the stiffening bodies left from his first encounter. He heard shouting in the distance, from up the long stairwell.

Gingerly, he placed Vara atop the first disc in line. The thing's circumference was twice the reach of his arms. At the rear, a cowl emerged from the bronze surface of the thing, offering Vara a modicum of shelter. The disc bobbed a bit as he climbed aboard awkwardly. When he had placed his weight square on either foot, the disc began to hum underneath him. He gently grasped the levers. A slight push sent the thing drifting forward. It began to bank slightly to the left, eliciting a muffled curse from its inept pilot.

Tyur relaxed his grip on the right lever and gave it more forward pressure. With some difficulty, he angled the craft toward the broad expanse of the large door the hunting party had used. At the disc's approach, the door began to open. Tyur's heart soared. The bright light of the sun spilled in through the widening space. Beyond was desert and finally freedom. The Dryth must be occupied with a fruitless search in the burning chamber. Perhaps they picked through the burnt corpses of Dryth thinking he must lie among them. Tyur smiled to himself.

"Defiler! Halt!"

Tyur spun, causing the disc to list. The Dryth were pouring from the double doors atop the stairs. Eyes wild with rage, they came with such reckless haste that some fell from the rails. Bolts flew from their weapons. At their head was a Dryth built like the warrior-leader but clothed in robes of shimmering gold, even more ornate than the priests Tyur had already encountered.

The hunter pushed the lever forward and the disc sped onward into the bright desert. Under his inexperienced hand, the craft pitched and bucked as it sliced the hot air on its way to freedom. The speed was nearly too much for Tyur. He felt his stomach flip as he watched the ground underneath, a dizzying blur. He frequently made the novice mistake; the disc would inevitably end up pointing in the direction in which he was looking. Then the mistake would be compounded by a tendency to overcorrect when realizing his error. From the sun and his knowledge of the way he bore north the best he could. Far in the distance, the mountains above his home could just barely be seen amidst the shimmering haze. Though the sun beat strong, the wind chilled his skin, recalling to his mind the thick robes he had seen hanging throughout the palace dome. He chanced a look toward Vara, curled under the cowl. She had lost consciousness. Tyur risked more speed. The disc vibrated under his feet. How long would it take? Tyur could not guess.

A glimmer of hope stirred within. Tyur had won free of the dome with his love and rode atop a device that rendered distances small. Tyur could fly directly to the Sorcerer's home and let the wise old man tend to Vara with his potent magics. But what of the Dryth? The old man was keen to keep his home a secret. And how long could Tyur himself live in the lands better suited to the Ithra? Would the air be too thick? Would he die of the cold come night? His savage mind was engrossed by these questions.

A great flaming bolt sailed past on his right. In his shock, he pitched the craft right. It banked hard as the steep angle sent waves of fear through the hunter. He was near perpendicular to the ground when he banked it back to the left, overcorrecting again and sending the craft into another banking arc. He risked a glance backward and felt anger and bitterness rise at the sight of his pursuers.

Atop a golden disc three times the size of Tyur's rode the high priest. The thing was like Tyur's but more ornate, and gold instead of dark bronze. Its curves wove from bow to stern, fanning into a fine filigree that belied the material's great strength. The Dryth sat on a throne while warriors guided the craft and manned two mounted spitters, large ones, the length of a man. They fired with a horrible noise, the sharp crackle of near lightning. Flanking the priest were another two discs, oblong in shape, longer to accommodate squads of warriors clothed in the heavy robes.

Tyur nearly flipped the disc as he pointed the lever north again. His panicked piloting made the small disc a difficult target. Bolt after bolt sailed past. Tyur bore down on the lever but there was no more speed to be had. With one hand on the lever he turned and fired the thunder-spitter one handed. He aimed at the priest but struck the warrior on his right. The Dryth reeled but recovered. Tyur cursed. The thunder-spitter was a powerful weapon but not at distance. Before he could solve the puzzle of racking the weapon with one hand on the lever, a bolt struck the rear of his craft. It bucked hard and began to spin. Tyur threw himself down, grasping the edge with one hand and Vara with the other. His stomach lurched as the spin gained momentum and the disc descended.

The craft struck the ground with a bounce that sent Tyur flying, though the spin kept Vara pinned against the cowl. With a jarring crunch, he landed upon the sand. His momentum propelled him along as his body rolled, finally coming to rest on his back. With a grunt of pain, he came to his knees. He reached for the shotgun only to find it gone. Drawing the dagger at his hip unleashed waves of agony from his right shoulder, causing him to fall again. He took the blade in his left hand and stood. He sought the disc but found himself blinded for a moment as blood coursed down his face from another cut on his head. He wiped it away and spun frantically as he searched for his love.

The disc rested at the end of a long furrow. He could see Vara, a bundle of cloth and dark hair curled against the disc's cowl. He limped toward her.

A shadow descended. Behind him the lead disc came to hover above the sands.

"Kneel before me, defiler. Your escape has come to naught."

Tyur turned, dropping the dagger. He bent to pick it up, an act that nearly caused him to lose consciousness as the blood rushed from his wound. He stood with the simple weapon at the ready as the flanking discs descended and the warriors leapt to the ground.

The high priest shouted his orders, "I want him alive!" He faced Tyur. "I will torture you with techniques gleaned from the Sleeping Father. I will prolong your agony for years. You will know true remorse. You will understand the great affront which you have committed. And your tribesmen will pay, too."

Tyur felt deep sadness at the mention of reprisals. His greatest fear would come to pass. He held the dagger limply. The warriors fanned out, walking slowly, enjoying themselves. The hunter's head wound continued to bleed, red-green liquid congealing near instantly in the hot air though it still kept coming.

I will kill at least one of you, thought Tyur, as the warriors advanced. He looked again to the priest, a duly impressive figure amongst the Dryth. The rich gold of the robes was set against the brown of his scales striped with soft black. He sat peering down at Tyur, cruel smile written across his long, lipless mouth.

Everything ceased for the briefest of moments. Tyur looked down to see that he hovered a little above the ground. He heard nothing, then a sudden roar filled his ears and he found himself flat on his back. Where the High Priest had sat a moment ago was now a conflagration. Within the white-hot flames, he could just pick out the robed figure, writhing as his limbs flailed impotently against the consuming fire.

A large shape passed between his gaze and the sun above. In its wake came more noise, a loud hum that was felt as much as heard. The shape sped away then banked to swing around again, and there was another roar as a bolt of heat was sent from its pointed bow. Tyur watched as Dryth flew in the air, limbs blasted, flung here and there. A hunk of the golden disc landed smoldering to his right. All was chaos as the Dryth scrambled to mount their discs. But the shape dived in again and again, blasting the discs and finally strafing the survivors until none were left.

The shadow passed over once more, close this time. The hum hurt Tyur's ears as he brought himself to his elbow. An expanse of dull gray filled his vision. There was a hissing sound as he watched a portal open along the thing's surface. The figure standing within was familiar but strange.

Tyur smiled. There stood the Sorcerer, odd looking as he wore a mask of some kind.

"Son of a bitch," said Tyur.

The astronaut laughed. "That's right, young man! I got you this time. Where is Vara?"

Tyur stood and shuffled to the bundle. The Sorcerer leapt to the desert floor and ran ahead. He gathered Vara in his arms and shouted to the hunter.

"More discs en route! Get in, hurry!"

Tyur stumbled toward the Sorcerer's craft, a long rectangle of gray broken by panels, lines, and forms, the purpose of which the hunter could not guess. The end tapered to a dull point studded with probe and antennae. A Dryth fire-spitter, one of the larger variety, was mounted just below the nose. The contrast between the two technologies could not have been starker. The ship was a model of utilitarian form while the weapon was an ode to cruelty written in dark metal.

Two small windows looked into a cramped interior. Behind stubby wings, a cluster of cylinders sent waves of heat to bake the sand to the rear. With the last of his strength, Tyur flung himself through the portal behind the Sorcerer and Vara. Inside was much like the Sorcerer's home, a dizzying array of blinking light and bright screen around simple furniture and strange objects.

The old man thrust a mask into Tyur's hands and sprinted the short way into the forward chamber as the portal closed with a hiss.

"Get that over her face! And get ready!"

For what, thought Tyur. The answer came in a sickening lurch as the craft lifted into the air. Tyur got the mask over Vara's ashen face with difficulty as the ship banked hard and gained speed and altitude. When the ship was set on a course, the Sorcerer came to Vara's side. He pulled a bench from the wall and gently set her down. A white case produced a series of objects he used to attend to her wound. The old man worked frantically, punctuating his efforts with shouts in his native tongue.

Tyur watched helplessly. He pushed himself to sit next to the bench, grasping Vara's limp hand in his.

The contrast brought sadness to his heart. Her hand was lithe and graceful, his bore scales and claws.

The Sorcerer made a noise of triumph. He fussed over his patient, making her as comfortable as he could. He looked to Tyur and said, "I have stabilized her. The wound will heal, and the antitoxins are undoing the effect of exposure to the foul atmosphere there. She will survive." His expression became suddenly grim and he continued. "She will never bear children, but she will live."

Tyur nodded. He cared not for anything but that she would live. He looked down at his arms, corded sinews sheathed by smooth scales. His own injuries clouded his mind with waves of pain and discomfort while the air inside the vessel felt heavy in his lungs. He spoke with some difficulty.

"I am in no state to start a family, either. I am a monster, after all."

Vara stirred. Her eyes took in her surroundings, and she showed a moment's panic before Tyur's voice calmed her.

"You are safe, my love. I am here, and we are with the Sorcerer. He is a powerful ally and friend."

She reached out to touch Tyur's face.

"Your eyes!"

Tyur shook his head. "There is much to explain."

The Sorcerer set his vessel down in the clearing near the cave. Vara stepped from the portal. Her own formidable strength had been marshaled during the short trip, and she stood tall as she called to her tribesmen. The Ithra, slowly at first, left their hiding places to gather, gaping in wonder at the ship. Kiom led them, eyes squinting as he drank in the most unexpected visitation.

"Vara! You live!"

Captain Alan Washensky stepped from the doorway to stand behind her.

"Alan! Do my old eyes deceive me! My heart swells to see you. But what of the Dryth! They will come! Old friend, have you forgotten the danger?"

The Sorcerer shook his head no.

"Kiom, old friend. Your warrior Tyur found me and beseeched me to help him on his quest to find Vara. I helped him as I could, and sent him on his way. In the days that followed I began to question my decisions. I sought to do no more harm when I made my mountain hideaway. But in doing so I permitted evil to continue."

The gray-haired traveler from distant times looked at each Ithra in turn as he continued. "No more. With the help of the Ithra, we will fight the menace of the Dryth once and for all. No more hiding."

Kiom shook his head. "Alan, though my heart soars at the thought, I am an old man, I am no war leader. And we have not the weapons nor magics."

Vara stepped forward. "I claim that honor. I know the Dryth. I have faced them. And my mind is keen and my body strong." She fingered the bandage at her belly as she spoke. "Let me be the mother to all the Ithra, mother to all the warriors. I will lead them."

Kiom beamed. He turned to the crowd of Ithra.

"I proclaim Vara war leader, fighter of Dryth and Mother of Warriors! Do any dispute?"

Their answer was a cheer, her name again and again as they raised spears in the air. The younger warriors could hardly contain their joy.

Kiom grasped her shoulders in joy. His face darkened suddenly. He looked to her and the Sorcerer.

"But what of Tyur? Did he fall?"

Vara answered, voice dark with grief.

"No. My love lives. But he can never return."

She looked to where the Sorcerer stood amidst a gaggle of young warriors. In the tone of a learned elder, he addressed the rapt crowd.

"We dealt the Dryth a heavy blow, but they will recover and seek vengeance. We have no time to spare."

In his hands he held out a weapon for their inspection.

"This is a shotgun…"

The hot wind was soothing against his scales as he stood perched on the jutting black rocks, an island in a sea of sand. His reptilian eyes stared toward the city in the distance, pondering its secrets. The black pyramid stood as ever, menacing, its mysteries as yet unknown.

Tyur took in a lungful of air, letting its acrid flavor soothe a throat still somewhat raw from the cries of battle. Resting on his sore shoulders was the thunder-spitter and on his arm the mark of the tribe American. He looked east and west at the sprawling wastes, hazy with the shimmering waves of heat from the sun god's gaze. This was now his home. Here he would wander until his death. Here he would hunt the Dryth, and the Dryth would hunt him. He fingered the small box at his belt. When the thing showed a red light, he would meet the Sorcerer at the appointed place. Otherwise, there was nothing but the wastes before him. And the hunt.

The Law of Wolves

A chorus of wolves sung their mournful song as Annathea's grandmother neared her meeting with Death.

Annathea looked to her father. He stood at the foot of his mother's bed, the hearth's warm glow behind him.

"Why do they howl so?"

The father brushed her question away and motioned for silence. Annathea looked to the frail, old woman in the bed, nearly buried in blankets of rough wool underneath the hide of a bear.

From where she knelt she could watch the old woman's chest struggle meekly to rise with new breath. It stopped finally. The hand she held went limp.

The family said quiet prayers. None but sentimental Theadra wept, as the woman had lived a long life, blessed in a greater measure than God had sent ill.

After a time, the father came beside Annathea. "The wolves that remain in the Old Forest are as old as the Garden, which covered all of the world before the fall. They have no love for us though they know our family. While they do not mourn, they recognize her passing and mark it in their own way."

Annathea's brow knit. "But they are not our friends."

"No, child, it is as I said. They would strip the flesh from your bones should you wander too far in the Old Forest. But they pay our family a respect nonetheless. Alone among men we live close to the Old Forest."

She nodded. "Because father is a woodcutter."

"Yes, my child."

Annathea looked down to the hand she still held. It was gnarled like tree roots, the result of a lifetime of labor in field or at the hearth. Her own hand was yet smooth and of graceful form. With a small private shame, she released the hand and stood. Her mother bent to give the old grandmother a kiss on the forehead and the rest of the family followed suit.

The father, the woodcutter, bent with a grace that belied his large size. Her sister Theadra was next. Tears glistened on her cheeks as she kissed her grandmother goodbye. Annathea was a year older than her sister but seemed wiser by many more. She kissed the old woman and stepped back.

The old woman's face was as peaceful in death as in life. She had obeyed the priests and raised many children. Only one had been lost to war, two to disease, and one to childbirth. Her grandchildren were faring even better, a source of great joy. She had come to her youngest son's spacious cabin to impart her wisdom to his wife and daughters and live out her days. The last chapter complete, the old woman died content.

The family knelt again for a time, whiling away the long autumn night in prayer before a frost-strewn dawn shone through the thick panes of the cabin's sole window.

The woodcutter took up pick and shovel and went to work on a grave as his wife and daughters worked, baking bread and preparing a stew.

Midday saw two arrivals, both expected, the woodcutter's son, now a gamekeeper, and a priest from the village.

The priest gave a mass in honor of the old woman and the two men gently lowered her rough coffin into the cold ground.

Annathea looked with an annoyance she could not hide at her sister who wept openly.

After the service the two gathered water at the well. Theadra had recovered some of her usual good cheer as Annathea had grown more morose.

Theadra tied back her long, blonde curls and bent to pull up the waterskin. She mistook her sister's cause of distress and said, "You should not worry. Grandmother is with God now, happy for all eternity."

Annathea sighed. "I think of us. Next year we will be married ourselves most likely. Then children and our own households. We will work and grow old. Our hands will tire and warp, our backs will stoop and our hair gray."

Theadra cocked her head. "Such is life. Why does this trouble you?"

Annathea replied, "Such is not life for everyone. Princesses live in castles and have servants. They wear their sables rather than trade them for silver. The men play games and ride horses rather than hew pine."

Theadra handed the full skin to Annathea. She laid the thick line over her shoulder and waited while the other skin was filled. The line hurt where the folds of her cloak offered no protection. She shifted impatiently.

Theadra shrugged. "The priests say all are born according to God's will. Brother gathers many sables for our dowry and father hoards the good lumber. We will have good husbands, men of the town perhaps. I hope mine is handsome, though mother says sometimes a fair countenance masks a foul heart. But it is not always so."

It was Annathea's turn to shrug.

The tall shadow of their brother fell across the path.

He was handsome if somewhat windswept and ill-treated by the open elements. His eyes, seemingly always squinting, regarded the pair with warmth.

"My dear sisters. Let me…"

He tossed the skins over his broad shoulders and the three entered the cabin. One skin was poured into the cauldron for stew while the other was poured in bowls for dough. The brother drank greedily at the remainder. The father laid his axe down and poured ale into clay mugs for his son and the priest.

His eyes were bright as he asked his son for news.

"My lord keeps well. I range across the west acres and watch for poachers and sign of wolves. On saint's days or by his leave I take game for myself. Bread and ale are there at the guard house when I wish."

The father laid an arm across the son's big shoulders and looked to his wife who knelt by the pot and stirred with a practiced hand.

"Our boy serves a good lord. We need find him a wife, now that he is secure."

The priest chimed in, "Here, here," and swallowed a gulp of ale.

The brother continued. "When the rut began my lord took the men of his household and honored me by asking me to lead the hunt. I bade the lords arrange their chargers in a line and we pushed the deer to the banks of the river. A blast of my horn sent the flank to wheel and many good stags were taken. My lord made a gift of this in thanks." Chest swollen with pride, the young man drew a fine dagger from his belt.

The father inspected it with wide eyes. "Good steel!" He ran his fingers along the relief on hilt and pommel, stags bounding amidst tall oak, horns woven in knots, which delighted and confused the eye.

Annathea came to sit beside her brother. "What do you mean, 'push the deer'?"

The brother warmed to the question. "With a show of force the herd will move as a great mass, heedless of direction. The trick is a wide front lest they slip behind you. Men and horses must act as one. The deer will throw themselves from great heights out of desperation, or run right into a trap, men with bows and spears."

Annathea nodded. Her brother pushed back a lock of her dark hair. "And how fares my sister?"

"I am well."

"Every time I see you and our sister, you are more woman and less child. Soon you will have your own households."

Annathea looked askance a moment and then left to help her sister knead dough.

The priest set down his mug. "That one was sour even as I christened her. She fidgeted so while her sister cooed like a little dove."

The mother said, "Both are good girls."

The priest raised his mug again. "Very true!"

When the sun sank behind the pines, the feast was laid out. Bread and stew with game. The priest brought forth a skin of wine and the family toasted grandmother many times. The woodcutter smiled at his mother's memory though his eyes shined at their corners. The priest told the young girls of the splendors of heaven where their grandmother would sleep this very night.

The next day the brother returned to the lands of his lord. The priest watered his mule and began the journey back to town. The mother pressed two coppers into his soft hand and he gave a blessing to their house.

Much work went to lay provisions for the winter. When the snows came the family could stay warm near the hearth. There the mother sang and the father told tales while the girls spun wool and played games and so Annathea's seventeenth winter was passed.

The first thaws saw the woodcutter inspecting the lumber he kept behind the cabin. A quantity of old oak was reckoned fully seasoned. Father announced the intent to take the lumber to the town for sale and the girls became greatly excited.

"Father makes ready our dowry. Come summer we will be presented to father's lord and there will be talk of marriages. Bar the coming of war, we may be married before the end of the harvest," said Theadra.

Annathea thought of the delights of the town, cakes and breads baked with honey, many cloths and trinkets in the market, the sight of the ladies of the lord's hall, bedecked in their gowns. Though they pleased her, she felt a cloud over her heart.

"Soon our fates will be sealed."

Theadrea shook her head, "'Tis strange to think so. It is good to make a family."

The image of grandmother's hands chased a reply from Annathea's mind.

Father spent the day lashing the thick timbers to his simple cart and as the sun rose the next day the family began the journey to town.

The Old Forest receded behind them as the cart rolled on solid wheels down the gently sloping track. Benwyth, their draft horse, plodded along, his nostrils steaming in the chill morning air. The track joined a larger road and soon the landscape was a quilt of small plots cornered by hovels and pens for goats or pigs. The peasants ploughed the land, each contributing his labor to his neighbor's plot. Many waved to the woodcutter though their manner was guarded as the woodcutter was reckoned strange by living so close to the Old Forest.

The cart passed through the town's gate. The woodcutter spoke with pride of its thick timbers, cut by an ancestor many years past when the pagan oaks fell to make the walls and beams that sheltered the men of the village as they returned to the Law man had been given after the fall of the Garden.

The houses and shops within were arranged along a lane leading to the lord's keep of gray stone. The plaster between the timbers of the houses was fresh and bits of colored cloth were strung across the lanes. A festival atmosphere lightened the steps of the many merchants and artisans who lived within the walls.

The cart was guided to rest next to the joiner's hall. Immediately a crowd began to gather, merchants in caps of colored wool and fine hose under tunics decorated with embroidery. The master of the joiners, a heavy man in robes of green marked with the crest of his office, discussed the lord's needs with the woodcutter while the merchants argued amongst themselves.

Theadra's foot tapped on the hard packed ground. She looked here and there, craning especially to see the center lane, its shops and wonders. The mother bade the father conclude his business with haste. Annathea's mood was light, if distracted, as she watched all around. A knight bearing the crest of the lowlands intruded upon the party. He was young, the dyes that colored his tabard were yet bright and the thread with which was woven an image of a heron shone white in the noon sun.

"Pardon me, woodcutter, I am milling about the town until the lord receives his subjects. I would like to offer myself as escort to your family until I am called to see the lord. My name is Ardwelgan."

The mother raised her eyebrows. Annathea tugged at the cowl, which covered her dark hair as she regarded the young knight. He had a strong face, though still soft with youth. His shoulders and long arms sheathed in mail suggested strength. As much as modesty permitted he dared looked at Annathea. He wore an expression the mother knew well, a wistful look, which heralds love in the way a warm breeze warms of a summer storm.

The woodcutter smiled. "I can think of no reason to refuse."

The mother made a snorting sound but did not protest.

With the business of the lumber concluded the party left to stroll the lane. Annathea permitted herself to be infected with Theadra's cheer as the pair darted from stall to stall. Theadra wished for a bolt of cloth and her eyes also lingered on broaches for their cloaks. The mother hovered behind, working to keep their desires within the realm made possible by the woodcutter's meagre purse of silver, much of which needed to be held back for the young woman's dowries.

Sir Ardwelgan walked with the woodcutter. He made polite conversation about the older man's work in the forest while his hand rested on the pommel of his longsword in a posture of exaggerated readiness that the woodcutter found flattering.

The family and the knight neared the center of the town. A crowded had gathered to watch a troupe of mummers. Their large cart sat in the center of the square. Banners of bright color fluttered in the wind above. One side was unbolted to lay flat; a small stage. A dozen figures moved about the stage, each with a different instrument. There were pipes and skin drums, a hurdy gurdy and bells, and one lute, played by an old man in the corner. The others were women, some young, others just coming into middle age. A man stood center stage as he danced and sang. He was Valkani, the balladeer known throughout the lord's lands and far beyond. He wore a tunic of buckskin cinched by a wide belt where hung a thin dagger. His leather shoes were cut in a southern style. A short cloak of deep red worn over one shoulder and secured with a gold broach completed his ensemble. He sung in a baritone, employing an occasional vibrato. The lyrics described the heartbreak of a girl cast from her family home after refusing the advances of an evil knight. She wandered to where the land met the sea and her beauty compelled the king of the waters to invite her into his household.

Annathea was enthralled. She stood rapt, watching him step, spin, and weave the tale with body as well as voice. He had a strong face, dark eyes underneath a dark brow. A wide mouth, pulled down at the corners, sat above a strong chin sporting a short beard. She pushed her way to the front. Her cowl fell away in the jostle. Valkani met her eyes, once, then again, and then smiled at her after the song ended.

The crowd shouted for another but Valkani implored the troupe be given a short break. One of the women handed him a cup of wine and he sat behind the cart, waving away those of his troupe that begged a word.

His eyes fell on Annathea again. He motioned her to come close.

The young woman looked back. She could not see her family in the press of the crowd. The bard sat smiling gently and motioned again.

Her heart beat in her throat as she approached.

"What is your name, young woman?"

Annathea whispered her name.

He looked her up and down. "A farm girl of great beauty, the source of many songs."

Behind him stood a woman many years older than Annathea. Her clothes looked fine when viewed on the stage but from close, the young woman saw the gold clasps were tarnished plate and her gems cut from colored glass. She was still beautiful, dark like Valkani, but stood petulant, her face in a scowl at Valkani's last comment.

Annathea blushed a deep crimson. She marshalled her courage and spoke, voice barely above a whisper.

"What is it like?"

Valkani cocked his head.

Annathea stammered, "This life…" She gestured to the cart.

Valkani threw his head back as he grinned, "It is wonderful. We sing and dance and go where we please. We serve no lord but are loved by them. We till no field but have good bread. It is the only life for me."

A hand on her shoulder startled the young girl.

She turned to see Sir Ardwelgan.

"Young lady, your mother is in fits. Permit me take you to her."

Valkani laughed, a pleasant sound that resounded through the square though the knight did not seem amused.

"A fair maiden rescued by handsome knight! A venerable tale if ever there was one!" He reflected a moment, then continued in a voice dripping with mock indignation. "Dear God, I suppose I am the wyrm in this tale! Me! Sweet Valkani!"

The woman at his side spat.

The knight led Annathea through the crowd. The people parted by habit to let the armed knight pass. The mother spied the pair and gave a sound of relief.

Annathea blushed again. Her stomach felt ill at the embarrassment. A boy squire barely as tall as Sir Ardwelgan's waist appeared with word that the knight was to appear in the keep. Ardwelgan pulled the woodcutter aside for a private talk then bowed low to the group and left.

The woodcutter nodded as he spoke. "Annathea's beauty has claimed its first victim. The young knight begs me send word to his father and offer a match. He has no lands but a place in his lord's keep and stipend enough to raise a family. He is lovestruck, and likely will not make a fuss over dowry."

Annathea stared at the ground.

The father continued. "I shall ask around regarding the quality of his family's word. If they are honorable then we will have much to think about."

The family made camp in the grounds outside the walls where many merchants did the same. The mother unrolled their supper from a cloth, cheese and dried meat supplemented with bread from the town, baked from fine white flour, a treat the woodcutter could not resist. The mother planted a kiss on his cheek in front of everyone to much laughter, happy as she was at the gift of a fine scarf, a length of silk from someplacc far to the east.

Theadra was jealous of the knight's attention to Annathea but not so much to be bitter or work to spoil the mood.

"He is a knight, better even than a merchant. On feast days you will dine in his lord's keep and listen to music."

Annathea picked at her bread. The sound of Valkani's voice echoed in her mind. Her strange mood could not escape notice by the mother. She reached to take the young woman's hand.

She spoke of the future, painting a bright picture of what may lie in store for the young woman.

Annathea held her mother's hands. She looked at them, tracing the deepening wrinkles and callouses. The knuckles were larger than Annathea remembered, the skin rough from labor.

Annathea nodded dutifully even as waves of panic and uncertainty swept over her.

The family bedded down on the soft grass of the field as the camp's fire burned. They slept in their clothes, wrapped in cloaks and blankets from home. Her father began snoring as Annathea lay awake, staring at the stars. Theadra slept soundly under the wool beside her.

The dark-haired sister tossed and turned until near dawn, when the horizon glowed with the faintest stripe of purple. A scream seemed to lie above her heart, threatening at any moment to burst forth. She thought of her mother and father, love and hate intertwined like two serpents. She had been born with no say, no part in any of the things which shaped her fate. The situation was intolerable. With equal parts terrible guilt and giddy exhilaration, she made her choice.

On shaking steps she crept away from the camp, strides lengthening until she ran to the town. The crisp air filling her lungs was glorious. The moonlight bathed her as she ran.

The mummer's cart stood clear against the lightening sky as she ran toward it. The troupe was already up, not wishing to miss any daylight for their long journey. The figures emerged as she approached, hazy in the murk of the new dawn. The women saw to the oxen, four of which were needed to pull the large cart. The thing was painted in gaudy colors now dull in the dim light. It stood a story and a half tall, boasting many doors and windows.

"And where are you off to, child?"

Valkani's voice swam through the misty air. Annathea spun and there he was, dressed the same as the previous day.

The young woman stared dumbly. She swallowed a gasp as he reached forward, taking her chin gently in his long fingers.

"Have you lost your tongue, my sweet?"

"I wish to join your troupe."

He smiled. He regarded her with a strange frankness, the nature of which she could not divine, and spoke with a new gravity.

"Are you sure? You understand there is no going back, do you?"

She nodded as her pulse raced. For a moment, she thought she would faint. But he smiled down at her. He stroked her hair a moment then took her hand.

"So be it. You belong to the troupe now. Will you take our oath?"

She nodded again. The other members of the troupe had gathered around. The mood was dour, Annathea noticed, but her mind was full of new hope and she pushed the doubts aside with little effort.

Valkani said, "Repeat these words. I give my life and my heart to the troupe. I disobey on pain of death."

Annathea did as instructed.

The woman perhaps ten years older than Annathea spoke in a low voice. "Haste, before the father comes searching."

Valkani sent the woman a cross look, an expression that sent a ripple of fear in Annathea though she was not the target.

The troupe found spaces atop and inside the cart. The old lute player snapped the reins and the oxen pulled. With a groaning creak, the cart moved on, out of the field and onto the western road.

Annathea marveled at the interior, spacious though packed with instruments and costumes and masks. The women of the troupe regarded her with suspicion and another emotion Annathea could not name. A pretty girl with a head of brown curls watched especially close, arms folded. She tersely introduced the troupe to Annathea, who sat quiet, watching all. Valkani sat atop the cart, speaking with the lute player, planning their journey.

The older woman was Maria, a woman from lands south that Annathea had never heard of. There were Yula and Alina, two women the same age who boasted of dancing for the king to which all the lords swore their fealty. The other names came too quick to recall. The girl with the brown curls was Melia. Until Annathea's arrival, she had been the newest member. While each of the women met Annathea with tepid warmth or disinterest, Melia was notable for her open hostility.

"I can't imagine why Valkani chose you."

The older woman spoke sternly. "Make no trouble, Melia. Valkani values youth and beauty, as you know."

The bard leapt from the bench to the runner then slipped through the door into the cart.

"I heard my name spoken." He looked to Annathea. "Are they mistreating you?"

She shook her head no. The older woman eyed her with approval.

As the morning warmed the sides of the cart were propped up to grant the riders air. Melia attended to an infant while the other woman dozed or played at an instrument. Annathea watched the hills rise along the western road. It was a familiar path. Soon the road would meet the track, which led to the woodcutter's cabin.

The sound of hoofbeats echoed between the hills. The women stirred and craned their necks to see the source of the sound.

A knight in mail galloped forward. He brought his mount to heel before the mooing oxen and doffed his helmet.

Sir Ardwelgan's jaw was set as he spoke to Valkani.

"The woodcutter wishes the return of his daughter. Is she among you?"

Valkani laughed. "She is sworn to the troupe. She belongs to me now."

The knight drew his sword. "Arm yourself, then." He donned the helmet and kicked his steed to a walk.

Valkani's eyes narrowed. "I shall, foolish boy."

The bard undid lashings on the carts' low ceiling and brought down a longbow, strung. He notched an arrow and took aim.

Sir Ardwelgan spun in the saddle, grasping for the shield tied to his mount's flank.

Annathea screamed when the arrow struck. The young man fell from the saddle and died, still clutching the arrow stuck through his neck.

The older woman took Annathea in her arms to quell her shock. She wept there while the troupe leapt from the cart to plunder the body of the young knight. Valkani ordered that they drag the body far from the road and set the horse to a run.

He grabbed Annathea's wrist and pulled her from the older woman's embrace.

"I had thought to take my pleasures tonight but the killing has whet my passions."

Annathea spoke through tears as Valkani dragged her into the forest. "What are you talking about?"

Valkani wore a deep scowl. "You belong to the troupe, now. You belong to me. You are my wife, as all the women in the troupe are, mine to do with as I please. Now, be still lest you know the back of my hand, sooner, rather than later."

He pushed her to the leaf-covered ground and lifted his tunic. She screamed and tried to push him away. He struck her and then redoubled his efforts. Her hands pushed here and there to no effect. Her palm closed around something cold.

It was the dagger. Deep in a primal madness she pulled, then stabbed upward. Her hands were suddenly awash in hot blood. The thin blade was stuck deep where neck and jaw met. Valkani reeled. He lurched to his feet, staggering as his life's blood gushed to the forest floor. His panicked eyes looked deep into Annathea's. She read only fear. The eyes, which had recently glittered with pride and lust, reflected now only naked terror, such as when wicked people near judgment. He fell to his knees and then curled on the forest floor and was dead. Annathea ran. She passed the cart and fled up the long hill. To the east lay her home but she ran north, heartbroken and panicked. Her dress was ripped by thorns and her cloak full of brambles. She ran until her vision swam. Her paced slowed but she moved on, now surrounded by tall trees and saplings and brush. She collapsed on a bed of moss by a stream.

She wept there, weeping for the wrong she had done her family, weeping for the evil she had witnessed. She wept for the young knight. Now that his body lay still amidst the brush she considered what life might have been like. His eyes had been so different from Valkani's. Would he have been kind? He would have, she thought.

She lay on the moss, mind adrift. Sometimes she thought that she must be dreaming. She would wake under the wool on the soft grass of the fairground and shake off the nightmare and return to the cabin with her family.

But she would not wake to her old world no matter how much she wished.

When the tears stopped coming she sat silent on the moss.

A shadow passed across the yellow rays that broke through the top of the forest.

Annathea gave a start and leapt to her feet.

Before her stood a wolf. The creature was much larger than she reckoned wolves to be. His fur was black, tipped with gray around neck and chest. The blue eyes that stared into hers showed a strange mix of expression, hunger, curiosity, and the innocent cruelty of the wild. She realized other wolves stood at his flanks. There was a beautiful specimen at his right side, silver gray with white ticking, fur glistening like mail in the streaks of light.

Perhaps a dozen stood watching her. Those in the back paced nervously while the black wolf simply watched. He stepped forward on large paws and spoke.

"Why has one born of woman come so deep in the Old Forest?"

She stammered a reply as she walked backwards on shaky steps.

"You talk…"

His proud head shook as he spoke again. "I speak, as all creatures did before the Fall. The Old Forest is the last trace of the Garden which once covered all of God's creation, though it be far removed from the splendor of old."

Annathea found herself backed against a tall oak. The wolves advanced.

The silver gray wolf spoke next. Her voice was not near as deep as the black wolf's.

"She is sent by God to fill our bellies. Give the word, my king. I hunger."

The black wolf shook his head no.

"Don't you smell it?" He brought his muzzle to sniff Annathea's trembling hands.

"She comes washed in the blood of an evil man. She is a murderer. What's more, I smell the family that lives close. She is of the woodcutter's people." He looked to Annathea. "Are you not?"

She nodded yes. "I am Annathea, the woodcutter's daughter. I ran away and then slew an evil man and now I have nowhere to go."

A younger wolf cocked his head and spoke. "Why can you not return to your people?"

The black wolf growled a little at what he reckoned a stupid question.

"She and her kind keep the Law of Man. They cannot kill each other except in war. When one kills another they hang the man from a rope until he dies. She is a murderer and cannot return."

The silver wolf said, "Just as well. She is in the Old Forest and thus is ours to eat."

The black wolf stood still. The silver wolf nudged him, her tail wagging.

"Please, my king. Our bellies are empty. We have had no deer for days. Every year there are less, as the magic of the Garden fades a little more."

The black wolf growled again. "So be it."

Annathea spoke quickly, struck with desperate inspiration.

"I can teach you the way men hunt. You will never go hungry. Let me live."

The King of Wolves wore a dubious expression.

"How can wolves hunt as men? We bear no iron nor wood in shapes of our making."

The silver wolf spat as she advanced. "She speaks nonsense."

"No! I swear on my father. I can teach you how the men hunt. You need no spear, only direction."

The king looked deep into her eyes, blue like his but glassy with fear.

The wolves howled in anger when their king called them back. He darted amidst their ranks, snapping, growling, until all were cowed.

The silver wolf, his queen, was most bitter.

"I beg of you, king. Her flesh will be so sweet and soft."

She yelped as he bit into her flank. She relented, whimpering on the leaf-strewn ground as he addressed the pack.

"She will direct us in the hunt. If she is successful we shall never be hungry."

The queen stared with hooded eyes. "And what then? She will live with us? She cannot. It is an affront to God. She lives by the Law of Man, we by the Law of Wolves."

Annathea's heart beat with new hope. She summoned her courage to ask a question.

"What is the Law of Wolves?"

The queen laughed as wolves laugh, high pitched, a cruel sound.

"Your question betrays your ignorance. The Law of Wolves cannot be spoken. Though we speak as all creatures once did, some things are not for words."

Annathea shrank against the tree while the king of wolves turned to address the pack.

"My wish stands. Oppose me and know the feeling of my fangs in your heart. We will hunt with the woman."

The pack idled with lowered heads as the king turned back to Annathea.

"Lead us in the hunt."

The young woman walked amongst the pack while her eyes scanned the landscape. To the north a low cliff of broken shale rose running east and west. Beyond the crest, the hill flattened to stretches bearing only clusters of pine.

She climbed atop a jumble of boulders. The king scrambled up next to her. Her hand shook slightly as she pointed in the distance.

"The pack must run on a line as do the men on horses. They should start there, far away, then sweep across the field of pine. Have two wolves await the herd at the bottom of the cliff. If the pack can stay on a line they will push the deer over the cliff."

The king nodded. "I see the cleverness of it."

With savage impatience, he barked orders to the pack. The queen and a younger male trotted sullenly to await the herd while the rest ran to the far edge of the pines Annathea had indicated.

The pack moved with animal grace across the sun-dappled forest floor. The young woman ran with them. Despite her hunger and fatigue, she felt a rush of strange joy. Her step was light as she scrambled over rocks and fallen timbers.

The pack paused deep amidst the tall trunks while the king arranged them, a difficult task to order creatures that had never known of such a thing. Finally ready, the king sprinted and the pack bounded with him, running their loping strides. He scanned left and right, letting loose a low growl when a wolf got out of line.

The field opened up before them and suddenly there were deer bounding ahead, disturbed in their daytime rest. The wolves' hearts soared and they gave their voices to howls of joy and greed.

The deer darted left and right but found always wolves behind. They ran with a growing madness. The cliff came sudden. Two doe reared up, but too late, skittering over the edge where the queen waited. They landed hard, legs broken, and she and the young male fell upon them. The others spun and bounded away only to be met by the line of wolves. Fangs sank into their flanks as they screamed and bellowed. Two managed to escape in the confusion but many were slain and the pack fell immediately to feasting.

The pack had never known such a bounty. They had hunt as wolves hunt, a bounding mass to winnow the weak from the herd. Now they ate of deer in their prime, stag and doe as well as the tender fawn.

The forest resounded with howls of joy.

Annathea watched the gruesome tableau. She smiled despite herself.

The king, muzzle stained with gore, stepped to her side and laid a hunk of torn flesh at her feet, a choice piece from the haunch of a yearling.

Hands still caked with wicked blood, she picked it up and held it.

The king said, "Eat. All share in the hunt, as apportioned by me, the

King of Wolves."

Annathea, murderer and outcast from the world of men, shared in the hunt and ate. At first she forced the meat down but soon it felt as natural as anything ever had. Was it the lingering force of the Garden or her own desperation? She could not say.

Bloated with the feast, the pack watered themselves at the stream and rested in a glen of tall grass. The king bade Annathea lie down.

The queen watched from the edge. She paced slowly while the rest of the pack lolled on the grass.

Annathea laid down and let the tiredness seep from her body. She felt a warmness and realized the king lay alongside her. The pack slept and Annathea with them.

The next day the wolves were slow to rise. Many wolves, especially the younger, came to nuzzle against Annathea, to her delight, as their full bellies made them feel warmly toward the young woman. The wolves returned to the remains of the feast and ate again while Annathea strolled nearby, searching among the brush and saplings for the roots that could be eaten, as taught to her by her father.

When not hungry the pack was idle. Some wrestled or chased each other while others teased and goaded until a mock battle ensued. Others dozed while some females labored at dens. Annathea found herself beset with questions as she lounged on a boulder.

"Why do you not eat your horses?" asked a young female.

The young woman shook her head and laughed, "I suppose they are needed for other things."

The young female nodded. "How did the man taste? The one you killed?"

Annathea shook her head. "I only killed him. I did not eat him."

"Oh, that is a shame. The others tell me the flesh of man is the sweetest."

The king looked up from where he lounged.

"Is it nice to walk on two legs? If I walked on two legs, I would become a king of men."

Annathea laughed quietly, "I am sure you would."

He was indeed beautiful to behold. His sleek form led from gray-flecked tall to the black fur on head and back that showed a silken sheen in the rays of sun that penetrated to the forest floor.

The queen stalked, placing herself between the king and Annathea.

"It is nothing to walk on two legs." She reared up and stepped with her back paws. For a moment, she held straight but a paw lost purchase on a smooth rock and she teetered this way and that. Her steps raced to recover her balance, sending her tipping the other way, until finally she tumbled to the ground.

The king and the rest of the pack howled with laughter.

He said with cruel glee, "Annathea shall be Queen of Wolves while this queen goes to live among men, if she can stand long enough!"

The pack howled while the queen scowled, nipping at the younger wolves as she skulked away.

So the spring was passed. Annathea's method of hunting fed the pack well though each time the herd was smaller. Soon only the swiftest stag and his harem of doe remained. Annathea kept her worry private as the wolves thought little of the future.

One day, as the summer blooms decorated the forest, the king made it known he would take the stag, the quickest and strongest they had ever seen. The pack came to a line and Annathea followed. Her dress was mere tatters at this point. Her hair was wild and limbs scarred by thorn and bramble. Her eyes shone with vigor though, as she drank sun- and moonlight in equal measure and ate of the deer and sipped from the stream and lived as a wolf.

The king of wolves sprinted through the woods, powerful shoulders catapulting his silken length under fallen logs and over boulders. Behind ran the queen of the wolves, shining in the summer's light though she was as sullen as ever. The king of wolves howled with joy. Ahead bounded the stag, as proud as he. The stag's bounds were long and graceful, muscles rippled across its brown flanks. He spared a look back now and again. The king of wolves was closing as the chase neared the cliff.

His heart beat as hard as it ever had as he strained, squeezing every last ounce of strength from his body in the service of the chase. His eyes grew wide as he neared the stag. The smell of the stag's fear filled his snout and covered his tongue. So close now. The king of wolves leapt and sank his fangs into the stag's haunch. Underneath him, the ground gave way. The stag turned midair, breaking the king's grasp, and the two plummeted downward.

Annathea stopped at the cliff's edge and watched the king of wolves fall. He landed badly, he and the stag.

The young woman ran back down the slope.

The pack stood around him. He strained to move but could only twitch his paws. He craned his neck to seek for Annathea and she knelt by his side. His blue eyes were awash in sadness and shame, for Death cannot be truly understood by those that live without sense of future. The king of wolves looked to Annathea. She noted the fondness he revealed in that look, kept for her even as Death approached. She wept, stroking the fine fur on his neck as he passed.

A shadow passed across them.

Annathea stood as the queen of wolves circled her. The pack stood away, silent.

A low growl sounded in her throat. Her eyes gleamed with the sense of something arriving that had been long awaited.

Annathea stepped backwards.

The queen of wolves said, "Now I shall teach you the Law of Wolves…"

And with that she lunged, fangs bared.

Mortu and Kyrus in the White City

"Who are the greatest enemies of the gods?" asked Mortu, shouting above the rumbling din of the iron steed upon which he rode. Kyrus sniffed at the question as he sat arms folded, eyes half closed against the wind.

Mortu pressed the issue. "Who laid waste to both church and temple so that man would lose his sense of hope and swear fealty to an alien emperor?"

Kyrus answered, "The Illilissy, of course."

The big warrior smiled and continued.

"And who broke the reign of the Illilissy? Who sent them back to their blue ships and onward to their far home?"

Kyrus sighed. After hundreds of leagues on the road, he knew hundreds of variations of this feeble line of attack. Yet the big northerner kept attempting, tenacity beyond reason.

The monk picked a nit from the fur on his thigh and replied, "The Mutinous Regiment of the Men of the North."

"Yes! My ancestors! Then tell me, wise one, tell me why the gods of Men of the North are not thusly proven stronger than your One God?" The monk frowned as Mortu spoke, though his hulking friend could only just see him from the corner of his eye, as Kyrus rode atop Mortu's shoulder. Kyrus reached down with his small hand and took up the locks of dark brown that hung swaying above the northerner's ear and yelled, syllables falling like hailstones.

"Because your gods simply do not exist! As I have said a dozen times, you cannot compare the strength of two things if one of the things does not exist!"

Mortu threw his head back and let out a sharp "Ha!"

Kyrus' long furry tail spun to save his balance. The monk settled back on his haunches with a muttered curse, then spoke with certainty.

"The One God works through all manner of servants when it suits him. His will is mysterious, inscrutable to mortals as we. Take my own case. Why would the Lord, our God, allow the most knowledgeable and capable of his servants to be imprisoned within the body of a small monkey? Do you need any more evidence of his mystery? I think not!"

Mortu smirked as he said, "Does not the One God value humility?"

The monkey brushed away the question. "Yes, but the fact is hardly germane."

Mortu smiled. "No. I suppose not." He shifted in his seat, leaning back on the long bar which protruded from the back of the steed, where his bedroll and meager possessions were tied in a bundle.

The barbarian continued, "With the war god's blessing the Men of the North mutinied and defeated their alien masters. The same favor let them rise in the wake of the Illilissy and become the sorcerer-kings of yore."

Kyrus stared a moment, peering across the dusty wasteland that stretched endlessly on either side of the highway. The view south was a haze as the flat wastes shimmered under the sun's gaze. To the north, the haze gave way as the orange-tinted wastes rose slowly toward a distant line of sharp peaks. Squat cylinders of orange stone rose from the desert at irregular intervals, the work of the long passed Illilissy.

Kyrus' small eyes squinted, peering ahead. He turned suddenly and leapt to the bar, bending to rummage in the bundle. After a shout of triumph, he hopped again to Mortu's back and stood, raising a set of opera glasses to his small, black eyes.

"Nomads!"

Mortu wore a puzzled expression on his strong brow.

"They are hardly blessed by the war god. I don't know what they have to do with any of it."

"No! Look, Mortu. Nomads! They attack a caravan!"

Mortu squinted into the distance.

"I see nothing."

"Up ahead, off the northern shoulder!"

The beating heart of the metal beast roared into the wind as Mortu opened the throttle. Kyrus nearly fell backward but caught onto one of Mortu's thick locks.

"A word of warning, perhaps, next time!"

Mortu did not reply as the steed shook underneath him. Forms began to emerge from the haze ahead. His ice blue eyes spied the line of carts off the northern shoulder. They were long metal rectangles atop rubber wheels as high as a man was tall. Each was bedecked with a dozen bundles and containers lashed to its sides. The roof of the carts boasted a short rampart that offered some cover to men attempting to return fire to the nomads circling below. The barbarian could just make out the silhouette of riders, circling the caravan. Details sharpened as he neared.

The din of many metal hearts filled his ears, a thunderous cacophony that heralded murderous doom.

Perhaps two dozen riders menaced the travelers. A few men of the caravan lay slumped over the edge, feather-fletching marking where the nomads' aim had been true.

Mortu watched with admiration. The nomads were skilled riders, zipping in and amongst each other. When one wanted to loose an arrow, he hooked a leg over the handlebar to free his hands. Mortu marveled at their prowess.

The iron horse thundered down the highway, gaining speed as Mortu held the throttle wide open. He grit his teeth in the dusty wind, wearing his odd smile as he always did before battle.

Kyrus yelled as he fumbled with the bundle, replacing the glasses into their pouch of patched velvet. "Wait, wait a moment, I have to get down first!"

Mortu stared ahead. The nomads, intent on their quarry, had failed to notice his approach.

The steed shook underneath him, speed building.

He dropped his left hand to the axe sheathed at his side and shouted his war cry into the wind as his right pulled on the brake.

The tires screeched against the pavement. The brakes of the machine were as powerful as the beating metal heart, which propelled it down the endless highway; both machine and the road it traveled were relics of the alien Illilissy.

Mortu was suddenly weightless, flying through the hot air. Kyrus' scream rang in his ear as his small friend held on for dear life. The monk lost his grip on the Northerner's hair and flew tumbling toward the carts.

Mortu landed on a nomad's iron horse, directly behind its rider. The man looked back in panic as the impact sent his steed's rear wheel sliding.

The two looked at each other for the briefest of moments. A cloth wound around the face protected the nomad from dust and hid his features. Mortu saw blue eyes stare into his with anger and confusion. The color gave Mortu a moment's pause; nomads were known to have eyes of dark brown, not icy blue like those of the north. Then the barbarian struck with the butt of his ax. The nomad flew from the seat and landed hard on the road, rolling, body slack like a doll.

The steed wobbled as Mortu reached for one of the grips. He

squeezed the handbrake and slammed his booted foot down on the other, leaning deep as he did so.

The steed slid sideways, coming into the path of the other nomads. Mortu leapt from the steed and lunged to the side just as a raider hove into view. He saw the panic in man's eyes as he made a vain attempt to brake but was too late.

The sound of metal crashing against metal resounded across the wasteland as the steeds collided. The nomad's iron horse flew end over end, pitching its rider high into the hot air.

The nomad following behind swerved to avoid the wreck and drew a blade. He bore down on Mortu, front wheel hovering above the ground as the throttle opened.

Mortu parried the strike away with the haft of his axe and swung, catching just enough of the nomad to send him sliding into the dirt beside the road.

More nomads came around the caravan.

The barbarian stood with his axe ready, bellowing a war cry, which echoed across the barren plain.

The nomads slowed their rumbling steeds to a stop. They looked to each other, uncertainty written across their windswept faces. One notched an arrow but another laid a hand on his arm, gesturing to their fallen comrade, the one Mortu had felled with a knock to the head. They conversed a moment, then the apparent leader waved to Mortu.

A high-pitched voice sounded from underneath one of the caravan's large carts. "What is happening?"

Mortu glanced over. From behind one of the giant rubber tires, Kyrus peeked out into the road.

"They seek parlay, I think. The fallen one was perhaps a leader and now they hesitate."

A nomad walked with arms raised, speaking in a strange language.

Mortu looked again to Kyrus. "Do you speak their tongue?"

The monkey stroked his chin as he answered. "Well, as a monk dedicated to spreading the Word of the Savior to a world lost in darkness, I have studied many languages. The Urkic dialects with their tendency to complicated agglutination did present quite a challenge. I recall my teacher, a man who spent his youth on these very plains before divine fate brought him to Zantyum and to my order. He always maintained the key was internalizing a particular schema, a harmony of vowels..."

Mortu snapped, "Do you speak the nomad tongue?"

Kyrus barked back, "The answer to your question is not a simple 'yes' or 'no'. You see, here again is the core problem evident in your intellect. You allow for no gradation, no nuance. It serves you well in questions of good and evil, commendably so, I should add, considering your stunted pagan morals. However, elsewhere it does you a disservice. The study of languages is complex, especially after the epoch of the Illilissy and their attempts to re-engineer humanity. I have studied various dialects of the peoples of the wastelands. It is possible that I…"

Mortu said flatly, "I have ceased listening to you."

The nomad came closer. He wore the loose, short cloak and tight breeches favored by the tribes of the wasteland. Protecting his shoulders were glistening plates of chitin culled from the massive centipedes that stalked the region. The wind toyed with the tassels of the cloth round around his head, revealing only dark eyes to Mortu's inspection. He spoke tersely, gesturing to the three fallen nomads.

Kyrus said, "I think he wishes to retrieve his comrades."

Mortu snorted, "I gathered as much. Are these folk normally so quick to parley and so concerned with their own?"

Kyrus shook his head. "Certainly not. All reports paint them as bloodthirsty and cruel."

Mortu stepped aside though he still held his axe ready.

The nomad made a quick inspection of the men and wreckage. Two of his fellows were gone from the world. The other, the one Mortu had struck with the butt of his axe, still breathed though the back of his head was bloodied. The nomad stripped the dead of articles of value and motioned for others to gather their weapons. His eyes showed regret as he regarded the wrecked steed. Its spine was cracked and its metal heart bled black blood into a pool on the dusty ground.

Two men dragged the wounded man back to the cluster of their steeds while the one acting as leader mounted the still living iron horse and kicked it awake. He guided the beast back down the road. Another pair rigged poles in a triangle to carry away the dead.

Kyrus looked out from his hiding place as the wounded man came past the cart.

The vest he wore fell open, revealing white fabric underneath.

The monk gasped. He scampered out onto the road, little finger pointing.

"He is a Knight of the Order!"

"What?" asked Mortu.

Kyrus ran to the man's side. One of the nomads kicked at him with a grunt of annoyance. The tiny monk ducked under the blow and leapt to the wounded man's chest. With his little hands, he tore aside the vest fully to reveal a tabard of white bearing the mark of a cross. He then pulled at the head covering, revealing a face fairer than the nomads.

Kyrus pondered, "Why does a knight of the West travel with bandits?" He gasped, "He must have forsaken his oath!"

Mortu's brow knit. "But then why does he still wear the tabard?"

Kyrus stammered. "Ah. But, yes, but if he hasn't forsaken his oath why does he ride with them? There can be no question. He has betrayed his vow and his sacred duty to God!"

Kyrus scrambled to avoid another kick and scampered back under the cart. The nomads viewed him warily now, not accustomed to seeing a monkey, nor especially one that spoke.

Mortu said, "They parleyed so quickly. It is strange."

Kyrus shook his head under the cool shadow of the cart's dented chassis. "Who knows? Perhaps they lost their nerve after your stunt, which nearly saw me splattered across the road. I suppose I should be thankful this body is a nimble one. What if I had been imprisoned inside a chicken? Or a rhinoceros?"

The wounded man was tied to a comrade lest he slip from the steed and the group thundered off across the open plain.

Mortu stood in the road and watched the cloud of dust recede in their wake. His arms, bronzed by sun except where scars ran in lines of white, twitched as the excitement of battle ebbed away, its exit hastened by the puzzling presence of the knight.

Kyrus hopped from the ground and scaled the big warrior to sit again on his shoulder.

"Well, we have faced battle once again and by the grace of God yet live."

Mortu raised an eyebrow. "We?"

"Young man, someday you might find yourself in danger, bereft of my wisdom and strategic sense, and then, alas! I do not wish to contemplate it! I have grown fond of you for reasons that even I, with my astounding intellect, cannot comprehend! Surely, a portion of God's inexhaustible love for His creation must reside in all of us. Perhaps even in pagans such as yourself."

Mortu shook his head no. "Were a falcon to carry you off I can't imagine being too upset."

Now Kyrus shook his head. "I know you jest." However, his small black eyes scanned the sky above.

The pair noticed simultaneously, atop the three carts of the caravan, a dozen pairs of eyes stared down. A few men held bows ready but not aimed. They wore fine leather armor improved with plates of polished steel but carried themselves not as warriors, but as wealthy men, tentative in motion and gesture outside the realms where they were masters.

The silence was broken by a man with gray at his temples.

"We give our thanks, lone rider!"

Kyrus's brow furrowed. "Lone rider? Are his eyes bad?"

Mortu nodded to the man and turned, walking toward his iron horse.

"A moment, warrior." The voice was feminine, educated, and despite its musical quality, heavy with authority.

Mortu turned. Stepping from the cart was a woman, tall and lean, of indeterminate age. She wore a tunic of red satin above breeches of dark gray and sandals, clothes that a wealthy woman might wear to travel. Her long, brown hair was tied behind her, fluttering in the wind. Her green eyes looked warmly at the tall northerner. She reached to stroke his muscular arm.

"You saved us."

Mortu smiled. Kyrus stared, arms folded.

Her features were high and angular, like Mortu's, but without the dour cast that typified the northern race. Mortu marked her as a highborn Imperial, likely from the far city of Zantyum, where his quest with Kyrus had begun. Her beauty was a severe kind, sharp, ever challenging. He stared a moment at her lips, painted a glossy crimson with a cosmetic.

She continued, "I am Leguna. What is your name?"

The monk spoke first. "I am Kyrus, Brother of the Order of the Light Eternal. This is Mortu."

Leguna laughed, a pleasant, youthful sound though Mortu could not guess her age. "I thought you his pet! How remarkable! Are you an exceptionally intelligent monkey or have you been transfigured? Was it sorcery or the workings of something left from the old epoch?"

"To the first part, the latter, to the second part, the former. The sorcerer Malathax entrapped me in this body to punish me for exposing his evil. Mortu and I travel east to seek a remedy."

She nodded. "Of course. And you, 'Mortu', have you no other appellation?"

Mortu said, "In the lands of my birth I am known as Kinslayer. In Zantyum I am known in the arenas as The Merciful."

"The Merciful?"

"I killed quickly," Mortu replied.

Leguna's eyes widened ever so slightly, then she smiled as she stared long at the warrior. He was nearly a giant, tall and upright, body heavy with thick muscle. His size, dark hair and blue eyes marked him clearly as a northerner, of those warriors of the frozen waste who bore equal measures of pride and shame; they were of a race created to serve the Illilissy in war but had rebelled, mankind's oppressor by birth had become the liberator. They were human, only just touched by the cruel experiments of the Illilissy, yet a faint aura of the alien hung around them.

A cry of pain interrupted the conversation.

Leguna turned and shouted to the people atop the cart.

"Have we lost anyone?"

No reply came but from the stillness above, the way the men stood with bowed heads, Mortu guessed one of their comrades had succumbed to his wounds.

A woman stepped forward.

She walked with head bowed to stand before Leguna. Though youth brightened her pretty face, her eyes seemed older from sadness.

"Ghan has passed; I could not staunch his bleeding. Hule and Mika will recover eventually unless fever takes them." She wiped her bloodied hands on her apron as she spoke. Mortu met her eyes. They were the color of deep water bounded by a band of gold, like where the ocean meets the shore. Her beauty was uncomplicated, earthy.

Leguna said, "I know you did your best, Nathia. Now, see to the children. I imagine they are frightened."

The young woman nodded deferentially and walked to the last cart in the line.

Mortu watched her walk a moment, then turned to Leguna and bowed his head slightly before turning to leave.

"But where are you going, Mortu?"

Mortu shrugged. "The road."

Kyrus bowed from where he stood on the warrior's shoulder.

"Praise the good Lord that sent us here to deliver you in your time of need. And now, needs must we resume our quest. It was a pleasure, my lady."

Mortu lifted his long leg over the saddle of his iron horse and kicked at the lever that brought the heart of the beast back to rumbling wakefulness.

Leguna shouted above the din. "Wait! You must let us repay the debt!"

Kyrus replied, "No need, my good lady! Doing good is its own reward!"

Leguna's expression became clouded with worry. "We are down three fighters. Our cargo is precious. Please at least ride with us to our city. We go east, as do you."

Mortu flipped a toggle near the grip and the steed became quiet again. He watched the woman named Nathia helping two children step down from the cart. She attended to each one in turn, soft voice, encouraging, comforting. The children regarded the bright sky and endless waste with trepidation. The pair were perhaps four or five years old. A tow-headed boy looked with wonderment across and up the road at Mortu's steed. The girl walked, holding one of Nathia's hands. Under her care, the pair seemed to brighten a little. She led them away from where a trio of men was digging a grave for their fallen friend.

Mortu spoke. "We will ride with you."

Leguna laid a hand on his thick shoulder. "You have my gratitude."

The caravan made ready to leave. Mortu stood before the grave of the dead man as Kyrus stood perched in his usual spot on the barbarian's shoulder and led a prayer for the departed soul. Mortu watched the men of the caravan as Kyrus droned on in the old tongue.

The men stood still but gave each other looks, irreverence at odds with their sadness. When Kyrus had finished one spoke.

"You are a restitutionist, I gather?"

Kyrus spoke haughtily. "Though the term borders on pejorative, I agree with the sentiment. Only when what the Illilissy destroyed has been rebuilt will mankind be whole again."

The man bowed slightly. "I meant no offense. I am Turnin of the White City. We follow a different creed. Mankind needs only unlock his inborn potential for true progress to be realized."

Kyrus smiled. "So many have said only to unleash woe upon his brother."

Turnin sighed and knelt at the fresh grave. "It was a friend I just buried. He shared our beliefs. We follow Leguna, as you should too." He laid a hand on the rough mound and continued. "If you knew what was lost with his death…"

"Every death is a tragedy, a loss of something unique. The sadness we bear is mitigated only by the knowledge that the soul returns to God and perfection."

Turnin shook his head. "This is no normal life lost, we of the city…"

"Turnin!"

All turned to see Leguna standing there. Turnin shrank visibly under her gaze.

Leguna regarded him with a look of gentle reprobation and then stared at the fresh grave. She took a deep breath.

Mortu watched her. She did not weep, only closing her eyes for a moment before turning them to her people.

"We should depart."

"Yes, Leguna."

The woman smiled at Mortu. "Would you honor us by leading the caravan?"

Mortu nodded.

The caravan sped down the long highway. Mortu's iron horse led the way. Behind the carts rumbled on, powered by hearts much larger than the one which propelled Mortu's steed, but slowed by their heavy burdens. The northerner's eyes were fixed ahead though in his mind he thought of Leguna.

Kyrus seemed to read his thoughts.

"I do not trust them, especially not her."

Mortu shrugged. "It hardly matters. We travel the same way. When we reach their city, we will part ways. At this speed we lose only a few hours, perhaps a day. If they were anything to be feared they would have seen those nomads off without us."

"Yes, quite."

When the sun began to dip near the far horizon, the caravan stopped to make camp. Mortu and Kyrus walked the plain, collecting scrub and dried grass for their fire while those of the caravan stretched their legs under the watchful eye of men on the roof. A man with light brown hair peppered with gray met the pair as they brought their burden back to where the iron horse sat idle, well outside the ring of carts. He bowed with casual grace and said, "I am Tomas. Leguna asks that you dine with us."

Mortu made an awkward smile then looked down to Kyrus. Leguna's strange charm was compelling but it competed with the natural standoffishness of the northerner. Kyrus was needed to break the tie.

His first thought was sharp denial, but furry hands rubbed a rumbling, empty stomach.

"We would be honored."

The mood was somber as the party remembered their departed. They sat around a large fire on rugs that Nathia had laid out. Eleven men of varied appearance, though generally all fit and apparently healthy, two women, Nathia and Leguna, and the children. Under Leguna's steady pressure the mood lightened, as they ate a stew made from dried vegetables. She conversed with both Mortu and Kyrus at once, culling the fascinating details of their very different lives. She spoke with a natural cadence, switching tone effortlessly to laugh at one of Kyrus' clever turns of phrase or gasp with awe at some detail of Mortu's far home. The desert air grew cold but the stew warmed them. The moon's rise saw Kyrus yawning as the group talked amongst themselves, periodically stealing a glance at the outsiders.

Leguna stood to her full height. Mortu stared at her face, half in cool moonlight, half in the warm light of the fire. He felt eyes watching and turned to see Nathia. She met his eyes for a moment then looked to the boy in her lap. Mortu puzzled. There again was the sadness in her eyes, but something more.

Leguna addressed the group, "I think it must be time we all sleep." She turned to a man with a bow across his back. "Ruyt, have you set the watch?"

"Aye, Leguna."

With a last smile for her guests, she made her way to the largest cart. Mortu and Kyrus returned to the steed. The big northerner laid a cloak on the hard ground while Kyrus stretched out on the steed's long seat.

"Mortu."

"Yes, little one."

The monkey sat upright as a look of irritation spread across his face.

"From dusk until the moon's rise we spoke with Leguna."

"What of it?"

"I know nothing more of her than when we first met. I know not where they came from or what the purpose of their journey is."

Mortu laughed. "Why did you not ask?"

"Because I was bewitched by her flattery! God forgive me!" Kyrus shook a little fist in the air as he continued. "Never again! That woman has something to hide! I know this!"

"You're mad. She is your equal in mind and it irks you. That is all."

"Ha, and ha! You are wrong twice!"

"The road, nomads, a fallen knight and strange woman. Our day was full and I wish to sleep. Silence yourself lest I tie you in a sack."

Kyrus snorted derisively but spoke no more.

The barbarian rose at dawn. Kyrus was curled in a tight ball on the seat as Mortu made ready. Terse inquiries revealed that the caravan would head off the highway some thirty leagues ahead, then ride north and likely reach their destination at dusk. When he returned to the steed Kyrus was yet asleep. He gingerly moved the furry mass backwards on the seat to make room for himself and then kicked the steed to life. Kyrus woke with a start and the caravan resumed its journey.

The road stretched on. The wind was hot and dry across Mortu's wide frame, lean muscle made dark by the punishing sun. In these climes, he wore only leather breeches and boots. Steel greaves covered his shins, a sole nod to the heavily armored warriors of his home. To either side stretched ochre wastes. Eons ago, before the Illilissy had wrought their strange changes across the earth, it had been a green steppe. Now clouds of dust rolled across a flat expanse, broken occasionally by great masses of jutting rock. Periodically a strange shape stabbed at the sky, graceful forms of dull white, the remains of the alien towers from which the Illilissy ruled. Abandoned now, windswept and forlorn, their mysteries beyond man's ken.

Leagues disappeared underneath the tires of the beast. The sun reached its apex as the barbarian and monk sat in their own reveries. A loud horn sounded over the roaring heart of the steed.

Mortu looked back to see Turnin pointing ahead and to the north.

There another track led from the highway, marked with two poles. The barbarian eased the throttle and guided the steed onto the track. The sunbaked earth beneath his wheels was nearly as smooth as the highway. The caravan followed. Ahead, far in the distance was a steep plateau of rock. White forms emerged, towers and domes; the Illilissy had improved the plateau. Upon the bare rock sat a disk of white. Flowing buttresses tapered down the side as towers rose from the top, gentle, twisting forms. Mortu and Kyrus both took in the vista.

Kyrus scratched his chin. "Before us is a city. My beloved Zantyum is a frenzy of towers and walls, quarters and bazaars. This," his furry hand shook at the plateau, "is the sort of ordered composition that only exists in men's dreams."

Mortu shrugged. "It has lain forgotten for centuries. Rightly so. A den of alien sorcery. I wonder how far beyond it lies the caravaners' village."

Kyrus spied a drake soaring above. The sunlight set the thin flesh stretched across its broad wings aglow. He pulled frantically on a lock of the barbarian's hair and pointed up.

"Aye, little one, I see him. Were we alone he might become a worry. But he won't attack a caravan. Keep your eyes up though, while I scan the ground for scorpions."

The monk watched the thing glide in slow circles above the caravan before angling south. He whispered a curse against the Illilissy whose tampering brought many new menaces to the earth. Or perhaps they had rebirthed old ones. None could say.

The plateau loomed ahead. Each mile it grew, taking up more and more of the cloudless sky. The western horizon began to glow orange, then red, as the alien city neared.

The horn sounded again. The man steering the cart in the cab gestured for Mortu to pull to the side of the caravan's path. Mortu obeyed, then watched with interest as the rumbling carts of the caravan made for the base of the plateau.

"Are we making camp at the base of that thing? Seems ill luck."

Mortu shook his head no. This close a great white portal could be seen at the base of the rock. As the caravan approached the door slid away with a smooth grace that belied its size.

The barbarian said, "I think not, little friend."

"Dear God! They live there!"

"So it would appear."

The pair stood ill at ease inside the great hall that opened to the desert. It was a large dome above a floor made out of a material Mortu could not name. It was hard like steel, laid out in long rectangles, but seemed to have the weight and texture of the countless clay roof tiles that covered the buildings of Zantyum. When all were inside the doors closed behind them with a great hissing sound whereupon the floor seemed to hum underneath them. The carts were parked neatly in a row while the travelers milled about, happy to be home. Mortu's steed sat quiet, resting on its kickstand, a thick layer of dust from the road obscuring its oily black shape. The children stared about in wonder at the size of the hall. Nathia stood with them. Mortu came to her as behind them the doors closed. He was at pains to find any source of light though the hall was as bright as day.

"You all live in this hall? Where are tables and beds? Where is the hearth?"

Her face showed puzzlement a moment, then she smiled and replied, "Oh no, this is the elevator."

It was now Mortu's turn to make a puzzled expression. He looked a moment to Kyrus on his shoulder but the monk was tense, eyes darting here and there as if expecting one of the invaders of yore to appear.

Nathia continued, "We go up, to the old city above."

Mortu feigned comprehension. The young boy clinging to Nathia's skirts interrupted the conversation.

"Will we not ride in the cart anymore?"

Her face darkened a moment before she smiled. "No, child. You will live in the city now."

His disappointment was evident.

Mortu addressed Nathia, "Are you not happy to be home?" He watched her face as she replied. Her beauty seemed at odds with the alien surroundings. A slightly upturned nose sat above her full mouth. While Leguna's angular face was a challenge, here was sensuality and warmth. What troubles were ineptly hidden behind the dark ocean blue of her eyes, Mortu wondered.

Her eyes looked at the ground as she replied. "I am happy. We are all happy here."

Kyrus spoke finally. "Indeed then, this is the end of your journey.

What of this precious cargo for which you risked life and limb?"

Nathia gestured to the boy. "The children."

Kyrus stood to his full two feet, steadying himself with a hand on the top of Mortu's head. His look became imperious.

"Young woman, slavery is outlawed in Zantyum, by the grace of God. I hope my companion and I were not drafted unawares to assist these people in delivering slaves!"

Nathia shook her head no. "The two children were orphans, adopted from Sisters of Mercy at Zantyum. So was I, nearly twenty years ago."

"Oh. Are all these people orphans?" He gestured at the milling group.

"No. The journey to Zantyum is made only periodically."

The young boy at Nathia's waist smiled up at the monkey. Kyrus bristled a bit, as he always did when children found him amusing. He reigned in his pride and hopped to the ground.

"Young man, are you eager to meet the children of the city above?"

The boy giggled at the figure before him but Nathia brought him close.

She answered for him, "There are no children above."

Kyrus cocked his head. A question died on his lips as another hissing sound erupted from the walls. The dome above parted in wedges that slid smoothly down to disappear underneath. The night sky greeted them with an abundance of shining stars, hemmed in by the multitude of white towers. They had reached the top.

Nathia said, "Now, the journey is over."

The elevator's domed roof had slid away to reveal a plaza of white stone. Curves flowed around walkways and fountains. The lines led to a plinth before the largest tower, taller than any in Zantyum. Men and women in white robes stood ringing the elevator, hands clasped. When the last sliver of the dome had disappeared they greeted the travelers with joy, making for loved ones or friends. The whole group numbered nearly a hundred by Mortu's quick reckoning. From the largest cart Leguna appeared. She strode purposefully to the platform and addressed the crowd.

"We have returned from far Zantyum to our beloved White City. With us are the children that will enable us to continue our way of life. Bless them, and bless those that aided me in the journey." She gestured to Mortu and Kyrus. "And bless these outlanders, kind and brave, who assisted us in our time of need. Our hospitality is theirs as long as they choose to stay."

Kyrus whispered at Mortu's ear. "Not bloody long in this alien place. What a wonder, men living in what the Illilissy left behind. It is unwholesome."

Mortu shushed his companion.

Leguna raised her arms in a gesture of generosity.

"Now, let us and our guests feast together and enjoy the warmth of fellowship."

From oval doorways more white-robed figures appeared, laden with trays of vegetables and fruits. On the opposite end of the plaza were long, curving shapes, arranged in no pattern that Mortu could discern, that served as tables for the feast. Men from the crowd hopped aboard the carts to drive them into enclosures well off the plaza while the crowd sat and ate. The men, perhaps ten, were armed like the caravaners with swords at their waists. They walked with confident purpose where others of the city were relaxed. Once the carts and luggage were dealt with, the men seemed to shed their serious mien and became like anyone else.

Smiles and laughter were everywhere. The children were shepherded off by a pair of women leaving Nathia suddenly without a charge and out of sorts. She took an apple from the buffet and sat alone.

Mortu inspected the food as Kyrus remounted his shoulder, laden with a bunch of grapes.

"No meat..."

Leguna was suddenly beside him. "Apologies, Mortu. We of the White City eschew the eating of flesh. The wonders of the ancients enable our wonderful gardens and orchards to flourish, providing all our needs."

Mortu stood close to her. She was perhaps older than he first reckoned. Lines radiated from around her eyes and her thinness seemed more pronounced.

He filled his plate with a thick stew and sat away from the crowd.

"Good bread, at least."

Leguna went to another table and then came before him, offering a glass. The barbarian took the delicate flute of clear liquid in his rough hand.

She smiled down at him. "Wine, of my own making. Please try it."

Mortu held the glass a moment, marveling at its delicate make. Kyrus reached over and grasped it with both his hands. He lifted it to his small face and sipped.

The monk's eyes widened. He sat down on Mortu's shoulder and sipped again.

"I don't know that I have ever tasted better. I… It is incredible. Light, yet with substance, accents of apple, refreshing, delicately sweet with a tart finish…"

He drank again. Leguna tossed her head back to laugh.

"Excuse me while I get another glass."

Mortu whispered to his friend. "How old do you reckon she is?"

"…such a pleasant aftertaste, and not too heady. What?"

Mortu repeated his question.

Kyrus shrugged. "Perhaps thirty-five, forty? Forty-five at the oldest."

"Everyone here, the men and women, all seem to be the same age save Nathia and the children. Where are the families? Where are the elderly?"

"In mankind's long history, many people have struck off in order to found their idea of a utopia. I suspect the denizens of the White City are such a group. All those that turn away from society in such a way meet a similar fate, gradual disillusionment and dissolution."

"Utopia?"

Kyrus' tone became pedantic. "A perfect society."

Mortu scoffed. "There is such a place, the north, where my people live as the gods intended."

"My young friend, once again essential concepts escape your grasp, like eels slipping from your thick fingers. While you may wrongly believe the savages that raised you to be of a perfect society, I refer to man's long dream of living without inequality or strife."

The barbarian scoffed again. "Life is conflict. We are but wolves that walk on two legs. Build your temples, write your books, nothing will ever change."

Kyrus took a deep breath, readying his words like a knight lowers his lance, but Leguna reappeared, denying the monk the pleasure of his rejoinder.

She handed a glass to Mortu and he quaffed it.

"Very good, though I prefer the strong ales of my home."

It was Kyrus' turn to scoff. "Pardon him, good lady. He has the palette of stray dog."

She laughed her musical laugh and laid a hand on Mortu's thick arm where a spiral of blue ink spelled the runes of his home. She traced the lines, crude but intricate, beasts forever woven in dire combat across his thews.

"I hope you two are not in a rush to leave. I find you both pleasant company."

Mortu felt eyes on him and turned to see Turnin looking his way. When their gaze met the man looked back down at his plate. He looked again and whispered to the man next to him. Both had the complexion and manner of members of the noble caste in Zantyum. Mortu looked to where Nathia sat. The young woman looked up at him.

Leguna gave his arm a light squeeze.

Kyrus spoke. "Our errand is somewhat dire, good lady." He sipped at the glass again, finishing it with a sigh of contentment. "I suppose a day or two doesn't matter overmuch." He wavered slightly as he hopped down and placed the glass on the table. He stood and peered, scanning the tables.

Leguna smiled. "I'll fetch you another glass and you can regale me with tales of theological and scholarly debate."

Mortu smirked. "I think I shall stretch my legs, if I am permitted."

"Of course, the city is yours, Mortu."

With no destination in mind, Mortu struck east from the plaza, long strides leading him down narrowing avenues. The buildings around him were a parody of those he knew from his time in Zantyum. There were no hard angles, only smooth ovals and circles, oblong lengths of the strange white stone. The windows had no glass. The barbarian recalled tales of the time when the Illilissy ruled the earth. They were reputed to be inured to extremes of heat or cold. By legend the aliens were tall and willowy; Mortu noted the scale of doorways built to accommodate beings taller than the average man. He peered into simple interiors. A clay bowl sat upon a wooden table. Blankets of cotton woven in muted colors spread across a plain divan. Away from the plaza, all was silent. No rat scurried underfoot. No dog howled at the moon above.

A cool breeze stirred a string of chimes hanging from a second story window.

Soft footfalls sounded from behind. Mortu tensed. He drew a dagger from his heavy belt and slipped into the shadow where a wall turned from the street. He crouched, waiting.

Nathia came into view, scanning left and right.

"You followed me."

She gave a start as he stepped from the shadow and sheathed his dagger.

"Yes."

"Why?"

Her beautiful eyes shined with worry in the moonlight. Words seemed to die in her throat as she tried to speak.

"Take a breath and say what you must, woman."

"It isn't so simple. These people raised me. This is my home, yet…"

She sat on a low wall, head sinking into her hands.

Mortu squatted down so her eyes were on a level above his. He was a man possessed of great reserves of courage and cruelty toward his foe, but before him sat a beautiful young woman in distress. The imperatives of nature, woven deep within the very cells of his blood, were difficult to ignore.

"What troubles you?"

Tears glistened in the moonlight as she whispered. "The children, this place…"

A voice sounded from down the alley. "Yes, Nathia, do tell us what troubles you."

Mortu spun to see Turnin flanked by other men. They wore the white robes of the city but belted. Short swords hung from the leather at their waist. They were the two dozen or so men marked by Mortu, the ones with the soldierly manner at odds with the peaceful mood of the city. Now their mood seemed positively grim.

Turnin gestured toward the plaza. "Go to the plaza, Nathia. Leguna wishes to speak with you. And you," He walked to Mortu. The barbarian stood to his full height, a full head and a half taller than Turnin. "The night grows late. Permit me to take you to your quarters."

The two men stared at each other a long moment. Mortu's hard face wore a plain expression as his blue eyes stared.

The northerner took a step forward.

Turnin's hand jerked to the hilt of his sword but Mortu's hand came up in a plaintive gesture, palm up.

His deep voice filled the quiet alley as he said, "Lead away."

Hatred simmered in Turnin's eyes as his hand slipped from the sword's handle and he turned to walk towards the plaza.

The feast was winding down. Mortu recognized no one from the caravan; fatigue had ended their evening early. A woman gestured to a small bundle laying atop one the tables.

"I'm afraid your friend is ill."

Mortu laughed, "Ill indeed!" He grabbed Kyrus' legs and slung him over his shoulder like a dishrag. Turnin and his men led them toward a row of domes lining a nearby street. At the first doorway he stopped.

"Inside you will find everything you need. Leguna begs your pardon for her absence." The last sentence was spoken through clenched teeth. He continued, "The city has important business this night."

Mortu stared at him until Turnin looked away. Then he entered the quarters. He gave a start at a hiss behind him, spinning to see the door close behind him, sliding from a thin seam in the doorway. He stepped to the door and it slid back open. A marvel, he thought, and turned back to the interior. A niche in the white wall held blankets, which he spread across a simple bed. He bundled one and placed it atop a low table.

Kyrus groaned as Mortu laid him down on the makeshift cushion.

"Goodnight, little friend."

The northerner made ready for bed in an adjoining room. He sniffed at the carafe of water that sat on the low table and took a swig. The bed was of simple design, rope woven across unstained lengths of pine, scaled for average people and thus slightly cramped for Mortu. He threw the palette to the ground and carried the frame to the other room. He laid it on its side, in front of the door, a measure against potential intruders. It was a habit, among others, he had adopted after spending time among those that called themselves civilized.

He lay on the hard floor wrapped in blankets. Through the high window, he could see the starry desert night. Somewhere above was the star, which the Illilissy had known as their native sun. Did the eld, which had once stayed in this room, still live; did he look upon the sky as did Mortu, this very moment? A fanciful thought, the barbarian smiled to himself. Traveling with Kyrus was turning him into a poet. Memories of the long day soon chased away other thoughts. There was Leguna, with her eyes that burned. Mortu had seen that look before but could not recall where.

And Nathia. What had she meant to tell him? Some secret of the city? Mortu suppressed a shiver. He had known cities before but none as bizarre. The wanderer in him, burdened by the past, still pined for the road. But what would he learn if he stayed? Thoughts of Nathia stayed with him beyond the veil of sleep and into dream. There she was his wife and he was happy, untroubled, but as he sat before the hearth her expression became distressed and she mouthed words that he could not hear. Shadows entered the hall and he raised his axe, all the while the sound of a child crying grew in his ears.

He woke in a sweat and snatched his axe from beside him. There was no one in the room. He sat up. The bed lay where he had set it.

The only sound was a high pitched snoring, as Kyrus did when drunk.

Rays of dawn spilled onto the floor in long streaks from the tall windows. Mortu lay awake listening as the city slowly came to life. It was not the cacophony of Zantyum but more like a village or perhaps a suburb. He stood and took the carafe and pondered Kyrus a moment before dumping the contents on him.

The monkey gasped and sputtered and rolled from the table only to leap back up, fist shaking as the water dripped from him.

"You son of a heathen cur!"

Mortu laughed. "Oh, you are up. Excellent. We need to discuss our plans."

Kyrus swore an oath and then sat, rubbing his face and head.

"Not until I have some of that water in me, and perhaps a piece of fruit."

Outside, a young woman in white directed the pair back to the plaza. There they found a long tent raised against the desert sun, under which was a buffet. The people of the city breakfasted on fruit and bread. Mortu pondered their garments, the white robes, as Kyrus tore open an orange. The barbarian wore a leather jerkin without sleeves, his breeches and heavy boots. Were he prone to such emotions, he would have felt out of place. The two sat comfortably on a smooth bench of white stone under the shade of tall ferns. The bread Mortu ate was hearty and delicious, enlivened with pieces of vegetables.

A man with light brown hair and wearing a pleasant expression walked by and stooped to pick up a piece of peel on the ground next to the table where Kyrus sat.

The monk said, "My apologies! I am not myself this morning."

"No trouble at all."

Mortu looked down on the man and wondered aloud, "How can one tell servant from master when you all dress alike?"

He smiled. The barbarian studied his face. He looked very much like one of the men who rode with the caravan but younger, a brother perhaps, thought Mortu.

"My friend, there is no servant or master here. We all follow Leguna for her wisdom and leadership. But all are equal."

Mortu scratched his chin. "In my far home, all warriors reckon themselves freemen; though among them no one is equal another."

"There is much strife, is there not?"

Mortu smiled. "Very much."

"There is no strife here." The man gestured, a sweep of the arm meant to take in the whole of the White City. He continued, "We have no need. All eat and drink their fill. The labor of the gardens is pleasant to some, thus they toil in happiness. The city the eld left behind contains many marvels that save labor. Some study its workings. The rest of us pursue our interests. I compose verse and study the martial arts. Others weave or make pots, perform theater. The keenest of our minds, Leguna herself among them, study the mysteries of the Illilissy."

Kyrus' brow lifted, his expression of disdain tempered with good manners. He said, "Nothing good can come of knowledge of the alien."

The man laughed gently and replied, "Look around, friend. There is only good."

The monk sniffed. "Yes, quite." He stretched his furry limbs and sipped again from a clay mug of water.

Mortu asked, "What of these martial arts? You would seem to have no need."

"Every now and again we must make the journey to Zantyum, where many of us were born. There is danger, as you know. Should the nomads' aim have been truer, and your steed slower, well, it is not pleasant to contemplate."

Mortu smiled his wolfish grin, typically a cue for Kyrus to begin rolling his eyes at the forthcoming comment.

"I suppose the little battle is the talk of the city."

The man shrugged. "I heard little talk of it. I was there."

Mortu scanned the man's face with puzzlement.

"I don't recall you being there."

"I am Tomas. I invited you to dine with us."

The barbarian stared a minute then said, "You seemed much older when first we met."

Tomas laughed. "Surely it was just dust from the road which seemed to age me. On top of that, we of the city find our home very rejuvenating."

Mortu nodded.

"If you two will excuse me, morning is the time for practice. Mortu, you are welcome to join me."

Mortu pondered a moment until Kyrus answered, "A kind offer, but he and I have plans to discuss."

"Of course. I bid you good day."

Tomas left the pair.

Kyrus said, "It must be this thin, high air atop the plateau that disagrees with me. My head hurts awfully."

"You are hung over."

"Nonsense. I had a glass or two of that pleasant, light wine after a long, taxing day. So, to leave this strange place I suppose we must beg our hosts let us make us of the 'elevator'."

"Hear this first, little friend. Last night, when you were discussing philosophy with Leguna, I took a stroll down the city's odd lanes. Nathia followed me and was about to tell me something of import when Turnin showed up."

"Oh really? Well, we cannot delay our quest so some pretty, young woman can 'tell you something'."

Mortu's face showed anger. "She meant to tell me something about the city and the children."

"Where are the children?" Kyrus thought aloud.

"Where is Nathia?"

Around them the people of the White City ate and went about their day. They clustered in groups of three or four. While buildings were a jumble of fanciful domes and towers, the lanes of the city were a sensible grid aligned north and south, east and west. From where he sat Mortu could see clear domes in the southeast quadrant. Were these the gardens? Many residents made their way there presently. Mortu saw Turnin and his men, perhaps three score, walking north, as had Tomas.

They were fit, as were all residents of the city, but carried themselves a touch more upright and more purposefully. These men are of a martial bent, thought Mortu. This is the pool of men who volunteer to protect the caravans, who study with Tomas and who wore steel last night to intimidate.

The sight of Leguna interrupted his thoughts. Flanked by two women, one fair and the other dark, she descended from the tall steps of the largest tower, north of the plaza. She came to the plinth where she had addressed the city and stepped down. She smiled when she saw Mortu and came before him.

"I trust you two had a restful night."

Kyrus said, "Indeed. We thank you for our hospitality."

In the morning sun she seemed radiant, youthful. She met Mortu's eyes and held his gaze for a long moment.

"We were just making plans to leave."

She frowned and looked down at the monk. "So soon? I would be bereft. It has been a long, long time since we had guests." She laid a hand on Mortu's arm. "There is much to interest both of you here. For the warrior, we have Tomas' hall. He has done wondrous work investigating the weapons of the Illilissy and their tactics. For the scholar, the north tower holds a trove of artifacts and texts left behind so long ago by the eld."

"Where is Nathia?"

Leguna answered, "She cares for the children. They are sequestered in order to acclimate them to their new home. It is so different from the orphanage."

Kyrus cocked his head and asked, "Why were they brought here?"

"We of the city live a unique sort of life. Few of us think of family. The orphans ensure posterity."

"Just the two? That seems hardly enough. There must be at least two hundred of you here."

Leguna shrugged and turned to Mortu. "Let me take you to Tomas." She took his arm and they walked to the north lane. Kyrus hopped onto his shoulder and sat with arms folded.

The hall was an oblong dome, high-ceilinged and long. At one end a raised wooden platform stood bearing racks and racks of weapons and equipment. The floor was sand. On the far end, a row of butts was set for archery practice. Two dozen men milled about in a loose ring, each clothed in only loose white pants gathered at the ankles. In the center was Tomas. He walked in a wide circle before his opponent, both armed with staffs. Mortu felt his pulse quicken. He was suddenly back in the ludi, the gladiator school in Zantyum, where he had spent many formative years. Leguna smiled at him and gestured to the circle. Mortu smiled back. He walked to the platform and doffed his shirt and boots and walked to the circle. He stood apart, respectfully, waiting until Tomas noticed him.

Kyrus sniffed where he stood at Leguna's feet.

"Like a fish to water. The boy loves fighting."

"It is in his blood. Him and his people. Born from tragedy and spared to shed blood for the Illilissy until the day when they rose up against their masters."

"Ancient history."

Leguna stared at Mortu as she talked. "Yet the legacy lives. You can see it in his strength, his bearing. Our old masters were remarkable."

Kyrus raised an eyebrow. "They turned mankind into slaves."

"They did. And in the process brought many wonders and stripped away illusion."

Kyrus felt his blood boil. He had heard such sentiments before in the rare times he had rubbed elbows with some of the elite of Zantyum.

"If the lady will excuse me, I think I will retire to the quarters you have most generously provided and take a nap."

Leguna replied to him, though her eyes were on the combatants. "Of course."

Kyrus made his way back to their rooms without difficulty. Inside he refreshed himself with the water and grapes that had been left on the table. He scampered up to sit on the ledge of a window, back leaning against the cool, white stone. The city was languid before him. The sun made the domes and towers pure in their brilliant white, hinting at strange reflections like an iridescent opal. Beneath them the lanes and streets were nearly empty. Here and there a man or woman walked without haste. A man on the street below him walked with a rug over his shoulder. Two women laughed where they sat at the edge of the plaza. Behind a low dome another man hung laundry on a line, stirring slowly in the warm breeze.

Idyllic, thought Kyrus.

From across the plaza walked the children Kyrus recognized from the caravan. With them were two white-robed women. There was a dash of white from the corner of his eye and he saw a woman running towards the pair. It was Nathia. She came before them kneeling, hugging the pair of them. Two men wearing swords jogged to catch up. Gingerly, though with menace lurking underneath, the two men separated the group. The children went one way, Nathia the other. Her head was down as she walked in between the men.

Kyrus stood as she rounded a corner, out of view. He wished for a moment Mortu was here, only to watch him acting impulsively.

He swore as he scanned his surroundings. An easy leap brought a clothesline in reach. He swung from that onto a ledge which wound its way across the second story of an oblong-shaped building. He scampered across, deftly dodging flowerpots and clayware left on windowsills. Another leap and he grasped a line hung back and forth across a cozy alleyway, decorated with triangles of colored cloth. He shimmied its length with ease, prehensile tail swishing this way and that to preserve his balance. A hop and he was scampering up the side of a dome. He paused to peer over the side. Had his guess been correct?

Yes. There was Nathia below. The two men with her wore looks of concern. One laid a hand on his shoulder as he spoke to her, for all appearances an older brother offering counsel. Kyrus chuckled inwardly. He was the scholar and monk, statesman and author, and thanks to his curse, now expert spy! He shifted his weight as the three conversed underneath. Panic ensued as his place on the dome became tenuous. He was sliding. Kyrus spun onto his belly, legs and arms flailing. A ledge arrested his descent but as he turned a shard of flowerpot was disturbed. He watched its descent. Slow as a feather, so it seemed to him, the thing spun in the air to land a few feet from the man speaking with Nathia. He gave a start and looked up.

There was nothing. In the distance, a few birds broke the blue expanse of desert sky. He looked back at Nathia and the trio continued down the lane.

Kyrus dared to breathe a moment later. When he heard their footsteps recede, he relaxed from where dome and ledge met, where he had crammed himself flat. He peered down the street.

The trio came before the entrance to a large dome. The door hissed open and they disappeared. With no rope across the street, Kyrus was forced to wait until he saw the lane was empty of people. When clear he sprinted across, a comical, loping gait that involved arms as well as legs. The monk caught his breath as he hid in the shadows where the dome melded into the structure next to it.

Now, how to get in, he thought.

Tomas and Mortu stalked each other in the ring, circling like two lions. Without warning Tomas lunged with his staff. With difficulty, Mortu parried the blow with his shield. He slashed with his wooden sword, a quick strike that missed yet succeeded in taking back the initiative from the wily Tomas. Mortu reckoned that back in the arena this match-up, a fighter with range set against one with more protection, was a classic. His normal tactics in such a fight were to use his shield and punish mistakes, letting his opponent overreach and become wrong-footed. But Tomas would not make a mistake. His attacks were precise. He never lost his balance or gave any advantage.

Mortu felt his frustrations grow. While both men were lean and muscled, Mortu had him in terms of height and weight. He thrust with his shield and stabbed under. Tomas planted his staff and vaulted over the warrior and kicked at Mortu's back. The barbarian grunted and swung the shield like a blade, bringing the sword behind it. Tomas dodged the shield with ease but the sword surprised him. He threw himself backwards, only missing its touch by a hair's breadth.

"Nearly had me!"

Mortu growled and charged, shield held forward. Tomas grabbed the rim and tumbled backwards until the shield pressed down on his feet. He kicked mightily, sending Mortu flying. He landed hard. The prone barbarian spun out with his blade but froze as Tomas brought the butt of the staff to rest on Mortu's throat.

The barbarian cast his weapon down.

Tomas reached for his hand. "Great match, my friend. I've never seen one so big as you but so graceful."

Mortu clasped his hand and stood. He felt his cheeks flush crimson as he regarded the men watching the bout. The rage subsided quickly. Tomas had fought and won an honorable contest.

Tomas' face showed delight as he said, "If your poise matched your speed and strength, you would be undefeatable."

Mortu bristled a moment. He was veteran warrior. Already proven in battle when he first set foot in Zantyum, the arena trained him in dozens of weapons and the skill of the duelist. Tomas was skilled, incredibly so. But it chafed to be given such advice from one of the same age, perhaps younger. Though apparently unschooled in social graces, Mortu's warrior society was governed by a raft of unspoken rules. Without these rules, prideful warriors would be forever at each other's throats. Tomas had committed a faux pas that might result in bloodshed in the far north.

His tone and manner though, seemed of a man far older, Mortu thought. Tomas laid a hand on his shoulder and handed him a mug of water. The two men drank as their chests still heaved from the exertion.

"I hope you stay a while. These men here," he gestured at the spectators, his comrades, "don't provide so interesting a challenge."

There was laughter and scoffing from the group. Tomas gave orders and the men paired up, selecting their mock weapons from the racks before exercising themselves. Mortu watched a moment with Tomas. As a whole, the thirty or so men acquitted themselves well. Tomas seemed to sense his thoughts.

"These are the men of the city like myself, of a martial bent. Perhaps another thirty men and the odd woman will train periodically. The energies expended here might become dangerous without release."

"Indeed. And you have men to protect the caravans."

Tomas nodded. "Rare as they are, yes. Well, have you had your fill?"

Mortu felt the shoulder that had taken the brunt of the fall. It was aching and stiff. He grinned and said, "Yes, I think so."

"Follow me. I've just the thing for your pains."

Tomas led Mortu to the southern end of the plaza where a low dome opened to tall stairs. Down they went, air growing humid as they descended. Glowing globes of light illuminated the way. The sound of rushing water grew in Mortu's ears. Double doors slid open at a landing. Tomas threw his trousers on a hook and stepped under a fount of rushing water. Mortu followed suit. The water was warm and soothing. He found soap in a niche on the wall and washed. Tomas disappeared into the mist with a gesture to follow.

Beyond the wall of mist was a great bath, a long pool of clear water bounded by white stone laid out in a design becoming familiar to Mortu, the slow curves so favored by the ancient makers of the city. Above more glowing globes shed light like miniature suns. Perhaps a dozen men and women lounged in the pleasant water. Conversation ceased ever so briefly as Mortu emerged, tall and lean, body crisscrossed with scar and tattoo, hair a wet black mop tumbling down his broad shoulders. He stepped in the water with haste, eager for the privacy it offered.

Tomas laughed. "Linger in the city longer and that modesty will surely give way." He leaned back against the stone and closed his eyes. "It feels good, doesn't it?"

Mortu admitted it did. The water was extremely soothing. He felt the pain ebb from his body. He shut his eyes and leaned back, sitting on a ledge. Time seemed to slow.

A shadow passed across him and he opened his eyes. Before him was a woman of the city. She was beautiful, light brown hair in wet locks across her face and neck. From the warm tan of her face, two eyes of dark brown peered at Mortu mischievously. She leaned forward. Mortu gave a start and nearly lost his footing on the smooth stone below.

Tomas laughed again. "Kara, dear, remember our guest is an outlander with customs likely different than ours. Careful you don't give offense."

She splashed water at him and replied, "You hush, Tomas." She turned to Mortu. "Do you not find me pleasing?"

Mortu nodded he did.

"Then we should make love." She came close.

All eyes were on the barbarian. He scowled.

"Am I some stud horse for you all to view?" He pushed her away.

Tomas made a plaintive gesture, "Dear Mortu, she meant no offense. Here in the city things are perhaps much more casual than you are used to. When two people wish to experience each other they do so without shame or worry."

A body slipped into the water beside Mortu. He turned to see Leguna. She came close.

"Forgive her, Mortu." She stroked his face. "Poor thing, it is too much too soon." Kara skulked off after a look from Leguna. Mortu blushed. Mortal danger was preferable to this awkwardness, he reckoned.

"Our ways may seem strange to you, but they serve us well. Can I ask you keep an open mind? A host may make small demands of their guest, may they not?"

Mortu nodded.

She nudged her way between him and the stone. Hands rubbed his shoulders.

"You are quite a specimen, doubly so from your novelty. Kara couldn't help herself. If there is one fault here, it is a lack of new faces. Meeting people is stimulating, isn't it?"

Mortu nodded again. He felt his composure returning, albeit slowly. Her hands were gentle, strong for a woman. The barbarian felt the tension seep from his body. There was a splash and Mortu turned to see Turnin had entered the bath. He waded to Leguna.

"I would speak with you." He addressed the city's leader though his eyes bored into Mortu. Beneath the gaze anger simmered like hot coals.

Jealousy, thought Mortu. Matters of love were not so simple here after all.

Leguna sighed. "I'm sure it can wait."

"It cannot."

Leguna leaned to whisper in Mortu's ear. "If I do not listen to him, he will become insufferable."

She slipped away. Mortu beat a retreat, lifting himself from the pool without a backward glance. Past the fount, he found his trousers were gone, replaced by a white robe. Sheepishly he donned it and made for his quarters.

Kyrus scampered around the dome, searching for a way in. The architecture of the city complicated his task. It was impossible at times to tell where one building ended and another began. As he skulked along a ledge, he heard voices growing in volume. From where he could not tell. He peered again and again underneath him but no one was there. He felt a breeze at his back and turned. He was standing in a window. Inside the airy room, Nathia sat at a table while the two men paced the room. Kyrus suppressed a gasp and flung himself around a corner, just as one of the men stepped to the window. The monk pressed his back against the white wall. The man leaned against the sill. Kyrus watched his profile. His pleasant face was a stern mask. Kyrus' tiny heart thumped in his chest. The man had to only look to his left and Kyrus' skulking would be discovered. He would then find how the people of the White City felt about a guest attempting to unmask its secrets. Kyrus breathed a sigh of relief as the man turned back to address Nathia.

"You need to let it go. Perhaps in another time and place, your sentiments would seem humane or noble. But you know better. You know what we have achieved here. Let it go."

Nathia cried quietly, "I am trying."

"Leguna worries you will make trouble with the outsiders. She has designs on the warrior. The monk will be a problem, but not a large one. You must understand how precarious our position is. The city is safe from nomads and the beasts of the desert, but not an army from Zantyum. We must be circumspect in our dealings with outsiders."

The other man snickered. Kyrus sniffed.

He continued, "The cost we pay to live as we do, it is something the warrior will grow to understand in time. I doubt a heathen from some accursed icy waste will care much, regardless. It is you I worry about. You are one of us, Nathia. You belong with us."

There was the sound of movement. "Now, sit downstairs. Meditate on the city and all the good therein. We are unique in human history, without want or strife. Help us preserve it."

Kyrus risked a peek around the edge of the window. Nathia had stood and now made her way to a stairwell. The two men watched her. Both were tall and well built. One was darker than the other. He stood, arms folded.

When Nathia was out of earshot the men talked in low voices.

The black haired man said, "We will leave her with her thoughts for a few hours. If she still seems unpredictable, any sort of risk, then we will do what must be done, as Leguna said."

"She should have been chosen when she first came."

"Indeed. She has always been willful. Her nature is more suited to farm than city, much less a paradise such as this." He took a deep breath and stepped to the window. Before him the city spread out, brilliant in the afternoon sun, an oasis of life in the punishing wastes.

"Such beauty. Peace, love, and laughter. This place would be a bargain at a hundred times the cost."

Movement caught his eye.

Down along the ledge, where the dome curved out of view, he caught a glimpse of furry tail.

He cursed and fled down the stairs.

Mortu lay on the divan, dreaming. His exercises with Tomas and the bath had made him drowsy. He had shaken off the awkwardness with ease, having some experience dealing with the strange ways of various city folk.

In his dream there again was Nathia. Shapes and impressions, gray shades and the distant sound of crying, only that and nothing more as he walked in the dream lands.

A noise.

Mortu shot upright, reaching for his axe.

Leguna stood at the doorway. She smiled at him and walked in, coming to sit at the edge of the divan. Mortu let the axe slip from his fingers and leaned back.

"I hope I have not disturbed you."

Mortu shook his head no.

"And where is your friend?"

"I thought to ask you."

Leguna wore a look of surprise. "I have not seen him since this morning. There is much to explore. I'm sure he will return shortly." She placed a hand on his knee. "If you were of a mind, I would like to show you the city. You've seen little besides the fighting hall and the baths, which I fear did not make a good impression on you."

Mortu shrugged. "I have seen many things in my travels."

Leguna waited a moment in expectation of further explanation. When none emerged she clasped her hands together and asked, "You will come with me?"

"Yes."

The pair left the quarters. The gentle breeze followed through the lane like cool water as they walked. The streets showed the slow pace of life that Mortu had come to expect already in his short time in the city. Passersby greeted them warmly. A few paused to thank Mortu for his intervention during the nomad ambush. The plaza would host no feast tonight but food graced the long tables. People came and went at leisure, sitting nearby to eat a piece of fruit and converse or headed home with a loaf of bread underarm.

Mortu looked around. "How did this all come to be?"

Leguna smiled. She wore her hair down around her shoulders, periodically pushing it back behind her delicate ears.

"That is a story perhaps long for this walk. Do you know of the Emperor's College in Zantyum?"

"I have heard of it."

"There was a time when people feared that the Illilissy may return. The emperor ordered that learned people leave the city and seek out the ruins of the eld so that man could learn ways of defending himself. So scholars scoured the earth looking for the cities and tombs that they had left behind."

She scanned the city before her with a faraway look in her eyes.

"I was the first to set foot here for a thousand years. I walked these lanes and explored underneath. What I found gave birth to the idea of making a home here. I returned to Zantyum and gathered together those like me, dreamers, people in search of a better life. We returned and made the city our own."

Mortu shook his head. "I mean no disrespect to my host, but…" He looked to Leguna.

She smiled warmly and said, "No, by all means, continue. Tell me what bothers you."

"This is a city of the alien. It is not meant for man."

The pair sat on a low wall. Another woman in white appeared with mugs of tea for Leguna and her guest. She smiled at Mortu.

"Thank you, Syra." She turned back to the barbarian. "Your prejudice is understandable. The reign of the Illilissy wrought many changes. But now I must beg your pardon and speak something that may offend you."

It was Mortu's turn to smile. "Go ahead."

"Of any that might belong here, wouldn't it be one whose people bear a trace of the Illilissy blood?"

The muscles in Mortu's jaw twitched. "My people threw off the alien yoke."

"Of course. And as soldiers bred to serve the eld, they were the only ones strong enough to meet them in battle. What a sight it must have been. The Illilissy, tall and inscrutable, their ruthless intelligence bound in the search for a harmony of their own understanding. The Men of the North, savage and beautiful, drunk on their rebellious freedom. Such battles they must have had."

Mortu's mind was carried away to the tales that illuminated his youth. There was the final battle, in a land of vast fields forgotten to memory, remembered only as Amerza. There was Sarai, whose beauty was so great it possessed the heart of Ulcyan, the favored knight of the emperor of all the worlds, the ruler of the Illilissy. Their scion was hidden from the world until he emerged as a powerful warrior. Marked for destruction, he was spared so that his descendants would make an army for the emperor, a race of warriors willing to obey and die without question, a trait more likely found in man than in the immortal eld.

The army grew and was sent into the stars so that the emperor's reach extended farther and farther across the galaxy.

The rebellion nearly wiped all life from the earth.

Leguna's touch brought Mortu back to the present.

"You do belong here. Of all of us, perhaps you the most. The blood of the eld runs through your veins. A great paradox; it gave your people the strength to overcome them, yet the blood marks you as one apart. The Men of the North are ever unwelcome in the wider world, are they not? You fought in the arena. Perhaps also under foreign flags. Good enough to die but not to live."

Mortu smiled. "My people are not prone to such musing. If any dislike the Men of the North it is because they envy us, our prowess and strength."

Leguna laughed. "Your arrogance is a delight. Here we are all of a more modest disposition."

Mortu shook his head sheepishly. They looked at each other a moment. She sat close. He could feel her warmth. A long moment passed. She smiled at him and then they both took in the sky. In the distance a falcon rode currents of hot air above the wastes, flying a lazy spiral. Nearly imperceptibly, Leguna shifted herself closer. Mortu watched the people idling in the plaza. He felt eyes on him and turned to see Turnin walking past, armed and with two men in tow. Turnin looked to Leguna next who studiously ignored him. He seemed about to interrupt but kept walking.

"Let us visit the gardens while we still have plenty of light."

The gardens were a line of two dozen connected domes. They seemed to be of glass but were of a substance unknown to Mortu. It gave under pressure but bounced right back into shape.

Long bays held wheat and corn while miniature groves boasted a variety of fruit trees ringed by lush flowers. The fragrance was nearly overwhelming. Amidst the bays, men and women were at work at all phases, planting, pruning, harvesting. The air was warm and humid. For comfort most worked wearing only loincloths. Leguna reached for an apple, full and red, shining in the light.

She bit into it and handed it to Mortu. The taste was sweet.

Leguna laughed and wiped a drop of juice from his chin. The fruit brought thoughts of Kyrus into his mind.

"I should return to the quarters and see if Kyrus has returned."

She frowned. "Must you? I am sure he is fine."

"I beg your pardon. But I have watched over him for several years and it has become habit. He is arrogant, bullheaded, and very tiny; a dangerous combination."

Leguna laughed her pleasant laugh. "Well, if you must. But come to the main tower, the one at the north of the plaza, at nightfall. We will dine together."

"I will."

They separated at the plaza. Mortu watched over his shoulder as Turnin intercepted her. Her face, careless and beautiful only moments ago, became grave and resigned as the pair talked.

Mortu shook his head. The city and its people were a mystery. Leguna was beautiful, without a doubt, but the warrior's heart guarded itself. He thought of Nathia and her earthy beauty against which he worried he had little defense. Where was she? And where was Kyrus?

Long strides took him to the lane where his quarters lay. He passed a man he recognized from the fighting hall. The man wore a sword. He gave Mortu a friendly nod when he passed. Further down the lane was another armed man, milling about.

Kyrus was not in the quarters. Mortu inspected every niche in case the monk was dead asleep somewhere. His apprehension grew. He stormed out.

Those he stopped in the street, those he asked, all were apologetic. None had seen the outlander's monkey friend. Mortu walked the length of the city as the afternoon wore on.

Finally he returned to the plaza. He passed a copse of ferns in a wide stone planter.

"Psst…"

Mortu's heart skipped.

"Kyrus? What are you doing?"

"Shhhh! Come close."

Mortu ambled about a little and sat on the edge of the planter. Kyrus' hushed voice came from within the dense ferns.

"Mortu. I am being hunted. I found Nathia and overheard too much."

"Is she well?"

"Shhhhhh! Yes. But in an hour or two, perhaps, she might be killed.

She has violated, or may violate, some pact or secret. Not all is what it seems here."

"Where is she?"

"In a dome two lanes over, to the east. Know it by its tall doors."

Mortu made a hushing sound as sword-bearing men passed. They walked quickly. Besides one awkward glance, they pretended not to notice Mortu.

The barbarian whispered over his shoulder. "What is your plan?"

The ferns made an exasperated noise. "Plan? We are surrounded by potential enemies with unknown abilities. I am marked for death but apparently their queen has something in mind for you. Every ounce of my considerable intellect and a great deal of luck was used to bring me here with the slim hope you would pass by. Do you have any ideas rolling around in that thick skull of yours?"

"I will fetch Nathia and return for you."

"I suppose that is all we can do."

Mortu walked with haste.

Long minutes brought him back to the quarters. With an oath he realized his axe was gone. He raised his hands in a fatalistic gesture and left for the dome Kyrus had described. Above him, the sky was painted in streaks of crimson and purple as the sun dipped towards the bleak horizon.

He found it without difficulty. The white doors hissed open. A man shot up from his wooden chair and stepped in front of the barbarian.

"Hold, friend. I'm afraid I must ask you…"

Mortu's fist swung out in a vicious hook that sent the man sprawling over the table. He bent and took the unconscious man's sword belt and cinched it around his waist. He drew the blade and inspected it in the streaking rays of dusk that spilled through the high window. A good blade, if short for Mortu's taste, no nicks or imperfections. Unblooded, thought Mortu. He grinned. Perhaps not for much longer. The city was a strange place that brought forth strange emotions in the warrior. There was Leguna and Nathia and peace like he had never dreamed could exist among men. But some darkness lurked beneath the surface that imperiled his friend and the young woman that had haunted his thoughts and dreams. No more time for the strange city of people that rutted like animals but spoke as scholars.

He flipped the blade in the air, end over end, and caught it with ease, then tested a few slashing strokes in the air. Tiny motes of dust swam in eddies in the blade's wake.

With no more delay he passed through another set of doors. Another man stood in his path, blade drawn.

Mortu recognized him from the fighting hall. Behind him stood Nathia, eyes wide.

He spoke, voice made grave by the nearness of death. "Step aside. I'm taking the girl."

The man shook his head. "I cannot let you do that."

"Kyrus tells me she will be killed."

The man's face showed sorrow. "We must protect the city. No one wants this to happen."

Mortu asked, "Why can she not simply leave?"

He shook his head again. "I wish she could. We all do, Leguna most of all. She herself brought Nathia here, chose her among those at the orphanage that day, twenty years ago."

The barbarian balked. "Leguna would have been very young."

"You have no idea what is happening here. Just leave. Even if I fall beneath your blade, you cannot defeat us all. And you can't defeat Tomas."

"Enough talk."

Mortu lunged. The speed and violence caused the man to reel back. He nearly lost his footing but parried with a desperate swing and stepped to the side. The barbarian offered no respite, slashing madly. The man fought off the blows, each time with a little less composure. His back hit the wall and Mortu stabbed low. The barbarian caught the man's wrist as he attempted a final attack, pinned to the wall and gasping.

His hand went limp and the blade clattered to the ground. Face white and lips gray, he whispered to Mortu, close as they were.

"Outlander, may you know someday, what I have given for the city."

Mortu pulled his blade free and the man slipped to the floor.

Nathia wept at the sight of the dying man. Mortu took her in his arms. He held her a moment.

"Whatever is happening here, I don't know, but blood has been spilled. Events will now take their course. We must go." Mortu made for the door, one hand on the blood-soaked hilt, the other grasping Nathia's warm hand, wet with tears.

Nathia took a deep breath. Mortu was right. Things would happen now. There was no more indecision, to leave or to stay, to live in the city or be killed by these men, to keep silent or bare the way of the city to these outlanders. There was only now.

"I must show you something."

Mortu turned to her. "What?"

She took the lead. Out the dome and through the narrow alleys off the wider streets. They ran, ducking clotheslines, peering around corners. Night was falling. Mortu could only presume he was now hunted as Kyrus had been. The darkness was comforting. He saw a familiar shape, the fighting hall.

"A moment." Mortu ducked inside. With a satisfied grin he found an axe similar in dimension to his own. He slung a buckler on his back and turned to Nathia. "Have you any skill with weapons?"

"Only the bow."

"Arm yourself, then."

She did as he bade and the pair stole back out into the night. It was the time the desert sky was banded in blue and indigo, before the stars came fully. They ran from shadow to shadow. Mortu pulled her close against the wall as a group of men jogged past. Nearly forty men, armed. Tomas lead them, grave look on his handsome face. Mortu waited a long moment until they had turned down another street. Then they were off again. The barbarian realized the plaza lay nearby. He stopped, pulling Nathia close.

"Kyrus waits for us in a copse of ferns. Can you fetch him? Put up your hood and walk slowly, no one will notice."

Nathia nodded. She took a deep breath. Mortu thought perhaps it was a bad idea. But after a moment the young woman was completely composed. She strode out of the alley with the casual, untroubled air of the city's residents. A few couples lounged in the plaza, lazily munching on the last of their supper. None paid the girl any mind.

She sat on the edge of the planter.

"Kyrus?"

The ferns rustled. "Nathia, is that you?"

"Yes. Mortu awaits us in a nearby alley."

"Excellent. Have you some sort of basket?"

"No."

The monk sighed. "How am I to be reunited with you two?"

Nathia thought a moment. "Slip under my robe. Grab the inside of my thigh and I will simply walk away."

"Young lady, that suggestion is highly inappropriate."

"Have you any better idea?"

"Not as such, no."

"No one watches us. Do it now."

With a sigh of resignation, Kyrus enacted her plan. She walked as naturally as she could with her passenger. She fought the urge to scan around her constantly. Finally she rounded the corner where Mortu waited. His face showed disappointment until Kyrus came sputtering out from under her robe. The barbarian laughed.

"You vanish for several hours and you lose all sense of decorum."

"Oh shut up, you great oaf." The monk composed himself with a dignity at odds with his tiny body and clambered up to Mortu's shoulder. Nathia motioned them both to follow.

Soon a great shadow loomed overhead. Mortu realized they had worked their way to the main tower at the plaza's northern end. Only they approached from the back.

Nathia pointed to a door. Inside was unlike anything Mortu had seen in the city thus far. The passage was lined with odd channels and bulging pipes, organic in nature. The material was nearly translucent, stretched thin over a bonelike latticework. Mortu reached out to touch the strange walls.

They were warm. His hand recoiled.

"Flesh."

Nathia nodded. "Of a kind. The city lives. We near the heart."

Down an uneven staircase they went. The air became hot and close. Another set of doors opened to a chamber with a high, rounded ceiling. Cables, more like veins or arteries, tumbled down from the ceiling. They were banded by the strange bone material and a soft glow came from in between its lengths. Kyrus stared.

"The light pulses."

Nathia nodded. All the cables led to an object in the center of the room. The three walked across a floor decorated with elaborate Illilissy runes. The floor hummed underneath their feet.

The object was a sarcophagus of sorts, festooned with the strange cables and wires.

Nathia wept quietly, though there was a cold anger in her eyes.

She said, "Here is the heart of the city, the source of its magic."

The three looked at each other. Though fear grew in his heart Mortu reached out. He grasped the lid and flung it open.

Within lay a child, a young boy. The interior had grown around him, nearly obscuring most of his small body. From a dozen places the strange cables were attached.

Kyrus crossed himself. He hopped down to the edge and looked to Nathia.

"The child lives."

Nathia shook her head. "No. Soul and body are one with the machine." She struggled to speak the next. "It is said to be agony. His soul will feed the machine until it is rendered into nothingness. When it is finally gone…"

Kyrus continued, "A new child is installed."

Nathia nodded. "As you saw, orphans are brought from Zantyum. In twos and threes, in case something goes wrong during the internment. That is how I came to be here."

Kyrus spoke with difficulty, questions coming too fast. He managed one, simply, "Why?"

Nathia shook her head again. "You don't understand."

Mortu looked to her, comprehension suddenly written on his stern face. "You are immortal. That is what the city grants. By means of these infernal machines," he gestured to the sarcophagus, "the Illilissy were immortal. And now so are those that live here."

"Leguna discovered this in her research. She founded the city, as we know it, some five hundred years ago."

Kyrus gasped in amazement. Words failed him again as he studied the boy. He laid a tiny hand on the ashen cheek.

He said finally, "How many children have been in this machine?"

"I could not say, nor even guess." She looked to the boy. "It might have been me. But for some reason, they deemed him more suitable. There was a ritual. The whole city took part. We surrounded the tower, each of us a candle in our hand. I was only a child. When I saw him thus, I knew, somehow I knew, he was in torment. Over the years the truth was made known to me. Everyone in the city knows. As an orphan I knew injustice and deprivation. Yet this… this." She trailed off. A step brought her closer. She touched the boy's forehead. "His name is Athal. He was kind to me during the journey, so many years ago."

Mortu reached into the sarcophagus. He tore the cables away. Arcs of energy lashed, then sputtered and died. The room seemed to shudder as the boy was lifted from his tomb.

The barbarian said aloud in wonder, "Light as a feather."

Free of the sarcophagus the boy was revealed to be not much more than skin and bones. Mortu knelt and cradled the child as Nathia and Kyrus came close. The boy stirred. With difficulty he opened his eyes.

"Nathia."

"Yes, Athal, I am here. Everything is fine."

"I have had a bad dream."

She stroked his face. "Please forgive me for not waking you sooner. It is over now. You may rest and be at peace. "

The boy smiled, ever so slightly. He closed his eyes again and was gone.

The three knelt a while. Kyrus whispered prayers over the boy's body. When he finished he looked at Mortu.

"What shall we do?"

Nathia spoke. "We must find the new children lest they wind up here."

Mortu laid the body down gently and stood. He took up his axe and made for the stairs. Kyrus tugged at his hand.

"Where are you going?"

"I am going to kill everyone."

The two hurried after him. Nathia held his arm but he could not be stopped.

Kyrus hopped onto Mortu's shoulder. "Mortu! We find the children and slip out of the city. We will carry word to Zantyum and they shall send an expedition."

Mortu scowled. Kyrus continued his argument. "Wanton slaughter is not the way! These people must face justice!"

"Justice is what I mean to dispense."

"Justice does not come from a blade's edge!"

"It most certainly does."

He turned to Nathia as he plucked Kyrus from his shoulder. He pushed the furry mass into her arms and said, "Is the elevator off the plaza the only way down?"

"No, there is a passage that leads to the surface at southern tip of the city."

"Where is my steed?"

Nathia thought it would still be with the carts in a shelter south of the elevator. Mortu told her to find the children and make for the passage. At the top of the stairs, he took in a great lungful of the night air and smiled at Kyrus.

"You may talk of cities and justice all you wish. Tonight, the pagan wins. My anger will be sated and these wicked people brought to ruin."

"There are too many, my big friend. You will be struck down."

Mortu shrugged and set off towards the plaza. Figures approached. The armed men were already on their way to meet him, fearing the worst, that the outlanders had interrupted the machine that bestowed immortality. Weapons drawn, they came at him, meeting him in the center of the plaza. He took the buckler from his back and gave the axe a twirl to test its balance. Then he ran towards his foes.

His war cry echoed from the tall towers and narrow alleys as he began his bloody work. The men of the city were skilled fighters. They practiced in their gymnasium and honed their skills and bodies to a high level. But they were not soldiers and never thought to act in concert. They met Mortu in ones or twos and so they fell. The barbarian laid a dozen low. The piled bodies, the wounded wailing in the agony of imminent death as they bled out on the white stone, this spectacle caused the others to waver. Soon Mortu was surrounded by a loose ring of men who retreated at his approach only to advance on his flanks. The northerner, muscles taut, hair wild in the night wind, seemed more beast than man to them. He spun to meet whoever advanced and they fell back again.

"Will no more of you test my steel? Who will risk what foul sorcery has bequeathed?" Mortu yelled, face contorted in rage. He spat on the ground.

The noise of mortal combat had drawn all the citizens to the plaza. In a larger ring beyond they watched, mouths agape.

A figure stepped forward to meet Mortu. He was lean and carried himself with a grace born of great strength and experience, a trained fighter par excellence. He bore a buckler and a long, thin-bladed sword.

"This is all very regrettable, Mortu."

"Tomas."

The man looked at the corpses that lay sprawled in the plaza. Grief pulled at his handsome face.

"I have known some of these men for five hundred years. You have no idea what you've done."

Mortu scowled. "They have lived too long. So have you. I know what it has cost."

Tomas nodded. "It is horrible, indeed. But what we have gained! We live as gods here! I cannot let you threaten it."

"Come then, try my steel and I will send you to hell where you belong. The gods of my people look down upon those that prey on the weak. There is no honor in it. There is no honor in you. I will enjoy killing you."

Tomas laughed. "I bested you once. I treated you as a guest and thought to go easy on you. Not this time."

In a flash Tomas closed the gap between them, springing forward like a bolt shot from a crossbow. Mortu reeled. His buckler angled to parry the sword but Tomas' shield came up instead, bashing Mortu across his temple. Stars exploded in his vision. Instinct took over and he tumbled forward. The thrust meant to skewer him struck a glancing blow instead. Before he could regain his balance another thrust came, then another. Mortu danced out of the way of each. Tomas grinned as he advanced. Mortu sidled across the plaza, putting a tree in between him and his foe, a moment to breathe.

Tomas slashed the air with his blade as he circled.

"I have not had such good sport in five hundred years." He feinted left then lunged right. Mortu parried with the buckler and swung his axe out in fury. Tomas ducked and slashed. The blade raked across Mortu's neck but the barbarian's speed saved it from being a mortal wound. Tomas spun and slashed again, leaping in the air this time. Before the blow could connect, Mortu lunged forward with a mighty kick that sent Tomas tumbling backwards. Tomas shot to his feet and stepped forward. Then he paused a moment, seized by a sudden fit of coughing.

Mortu watched in fascination. Tomas cleared his throat. When their eyes met Mortu saw new fear. And there was something else. The hair at Tomas' temple had gone gray again. Tomas composed himself and advanced again.

The strike was more restrained. Mortu parried with ease and aimed his axe down. Tomas sidestepped backwards but no counter came.

Mortu asked, "Are you feeling a little less spry now that the infernal engine is stopped?"

Tomas replied with a flurry of strikes. Mortu parried with buckler and axe blade. The two became locked together, arms intertwined. Mortu was stronger but Tomas knew how to use his weight. The strain was written across his face as Mortu smiled down at him and spoke. "The souls of the children cry out for vengeance."

"You and your friend will die. You should not have come. You could have simply walked away."

They pushed each other apart.

Mortu scowled as he stalked in a circle. "It is better to die than live out your years knowing you did nothing when confronted with such evil."

It was Tomas' turn to scowl. "Evil? Look at all the good the sacrifice brings us. Immortal life. Food and energy, all we could ever need. You traveled from Zantyum. Look at the evil there as people starve, waste away from disease, or die in the arena."

Mortu nodded. "No clever words will change what you have done or make it right."

He raised the axe above his head and lunged, letting loose a horrible war cry. He struck with all the barbarian fury for which his people were known. Muscles straining, sweat gleaming in the odd light of the plaza, hair wild. Tomas unleashed a vicious counter that would skewer the barbarian. But the northerner had thrown himself sideways. He let the axe slip from his grasp and reached to grapple the smaller man.

Before Tomas could react the two lay on the ground. Mortu's thick arm was around Tomas' neck, the other locked around his torso. The barbarian used all of his great strength. Tomas thought to scream but no air would come. He felt the grind of bone and the snap as his neck was broken.

Mortu stood, panting in the night air. The plaza was silent. The people of the city stood frozen, faces pale with shock. A woman's voice, melodic and sensual, broke the silence. Leguna stood on the stairs before the north tower. At her side were the children.

"Mortu, what have you done?"

Mortu walked toward the tower. "I'm taking the children. No longer will any suffer in the alien machine. Your time is up."

"You could have ruled at my side. You could have lived forever."

"If you knew how to live you would not fear dying."

Mortu took sudden notice of the bow in Leguna's hand. She drew an arrow from a quiver at her hip. The barbarian growled in desperate anger. Even if he sprinted from the center of the plaza Leguna would get off two, perhaps three shots. The fact that she had the children was most troubling. Kyrus and Nathia had failed. Perhaps they were slain. Mortu screamed as he ran. Leguna took aim.

The arrow sunk into his leg just above the knee. He stumbled, though in his rage he felt no pain. The steps loomed close as the next arrow grazed his hip. He lurched forward and stumbled again. Mortu reared back and hurled his axe with all his might. The weapon shattered the great white doors behind Leguna. She stood back up. Her eyes were sad as she pulled back on the string.

Mortu's anger faded away in that pregnant moment. He had done all he could. He would meet his father in death's hall with his head held high.

There was a blur of motion, a flash of white. Leguna's arrow fell from her grasp and the bow clattered on the ground. An arrow had buried itself at the point where neck and chest meet. Her hand grasped it feebly as her eyes went wide with incomprehension. She leaned against the white stone of the doorway's delicate arch and slipped to the ground. Leguna mouthed words but no sound came before she died.

Mortu turned. Nathia stood with her bow a moment then ran past him and up the stairs. She wept as she held the terrified children. The barbarian limped to the steps and sat down. He looked to see Kyrus beside him.

The monkey whistled. "Arrow to the knee. That must really hurt."

"Not yet. Make yourself useful and fetch me some wine."

Kyrus' voice became grave. "Mortu, look."

Mortu turned his tired eyes to the plaza. The men and women in white robes had collapsed. Mortu stood wincing and limped after Kyrus. The monk's loping gait took him to one of the citizens. The man lay on the ground, breath labored.

Mortu gasped and took a step back as he understood what he saw. The city people were aging right before his eyes. Turning off the machine had begun a process that accelerated with each moment. After a few more gasping breaths the chest no longer moved. The skin became like stretched parchment, finally splitting to spill dust onto the stones. The form continued to desiccate until nothing but ash remained.

A wind came from the desert. Mortu stood amidst the swirling eddies as the remains of the people of the White City were scattered to rest in the wasteland and beyond.

Kyrus took a tiny handful and tossed it into the air. "Heaven and earth will pass away. But my words will not pass away."

"What was that?"

Kyrus leapt to Mortu's shoulder. "Nothing for your heathen ears."

The barbarian's step faltered as Nathia embraced him. He held her close. Kyrus averted his eyes as the two kissed. Mortu drew back wincing. There was a sharp pain in his wounded leg. The children were holding onto his legs, one apiece.

"All these people and no one can get a wounded man some wine."

They lingered in the city only long enough to treat Mortu's wound and gather food and water. The back passage that Nathia showed them was a long tunnel that wound its way down the plateau. Mortu rode his steed gingerly with his wounded leg. Nathia sat behind him, arms wrapped around his waist, while the two children sat in front. The tunnel wound on and on until finally a void ahead signaled the end. Below the steed's wheels was hard packed ground while above the desert sky shown with countless stars.

Kyrus watched the towers recede as Mortu rode for the highway. To their left the horizon began to glow. The barbarian let loose an oath.

Ahead on the highway, a party of nomads waited. Kyrus yanked on a lock of his hair and pointed.

"I see them!" he shouted above the din.

Mortu's mind was wracked with calculation. He was not fit to fight but he had fought with worse wounds. But there were too many, about two dozen that he could see. Flight was likely to fail. The nomads' steeds were light and fast and he carried extra burdens.

His heart began to burn. To have succeeded atop the city only to be slain by nomads, it was enraging.

He opened the throttle. Nathia squeezed him tighter. The steed neared the highway. Mortu leaned forward, an unconscious act as he tried to wring every last bit of speed from the iron horse. He turned east and the nomads followed.

They soon overtook him. Mortu reached for the axe at his side. A flutter of white caught his eye. One of the nomads held a white cloth. He pointed to the side of the road.

Kyrus shouted. "They seek a bloodless victory!"

"Monk, look at him, look at his clothing!"

Kyrus squinted in the wind. The nomad wore a tabard emblazoned with the cross.

He yanked on the barbarian's hair again. "The fallen knight?"

"I am not so sure but it is time to find out."

He slowed, bringing the steed to halt just off the road. The nomads did likewise. The man who wore the cross dismounted and approached with hands raised.

"Explain yourself! You fought with the wicked people of the city and now you ride with their children. You gave me quite a knock on the head."

"The wicked people are no more. They are dust in the wind and these children are spared."

The man's grizzled face broke out in a wide grin. "God be praised. I am a penitent, sent to minister to the nomads. When they told me of the city and its evil I was resolved to destroy it."

Kyrus stood and leaned an elbow on Mortu's head. "Well, sir knight, I hope you will forgive us for taking the liberty."

The man laughed. "Come, rest at our camp."

They took a winding track through the heart of the wasteland. The oasis was nestled in a rocky ravine, a miniature Eden cradled by walls of jagged rock. The nomads' carts ringed a small pond and several date palms. The group was feted like heroes. The knight, who identified himself as Gunlar, beamed with pride as he described how the tribe had accepted Christ and how they were making inroads with neighboring tribes. Kyrus did his best to hide how impressed he was.

In the days while Mortu's wound knit, he lounged on the grass by the pond, Nathia with him. The two talked of past and future. Neither had a home proper. Mortu had the road and Kyrus' quest, and she had less, only memories of the White City and the two orphans which she was determined to protect. Love blossomed between them. She did not begrudge him Kyrus' quest but bade him swear an oath to return.

Kyrus was apologetic. "Perhaps life in this body would be acceptable."

"No, my little friend. Oaths were sworn. We shall continue east and find the sorcery to change you back. Then we will return."

Kyrus looked around. "I wonder. These nomads are energetic, and in civilizational terms, very young. The tribes may unify under the cross.

Gunlar teaches them writing, organization. Perhaps one day they will emerge from the wastes and replace the rot in Zantyum."

Mortu shook his head. "You either speak nonsense, or speak of things that have nothing to do with anything."

"The ceiling of your intellect is so low, even I have to duck. Mark my words! We shall return here one day. They will need strong fighters such as you when they head out to return the world to righteousness! Perhaps by then you will have seen the light and abandoned your heathen gods."

Mortu shrugged. "Unlikely." He made fast their belongings on the steed. Under the shade of a date palm he kissed Nathia and held her and shared private words. Then Mortu mounted his steed and Kyrus hopped to his shoulder. He kicked it to life and pointed it down the track that led to the highway. He glanced back once to see Nathia and the orphans waving goodbye.

On the highway, he opened up the throttle as far as it could go. Kyrus reeled back. The barbarian sat forward in the saddle, feeling the wind rush by.

He needed haste.

The Star-God's Grave

The shrill wail of the alarm bird echoed within the damp confines of the barrack's stone walls. Tunkal was up first, having had a restless night. Across the cold floor he shuffled, wincing and cursing. Reaching into a niche underneath the creature's small alcove, the young man removed a vial from its velvet case and loaded an eye dropper with the nectar contained therein. The bird ceased its caterwauling only when the dropper was raised to its beak. After it had drunk its fill, the creature cooed appreciatively. Tunkal gave its red feathers a pat and returned to his bunk to prepare for the day.

Like those of the other apprentices, his worldly belongings were stored in a wooden chest at the foot of his cot. From it he drew his robes, maroon trimmed in black. He laid them on his bunk and smoothed the thick fabric, wary of wrinkles and ever irritated at the faint scent of cedar which clung to the garment.

The apprentices took their turns standing under the fount of cold water in the washroom. Tunkal stood for a moment under the torrent and then stepped aside to wash. The soap was caustic and unpleasant—all he could afford on his meager allowance. Next to him, Dallis whistled as he washed with a bar infused with lavender, a part of his monthly care package. Properly scrubbed, the apprentices took turns rinsing in the chill flow.

The company was unusually silent, so Dallis attempted levity with a tug at Tunkal's necklace. The youth clutched at the leather thong around his thin neck, and all who watched did the same—a reflex.

Dallis affected the gait of an elderly man and spoke in a rasping soprano. "Grim Tunkal! You must be vigilant! A wizard without his crystals is merely a literate man, defenseless against the perils of a hostile galaxy, at the mercy of any cretin bearing a sharpened stick!"

The imitation of their master brought laughter finally to the company. Dallis's grin contrasted with Tunkal's frown, ever-present on his dour face, high cheekbones underneath sunken eyes, hair thinning though only nineteen solar years of age.

Dallis laid a hand on his bony shoulder. "Just a bit of fun, Tunkal, I meant no harm. And just so you know, if today you are selected for promotion, I will be the first to congratulate you. You have mastered four crystals. You are punctual and hard working. You deserve it."

Tunkal managed a smile even as he shook his head. "I don't know. I have been passed over twice."

A commotion at the window ended the conversation. The younger apprentices stood on tiptoes to see as the company crowded around.

"Gorgeous!" exclaimed Munj, a youth remarkable for remaining portly though he ate the same diet as his fellow apprentices.

The yacht floated past, a vessel grown with great skill from prize bixbite. The vessel's simplicity described the minimalist elegance currently in vogue among wizards and members of the aristocracy that deigned to care about such things as space travel. Its four sides tapered gradually to a sharp point, a pyramid laid on its side. No doors or windows ruined its smooth planes, faintly shimmering in the weak light of Tau Ceti.

Tunkal joined the throng marveling at the vessel's simple beauty. "It must have taken years to grow."

Dallis smiled. "Four years, in fact."

"How do you know?"

"My father had it made. It is a gift for our master."

Tunkal's frown deepened.

The ceremony to raise Dallis to the level of Apprentice 1st Order was a simple one. The master bade Dallis step forward and intoned on the solemn nature of the position and Dallis's eminent suitability. Then he added a crystal to the young man's necklace—a square of white quartz, a stone imbued with energies related to various endeavors: the finding of missing objects, the making of furniture, and the creation of explosive force.

The event was a mix of joy and lingering sadness, as the former Apprentice 1st Order had only been dead for three days.

After the ceremony, the master pulled Tunkal aside. The young man kept his head bowed appropriately though his fists were clenched within the long sleeves of his robe.

"You are a good student, Tunkal. Were your connections better, I would imagine you would be going far in this world. As an orphan you naturally lack any backing—not in the Order and certainly not at court. So you must adjust your expectations to reality. It is a difficult thing for young men to do. But the alternative is worse. I remember my tutor, Galzimontok. In his one-hundred-and-seventies, he went through a phase studying the effects of various crystals upon dormant genes. He had the goal of assembling a menagerie of dangerous creatures in order to impress the Duchess Caroline Impinga, a woman whose beauty was only equaled by her love of the macabre. For use as base stock, he ensnared a wolf on a world orbiting far Cancri. The poor creature fought against its collar with such persistence that a wound opened, eventually killing the wretched beast." The wizard fixed his small eyes onto his pupil. "Do not be like that wolf, young Tunkal."

His reminiscing continued. "In the end, Galzimontok won her over by constructing a bedchamber nestled within a rhombus of clear glass. The vessel was lowered into a large tank full of aquatic predators. The pair made love amidst the cloudy red spectacle of the beasts feeding upon convicted murderers." The master shook his head at the memory.

"The whole thing was in such horrible taste that I resolved to poison the old man at the first opportunity after the completion of my studies."

Tunkal stared at his master. The old man smiled down for a moment then cocked his head.

"What were we talking about, my boy?"

"You were telling me not to chafe against the bonds fate has imposed."

"Ah yes, platinum advice." The wizard stroked his beard as he eyed the young man. He continued, "I find myself wishing to reward your patience. Shall I tutor you in an additional discipline? Perhaps one above your grade? We don't have to tell the board. It will be our secret. What do you say?"

"Thank you, master. I wish to study post-formation reds, with an emphasis on telekinetics."

"Excellent. It is, in fact, not a challenging field, however practical. The only reason lower grades aren't instructed in that discipline is to keep young apprentices from the temptation of stealing a ship and flying willy-nilly across the galaxy. The course will last a month. See me in the west laboratory tomorrow and we will begin."

"Thank you, master."

Tunkal applied himself to the discipline with single-minded zeal, earning praise from the master. After a month, he could manipulate red crystals with ease, sending them through space at will.

The following evening he stole the yacht.

His fingers worked the control crystals with nervous enthusiasm, setting the vessel on a course for the galaxy's rim. The asteroid upon which sat the wizard's jutting towers receded in the distance as the pyramid of red crystal gained speed. Tunkal dropped a shard of aquamarine into a slot, and the ship was swallowed by a burst of brilliance, a rainbow of swirling colors emanating from the sharp point of the ship's bow. The ship was now freed of its bonds to the material universe, hurtling through null space at incomprehensible speeds. The course was set, and the former apprentice could relax the mental discipline needed to steer the vessel.

Tunkal leaned back in the hard chair and inspected Dallis's square of quartz, stolen from his necklace in the dead of night. He fed himself with a parcel of sweets taken from the fair youth's care package and pondered his situation.

Desperation and impetuousness had conspired to make him an outlaw. He would journey outside the space governed by the Empire and make his fortune in the lawless lands beyond. His young heart was a frothing cauldron of competing emotions—fear, excitement, and a determination unchecked by experience or common sense. Despite himself, he nodded off at the controls and slept a dreamless sleep.

Jun Tette was a stocky man with poor posture, careworn from years plying the spaceways in his freighter, *Regret.* With narrowed eyes, he regarded the pair addressing him across the table. To his left was a hulking red-haired man. Half a dozen weapons hung from his belt and cross-belts, the accouterment of life outside the Empress's law. To his right was a thin man, athletic and graceful, bearing faint traces of the Eld in his fine features. A shiny blond braid hung down his back.

The thin man continued, "It isn't that far into Lord Molker's space, my dear Jun. A simple taxi ride is all we need, in and out. When would you ever get such an offer? A few weeks' transit, a dip down to the surface, perhaps a refreshing nap as me and Thuf retrieve an object, then away back into the void and voilà! We are prepared to offer twenty percent! This artifact we seek, well, I don't wish to say too much, but it is the stuff of legend! The take is such that you may even retire! Think, my good man! You can finally rest! Those horrible bags under your eyes, your unhealthy pallor, the unsightly bulge at your waist atop those thin legs, atrophied from a life sitting in the pilot's chair, all these will be a thing of the past as you rest at the shores of a green sea, sipping wine and recuperating. A worthy reward for a lifetime plying space!"

Jun spoke through clenched teeth: "Two things. Firstly, Lord Molker's space is vast and uncharted. Legend populates it with a thousand savage worlds hosting all manner of creatures cast from nightmare. Any voyage into his space is suicide. Secondly, my legs are perfectly proportionate to my body. Good day, sirs."

The freighter captain left the bar on heavy steps, slamming the door behind him.

The warrior Thuf sighed. "The good captain is an umbrageous man. Perhaps in the future you might avoid insulting prospective partners."

"I am sure I don't know what you are talking about."

The two sipped their ale from oversized clay mugs. Near the hearth, an Ixxinni placed a decaphone to his spiracles and blew a mournful tune. The notes drifted through the smoky interior as a few gave their voice to the song. The lyrics described a common tragedy, a woman waiting in vain for the return of a spacefaring lover who had lost his life. Thuf was at the verge of growing maudlin when a patron shouted for something more cheerful. The Ixxinni made a clicking sound in irritation.

The hulking fighter leaned back in his chair and spoke.

"Mouve, my dear friend, let us take stock of the situation. In the last two weeks, we have spoken with no less than fifteen pilots. None are willing to go into Molker's space. I think the project must be abandoned. Perhaps it is for the best. Just the two of us robbing the grave of a star-god, deep within the Dark Lord's realm? Jun was right. It is suicide."

The muscles at Mouve's jaw twitched. "I shall not give it up! Since released from the Empress's service we've had barely more than a crust between us. We drink here on credit. And only this face of mine, these chiseled good looks, have thus far saved us from starvation. We need this! The two of us are the last that's left of the battalion. To see so many of our friends dead so that we may become indigent? We owe their memories better!"

"Well, it wasn't my idea to pool our severance and bet on the dogs."

Mouve affected a wounded look. "It was a sure thing! I had it on oath from Monetti!"

"Which head?"

"The left one."

Thuf sighed. "And there was the problem. The left one is a notorious liar."

"He assured me he always told the truth and the other one was the liar."

Thuf's scarred hands clenched into fists, and he breathed deep. He opened his mouth to speak but abandoned the effort at the last moment, shaking his head.

Mouve made an impatient gesture and stood, making for the back of the bar. A moment later he stood in the humid gloom of the filthy bathroom, admiring his fine features in a cracked mirror.

A shape hovered behind, a man in robes. An arm reached up.

Mouve spun, knocking the arm aside as he drew a dagger and lunged forward. His free hand grasped his assailant's neck as the blade stood poised to strike.

Before him stood a gangly youth of dour mien, now gasping for air and pleading for mercy. His hands were raised in supplication. Mouve relaxed his grip.

"What do you mean by sneaking up on me like that?"

"Nothing, sir! I apologize. I am new here. I only wished to inquire where pilots may secure work. I asked outside but no one would answer."

Mouve smiled as he sheathed his dagger.

"Well, friend. It is a good thing we met. Here on Made's World, many people follow a very elastic moral code. Someone might have attempted to take advantage of you. But now you are under the protection of Mouve Llansal! Come sit with me and my friend and I will let you in on a very exciting opportunity."

After introductions, the three sat huddled around the table. In desperation, Mouve made a snap decision to tell the young man everything. Perhaps his vagueness had been off-putting during his many failed attempts to recruit a pilot.

"So a few weeks ago I found myself enjoying a tryst with the Lady Ulgoun Kagginov. Do you know of her?"

Tunkal shook his head no.

"She is a regular at court and a woman of robust health and large appetites. Her generosity is famous among young, handsome officers of limited means. She typically favors the company of hussars; no further proof of her good taste is necessary. Her husband is Admiral of the Imperial Fleet Amos Zaster. He is an imposing figure but apparently unable or simply uninterested in the demanding task of dousing the roaring fires of his wife's ample passions. It was a marriage of political purpose from what I understand."

The young man's eyes lit up. "I know of him! His fleet is the finest in the universe, supervised by the Wizard Kalimsis, an expert in conglomerates, blues, and spontaneous formations. I have read some of his works."

Mouve looked to Thuf. "See there? Our young friend is an expert, a widely read wizard!"

"Apprentice, technically."

"Now, now, Tunkal. We are at the limit of the Empire and its boards. Here you are a wizard by virtue of mastery of crystals, not because some group of old men bestows you a diploma. It is liberating, is it not? Where was I?"

The warrior said, "Lady Ulgoun Kagginov."

"Ah yes. Insatiable! So there we were in her private suite. I was at the bar refreshing myself, replacing lost fluids after a strenuous few hours. The Lady lounged on the bed, talkative as ever. While the imps daubed sweat from her brow, she began to spin a tale concerning a dear friend, one Leftenant Willy Werman of our Imperial Highness's Navy. Poor Willy had recently gone missing. His ship had gone off course, finding itself deep in Lord Molker's realm. The green officer had landed on some Godforsaken world of purple sky and windswept dunes and has not been heard from since. But in his last communiqué, Willy claimed to have found the corpse of a star-god!"

Tunkal's eyes widened. "It has been centuries since one has been found. Was the soul crystal intact?"

Mouve shook his head. "We don't know. No one knows. Dear Willy said nothing of venturing within. He said very little at all except professions of undying love and pleas for help. Rather naïve, really. It is not as if the Lady would ask the Admiral for assistance in such an indelicate matter. From what I gather, Willy was not the brightest star in the sky. The letter's composition was abominable. As a boy, I was penning better metaphors to the nun that taught multiplication at gymnasium. That woman stole my innocence, God bless her. I think I first caught her eye during an athletic event. We were running—"

Thuf coughed. "Mouve, please. The matter at hand…"

"Ah, yes. Well, you have the gist of it, my friend. We have the report of the location of the remains of a star-god. We will fly there and retrieve the soul crystal. We need a fast ship and a skilled pilot." Mouve fixed the young apprentice with a confident stare and continued, "I think you are our man."

Tunkal nodded his head. "Yes, thank you!"

Thuf raised both his hands, a habitual gesture that meant he believed he had something important to say. The warrior's icy blue eyes narrowed as his brow furrowed menacingly. "Boy, are you ready to face danger? Death? Do you see this, boy?"

Tunkal's eyes traced the pale scar that slid down the length of the burly warrior's face. He nodded yes.

"It's from my arena days, long before I entered Her Highness's service. Daily, my soul felt the brush of chill fingers. Death and I are old friends."

The apprentice grew pale, though his face betrayed no emotion.

Mouve admonished his friend. "Brother Thuf! Let's not put a fear in this young man. Our errand won't be so dire."

Thuf scoffed, "What about the aforementioned creatures of nightmare?"

"Oh, I expect nothing more than some exotic local fauna. At the worst, perhaps an emaciated phung or a ghaut made irritable by lack of sleep."

"Hmmpf. Well then, young man, are you interested?"

Tunkal nodded. The three swore oaths, and the compact was sealed. Tunkal would ferry them to the location whereupon the trio would venture into the ancient fastness of the star-god's remains. The young apprentice would provide whatever support he could with his ill-understood magicks while the two veterans would meet foes head-on with saber and pistol. The pair made a great show of their generosity, granting the young apprentice an entire seven percent of the take.

On the dusty field outside Made's Tavern, the two ex-soldiers found themselves speechless. The yacht before them gleamed in the afternoon light of G678.09002, known locally as Mina's Star. Mouve ran his hands along its flawless exterior, starting at its sharp point, caressing its lines until they rose beyond his reach.

"Mother of God. If I had known this was in your possession, I would have simply robbed you, young Tunkal."

The young man wore an expression of alarm.

The lithe fighter continued. "Not to worry now, young wizard. Oaths have been sworn."

Thuf grunted, "Your comment was poorly thought out. We could not pilot this craft even if it did come into our possession."

"Yes, of course not."

The vessel's clean lines concealed a cramped interior. Tunkal sat in the pilot's chamber, accessible to the cabin by an opening so small as to necessitate walking on all fours. Within the cabin, Mouve and Thuf made themselves as comfortable as possible. A sofa of utilitarian design sat atop a floor of hardwood panels. One cabinet sat taking up space in the corner opposite the door which opened only on Tunkal's mental command. A small door behind and to the left of the sofa led to the head. Their equipment and sparse luggage were stowed under and around the sofa. Mouve expressed anxiety as the apprentice entered the cabin, stooping to inspect the cabinet.

"On larger vessels there is typically an airlock. It gives one a sense of safety."

Tunkal replied, "Once sealed the cabin can only be opened by a specific sequence enacted by myself. There is no danger of a breach or accident which would expose pilot or passengers to the void. As a matter of fact, larger vessels are much more prone to leaks and failures."

Mouve scratched his smooth chin. "A hypothetical situation; what if while underway you were struck down by an undiagnosed heart ailment? Neither myself nor gentle Thuf have the slightest knowledge of crystal theory. The regiments are ferried around the galaxy on vast ships with numberless crew, thus there was no need to concern ourselves with the vessel's operation."

Tunkal smiled. "I suppose, in that case, the vessel becomes your tomb. Oxygen will hold out as long as the recombiners in the cabinet are functioning, another few years, perhaps, based on their age. The dials can be set to dispense a nutritional paste, thus avoiding starvation. Removing a particular crystal at the helm will drop the vessel from null space. There is a chance you might materialize within a star or asteroid. But even if you re-enter reality safely, you will not be able to guide the vessel to harbor."

Mouve ran his hands over the smooth walls, testing. He said, "I suppose we would eventually go mad."

"This is typical." Tunkal suddenly let loose a wracking cough, clutching his chest as he did so, free hand steadying him against the red wall. The fair man regarded the scene with eyes wide with creeping fear.

The apprentice smiled, suddenly back in perfect health.

Mouve punched Thuf on the arm. "Did you see that? He makes sport of my well-founded anxieties!"

The warrior was unconcerned. "Have we left yet? There is no window."

Tunkal replied they would leave shortly. He wriggled his way into the pilot's area and began manipulating the crystal controls. Mouve related the last known position of Willy Werman as the ship rose from the dusty ground. A bass hum throbbed through the hard material. The sharp point of the vessel turned skyward, and the red pyramid left the thin atmosphere of Made's World. Tunkal grimaced with the mental exertion of steering the ship as it fought against gravity. In the cabin, Mouve and Thuf fought over possession of the sofa.

Tunkal shouted back.

"A vessel such as this is controlled by a complicated mental discipline, arranged and organized by this panel before me. A tranquil environment makes my work all the more easy."

The two ex-soldiers made themselves comfortable without further disturbance.

The journey took three weeks. Thuf and Mouve played cards incessantly, only breaking to sleep or occasionally read. The hulking warrior thumbed through a well-worn anthology of verse while his lean comrade stretched languidly, a dog-eared romantic novel, profusely illustrated, held before him as he mouthed the words, stopping periodically to explain a lurid twist to his fellows. Thuf eventually began to pester Tunkal regarding the techniques by which wizards manipulated and controlled crystals. The young man could expound on the topic at length.

"The first thing to understand is that all matter and energy are in constant motion at specific frequencies. To make maximum use of this fact takes a lifetime of work and study. It begins before puberty when young apprentices undergo a series of procedures to awaken the dormant telekinetic abilities of the pituitary gland. Next, a course of rigorous mental discipline is undertaken which grants nascent wizards the ability to stimulate or modify the frequencies of matter. Crystals, in their natural forms, are the most susceptible to these forces. They may also be grown purposefully to further enhance their capacity for manipulation. The crystals around my neck are typical examples, artificially grown for purity and receptiveness. The potential is limitless. The greatest wizards have been able to raise entire cities from the force of their minds. Though truth be told, the Grand Order, the governing body of wizards, has become ossified of late, falling prey to internal politics and a rigorous conservatism."

Tunkal bent low and craned his neck to view into the cabin. Thuf and Mouve slept soundly amidst a mess of playing cards, weapons, and bandoliers.

Tunkal's announcement that the planet lay below was greeted with throaty cheers from the two ex-soldiers. Thuf managed to cram most of his heavy frame into the pilot chamber to see the planet below, the last known location of Leftenant Willy Werman. Greenish seas between gray polar ice dominated the surface. The sole continent visible from their vantage point stretched wide across the equatorial region, tapering to an archipelago that trailed south into the ice. The landmass was largely desert, fringed by areas of vegetation around the coastal areas. Lying lengthwise along it were the remains of a humanoid form, a thousand miles long. The head was oblong, half submerged in the sands. Ribs jutted from the surface to poke up into the planet's mesosphere. Arms and legs lay largely straight, long hands folded across the empty expanse of the torso.

Thuf's bass voice filled the cramped compartment. "'Look on my works, ye Mighty, and despair!'"

Tunkal was speechless. The heavyset man continued. "He must be dead, now, twenty thousand years. Looks rather peaceful, wouldn't you say?"

Tunkal nodded.

The warrior craned his thick neck to address Mouve. "You simply must see this. He's lying there like my uncle in the drawing room before we put him in the grave."

"I would like nothing more than to see this wonder of the universe if you would simply move your impossible bulk!"

After his hazel eyes had drunk their fill, Mouve discussed strategy with Thuf as they switched places again. The soul crystal was reputed to lie in the base of the skull. The plan was to descend slowly, surveying the area for a place of easy entry. Tunkal brought the yacht down in lazy circles. Thuf's hot breath filled the small compartment as his small eyes strained at the pane of quartz upon which was displayed the world outside.

"There!"

A yawning hole became visible on the southern side of the skull. It was several dozen miles in diameter with jagged edges.

Tunkal cocked his head, brows creased with sudden confusion.

The warrior noticed the young man's expression. "What is it?"

"You don't hear that?" Tunkal's eyes grew glassy. "A song. Very faint. Very beautiful."

"My boy, these ears were present at the Battle of Moleno when the Empress's batteries of star cannons unleashed their fury on the forces of the rebel Hlati. I am lucky I hear anything."

Tunkal seemed not to hear. His face went slack. His hands seemed to lose their dexterity as they worked the controls.

The craft tipped violently, pitching Thuf's bulk forward.

Mouve screamed from the cabin as the descent robbed him of weight. He twisted in the air as he yelled. "What is happening?"

"I think the boy's gone off! His mind is gone!"

"Do something!"

In the awkward press of the chamber, Thuf shook the apprentice violently. But he was beyond reach.

His mind was consumed by a particular sensation, a feeling linked to a particular memory. During rare festival days, Tunkal and his fellow apprentices had been granted short liberty. There was only one place to go, the small port that served the looming tower in which they and their master lived and pursued their craft. Under its silver dome were a few dozen shops and taverns that served the small army of tradesmen, cooks, and laborers that met the tower's needs. The port typically saw a few vessels a week, craft laden with goods headed for outside the empire, explorers, or bounty hunters. One liberty Tunkal worked up the courage to patronize a tavern with a mild reputation, a place laboriously named Saint Nicolas's Home of Brief Respite. There at "Nic's" he spent a portion of his savings on a pint of ale and a slice of sweet bread and jam. The maid, a vivacious young woman whose bright smile and mischievous eyes inspired more than a few apprentices to try their hand at verse, inquired after his maudlin mood. Tunkal's composure collapsed and he murmured a nonsensical reply. From his mumbling, the young woman somehow interpreted that Tunkal had admitted that it was his birthday. By way of a gift, the maid bent and kissed his cheek.

Her scent, the soft touch of her lips, the warmth of her breath, sensations like these flooded his mind. Beneath him yawned the great hole in the skull. Within its blackness nested an abundance of such sensations, of this he was sure.

The ship fell like a stone toward the hole in the star-god's skull.

"Young man!"

Tunkal did not answer. Thuf puffed out his cheeks.

"This gives me no pleasure!"

His big hand cuffed the young man about the ears. Tunkal stiffened in his seat suddenly. He massaged the side of his head and shot a wounded look at Thuf.

"What'd you do that for?"

"Regain control!"

The young man saw the display with a start. His hands shot over the panel's crystals, and the craft jerked to a halt.

Mouve stood, smoothing his braid as he inquired, "What was all that about?"

Tunkal shook his head. "I don't know. I felt a mad urge to drop the vessel into the hole."

Thuf eyed the apprentice. "But you are fully in control now, no?"

"Yes."

"I suggest you put us down."

Mouve wondered aloud, "I wonder that we now know what marooned poor Willy."

Tunkal sniffed and began a slow descent into the skull of the star-god. A stark ray of light from the local sun illuminated the path down. The hole swallowed the ship and the quartz flickered as it adjusted to the darkness. The interior ringing the empty middle revealed itself a riot of bizarre vegetation. Great purple stalks, something between a tree and a vine, twisted upwards in coiling lengths. They wore crowns of maroon leaves around which flitted leathery beasts with four thin wings. They were many gnats in the distance but Tunkal's stomach grew sour as he realized they must be larger than the ship in actuality. As the craft descended broad plateaus of bone fragment stretched across the empty center below, dotted with dunes of sand deposited there by millennia of desert wind.

Thuf remarked, "A desert within the jungle, within the skull, within the desert." He looked to Tunkal and continued, "Get us as close to the center as you can."

The young wizard nodded. He guided the craft towards the base of a small range of jagged white hills, fragments of shattered skull knifing upwards from the dunes.

"Another quarter of an hour at this speed."

The big man slapped the wizard's shoulder.

Mouve shouted from the couch, "Time for one more game!"

He shuffled the cards as Thuf made his way back.

With a long sigh, Tunkal disengaged his mind from the mental posture required to pilot. He massaged his temples for a moment and then concentrated again to open the side door. Thuf and Mouve made to exit at once, tumbling onto the sandy ground with exclamations of relief. The pair stood and stretched, groaning.

"I feel as if my entire musculature has completely atrophied. My joints creak like an old man's."

Thuf nodded in agreement. "I do not relish the thought of our return journey."

"Nor do I."

Tunkal exited the craft and walked the length of the ship, bending to rub his thighs as he did so. To his left stretched the dunes, caps trailing tendrils of sand carried aloft by a warm wind. Hidden by dim haze the shadow of the jungle could be seen beyond. The great shards of bone to their right shot towards the distant sky like great slabs of rock.

After they had stretched all they could, the two ex-soldiers arrayed themselves in the tools of their chosen trade. Thuf slipped his bandoliers over his shaggy head, wide belts of leather festooned with charges for the heavy pistol that hung from his hip. He shoved a tomahawk into his wide belt opposite his saber's ornate scabbard.

Mouve wore coiled line over his lithe torso, clothed in a short jacket of faded navy, decorated with heaps of gold braid. His pistol dangled from a sling, a smaller weapon than his partner's but boasting a stock to improve accuracy. Around his waist were half a dozen pouches. His sabretache hung low against his thigh, sheathed in breeches of leather dyed crimson. Canteens were topped off from the yacht's cabinet and sabers were inspected before Thuf adjudged the party ready to proceed. Tunkal looked to his companions in their panoply and felt suddenly under-dressed in his robes.

Mouve regarded his reflection on the ship's smooth hull as he stood contrapposto.

"Whether in formal dress or arrayed for war, I cut a fine figure. What did the old poets say? 'Weapons are the ornament of man.' Or something to that effect." He turned to smile at his companions, a grin slipping from his face as he regarded Tunkal. He addressed the youth, "My young friend, you look a bit peaked suddenly. Are you ill?"

"No, I am fine."

Thuf's gruff voice expressed concern. "Indeed, he is as pale as a ghost. What troubles the young master?"

Tunkal stared at the ground. "Nothing. It is simply that I suddenly wonder what peril lies within. Seeing you two kitted out so brings a sense of impending danger."

Mouve gestured, a flourish as he spoke, a wave of hand and arm that seemed to encompass the entirety of man's mortal condition. "Whatever will happen will happen. And besides, young man, you travel with two of the greatest soldiers to have ever lived. Gentle Thuf has eased scores of men into the next life, and I have fought a time or two, myself."

The young apprentice nodded, smooth face stern as he marshaled his courage. The fair fighter continued.

"Also know that if you fall, Thuf and I will be marooned. So rest assured, beyond the typical considerations of honor and loyalty, we have a powerful incentive to keep you alive. If you don't make it out, no one will. If such be our fate, then so be it."

Thuf grunted in agreement. He took in the opening with a forlorn glance as he said to no one in particular, "'No one can hurry me down to Hades before my time, but if a man's hour is come, be he brave or be he coward, there is no escape for him when he has once been born.'"

The dunes drank the gruff bass of his voice. No echoes sounded despite the wide expanse.

Tunkal massaged his forehead. "The soul crystal must be as powerful as I have heard. I can already sense it though we must be a fair distance from the base of the skull. We must search where dune and shard meet and find a gap that might lead downwards."

The trio walked along the hill's base only a short while before a gap between two shards presented itself. It was a triangular opening wide enough for two men. Mouve thought it looked like the opening for a primitive tomb. His perfect features became furrowed with concentration as a sense of impending danger gripped him. He displayed a hand signal to Thuf, and the big warrior dropped to one knee, pistol at the ready. Tunkal craned his neck to see, curiosity and fear locked in a bitter battle inside his mind.

Mouve lowered into a crouch and peeked around the edge, straining to pierce the gloom within. The fair hair on his forearms stood straight as the sense of nearing peril became palpable. He shifted back, obeying a sudden impulse.

A shot rang out, shattering the ominous silence.

Mouve let out an oath as he leaned against the bone. Another shot sounded, then another. The rounds impacted in the dunes, tiny explosions of heat and sand.

"Did you see that, Brother Thuf? Blessed Mother Mary gave me a touch of prescience, thus I was able to evade the attacks."

"I think the dark interior of the cave and its ominous aspect were warnings enough."

"I find your skepticism disheartening. Don't hold your breath waiting for intercession on your own behalf."

The silence was deafening after the sharp reports. Thuf cocked his head, squinting in concentration.

"Upon reflection, I do believe those shots were from a standard issue concussive pistol."

"I believe you are correct." Mouve looked past Thuf to regard the young apprentice with an upraised eyebrow. The young man stood facing the skull, robes gathered up around his waist. "Good Lord. Tunkal, what are you doing?"

"Relieving myself. The shots… I suddenly had the need."

A voice rang out from within the skull.

"I hear voices! Who is there? Are you humanoid? Name yourself!"

Mouve's pleasant baritone answered, "Mouve Llansal and Thuf Kowalski, recently of the Empress's Hussars, now independent agents, traveling with Tunkal the Wizard, master of crystals and star-pilot. To whom am I speaking?"

"Leftenant William Werman vom Kühlungsborn, heir to his most Serene Highness Baron Gunthan of Alpha Artu."

The bedraggled young officer sipped greedily at the proffered tea. He scratched his short beard as he spoke, eyeing the dunes constantly as the party stood outside the yacht.

"All I could salvage from my vessel before the sands consumed it was a cabinet and a box of shells. I have been surviving on water and paste this whole time, just waiting for the recombiners to give out. The landing was rough. As we neared the surface the wizard was seized by some paroxysm and attempted to fly the vessel right into a cave mouth up yonder, to the north. I cuffed him hard, and we wound up in the dunes. He broke his neck in the landing, and Boffe, my aide, was lost in the sands. Everything in the cabinet was cracked. It is a miracle it still works. I managed to get one message out before the vocquois shattered." Tears welled in his reddened eyes. "But my darling MuMu has sent help. My love, my lady, she has sent deliverance!"

Thuf addressed Mouve, "Is he referring to that lady with whom you had the tryst?"

Werman's eyes narrowed. Mouve forced a smile as he replied, "I am sure you are confused, dear, dim Thuf."

He next met the lieutenant's eyes. "Indeed, the Lady Ulgoun Kagginov enjoined us to come to your rescue. You are safe and will return home, shortly."

The officer replied, "Thank God." He spared the dunes his glance to let it fall upon Mouve. He continued, "Do tell, how do you know the Lady? I do not recall seeing you at court or at any reception, or ball or recital. Oh, and by the by, it would be proper if you addressed me as 'my lord'."

Mouve filled his cheeks with air then exhaled slowly, eyes fixed on the ground. He was silent a moment before his smile returned and he replied. "Yes! I recall now, my lord. The good Lady inquired of my former Colonel, asking for a few volunteers. She wanted men of good repute but currently unengaged, without responsibility, thus able to handle a delicate matter. Naturally, my Colonel recommended Thuf and I, recently cashiered. The arrangement was handled through intermediaries; I never laid eyes on the good Lady herself, my lord."

The officer regarded Mouve with a haughty expression and spoke, his words accented with the elegant confidence of one raised at court. "I would think not with regards to your relative station."

Mouve's back stiffened. "Here we must disagree, my lord. As a hussar, I was twice mentioned in dispatches for gallantry on the field of battle. And though my father was an artisan, my godfather was a Prince of the House of Ranulf. I would not be out of place at a reception, or at any occasion, as a matter of fact."

Werman finished his tea and handed the cup to Thuf before continuing, "That is very nice. Your father and mother must stroll Ranulf's unpaved roads with their heads held high. Indeed, what you say is true. Sometimes those of wretched birth can find a place at court after meritorious service."

Color rose in Mouve's cheeks. "Yes, indeed. And further, at times the good ladies at court may crave the companionship of men of dynamic disposition, those less bound to tradition. I think at times they long for the sort of primal virility absent in so many of our well-born betters. At least, so I have heard."

"Now that you mention it, I recall my underlings reading popular novels that concern such assignations, among other things. I must confess, I do find the grotesque tastes of the plebian to be morbidly fascinating." The officer's tired eyes took in the lines of the yacht. "But perhaps we should continue this discussion while underway. As you can imagine, I am eager to leave. Night will come in a few hours."

Tunkal asked, "What happens at night?"

The aristocrat gestured upwards, to the ring of purple jungle that grew in jumbled terraces around the edge of the desert. "When the sun sets, the flying things are emboldened to hunt the desert. Without my pistol and the shelter of the shards I would have been supper for them." His knuckles were white as he clutched the pearl handle of his sidearm in its ornate holster.

Mouve said, "Be that as it may, I must ask forbearance from my lord. Since we are here, it suddenly occurs to me that we might explore the skull of this fallen star-god. Does my memory serve me correctly? We might find the soul crystal, no? It is worth a bit of a delay, I should think."

The lieutenant adopted an imperious tone, incongruous with his disheveled appearance. "Now, listen here, you nameless scroungers! My store of patience is completely exhausted. I wish to leave at once. During my stay here I explored the skull briefly and found no crystal. Regardless, we will leave presently."

Thuf sighed. "I also grow impatient. Tunkal, open the door."

A rectangle of empty space appeared in the hull. Thuf stepped forward and grabbed the officer's elbow. "We won't be but a moment, my lord. Just recline on yonder sofa until we return." The once gladiator lifted the officer like he was a small child.

"Unhand me! And you, pilot, get in there and take us aloft!" His shrill cries ceased abruptly as the hull resealed itself at Tunkal's mental command.

Thuf wondered aloud, "Is he secure in there? Can he not just open the door?"

The wizard shook his head no. "He is a naval officer, not a wizard. Naval vessels are constructed in such a way that mundane functions are automated. If aristocrats could directly manipulate crystals, then the natural order of the Estates would be completely upended."

Mouve made a noise of irritation. "While I am happy the sanctity of the social order is sound, this represents an annoying wrinkle in our plans. Whatever happens in the skull, we will tell the young officer that we didn't find anything. I will toss the crystal in a well before I cut that fool in."

Thuf grunted, "Indeed."

Presently the three stood at the opening. Above them the bone wall of the skull shot upwards into a sky tinged purple. Before them was yawning blackness. The former soldiers produced torches, cylinders of brass mesh that contained low-grade growths of cheap lumicite. Tunkal caused the square of quartz at his neck to glow. Once past the thick bone, the entrance opened into a chamber of uneven walls formed by a porous, purplish-white substance, hard and brittle, of unknown provenance.

The young wizard essayed a theory. "This must be the fossilized remains of what served as the brain."

"What explains these passages?"

In every direction passages of different diameter led off into the unknown.

"Vessels for blood?"

Close against the wall of bone sat a cabinet and uniform coat.

"There must be where Werman slept. A far cry from the quarters occupied by young officers of the aristocracy." Mouve kicked an empty ammunition can, disturbing some of the spent brass scattered over the sandy floor. Tunkal took up the ammunition can, dusting it off and checking the lid as Mouve watched him.

The young wizard said, "We'll need this for the crystal. It isn't good to go around holding such an object in your bare hands. If its powers are not exaggerated, then all sorts of things might happen after prolonged exposure."

Mouve sniffed. "Do you mean something like a curing of minor ailments, or perhaps growing an inch or two taller?"

Tunkal shrugged.

Thuf stood before the largest of the openings. "So, we expect to find the crystal near the base of the skull, correct?"

Tunkal peered around the warrior's broadness. He replied, "Yes, if my readings are to be believed. It is difficult to estimate from the ground, but I believe we need to proceed down and to the right, or west, more accurately. If these channels are the remains of a vascular system, then it would seem that we should proceed always to the larger channel, heading for the torso which would bring us through the neck first and thus passing the base of the skull. It is difficult to reckon the scale of this fallen monster. We are fortunate the great hole in the skull enabled us to land so close. With luck this journey will take a few hours. Otherwise, a few days."

Thuf nodded. He looked to Mouve. "Do you concur?"

"Certainly. I didn't really understand it, but I am eager to get moving. The sun sets, and I do not wish to meet whatever gave Willy such a fright. Surely in the labyrinth of the star-god's remains there is less peril."

Thuf snorted.

The trio entered the channel.

Thuf took the lead, stooped low in the narrow tunnels, saber held out against whatever danger waited around the many sinuous bends and dips. The porous walls were uneven, bulging here and there, floor and ceiling the same, so the trio walked without rhythm, picking their way down the gently sloping tunnels. At each branch, Tunkal picked the route most likely to lead to larger passages. His instincts were soon validated as the tunnels became larger and larger. Eventually Thuf could stand at his full height. Presently the trio stood in a passage wide enough so they could stand abreast. Moisture dripped from the ceiling above, pooling at their feet. The liquid was tinged purple and gave off an acrid odor.

The gruff warrior slapped the wizard's back. "You were right. We appear to be heading in the right direction."

Tunkal frowned, shaking his head. "I am not sure."

Mouve wiped his forehead with a handkerchief. "Why not?"

"I do not feel the presence of the crystal."

The ex-hussar's handsome face was tinged with sudden worry. "Have we gone in the wrong direction?"

The young wizard threw up his hands. "I suppose we have. The crystal is supposed to lie at the base of the skull. Our route, as best as I can tell, will take us there. In general, we need to move deeper and to the west. We have been, of this I am sure. But I sense the crystal much less than when we began."

Thuf inquired, "Do you think the officer had it?"

Mouve shouted his anger, voice reverberating within the brittle passage. "Son of a bitch. Leftenant Willy Werman vom Something Something. That ridiculous court creature has the crystal. My God, how could I have been so stupid!"

The big warrior shrugged. "Well, he can't have gone anywhere, so we needn't worry overmuch. He played his little joke on us, and now we will return to the surface, get the crystal from him and be on our way. If he gives us any trouble, we will feed him to the desert."

The trio began the return journey. Tunkal now walked in the lead. Mouve bent to wipe the purplish sludge from his boots as the young wizard proceeded around a bend. There was the sudden sound of running feet, then the world was upended. Mouve picked himself up, extricating himself from the tangle of Tunkal's limbs.

The young wizard sputtered, "Something ahead, it tried to kill me…"

"What is it?"

"Don't know! Humanoid in shape, but hunched, sort of scuttling. Maybe more than one."

Before Mouve could prod for more information Thuf darted around the corner, saber ready and pistol drawn, eyes gleaming. He entered a larger chamber, room for perhaps three abreast. At the other end, glittering eyes shown through the dank dimness, rising like a frothing tide toward him.

"Thuf! Wait!" Mouve swore an oath as he drew his sabre and rushed to catch up with his friend. He turned to Tunkal, "Now would be the time for you to dazzle your new friends with a display of what you learned at that school."

The lithe fighter made it around the bend in time to see Thuf hurling himself at a cluster of creatures brandishing clubs and short axes of roughly-shaped stone. They stood at around five feet with thick trunks sheathed in oily chitin. Their many limbs terminated in broad paddles, the underside of which boasted three digits. Agitated, they made a chittering sound as they rushed to meet Thuf's charge. The hulking ex-gladiator fired his weapon at point blank, the report nearly shattering the ears within the confines of the passage. The lead ball sailed through a pair of foes, impacting with a sickening crack. His saber met those that clambered over their fallen comrades. His heavy arm propelled the blade deep, cleaving from shoulder to groin. He fought in grim silence, a butcher at his work.

But then the big man yelled in frustration. His blade was stuck fast. Enemies crowded around the warrior, a tableau of intermittent light and black shadow as the rays from his crystal torch jerked from foe to foe.

Mouve entered the fray. His blade separated head from shoulder then thrust deep into the back of another. Foes continued to pour in through the passage, surrounding Thuf completely. Clubs battered the big man to the floor as the new arrivals formed a phalanx in the confines of the passage to face Mouve. Artfully he parried again and again, taking whatever chance he could to strike out, less and less as more flint blades came against his steel. He shouted back.

"Tunkal!"

The young wizard stood at the entrance to the chamber with mouth open, expression of shock written across his smooth face. He watched as Mouve danced, parrying, ducking, lashing out whenever he saw an opening. And there deeper in the passage was Thuf. A cut on the head had made his face a mask of bloody rage. He had managed to get back to his feet and now made weapons of his foes, lifting one and hurling it into the mass of its comrades, dashing another against the passage wall, roaring in anger when a stone blade found his back. He loosed the tomahawk from his belt and struck with a viper's speed, swinging the wicked axe in great arcs. He struck in all directions, precision gone now that the only source of light in the cave was Tunkal's glowing crystal.

In the heat of battle his new companions were revealed to be the fell warriors they presented themselves. But the numbers were telling. Any moment now Mouve would slip or make a critical misjudgment, and his foes would swarm over him. Any moment Thuf would drown in a sea of black plate and rough blade.

Time seemed to slow for the young wizard. In odd clarity, he realized that very little of what he had learned was of any application here. Spells of a martial nature were reserved for those of much higher level than he. He fingered the crystals around his neck as his mind raced, leaping from spell to spell. The square of quartz was smooth in his grip. Thuf cried out in pain, again. There was no more time to ponder, action was needed. He would have to trust to his natural talent, working in broad concepts.

The wizard held the crystal as he cleared his mind. A series of mental sequences were enacted in a fraction of a second. He raised his left hand, palm toward the center of the melee, the cluster of insect men between Thuf and Mouve. Tunkal intoned the final sequence. The force of his will vibrated in tune with the crystal in his hand, sending a wave of energy forward, heralded by a great bass throb that hurt the ears and turned the stomach.

The blast knocked them all down. Those foes at the center of the explosion were blown to bits. Pieces of the hard shells were lodged in both ceiling and floor. Those further away were stunned. Thuf stood first, eyes glassy but still enraged. He struck down at those insect men struggling to get to their feet. Mouve was unconscious but so were the foes that had engaged him. Tunkal, now beaming with martial pride, rushed forward to take the heavy saber from Mouve's limp hand. The young wizard hacked clumsily down at the pile of enemies at Mouve's feet, striking those unconscious, dead, or near dead, without discrimination.

Thuf's rage ebbed after the last enemy was still. He stepped over the ruin of bodies to regard Mouve as Tunkal leaned against the saber, breathing hard.

The young wizard smiled up at Thuf. "That's the last of them! I used a spell! In battle!"

"Indeed. So that explosion was your doing?"

"Yes. It was the first time I tried that particular sequence." Tunkal regarded the cracks running through the passage. "The effect was a little more robust than I had anticipated."

Thuf grunted. His glance followed the young apprentice's. The cracks were deep at the explosion's center, thinning as they snaked up walls and even into the ceiling.

The big man stomped his boot down twice on the floor. He pondered aloud, "I wonder if it is safe here now."

There was a cracking sound, then a tumbling sensation. Their torches spun in the air as they fell, painting the walls of the pit in stark streaks of momentary bright, chaotic and disorienting.

Mouve woke to blackness. He was afloat in the void, his own breath loud in his ears.

"Oh no. Limbo! Lord, hear my prayers, let me repent and leave this place! Thank you for not sending me to perdition!"

"You are not in Limbo. Firstly, Limbo is reserved for unbaptized infants, or so I have heard. You must be thinking of Purgatory. Secondly, you are not dead."

"Thuf! God be praised! What are you saying?"

Mouve twisted in the gloom, desperate to see his friend, see anything in the blackness. His efforts were rewarded with a mouthful of thick, bitter tasting liquid. He thrashed about until his head broke the surface, gasping.

"Make yourself still and you will float back to the surface, you ridiculous man!"

Mouve thrashed around a moment then seemed to get the hang of it.

He said, "I don't suppose you or the wizard know where we are or what is happening?"

The young apprentice's voice, both dour and youthful at once, sounded in the gloom, "I believe we have fallen through into an extremely large vessel, or perhaps a reservoir of sorts. A moment…"

His quartz glowed, revealing a great cavity of unknown dimension, borders falling outside the reach of the eerie light. The lake of viscous fluid upon which they floated was purple under the light, fading to black.

Thuf sighed. "I suppose we should just pick a direction and begin paddling."

Mouve's face frowned in frustration. "I can barely hear you—what?"

The wizard interjected, "Wait, an island!" He pointed to the far distance.

There, a long beam of sunlight shone from a hole in the high ceiling.

The light streaked down in diffuse rays, finally losing its battle with the dark just as it alit over a strange mound.

The trio made their way as best they could, paddling and kicking, frequently slipping beneath the surface to emerge again, sputtering oaths that echoed in the vast chamber.

Tunkal's light revealed the mound to be a jumble of hard edges, cracked crystals of all description. With some difficulty, he pulled himself into a niche between two jutting formations where the liquid met the mound. He leaned back and tried to catch his breath, wet robes as heavy as armor on his thin frame.

Mouve pulled himself up beside the apprentice. He let out a sigh and complained in a voice overloud.

"Mother of God! That liquid is something! Were we swimming in the blood of a star-god? What a thought!"

Tunkal shook his head. "I don't know. Perhaps blood is too simple an explanation. The star-gods are the things of ancient dreams."

Mouve moved his head to the side and back, tapping his ears.

"What? I can't hear anything."

Thuf lay panting on a smooth outcropping. A look of alarm spread out on his wide face. He dug through his pouches. Relief washed over him as he realized his book was untouched by the liquid, safe in its leather case.

Tunkal grabbed Mouve's sleeve. "There is something up there!"

"What?"

A voice came from above, sensual, a sound out of time. It came like a cool mist flowing down the wreckage of the mound. Its pitch was decidedly feminine. Beneath its pleasing delicacy throbbed an undercurrent of strange power.

The voice spoke, sibilant tones that reverberated gently through the entire body. "Why have you come here?"

The sound of it seemed to wrap itself around Tunkal's soul, a python's grasp sheathed in warm silk.

The young wizard answered before he could think. "We seek the soul crystal." His voice bore a strange bass echo. He realized Thuf had replied at nearly the same moment.

Mouve's eyebrow arched in confusion. "The soul crystal? What did you say?"

The voice continued. "The soul crystal. So many have come in search of it. What is it understood to be now? I have heard so many versions over the long years."

Tunkal swallowed and replied, "It is the nodule through which the star-god's energies were directed. Within its molecules resonate traces of the monster's incalculable power."

"Star-god. Such a primitive, grotesque way to describe them. I watched as they strode the galaxies so long ago. I know what they called each other. I know their names. I would speak them, but you could not hear. Come closer."

Warmth and contentment washed over Tunkal's body. He found he desired to hear the voice again, wishing to be immersed in its sensuality. Movement distracted him. Thuf was scaling the slope, picking his way along the broken terrain. His eyes were glazed and his movements were clumsy; for all appearances he was drunk. Tunkal stood, suddenly fearful that Thuf would reach the peak before him.

Mouve looked on. "Who are you talking to? Hey!"

Thuf and Tunkal scrambled toward the peak. Despite their enthusiasm, it was slow going, picking their way up a slope of jumbled angles and slick surfaces. Each handhold sent tremors up Tunkal's arms; these fragments were apparently crystals themselves, the debris of a thousand crashed ships.

The ex-hussar strained liquid from his long braid as he watched his companions. He shouted, voice loud in his own ears. "What in God's name are you two doing? Is it a race?" His tone became strident as he swore. He began picking his way up the slope. His body was stiff from his exertions, and the slick liquid coating him made climbing the smooth crystals all the more difficult. He pondered the mound.

"Are these crashed vessels? Must be hundreds of them!"

In the dark of a crevice his hand found something, a different texture, light and organic. He pulled the thing into the dim light.

A skull. Time had turned the flesh into a few scraps of damp leather. A few wisps of hair remained on the scalp. Mouve let loose an oath and tossed the thing aside. It clattered down the mound until finally splashing into the purple lake.

He looked up. His friends were nearly at the top.

"Wait, you idiots!"

Tunkal's soul soared. Somehow she was there. The woman from Nic's. She sat upon a throne of jumbled crystal and regarded him with a warm smile. She was exactly how he remembered her. Dark hair tumbled down over smooth shoulders tinted warm olive, bare in her peasant's dress. Everything about her suggested an intoxicating abundance. Tunkal longed to wrap his arms around her full hips. Her blue eyes stared deeply into his.

"Hello, Tunkal."

The young wizard stumbled forward.

She spoke again, voice like warm water from the bath, enveloping the young man in a sensuous mist. "Do you wish to kiss me?"

"I do."

She beckoned him forward. Tunkal made his way awkwardly over the wrecks toward the throne. Thuf stood stock still, eyes glassy and unfocused.

Mouve clambered up with some difficulty. He found more skulls and other bones, each new discovery met with another gasp.

Atop the mound, he was greeted by a strange spectacle.

His big friend stood motionless while the wizard kneeled before the makeshift throne. The young man was held in the grasp of a creature of nightmare. Dozens of segmented legs sprouted from an oily, eel-like body dotted with short, black hairs. Its face was a mass of bluish tentacles which engulfed the young man's head. Pulsing energies danced down the tentacles as the thing twitched with pleasure.

Mouve made a sound, something between a scream and a yell, and drew his dagger. He made for the monster, but an iron grip encircled his wrist.

He looked at Thuf and his stomach sank. The big warrior's eyes betrayed his bewitchment. Mouve wrenched himself from the grasp.

"Now, Thuf, I know you can hear me in there…"

The big warrior lunged at his friend. Mouve scrambled underneath the great arms, moving awkwardly across the terrain of hard angles.

"It's me! Your dear friend! Barracks, battlefield, brothel and bar, we have been beside each other for a decade!"

Mouve spun away a hair too slowly, and a hand closed around his shoulder, grasping his wool jacket and epaulette. The big man bore down and Mouve found himself on his back. He fought desperately yet still checked his blows, having not the heart to brain his friend. Thuf simply attempted to hold him still, preserving him for the grim kiss of the thing on the throne. Mouve's frustration grew. He was in the corpse of an impossibly large alien, on a mound of greasy wreckage. He was about to be killed by some bizarre creature, and his own boon companion was aiding in the murder. The young wizard was likely near death. A wave of guilt washed over Mouve, and his anger bubbled forth.

"To Hell with you, you big oaf! Ten years in your company! Utterly tiresome! Ten years of you telling me not to spend all my money! Ten years of listening to you drone on about the arena! Like you were the only man to ever face death! Ten years of listening to you quote those inane, pointless poems!"

There was a flicker across Thuf's meaty features. Sudden clarity came to his eyes, followed by anger. He raised his fist as his deep voice bellowed in the cavernous depths.

"'Those inane poems' are masterful works of literature that have survived through the millennia. Through war, through epochal shifts of human history, through mankind's spread into the stars, those poems endure!"

Mouve grinned. "Thuf! You are back!"

Thuf stood still a moment, looking about in confusion. His head turned to the throne where Tunkal still knelt.

"My God!" Thuf lunged toward the throne as Mouve scrambled to his feet. The once gladiator hesitated a moment, hands in the air. His face screwed up with determination, and he grabbed the vile siren, ripping it from the young man's face and dashing it to the ground. There was a horrible screeching sound that called up waves of terror, welling up from deep within the soul. The sound ceased as the pair crushed the creature to pulp under their boots. Panting, they stood to regard Tunkal. The young man was a bundle of damp robe and pale limb on the uneven ground. Mouve knelt beside him and put a hand to his forehead.

"Young wizard, how fare you?"

A weak voice answered, "Where did she go?"

The two men looked at each other.

Thuf bent and scooped up the young man in his great arms and placed him on the throne.

"She's gone, my young friend. How do you feel?"

"Weak."

"I'm sure your strength will return soon."

Tunkal asked for water. Thuf's canteen was gone, but Mouve still had his. He lifted the metal spout to Tunkal's lips. The big warrior sat down with a sigh. From a crevice he drew forth another skull and regarded it with a wistful expression.

"Voices sweet, from far and near, Ever singing in his ear, Here is rest and peace for thee!"

Mouve sat next to Thuf, as the young wizard rested. Before them yawned the dim cavity. They discussed strategies for leaving. Thuf postulated that outside their view were numerous channels leading back to the circulatory system. Mouve tapped his head, removing the last of the viscous fluid from his ears, and expressed doubt about the lengthy swim that might be necessary to find a channel.

"We could fly out."

The pair turned to regard Tunkal.

Mouve asked, "What do you mean, young man?"

"We are sitting upon a mound of crashed ships. We need only to find a bixbite or some other red, and there is a chance I could pilot the craft out, through the opening above."

The two ex-hussars looked at each other.

Thuf shrugged. "It is certainly better than my plan."

Under Tunkal's instruction, the three set to work. They were to scour the mound in search of a vessel of red crystal. Tunkal was yet weak but soldiered on.

"In this dim, weird light I am having difficulties."

Tunkal waved off Mouve's comment and called the pair to him. He stood on a jutting ledge near the base of the mound. His hand lay on the surface of the ledge.

"I feel it. Stand back."

The young wizard stepped from the ledge. He grasped his necklace and with the other hand began a series of complicated gestures, a ritual to focus his thoughts with inhuman precision. Thuf and Mouve scurried up the mound.

Minutes passed as sweat rolled down from Tunkal's forehead. He swayed slightly, and the ex-hussars stood, thinking to catch him. But the young man's spine stiffened and there was a sudden, crashing lurch.

The vessel hovered free. It was a rectangular slab, perhaps thirty feet long and fifteen feet at its highest point. With a wave of his hand, Tunkal caused the cockpit to open, revealing a single seat formed from the hard crystal.

Thuf said, "A one-man scout."

Tunkal nodded. "I'll leave the cockpit open, and you two can hold on as best you can."

Mouve wondered aloud. "Would it be best for you to rest a bit before we take off?"

The ship quivered in the air a bit. Tunkal shook his head no.

"This vessel is riven with fissures. It takes effort to merely keep it afloat and still. I'm afraid if I stop I won't be able to get it aloft again."

"Fair enough." Mouve and Thuf climbed to the top of the craft as Tunkal settled himself in the cockpit. He looked with consternation at the controls. He puffed out his cheeks and exhaled.

"Hold fast."

His smooth, bony hands worked the controls. The vessel shot up with a gut-wrenching lurch.

Thuf yelled, "The hole! To the right!"

Tunkal adjusted and the vessel shot through the hole. The rough walls were porous and uneven. The light above grew stronger. Here and there sand had collected in crevices; the desert inside the skull was just above.

They crested the edge and continued to rise, the desert now beneath them. The hole was soon gone to sight, hidden by a trick of the light. The airy interior of the skull was as before, sand underneath and strange jungle ringing the inside.

Thuf shouted, "There! The shards where we landed."

Tunkal grimaced as he fought the controls. The vessel continued to rise. The air became chill as he worked. Finally, in frustration he removed the elevator crystal. The ship was still for a moment and then began to descend, momentum building.

Thuf lay back while Mouve clutched a rosary. Tunkal reseated the crystal, and with another lurch the craft leveled off and then began a slow, turning descent.

Thuf shouted above the wind. There, where they had left it, was the red yacht. The landing was awkward, sending the two ex-hussars rolling across the sand. The new vessel bounced once from a shard of bone and buried itself a few inches in the hard ground near the dune's edge. Tunkal leaned back and let his mind rest.

Thuf and Mouve whooped at the miracle of survival.

"You comported yourself excellently, young man!"

Tunkal nodded at the comment and slid to the ground. Sudden pains attacked his temples. Mouve slapped his shoulder.

"All that exertion takes a toll, I imagine."

Tunkal shook his head. "It does indeed. But there is something wrong." He massaged his pale temples while his tired eyes scanned the surroundings. "Something very wrong."

The two hussars tensed, scanning the sand and horizon with him. The landscape was becoming dyed in dark purples and warm crimson as the star that served as the world's sun dipped to the horizon. The wind danced across the tops of the dunes, a rustling, low whisper that unsettled Mouve.

"I see nothing."

Thuf said, "Me either." He turned to Tunkal. "Open the door of the yacht and let's be gone from this place."

Mouve's handsome face was lined with anger. "I shall be giving that high born ponce a piece of my mind. Letting us look high and low and risk life and limb while he had the soul crystal. Galling!"

Tunkal waved his hand and the door of the yacht disappeared.

He screamed and fell backwards onto the sand. Pouring forth from the opening was a mass of flesh, an amorphous blob sprouting bloated tendrils. From somewhere near the center a mouth gaped, moaning, screaming, babbling unintelligibly.

"Mother Mary!" Mouve dived backwards as a coiling tentacle sought his waist. He reached for his saber only to realize it sat at the bottom of a pool of purple liquid deep in the depths of the star-god's skull. He brought his pistol around instead. The sharp reports echoed across the wastes as he fired into the mass. The thing was a mockery of nature's slow deliberateness. It was flowing and changing even as they watched. A great eye appeared from a fresh slit, and Mouve fired again, screaming.

Thuf found himself aloft, wrapped in a tentacle as thick as he. The mass was growing, more and more spilling from the door. With difficulty, he pulled a dagger from his belt and hacked at the appendage. He sliced through the translucent skin, deep into the tissue underneath as the gaping maw howled in pain. Thuf kicked viciously as he was brought close. Rounds whipped past him as Mouve fired. The grip loosened and the big man was free, scrambling away. He scrambled underneath another tentacle. One slid past, a thick one, and he realized with a start that the young wizard was within its coils, wrapped nearly head-to-toe. Thuf swore and stabbed madly at the tentacle. With a squeal of pain, the thing released its grasp, and the big warrior dragged the young man away.

"Ideas?" Mouve shouted as he shoved thick rounds into the chambers of his smoking pistol.

Thuf shook his head. "Flee into the dunes. Pray that it will forget about us?"

"Off we go then." He grabbed Tunkal's other arm and the trio ran for the sands. Mouve turned to fire, once, twice, and swore.

"The damned thing follows us! What in God's name is it?"

Thuf's expression was grim. "It is Leftenant Willy Werman. Exposure to the soul crystal in such confines as the crystal yacht is apparently quite deleterious."

The three stumbled on the shifting sands. They ran all out, lungs aching with the effort as their feet sank into the dunes. Above, the sky continued to darken. Thuf spied movement ahead. A dune was shifting, collapsing as if the bottom of it had been knocked out. Then another, and another, gathering speed as it turned toward the trio.

The big warrior pulled his friends short as a dune rose right before them. It emerged with a hissing shriek, a great worm sheathed in hard segments. The thing was colored a sickly mauve in the strange light. Rings of bristles wound around the edges of the segments. Spirals of yellow teeth the size of daggers wound down its gullet, pointed inward so that no prey could crawl out.

With a speed that seemed impossible for its size, the worm struck, rearing back and flinging itself upon the three men.

Mouve leapt to the left, Thuf to the right. But Tunkal stood still, frozen with fear. The worm swallowed him up. It reared back, and Mouve watched with horror as the shape of Tunkal could be seen as it went down, down into the depths of the thing underneath the sand.

He yelled in anger and fired at the maw. He felt an arm around his waist, but it was no arm. The air left his body as a tentacle began to crush him, lifting him high. Below, Thuf stabbed ineffectively at the blob.

The worm struck again, and suddenly Mouve was thrown, landing awkwardly in the sand. By the time he got his bearings the worm was half done with the blob, taking it in, mouthful by mouthful.

Thuf screamed, "Tunkal!"

Mouve ran to his side.

"We lost the boy."

Tears welled in the corners of the big man's eyes.

"I know."

The worm finished its meal, finally silencing the shrieks of the blob. Its segments strained to accommodate the mass it had just swallowed. It was sluggish as it began to bury itself again, forcing its way back under the sands with a sinuous motion.

"What do we do?"

A mad gleam showed in the big man's eyes. "We'll cut him out!"

The two rushed forwards towards certain death. The worm, more than sated with its unexpected repast, ignored them. The last of it was disappearing beneath the sands as Thuf stabbed ineffectually at a segment.

"Dammit!"

A terrible noise erupted from under the sand. It reminded Mouve of a cannon, so loud as to make everything seem quiet, a sharp boom that reverberated through the body. The lithe warrior saw the sky, then the ground again, and realized that he was aloft, spinning in the air, thrown by some immense force.

He landed hard. It took moments to regain his wind, and he stood. Thuf groaned from nearby.

The dunes had parted. Where the worm had disappeared was now a crater, ringed with purple gore. At the center, amidst the smoking remains of the worm and the blob, sat Tunkal. He was drenched in ichor and bile but apparently uninjured. Mouve skidded down its slick sides. Tunkal's face was expressionless as he looked up at the lithe warrior.

"I managed that spell again."

"You did. Good job, my young friend."

Thuf ran into the crater and grabbed the young man's arm.

"On your feet. The dunes shift all around us."

Mouve looked up. The big man was right. Here and there dunes were on the move, converging on this spot. He scanned the ground, hoping the soul crystal was somewhere at his feet, poking out from the scattered gore. No such luck.

The dunes were closing in. He heard the sands hissing as they fled.

"Damn you, Willy Werman!"

The three ran back to the yacht where a patch of hard packed earth offered relative safety.

Tunkal was pale and weak from his trials but able to take the yacht aloft and away.

Mouve let out a powerful sigh as he lay on the couch. The cramped interior was filled with a cloying, fetid odor. Thuf sat in a corner. He removed a heavy boot and upended it, pouring purple liquid onto the floor. Now that the party was relatively safe, his wounds from the fracas in the cave began to ache. He set about to clean and bind his numerous cuts and scrapes. Tunkal leaned back and let his mind rest as well as it could while in control of the craft. He was sore in a dozen places, and his ears still rang. His robes were damp with worm bile, and the tiny part of his mind that could wander thought only of a warm bath.

Mouve spoke, his pleasant baritone filling the small chamber. "While it's true we did not secure the soul crystal, I feel gratified to be alive at the moment."

Thuf held the end of a bandage in his teeth as he tied a dressing around his forearm, the act effortless with much practice. He spoke to no one in particular.

"A man my age should be settled with a family. My cousin has a farm on Silesia IV. Grows corn and keeps a herd of goats for cheese."

Mouve raised one eyebrow.

"An admirable goal. Good, clean work away from danger. Responsibility and solidity. I imagine you could become a leader in the community. Raise many polite children."

Thuf nodded his head, warming to the idea.

Mouve came to sit before him. "Just one problem."

Thuf looked at him.

The lithe warrior continued. "You are stone broke. You need capital to start such a venture."

"True."

Mouve smiled. "This whole escapade has reminded me of something Ulkelrt, that crusty sergeant, used to talk about. A tomb full of riches deep in the jungles of Rett's World out on the Far Rim."

Thuf smiled and shook his head.

Tunkal shoved his head out the pilot's chamber. His expression was dire as he massaged his temples and spoke with teeth clenched.

"I'm more exhausted than I have ever been! You two keep quiet a while or I'll open the door and blow you out into goddamned space!"

The two wore wry smiles but became quiet. After a minute Mouve said in a soft voice, "After you've rested a bit, my young friend, we'll make some new plans."

Printed in Great Britain
by Amazon

81823064R00140